The
CHATEAU

Also by Jaclyn Goldis

When We Were Young

The
CHATEAU

A Novel

JACLYN GOLDIS

EMILY BESTLER BOOKS
ATRIA
New York • London • Toronto • Sydney • New Delhi

ATRIA

An Imprint of Simon & Schuster, Inc.
1230 Avenue of the Americas
New York, NY 10020

First Emily Bestler Books/Atria Books hardcover edition May 2023

EMILY BESTLER BOOKS/ATRIA BOOKS and colophon are trademarks of Simon & Schuster, Inc.

For information about special discounts for bulk purchases, please contact Simon & Schuster Special Sales at 1-866-506-1949 or business@simonandschuster.com.

The Simon & Schuster Speakers Bureau can bring authors to your live event. For more information or to book an event, contact the Simon & Schuster Speakers Bureau at 1-866-248-3049 or visit our website at www.simonspeakers.com.

Interior design by Dana Sloan

Manufactured in the United States of America

1   3   5   7   9   10   8   6   4   2

Library of Congress Cataloging-in-Publication Data
Names: Goldis, Jaclyn, author.
Title: The chateau : a novel / Jaclyn Goldis.
Description: First Emily Bestler Books/Atria Books hardcover edition. | New York : Emily Bestler Books/Atria, 2023.
Summary: "A girls trip to a luxurious French chateau turns from dream vacation to nightmare"—Provided by publisher.
Identifiers: LCCN 2022046961 (print) | LCCN 2022046962 (ebook) | ISBN 9781668013014 (hardcover) | ISBN 9781668013038 (ebook)
Subjects: LCGFT: Thrillers (Fiction). | Novels.
Classification: LCC PS3607.O45424 C47 2023 (print) | LCC PS3607.O45424 (ebook) | DDC 813/.6—dc23/eng/20221214
LC record available at https://lccn.loc.gov/2022046961
LC ebook record available at https://lccn.loc.gov/2022046962

ISBN 978-1-6680-1301-4
ISBN 978-1-6680-1303-8 (ebook)

For Suz

CHAPTER ONE

Jade

In the prelude to sunrise, just after I've returned to my room and drifted back off to sleep, I awaken to a scream. I bolt up in bed, shove my sleep mask off my face. I reach out to toggle the lamp, but where is the switch? Disorientation in the dead of night is doubled when you're across the world, in someone else's home. Finally, I grasp the switch and wince as light illuminates the cavernous room, the herringbone marble fireplace and towering windows framed in gauzy cream drapes, the leafy branches of an oak tree swishing against the exterior of the panes. In the thick silence that has ensued, I analyze the sound I thought I heard—its scratchy, desperate contours. Did I dream it? I sag back into my nest of pillows. I suppose I did.

I grab my phone to see if one of the girls has texted. No text, and mercifully no Instagram notification from @imwatchingyou88. Only the time blinks back at me. 6:05. So I stole not even ten minutes of sleep after returning from my little errand. My heart slaps my chest—did someone see me? Does someone know?

No. Impossible. I force my mind to turn over other affairs—the fact that my birthday is officially over. Forty. Thank the Lord. Thirty-nine felt like a forced march, but now that I'm here, in this new decade, I remind myself, again, that I have everything I've ever wanted. A kind, gorgeous husband; two amazing kids; a career that has steadily skyrocketed. And I'm hotter than ever, hotter even than most of the twenty-four-year-olds who clamor to take my spin classes. Forty isn't our grandmothers' forty, right?

My unconvincing pep talk is interrupted by another scream. My breath stalls, hovers, until I gulp for it. The sound rollercoasters my eardrums. I've never heard anything so primal. And its origin is clear. Darcy.

I hear footsteps outside my door. Arabelle?

"Belle?" When there is no answer, I shout, "I'm coming!" The few words I manage sandpaper my throat. Darcy needs me. Us. Someone. But still I am fixed in place to this linen duvet.

In the twenty years Darcy Demargelasse Bell has been my best friend, I've hardly ever heard her scream. Darcy is exceedingly patient and compassionate, not the type to overreact. Recently, though, I've witnessed her in a couple of disproportionate blowups—an unusually short fuse with her kids, with Oliver. It's not nice of me to say, and I wouldn't aloud. These are the kindnesses best friends pay each other, to trip over each other's failings and then straighten out the rug.

Silence has once again descended like a tarp on the chateau. I pad down from the bed and reach for my tee draped on the olive velvet chaise, then tug it back on. My feet shiver against the terra-cotta tiles. For a moment the view from my window transfixes me: the manicured grounds, the still swimming pool, the shimmering moon. It is a *Starry Night*, like the one conceived by Vincent van Gogh, who painted his most acclaimed works at a sanitorium nearby. His muse was this very horizon that has shaped me in indelible ways.

I think about what I vowed before coming here. What I still must do.

Then my eyes catch on a shadowy figure on the outskirts of the pool, wandering past the hedges. Raph? The groundskeeper. But why would he be walking about before morning? I step closer to the window, but then he's gone, disappeared around the corner, back to his little cabin on the outskirts of the property, I presume.

It is the lovely part of summer in Saint-Rémy-de-Provence. June. I've never been here in summertime, but this isn't my first time at Séraphine's grand chateau. Darcy used to bring all of us to visit her grandmother during the semester we met, when we studied abroad in Avignon, fifteen miles away. This time of year, lavender fields swathe the countryside, providing endless backdrop fodder for all the tourists who flock. But summer aside, my teeth are now chattering like someone banging on a door knocker. My nerves are the obvious puppeteers.

Darcy is staying upstairs, down the hall from her grandmother's suite. Across from Vix's room, too. Arabelle and I are on the main floor in the hall by the stairs, across from each other. For me to hear Darcy scream from upstairs in this massive place, she had to scream really loudly, right? I bite down on my lip, then set out the door. Shuffles of feet echo ahead of me.

"Arabelle?" I call out. No answer. Anyway, didn't she pass by before?

My head is fuzzy from the previous evening's revelries, and buzzing from what I just did, only a little time ago. God, how much did I drink last night? I'm usually a strictly kombucha girl. Why did I let Darcy insist on that last shot of *pastis*?

Voices above, but I can't yet make out their edges. Shadows ping off the walls like intruders.

Suddenly I hear weeping and then a different cry overlaid, more strangled. It is clear now that life will divide into a before and after this morning. This pronouncement may sound dramatic, but I have a compass for trauma. Not mine, necessarily, but that of those who came before me. And is there really a difference, when it all converges in your bones?

The cold stone floor absorbs my tentative footsteps. Somehow, I can't coax myself up the last step. My icicle feet make me think of Darcy. When for years she struggled to get pregnant, one doctor asked if she wore slippers. When she said no, that she liked the feel of wood floor on her soles, he shrugged. *Cold feet, cold uterus.* When I heard this, I felt like punching the guy. Instead I brought her UGG slippers. I remember how we hugged, and I said, fiercely, *Warm fucking uterus. Okay?*

When I finally dart past the landing, I see the door flung open to Séraphine's suite. Inside the opulent room, Arabelle hovers at the mouth of the door, her face sucked of color—the same gray as her silk pajamas. Then Vix is standing and Darcy kneeling, both beside the imposing poster bed made of mahogany wood and rich-people carvings. I walk slowly over. My eyes rove to the crimson stains on the sheets. The unmoving shape. The knife plunged in her chest.

Yes, the old bitch is dead.

I close my eyes, and my hand goes to the necklace at my throat. One diamond. The only one that remains.

When I open my eyes, I'm going to have to rearrange my face into something that resembles upset.

CHAPTER TWO

Darcy

Two Days Before

Come mark your collective onset into middle age with a woman so old she will make you feel young again.

I run my fingers over the thick cream invitation, embossed with Grand-mère's coat of arms. Three lions pawing at a crown. In case the calligraphy doesn't scream it, the coat of arms does: *We are important people.*

Well, Grand-mère's money screams it, too.

I like the coat of arms. I use it on my own stationery.

Middle age, though—is forty middle age? Surely not. That's fifty, right? Or at least forty-five. Leave it to Grand-mère to subtly twist the knife.

Anyway, yes, I am forty, two months in. Vix turned forty six months ago. Arabelle, two years ago. She's the group grandma, and she accepts the label with grace. Probably because she's the hands-down stunner, the one who most turns heads. Also, she looks like she's thirty-two, max. And Jade is the baby. Still thirty-nine. Her birthday is tomorrow. We'll be at the chateau together. Jade says not to go out of our way, that she wants something small—yet we will give her something big. Or I will. I'm the one who plans these things, and I'll say it's from all of

5

us. Forty deserves it. A grand surprise. Though when I said I wanted something small for mine, Jade threw me a cozy dinner party at her Hamptons place. With quail. Somehow the quail of it makes me irritated all over again.

"Mama." Sticky Mila fingers on my biceps. "Are we there yet?"

"Not yet." I gaze down tenderly at my four-year-old daughter's perfect, innocent face—strawberry blond hair like me, big blue eyes like Oliver's. The best of us, both her and Chase. Deservedly so. In the end, the reward did match our effort. "We're still on the descent, angel. Nearly there."

"Well, when we get to France," Mila says it with her father's Midwest *a*, "can I take a picture of the world?"

"Of course." I grin at Oliver on Mila's other side—a genuine smile, even though my stomach crimps. Oliver grins back, pinned down by our sleeping one-and-a-half-year-old son, Chase, who still qualifies as a lap child. I know that later we will quote Mila's take-a-picture-of-the-world to each other, smiling in satisfaction at the perfect humans we have created.

Mila focuses back on the goats she is coloring in her Provence coloring book. I found it at one of those niche Francophile stores in Williamsburg where Brooklyn parents swarm to infuse their children with culture.

I glance back at the invitation, reading again the peculiar sentence scrawled in ink in French, right below the calligraphy. The translation of it being:

And Darcy, I must speak to you about my Last Will and Testament. Remind me, if I don't remember.

Grand-mère's Will? Fear scratches my insides. And why would Grand-mère not remember?

At ninety-four, Grand-mère's memory is still exceptional. She remembers every maid and the decades of their transgressions. All of my friends, and their transgressions, too. Her memory for the wrongs has always superseded the rights. But I haven't seen her in a year. Has there been a decline? We don't speak on the phone. Grand-mère doesn't believe in the phone, or the internet. She believes in letters. Letters are civilized. (The fax machine is, peculiarly, allowed. It's why I am the only person in the greater New York area who still owns one.) Grand-mère has a lot of beliefs, and she expects everyone around her to share the same, precise ones.

Why did Grand-mère invite my friends and me for this trip? This question has been circling my mind for the few weeks since she summoned us. The last time Grand-mère had us all together was nearly twenty years ago. Grand-mère likes my friends, of course. We used to visit her chateau on the weekends when we studied abroad. But that was ages ago. And why invite just us? Women only. No husbands? No kids?

The rest of the girls think the invitation innocuous—an old lady looking for some kicks. But I know her well enough to be certain there is more to it.

My eyes flit toward the window to take in the view, but on their way my eyes are distracted by Mila's mussed hair and Chase's wispy baldness and Oliver's thick black hair that he's recently grown out so the top part swoops up, with the sides shorn. I think of the thousands of times my hands have tangled in my husband's hair. I love looking at their heads, all three of them. Counting them. Reassuring myself they are there. Remembering. Hair turns to love turns to sex turns to . . . darker things, too.

But now I need the treetops. My eyes greedily mop up the view. We are almost to Avignon, but it's not the same somehow. Disappointment floods me, but not surprise. I expected this, the dulling of what this place used to do to me. I am like an addict who has turned to my drug one too many times. There isn't a dose big enough now to make me forget. It used to reassure me, the first glimpse of the trees, but now as the clouds have gone and green twists across the brown, I feel like a dinghy bobbing unmoored in a deep ocean.

Even though Oliver and the kids weren't invited, we decided to make a family vacation out of it. Oliver and the kids will stay in town and do their own thing, and then after the reunion, we'll all go to Paris. It's been a bit of a sticking point between Oliver and me, because our finances aren't exactly conducive to such a trip, but Oliver insisted, saying it would hardly make a dent in our credit card debt. Which is frightfully true. But in the end, Grand-mère covered most of our travel costs. And I'm enormously relieved that my first time ever sleeping away from my children will be mere miles, not across oceans. Jade has decided to come without her family, because her kids are older, in sleepaway camps now, and her husband is a principal in a venture capital fund, which is code for work-around-the-clock. Vix and her girlfriend recently broke up, and she doesn't have kids. And Arabelle, also childless, lives in Nice with her husband, who stayed behind to run their hotel, one of the poshest in southern France. She's driving into Saint-Rémy today.

I could be insulted that Grand-mère doesn't care to see her own great-grandchildren, but what good would insult do? It is useless to feel emotions that have no hope of rectification. That's a belief I inherited right from her. Anyway, I remember how long it took Grand-mère to engage with me. I was six, and we had tea, and my hands shook as I tried not to spill anything or leave behind crumbs on the antique brocade sofa.

The five of us together again. Grand-mère and her girls. That's what she used to say. The most affection I'd ever heard her express, and it wasn't directed at my grandfather, or my father or me. It was directed at my friends. Or maybe it was just directed at Vix—her beautiful, precious Victoria.

Can I do it, I wonder?

I am a mother. *The mommiest mom*, Jade recently accused me of being. She didn't intend to wound me, but it hurt. I know I have taken mother as an identity—what defines me. I was empty before it, and mothering has filled me.

But for Jade it came easy. The first time she went off birth control, when she and Seb weren't trying, but weren't *not* trying. Those oops-I-got-pregnant girls still make my fists ball. And then just after Jade got her period again, when Sea was not even a year, she conceived Lux. I've always been happy for Jade, don't get me wrong. Though even as I insist it to myself, I know there are layers underneath that I don't feel like unpacking. Just, Jade is that type of person, who thinks life simply bends to her will. And because she thinks that, it does.

Whereas I tend to think life is a game. A deck of cards, really. And you don't get to choose your hand, but you do get to choose your play.

This week with Grand-mère and my friends: This is my hand. And I have a plan. The only question is—do I have the guts to follow it through?

The plane makes a sharp, stomach-dropping descent, and my eyes catch on Oliver. He gives me an easy grin enunciated by the dimple in his left cheek, the same intoxicating package of a smile that just over a decade ago made me a goner. I used to think it was a smile that conveyed, *I am a good man. I will love you and take care of you until the end.*

I think we only see what we want to see, one hundred percent of the time.

"Almost there," Oliver mouths. I convince my lips to smile back.

Then his eyes flutter closed. His head shifts to rest on the window, and I know my husband will fall into a quick sleep. Ten minutes until we land, but he will maximize it. Oliver is a gold-medal sleeper, fast and hard and long, difficult to rouse. The opposite of me.

My fingers find my phone. I flip quickly to our family album, thumb up through the icons until I land upon one picture in particular. The kids in coordinating Easter wear, holding chocolate bunnies, with Chase's teeth gnashing, aiming to lop off a head. Chase: my miracle baby in more ways than one, having survived open-heart surgery as a newborn. If pictures could speak their view count, this one would say that I've hovered over it, zoomed in, stared until my eyes ached from the screen glare, at least a thousand times. My children are here, right here, but still, I like soaking in their sweetness from all angles, especially those of the near past. Mere months ago, but a far simpler time.

All of a sudden, I am certain. I can do it. I can, and I will.

CHAPTER THREE

Vix

"I still can't believe you checked a bag, Vix." Jade isn't looking at me or my admittedly overstuffed suitcase; she's reapplying her Pillow Talk trifecta. Lip gloss, lipstick, and liner, the latter of which glides on via this trick she learned on TikTok that involves her pouting her lips so she looks like a walrus.

I shrug. "You and Arabelle are always doing runway-esque looks. I decided to step up my game."

There's that pleasing sound of an expensive lipstick clicking shut as I sip on my *café crème*. I even ordered it like the cool French girls do, by referring to it as *un crème*. It's about the only thing that's stuck from study abroad. Which says more about my need to caffeinate than anything.

"You're the girl who insisted on a carry-on backpack through Cambodia, Vixen," Jade says. "Er . . . Vix."

Silence. I look at the floor, compose myself. It's strange how that nickname—what my closest friends have called me forever—can suddenly rouse in me something red hot.

"We were practically infants in Cambodia," I say, shoving Vixen from my mind. "In your early twenties, you can actually wear a pair of flowy elephant pants every day, and still look hot. By the way, I *did* look hot. Do you want me to resurrect elephant pants?"

Jade smiles. "I don't want you to wear elephant pants. I mean, well . . . you do you."

"I always do."

"Actually, please do wear elephant pants. To dinner. I'd like to see Séraphine's face."

I smile tightly. Jade is still scrutinizing me with an air of suspicion, like a private investigator, which I get. Minimalism is one of the qualities on which I pride myself. For instance, after the plane, I changed out of my sweats and into street wear: black bike shorts and a beige tee with shoulder pads, paired with my studded black sandals that Darcy calls orthopedic. (But Gen Z would call all the muumuus she wears cheugy. So really, who is the cool barometer here?) I can, and will, wear each of these items with several other things I've packed, all of which are currently rolled into compression cubes in my carry-on. I don't get Jade's reticence to re-wear items. When you buy your perfect piece, the nicest of its category that you hunted down and invested in, why wouldn't you want to wear it over and over again?

I'm the friend Jade calls when Seb makes her cull the ten pairs of shoes she wants to bring for a weekend in Copenhagen. *No, you don't need two pairs of black boots. No, wedges aren't their own category.*

I won't argue this point now, not when I am eager to switch off the topic of my luggage.

"Guys! *Bonjour!* Raph is here!" Thank God. Darcy. She whooshes in, not with her typical calm and even keel, but in a wave of frenetic energy, bags hanging off her like she's a human coatrack.

"Who's Raph?" I ask.

Darcy gives a quick cheek kiss to Jade, whom she no doubt saw within the past couple of days because those two do everything together. All three of us live in the New York area, but they do the type of things you do when you have kids, which unites them more frequently. As for me—it's been a week since Darcy and I saw each other. She moves in for a hug, and I have that familiar debate with myself: hug, or awkwardly beg off. It's easier just to hug. But still I can't help but wince.

"Oh shit." Darcy flings herself back and studies me with that concerned look I've come to despise. "Shit, Vix. I don't know how I forgot for a second." She pauses, then says, "They feel bigger."

"The doctor expanded them again."

Four months ago, I had a preventative mastectomy and reconstruction. It was the responsible decision. Can't explain how many times I've heard that echoed back at me. I was one of the lucky ones. Stage zero. The cancer was in my milk ducts, hadn't spread. But it could have. I didn't want the mastectomy; most stage zero breast cancers don't ever progress. But Juliet really pushed it. Because you see, I have the BRCA mutation. It was a one-two punch—breast cancer and the genetic risk of getting it again, and much worse. She said I had to think about the people who love me, not just myself. So I agreed to the surgery. And then after I did it, Juliet left me.

That's unfair to her, I suppose. It's more complicated than that, as all relationships are. It involves little lies and big ones, and Séraphine and this trip, too, in fact. But Juliet isn't blameless, either. She left me at my smallest, my weakest. Now I am hurt and sad, and trapped inside a body that doesn't feel like mine.

I hadn't realized that reconstruction is painfully drawn out, part of the whole wide world of cancer that only those in the unlucky club can fully understand. Some women get permanent implants placed in their chests at the time of mastectomy. Others, like me, aren't eligible for that, so the process takes longer. Now I have a balloon-like tissue expander placed over my pectoral muscles. (Whenever my surgeon says *pectoral muscles*, I feel like a male bodybuilder.) Over the course of months, my surgeon fills the balloons with saline until my breasts are the right size. But for now, I have these painful half breasts. Saggy little lumps. Raisins on a log.

"I'm sorry," Darcy says again. *Sorry* is my current least favorite word. It's what the doctor said five months ago when the biopsy results came in. It's what Juliet said two weeks ago when she left me.

"It's okay." It's not okay, but it's not Darcy's fault. And she's been amazing through this. Still, my chest stings in some unknown place.

"How are you doing?" she asks, a question I also hate. But she means well. She calls me every day, asking it.

"Fine," I say, the same thing I always say, forcing a bright tone. "Hey, where are Oliver and the kids? I want to say hi."

"They already left for town." She smiles, but I know it's an effort. Darcy has never left the kids before, not even for a night. She's a Supermom, capital S. Not being derisive. She really is the best mom, so loving, so involved. But she worries so much. Every object, like a simple rubber band, becomes an evil device bent on harming children. She could find safety defects in a rainbow. Jade is a wonderful mom, too, but far less ruffled. But Darcy's path to motherhood was different, arduous. It's like she is so grateful she finally has them, that she must savor every instant and cushion every stumble.

"How are you feeling after the flight, Vixie?" Darcy is staring at me now, trying to see inside me, it feels like, to figure out where my brain is zigging. To figure out how I really am.

How am I? Hell if I really know. I miss being the girl without cancer. And I miss my boobs so much, I want to scream. I loved my boobs. I was always known as the girl with good boobs. Back when going-out tops were a thing, mine were all the plunging, sequined varietal.

"I'm fine," I finally settle upon before reaching for a new topic, anything else. "God, I forgot how the air is here. Even in the airport, I start to feel inspired." I gesture vaguely around, my hand landing in the direction of a striking woman in palazzo pants who's hastening past with a cream carrier case. "I've been blocked for months, you know, with my art. Maybe France is the *je ne sais quoi* I need."

"Great!" Darcy frowns and types off a text.

"So who's Raph?"

"The new groundskeeper."

"Oh, right. Croissant?" I flake off a piece.

"Ooh, God yes, please." Darcy shares my belief that carbs and sugar unite to form one superessential food group. I don't even bother offering the croissant to Jade.

Darcy is wearing the Insta-mom famous Nap Dress—the one that sells out the second it hits the website. To be honest, the dress's popularity baffles me. It looks like a potato sack with frilly cutouts for arms, like a Victorian nightgown. Darcy's strawberry blond hair is shorter now, blunt cut and shoulder-length. It reminds me of the shy girl I first met in a nude drawing class in Avignon, whose face was even redder than her prim, straight, strawberry hair. When we all finished our drawings, hers got the biggest laugh. She hadn't even attempted the penis—just chopped it fully off and castrated the poor guy, to boot. Whereas I had been riveted by the first penis I'd ever seen in real life. And in the decades since, my experience of penises has remained relegated to nude drawing workshops.

I'm not surprised Darcy cut her hair before this trip. Séraphine doesn't approve of long hair. Except mine. My natural hair is a rich chestnut, but recently I had it highlighted with some blond. Something—anything—to distract myself from the rest of me, or the parts that are smack dab in the middle, at least. The hairdresser called my new color bronde, and said the streaks complement my olive skin and pull the flecks of gold from my brown eyes. She swore I could pass for twenty-five, and for some moments I felt that young and free again, with my bouncy blowout and her fanning out my hair, lavishing the compliments. I was like a puppy, lapping them right up. I called her my fairy godmother. She smiled, then told me the exorbitant price for her services. *Bibbidi-Bobbidi-Boo,* she said, laughing, as I winced and paid, and then she waved me off as if into a fairy-tale ending. It was only later, alone, that I looked at myself in the mirror, and saw the same tired, sad, wrinkled me, but with admittedly beautiful hair. Now I play with a curl, nearly down to my butt. My long hair is the one thing that still makes me feel feminine. Séraphine won't deprive me that. She's been amazing through my whole breast cancer experience this past year.

Actually, she's been amazing always. Full stop. She's encouraged my art, believed in me more than anyone. Perhaps even more than I believe in myself. She's like a second mother to me. I wonder if that's why there is always some subtle, invisible distance between Darcy and me. Sometimes I think Darcy regrets having brought me along when we spent that first weekend at the chateau.

"You checked a bag?" Darcy's eyes flitter from my suitcase back to me.

"Right?" says Jade. "Who is this, and what has she done with our friend?"

"Get over it, guys."

Silence, the awkward kind. Because normally they wouldn't get over it. One of them would try to unstick a zipper. When I'd swat their hand away, they'd keep pressing on. Jokes, insults. The kind that people who have known you for twenty years have built into an arsenal. But nope. I'm the boobless cancer girl whose girlfriend just broke up with her, to boot. So for now, my luggage is safe.

"Okay, let's go," says Darcy. "You *guys*!" Now her face spreads into a smile, with giddy, excited kiddish energy that for once doesn't have to do with her kids. "The four of us together again, in Provence."

"I can't wait to crack open some champagne," Jade says.

"You're drinking?" I ask. Jade never drinks. It's not just the calories, she says, but the puffiness. And how the alcohol impedes her fasting window. "What about your fasting window?"

"No fasting window today." Jade grins.

"I'm very glad to hear you say that." Darcy pulls out a bottle of champagne and paper cups from one of her many bags. "Come on, ladies."

"Ladies?" I groan. "When did we become ladies?"

"When we turned forty."

"Speak for yourself. I'm still thirty-nine." Jade winks. You'd think she was twenty-nine for how frequently she reminds us she's the baby. Well, who wouldn't enjoy being the babied youngest? I certainly wouldn't if I still had a three in front of my age, even if for one more day.

I watch Jade set off to the exit. She's wearing one of those matching workout sets with a revealing burgundy top that has an inexplicably numerous amount of straps, crisscrossing in ways not requisite to hold its shape. Not the most appropriate to see Séraphine after all these years. Which I feel like Jade relishes a little bit.

Still, I'd toss her a sweatshirt if my suitcase actually had clothing inside.

CHAPTER FOUR

Darcy

"**S**hotgun," I say, claiming the front seat. My cheeks flame when I realize that I've probably not said that since I was twelve. I hold a perspiring water bottle to my right cheek, then my left.

There are buckles clicking and champagne popping. I made it. I slip my sunglasses on and down half the glass Vix passes me.

"Your grandmother is very excited to see you," Raph says as he navigates across the Rhône on our descent south. His voice is deep, but lighthearted. It's always strange to hear a person's voice, how different it might reconcile with their name. Not that the name Raph isn't conducive to young people, but when Grand-mère wrote me about her new groundskeeper, I assumed he'd be older, grayer, like groundskeepers of past. I was wrong. I peg Raph as a few years younger than us, maybe. But is that how everyone looks to me now? He's tall, lanky, boyishly cute, with a distinctly Southern accent. When he was speaking with the parking attendant, I heard him pronounce all the syllables, unlike Parisians.

I think about switching to French, but my French isn't as good as it once was. And right now I can't muster the energy to do yet another thing I will fail at.

"How is she?" I ask him.

"*Bon, bon,*" he says absently, making a sudden turn. Not that a man would notice the nuance I am digging for.

Jade and Vix are chattering in the back, and I gaze out at all the happy people picnicking on the river shores, spread out on the grassy banks among baguettes and cheese and charcuterie spreads, as kids frolic down to the quays. I down the little champagne that's left in my glass, then pass it back. "Refill me?"

Vix is holding court over the champagne bottle. She takes my glass.

Normally I would have crammed in back with the two of them. But I didn't call shotgun because I get carsick, or because I'm particularly keen on sitting next to Raph. My eyes rove over to him as he runs a hand through his curly mop of brown hair with zero style, whose shade of brown if it were to be identified in a flip book of paint swatches would probably be called Regular Brown.

God, I'm being a bitch. He does have good eyes. Excellent blue ones. If my past could speak, it would say I've always been a sucker for blue eyes, especially ones like Raph's, which are more turquoise to Oliver's navy. Honestly, Raph is cute. On the hot side of cute, really. I'm married, not dead. He's wearing a dark gray T-shirt that highlights his tanned biceps, and skinny gray jeans a smidge darker than his shirt. He has a mole by his mouth that, strangely, doesn't detract from his cuteness.

I jolt when I realize I'm staring. He's driving, but a person can tell when eyes are on him. And by his perplexed glance over at me, I know that he has noticed me looking. I swivel toward my window, gazing defiantly out. It's all just nerves about seeing Grand-mère. About being back at the chateau, all of us together. About my financial troubles. About sleeping away from the kids for the first time. But mostly it's about *her*. Sitting right behind me, like everything is fine. Like she has succeeded in deceiving me. Like I'm not going to fight back. Seeing her at the airport—it was harder than I expected to fake it.

I make myself do that box breathing thing that every holistic therapist I follow on Instagram endorses. Four in, hold, four out, hold. After one round, I stop. I scan myself to see if the anger is still there. Yes. Why yes, it is. Eight rounds of this breathing technique crap—can anyone manage it, other than monks on top of mountains?

In hindsight, I can't believe I survived the flight, kissing Oliver goodbye, kneeling down and hugging my children and watching them trot off, and then reuniting with Jade and Vix—as if nothing were amiss.

"How long have you been working for my grandmother?" I ask Raph, in lieu of pointless breathing. Out my window, the countryside is green and cheery and seemingly teeming with women in floral dresses and espadrilles, carrying straw totes and red-and-white-checked picnic baskets, shuttling children along walkways shadowed in willows and poplars. Everywhere are crumbly houses with red-tiled roofs and undulating hills. So many memories fling themselves at me. We are in la France profonde, deepest France, a place that feels simultaneously like home and also like an itchy sweater you can't wait to shed the moment you leave. A perfect conundrum. It's been this way ever since my grandfather's death.

"I've been working for Séraphine nearly a year now." Raph makes a turn, yielding another expanse of green. "We play *pétanque* together," he says, referring to the popular French game played on gravel, where the object is to throw small silver balls toward a target ball and get your balls closer to the target than your opponent's.

"Really." I can't imagine it at all—my grandmother in her perfect blond bouffant, in cream trousers and a Chanel knit blazer, out on the lawn in the *pétanque* field, playing with her help.

It's not that Grand-mère isn't kind to the people who work for her. Sylvie, for instance. She's been my grandmother's housekeeper for the entirety of my lifetime. She's part of the family, dear Sylvie. I feel the tug in my heart, imagining how Sylvie will fold me into her arms. She's round and pillowy and perpetually covered in flour dust from the pastries she bakes up, still vigorous and youthful in her early eighties, eleven years younger than Grand-mère. Sylvie is smiles and lightness and receding into the background where Grand-mère is witty and prickly and dominating of both the foreground and background. I wonder what Grand-mère will do once Sylvie retires. Somehow I can't imagine it. Sylvie is rooted to the chateau as much as the towering plane tree in the yard.

"I heard about your *pétanque* games," Vix says from the back seat, laughing. "Séraphine said she's whooping you."

Immediately I swivel around. "You talked to Grand-mère? Like, on the phone?"

The harsh *brrr* of the air conditioner is the only reply. Finally, Vix says, "Well . . . yeah. I thought she called all of us, you know, to invite us."

"The invitation invited you, though. You got an invitation, right?" My jealousy is spilling out of me so obviously. But calling Vix and not me? It's insulting.

"I got the invitation," Vix says quietly. "Sorry, Darce. I really thought she called all of us. It wasn't a big deal. We didn't talk long."

I mull it over. I could drop it. I *should* drop it. Instead I say, "Did my grandmother call you, J?" There's a long pause, pregnant of everything. "Never mind. She didn't."

I don't add that she didn't even call me, her own granddaughter. Or that to my knowledge, my grandmother hadn't picked up a phone since 1991, when she dialed for an ambulance. That was when my grandfather slipped on a slick of water and hit his head on the bronze statue that presided over the pool: three lions pawing at a crown, all on a plinth. A mimic of our crest. To be precise, he hit his head on the left-most lion. The doctors said later that he died instantly. An internal hemorrhage of his brain. My grandmother had the unfortunate luck of watching it all happen from her bedroom window. I didn't see it happen, however, because I was in the pool doing a handstand, trying to keep my legs from wobbling, to demonstrate to my beloved grandfather how good I was at handstanding. I only realized something horrible had happened when I stood up in the water and rubbed my eyes, all proud and poised for his torrent of praise—and saw that the water was turning red.

"Darce, I'm really sorry. I didn't mean to upset you. You know your grandmother and I, we just—"

"It's okay, Vix," I say, even though it isn't. "It's not your fault, anyway." I try to push my hurt away, push away the red water, too, and then the horrible sight my eyes had to see after. The chateau is the receptacle of some of my best memories, but also my worst. "Let's change the subject." I reach for my second glass of champagne. "And keep drinking."

"Did Séraphine say why she wanted us to come?" Jade asks. She's barely drinking, I've noticed, despite her hype. She hardly ever does. But she's the life of the party, and everyone thinks she's reveling along. Only I know she's always in full control. "Sorry, Darce," Jade says. "I don't want to twist the knife, but . . ."

"Why now, after twenty years?" I fiddle with my wedding band, the Cartier love ring in gold. Basic bitch. But no one would know it's not real. That I had to sell the original. God bless Amazon and their decent fakes. "I have no idea. Who knows why Grand-mère does any-thing?"

"She just said she wants one last visit with her girls." In the rear-view mirror, I can see Vix twisting her hair into a topknot. "And to make things right."

"Make things right," Jade says. "Really? But what does that mean?" The hopeful lilt to her voice is unmistakable. I know exactly what she is thinking.

"She didn't elaborate," Vix says.

"One last visit with her girls." That cycles round my head.

"I'm sure she didn't mean last as in . . . last," Vix says. "Just, she's ninety-five."

"Ninety-four." I feel a hit of satisfaction that Vix got it slightly wrong. That I know something about my grandmother that she doesn't. Even if she gets the phone call.

"Right." I can see by the sag of her face that Vix feels bad for mak-ing me feel bad. She deserves this trip, more than any of us, really. It's just—it's easier to be there for someone in their moment of crisis when your own life is going swimmingly. And my life is not going swimmingly at the moment.

I check my phone to see if there's something from Oliver or the kids. Unease swarms me like a beehive. Perhaps I should have aborted it, last minute, this plan to have them join. Out of sight, out of mind only applies when there isn't a stone's throw between you.

"Hey, so . . . I saw your last Instagram post, Darce," Vix says, and I can tell she's trying to get my mind off her phone call with my grandmother. "It was really vulnerable. You're amazing, how many people you're helping."

"Oh. Thanks." The Fertility Warrior. It feels like years, not just a week, since that post. I wrote something last week about what it meant to feel like a failure to your husband. That you were the one who had promised to give him life borne of you, and your body wasn't cooperating. I wrote it just before I found out how else I was a failure to my husband.

"I wish I'd known the extent of what you were going through," Vix says.

"Yes." I push back the anger, the helplessness that bubbles up from that time, even now, with two healthy, beautiful kids. "Well, you couldn't have. That's why I'm trying to expand the platform. Imagine if you're struggling to conceive and only a few clicks away from inspiring stories of women who became mothers with the very same odds, and doctors who can help, who won't turn you away just because your FSH is subpar. . . ." I knead my hands in my lap.

"You're gonna help so many people with the new subscription database," Jade says. "Hey, whatever came from that meeting with the investor Seb hooked you up with? The one you flew to DC for? I totally forgot to ask."

I make my voice light. "Didn't pan out."

"Oh, well, investors will be clamoring, just wait. It's something so needed, Darce. Connecting with women going through the same—"

"Thanks," I say briskly. I can't bear it now, if she goes off on needles and doctors and all the rest.

I can see Jade in the rearview, surprised, maybe a bit hurt. Her startling eyes—the right a clear ice blue, the left a murkier blue veering on hazel—are perfectly rimmed in black eyeliner, her signature, the same inky color of her hair. Everything about her, other than her

21

eyes, is dark and hard angles. She certainly looks more stereotypically French than me, which I've always been a bit envious of—although she can't speak a word of the language, and I'm fluent. "Hey, Darce, are you okay?"

"Here we are," announces Raph, before I can reply. I let Jade's question evaporate, and I can see her wrestle with whether to reinstate it. Eventually, she fluffs up her hair, the volume at the roots, so it looks even more perfect than her typical perfect.

We turn right onto the dirt road surrounded by pines, with the French version of a lemonade stand at the mouth, operated by a new contingent of kids. They're peddling *diabolos*, homemade lemonade mixed with a bit of Teisseire syrup, and the sign advertising their product flaps in the breeze as we pass and wave. The road is reassuringly the same as it's been the entirety of my life, lined by ancient stone walls covered in moss. We're at the foothills of Les Alpilles mountain range now, about a mile-and-a-half past Saint-Rémy. The town is often called the Hamptons of Provence, with chic boutiques and restaurants, and a grand market every Wednesday. It's quiet here, outside of town, but still less than an hour's day trip to Arles, Avignon, Aix-en-Provence, and L'Isle-sur-la-Sorgue. Or the vineyards at Châteauneuf du Pape. Or you can just laze at the chateau, and nurse *cafés au lait* on the terrace.

My breath stalls as we rumble up the drive to the gate, announcing Chateau du Platane in curvy script. Our family crest is just below, the lions fierce, wrought in bronze, making any trespassers think twice—or at least that's the goal, I assume. The gate flings open; it is now keyed to a clicker in the car, but decades ago, when I was delivered to the chateau in the summers, a staff member would have to come with a key to let me in. We drive through the gate, past the vineyard whose land the chateau still owns but no longer operates, toward the grand house with pale stone that makes me feel instantly small. The chateau was built in the early seventeenth century, around the same time as the palace of Versailles, as a country retreat for the noble Provençal family from which my grandfather descended. The house is palatial, imposing, which is what I warned Jade and Vix before I first brought them here twenty years ago. It is not a warm hug, a cozy spot; it is more like a castle in a fairy tale where children are raised by servants. I remember watching my friends' eyes goggle, and how Vix said *palatial* was too underwhelming a word to describe it. I understand it, the same wide-eyed awe I felt as a child, pulling up each June to spend the summer with my grandparents.

The chateau is two stories, an imposing block of beige stone with that appealing, inexplicable European quality of appearing both pristine and crumbly. Each story features evenly spaced small windows framed by limestone ashlars, no shutters, and in the center bottom is a giant arched mahogany door with carvings. To get to the door, you walk down a little gravel *allée* between two rows of towering pines. There is nothing soft about the house or accessing it—the whole thing is severe. It's not your cute French country house with a porch swing, with trellises carpeting the house in green. Most everything is neutral, both outside and in, with antiques next to designer pieces, all shades of creams and tans and browns and terra-cotta. Even the impressive art collection falls in line with the color palate: tan nudes, marble sculptures, modern acrylics splashed out in neutrals, antique alabaster vases. The only real dash of color exists in the crown jewels of the curated art. Exceptions made for names like Degas and Renoir. And, of course, the swimming pool out back, and the dewy green of the landscape. You can't escape green in Provence.

I stare out the window and don't realize how close I am to the pane until my nose hits the glass. The car grunts to a stop. How many times did I walk this path as a girl, all freckled, flinging limbs, excited for a new day in paradise, completely thrilled by the love of her two beloved grandparents? For a fatherless girl, with a self-absorbed mother, I always wished I could freeze summers here, suspend them in time—make them last forever.

Raph halts just before the pines, and I open the door to everything familiar. And yet everything feels wrong.

CHAPTER FIVE

Arabelle

"*Oh fan!* They're here!" Mamie announces, scuttling past me in the kitchen, but not before pinching my side in affection. If my grandmother knew what the term *love language* was, hers would be touch. And as her only living relative, who lives in the far-off land of Nice (read: one hour away), she doesn't stop touching me from the moment I arrive for a visit until the moment I leave, laden in food, as if I, a chef, am liable to starve.

I admit that I like it. No one else wants to touch me that much, including my husband.

"Arabelle, they're here!"

Mamie has already switched to English, in preparation for the descent of the Americans. Mamie adores my friends, though she hasn't seen them, other than Darcy, in forever. Mamie has been Séraphine's housekeeper since before I was born, but now her role is more accurately described as Séraphine's caregiver. Her minder. Even though Séraphine is far too proud to acknowledge the transition, to admit to needing care.

I was raised at this chateau. When I was four, my parents died in a car accident with me in the car. People get inevitably shifty in their chairs when I am asked about my parents and then have to let out with this story. I know the drill. They avoid eye contact. Mumble their sorries. But I tell them the truth: I have one solitary memory of my parents, well, of my father, at least. It was the best way to lose them, if there were a best way. Before the rush of memories that could return and haunt you. I grew up with Mamie, who gave me the love of a world of parents, rolled into one person. So I consider myself blessed. And although we never had much money, and I never had the same beautiful clothes and toys as Darcy, for instance, I got to grow up here, in paradise.

In the summers, Darcy would come for her months-long visit, so in a way, we grew up together. But I am two years older, so there was always a bit of distance between us, a lag between those things in which we were interested. I was usually tucked into corners, flipping through cookbooks. Mamie would pick up secondhand ones for me at the markets, and they were covered in my notes, and previous owners' oil splashes. Whereas Darcy would be off with her grandfather, on some adventure or another, picking cherries or checking on production at the vineyard, or learning the dos-and-don'ts of hostessing a party and setting a table with her grandmother. When we were younger, I do remember us playing hide-and-seek. How I always found her, just after singing, *Come out, come out, wherever you are!* It was Darcy who taught me that Americanism that accompanied our game. But aside from those limited childish interactions, our paths didn't cross often, even when we spent entire summers in the same chateau. Because the chateau is big, and I had my school friends in the area, besides. Whereas Darcy kept closer to home, soaking in time with Séraphine, and especially with Rainier, before his tragic accident. But to tell the truth, I often think some of the distance between Darcy and me as kids wasn't just our age differential, but because of Séraphine herself. Even though Séraphine adores my grandmother, I am still the granddaughter of the help. Not of Séraphine's, or Darcy's, high genetic social standing.

But then, when Darcy was twenty-one and I twenty-three, she studied abroad in Avignon, and came here often on the weekends with her two new friends from her program, Jade and Vix. I was living at the chateau, enrolled in a local culinary school. The age difference among us was nil by then, and the four of us have been best friends for nearly twenty years. Because Darcy, Jade, and Vix live in New York, I see them less than they see each other, but I'm not a fear-of-missing-out person. I know what we have together, and how cherished I am by them. Anyway, I manage to get out there a few times a year. And we try to do occasional girls' trips, although Jade and Darcy can't always join because of their kids. But Vix is usually up for a weekend away, which is why she and I have grown closer over the years. Jade and Darcy have other singular bonds, like their kids and their more regimented schedules. Jade once termed us the Mamas and the Rihannas, after Vix and I stayed at the Hotel du Cap-Eden Roc the same weekend as Rihanna. Jade said it in a lighthearted way, but I could feel the division that underlay the comment. She and Darcy are the Mamas; it's true. And Vix and I are a bit more inclined to flow and pleasure. I suppose that is natural, though. Things aren't ever equal, or fair.

"Arabelle, *allez!*" Mamie pats her coarse gray hair, swept into a tight bun. Tendrils escape, as always, and she mops sweat from her brow with the sleeve of her purple floral dress. Mamie epitomizes the plump, adoring grandmother of sitcoms.

Her apron sweeps my arm as she pads past the giant hutch painted in thick, clumpy swirls of cream and mint green, almost like a talented child was told to go to town. The hutch's glass doors spotlight a mismatched jumble of pottery from local artisans: pastoral scenes done in blues and browns, little dishes rimmed in gold, teacups perched atop stacks of china; serving dishes interspersed. The jumble is intentional—it is an organized jumble. Everything in this house is intentional. For the most part, the people inside it, too.

"Coming! *Un moment.*"

We've been in the kitchen all afternoon, cooking. The family kitchen, I should clarify. During significant, prize-winning renovations a decade ago, a chef's kitchen was added to the chateau, which the family does not often enter. Needless to say, I find the chef's kitchen beautiful but a bit sterile, with its La Cornue range and other industrial elements, and this smaller one far more suited to my tastes. It has more color, too, which the rest of the chateau by and large avoids.

26

I take in the original stone walls and ceiling beams, juxtaposed nicely with the row of copper pots. Mamie consulted me on which ones to order, and of course I chose Mauviel. And then my eyes rove over the display of blue-and-white antique Delft plates mounted above the stove. I remember the triumph of finding each one, when Mamie and I used to go to the markets and search for them.

Séraphine employs a chef, but when I come to town, I like to cook, too. It's the way I love, I suppose. And it's my job after all. I'm a chef and entrepreneur with 1.7 million people following along on Instagram as my husband, Giancarlo, and I run our inn and our cooking workshops for tourists. I've also done several collaborations, most recently with a perfumery to develop my own signature fragrance (a combination of sandalwood, orange blossom, and neroli, without synthetics; it sold out after an hour and a half, and we're planning a reprisal). I've also written three cookbooks, the last of which was a #4 *New York Times* bestseller, and I'm working on my fourth.

I undo my apron and admire the tomato *tarte tatin*, to which I add a few sprigs of thyme. "I just want it to be perfect for them." I scrutinize the tarte, removing one sprig of thyme. "We're never all together like this, and with you and Séraphine. I want it to be a perfect week."

"*Qui vivra verra*," Mamie says cheerfully. *The future will tell.*

I think about that. How deceptively opaque the future is.

"*Alors*, come!"

With one last tweak of the *tarte*, I follow Mamie out the door, past the fireplace logs stacked against the wall, and down the limestone hall. Everything is huge in this chateau, most especially the spaciousness. Séraphine exercises maximal restraint in filling a room. She prefers empty space. Finds it more interesting. Which creates, paradoxically, the Big Dick Energy version of a house.

Even though it is bedecked in neutrals, cool from the blue-gray stone, the chateau somehow maintains a warm, inviting atmosphere. The walls are gray, but plaster-finished and overlaid with limewash, so the lime melds into the plaster, lending it a patina that looks almost sponge-painted, imperfect. Séraphine greenlighted the restoration but insisted there be no evidence of her concessions to modernity. You'd be hard-pressed to spot an electrical duct; they are all cleverly concealed. The experience of traversing the chateau is like that of wandering through a well-appointed cave, and every so often stumbling upon a pristine, magazine-worthy vignette. A framed Perle Fine painting with a cream backdrop and horizontal blurred gray lines that are almost trippy, conjuring brainwaves, set above an ornate table arranged with alternate-height cream-colored candles. Then you catch the flimsy white drapes adorning a window, and your eyes flicker on over to the oversize Noguchi lanterns. The art is alternately abstract but subdued, like acrylics in grays and creams by Roseline Al Oumami, interspersed with eighteenth-century alabaster urns that sit astride bold sculptures by Laurence Perratzi. My favorite is *Head in the Clouds*: a naked woman carved out of black jesmonite with her head subsumed by clouds. Perhaps I gravitate toward the sculpture because it feels the very opposite of me; for better or for worse, my head has never gotten lost in the clouds, not even once. Airing everything out are the myriad windows—*The art must breathe*, Séraphine has always said, *and the people, too*. Most windows are flung open, each a perfect little vista onto the rolling countryside, or the terrace where we take breakfast. The *mistral* is blowing in from the north, harsh and warm and familiar, and I rub dust particles from my eye.

I arrive at the *entrée*, with its palatial ceilings and its centerpiece crystal chandelier, and the giant curving stone staircase with wide banisters carved out of identical stone. Then the front door creaks open, with Mamie peering out. I hear their voices. Jade's, laughing about suitcases. Something heavy dragged against gravel. We don't have a butler, a fact which can surprise people. Raph is the groundskeeper of the past year, who lives in a cabin by the pool. Then we employ a chef and a cleaner, both of whom live in town and come in just for the day. Mamie doesn't clean anymore, not for decades, although I have memories of her down on her knees, scrubbing floors. But no butler is needed; Séraphine is only one person, after all. Besides Mamie, no one else has lived in the chateau since Rainier died.

Footsteps up above on the landing, at the top of the stairs. I can't see her yet, but there is no doubt to whom those steps belong, with their heavy, unmistakable tread, belying her tiny stature and ninety-four years. Mamie has told me that for years she's been trying to convince Séraphine to move into one of the ground-floor bedrooms, but she refuses. This rankles me a bit, because Mamie takes care of Séraphine, and thus lives in the suite next door. Even though she's eleven years younger than Séraphine, Mamie isn't meant to be walking up and down steep stairs, either. They should have added an elevator in the restoration—I did suggest that.

"Belle!" That's Darcy, coming toward me.

"Darce!"

We hug the American way, tight, close, and she says, "You got skinnier," which she says every time, half admiringly, half enviously.

"I didn't." I have, unintentionally. I prefer my curves, but sometimes I am absorbed in a task, and a task becomes a day, and a day becomes a week, and I look at myself in the mirror and think, *I am forgetting to eat*. I realize it's not the sort of thought for which most women have sympathy.

Darcy has never been big, but lately she makes occasional self-disparaging remarks about how she's still holding on to post-Chase baby weight. It's why, I suspect, she now heavily favors those potato-sack dresses. I think she looks wonderful, though, if a little tired, certainly better than when at her smallest. I remember vividly her rigid wedding diet plan. She's petite, barely skimming five feet. My thin is the tall kind; hers was the sort where I wondered if she was trying to disappear. When I helped her into her frothy white wedding concoction, I had to hide my wince at the pronouncement of her ribs.

"Anyway, I can't look that different," I say. "You just saw me!" It's only been a few weeks, after all, since I had a couple of events in Manhattan for my latest cookbook.

"I know. It's not enough." She searches my eyes, and for a moment, I wonder if she knows. I keep her gaze. Darcy's eyes are green and clear, without nuance. Perfect. Whereas mine do not have one defined color—I've been told they are like a chameleon's, sometimes they look green, sometimes brown.

"I know. If my next cookbook takes off, maybe we'll buy a second place in New York."

"Don't tease. I would die of happiness!" Darcy squeezes me again. Now Jade is coming toward me, but I hang on to Darcy's embrace a little longer. I love Vix and Jade, to the end, no doubt. But Darcy and I—we are connected, by this place, by our grandmothers.

We are the closest thing to sisters. The only family besides my grandmother, and my husband, that I have in the whole world.

CHAPTER SIX

Séraphine

I appraise myself in the mirror at the top of the stairs, before I begin my descent. A pause before the mirror ceased being for vanity's sake at least forty years ago. But appearances matter. That is the mantra I have lived by, among others. My mother died when I was young, so I didn't have the chance to winnow her wisdom. Rainier's mother became mine when we married; I called her Maman. At first, I was so happy to have a mother again.

On our wedding day, she told me, "Séraphine, all you have in life is your good name. Now your good name is our good name. Our reputation. You must protect our name with everything you have."

I avoid my eyes as I scan myself. There is something in the eyes, I suppose, that is too bracing, making you take stock of yourself, where you have done right by your soul, and where you have not. I have already taken stock of my soul—no use dwelling upon my low marks. That is why the girls are here, after all. I note my hair in the mirror, its sparse locks plumped up with a hairpiece, all dyed to the same pleasing shade of warm blond. It's the color to which old ladies gravitate, as it helps the grays blend in. Canvass old-lady land, why don't you? All of us raven beauties go blond. Not that I was a beauty, mind you, but I was striking. I know I still am.

I inspect my clothes for errant threads. I am wearing a cream pantsuit, with a McQueen scarf covered in skulls. I do like donning the unexpected, the irreverent. My heels are two-inch quilted red Chanels.

Sylvie tells me to quit it with the heels. Apparently, I'm asking for a death sentence by insisting on continuing to live in my master suite upstairs, and then merely walking down these stairs in anything more than a flat without her shepherding me along with her outstretched arm. As if eighty-three-year-old Sylvie is the best vehicle to break my fall. She even tried to talk me out of the authentic stone from the Dordogne region we used in the renovation. Stone is hard on old bones, if you fall. This is what it means to become old. The smallest, most foundational things, like staircases and stone floors, threaten to be taken away from you.

Thankfully, I still wield the pocketbook, which always equals power.

I hear the girls downstairs, reuniting. Those young, untroubled voices. Arabelle and Jade. Those two provoke many complicated feelings in myself that I shove aside. Then my Darcy peels laughter, and my Victoria, too. Victoria is special to me, even though she isn't my blood. Darcy can get jealous—I do notice these things. But she has no reason to be jealous. Darcy is the grandchild of my soul; Victoria is the one whom I chose. With Victoria, I can feel like a bird, soaring in the sky. Whereas with Darcy, I can feel like a squirrel, burrowing into dark soil. This has nothing to do with them, and everything to do with me. Besides, any parent or grandparent knows that you don't love any child more. All four of them here at the chateau together, it gave me some happiness one summer many summers ago. But that is not why I have called them all back here.

There is so much they don't know. And time is running out.

I must protect my name with everything I have.

I understand it now. Maman was right in a way, but also wrong. It only came to me later. Much too late.

I wasn't meant to protect my name at all costs so that people would like me, so that people would respect me. I was to protect my name at all costs so that *I* would like myself. So that *I* would respect myself.

There is a giant chasm between, and for much too long I have been terrified to leap. Here is the truth: Americans fear not being liked, whereas we French fear being accused of a *faute*. Of making a mistake. Of being blamed. Indeed, these fears live deep in my bones. But I have made many mistakes. I deserve mountains of blame. And now I must forge forward and dig up the truth, however difficult and painful it will be, for myself and also for the ones on whom the truth lands.

I fight a wave of nausea that is all too frequent these days. Sylvie is concerned that I spend so much time in bed.

"I am an old lady," I tell her.

I do not tell her that I have cancer. Cancer of the blood—a death sentence, as my doctor told me regretfully. That it has taken over my body. That I don't have much time. If I told Sylvie these things, I would have to contend with her heartbreak, and my energy must be conserved for what I must do.

I hesitate at the top of the stairs. I am not afraid to descend them for safety's sake, as is everyone else on my behalf. But today I am indeed afraid of what awaits me at the bottom.

I smile now at the woman in the mirror, to give her courage, to remind her of her purpose. Given enough time, a fake smile can become a true smile. Sure enough, soon I am not fake smiling at my reflection. Now my smile is true because I cannot wait to fold Darcy and Victoria in my arms.

Some moments of pleasure, before I attempt to make things right.

———

There is much fuss made of my arrival. A lot of exclamations about stairs and their dangers. A story about someone's great aunt's cousin's friend—some fossil or another—who toppled down mere porch steps, to great damage.

Darcy, I've seen, of course, but not enough. Is it ever enough when your grandchild lives across the world? She is forty, and looks it. Tired. She's gained a little weight. Perhaps more than a little. She has her mother's lips, those perfect bows. Her pale, freckled skin.

But the rest of her—especially those green eyes—is her father. My Antoine.

"*Tu m'as manqué, Grand-mère,*" Darcy whispers against my neck. *I missed you, Grandmother.*

"*Oui, oui, ma chérie.*" ·

This is our big hug, maybe our last. We are not a touchy family. Generally, we just *faire la bise*—the French custom of air kisses by the cheek. Hugs are relegated to beginnings and endings. The reunion and the parting. I once overheard Darcy tell Jade that hugging me was as satisfying as hugging tissue paper. I wasn't offended. It is a true statement. I am a slippery person. It is hard to pin me down, get up underneath all my layers. As I smell Darcy's lemony skin, I hold tighter. Maybe I was wrong all these years. Maybe I should have been gripping on, instead of slipping away.

Darcy sets me back at arm's length. I steel myself for her appraisal. She can't know I am sick. There is much to be done this week, without a fuss to be made.

I can tell by her softened gaze that I have passed whatever test she levied.

"You saw the money?" I say quietly. "You got it?"

I gave her ten thousand euros, five thousand of which I intended to support her start-up. It's called The Fertility Warrior. She began it a year ago, inspired by all those pricks and jabs and doctors and operations it took to give her children. Does the world need a Fertility Warrior? Perhaps. I am not the one to say. I know she needs a bit of money, and I am happy to give her some. The extra five thousand euros I gave her after I found out that Oliver and the kids were coming to France, too. All those flights, hotels. It is my pleasure to help. I don't tell her that soon when I am gone, most of this will be hers anyhow. She will be financially fine. She will be rich. *En effet*, she will be *very* rich. I must talk to her about my Will. It is one of the things on my list.

Her gaze shifts off me, to her nails. They are a ballerina pink, like mine. "Yes. Thank you, Grand-mère. I can't thank you enou—"

"*Arrête*. It's my pleasure, I told you."

"Séraphine." That's my Victoria, on my side. "It's so good to see you."

"You too, *ma chérie*." We do not hug. That is not our way. But we *faire la bise*, and when we step back with some distance, my eyes shine at her, and hers back to me. She's bigger, heftier, than the other girls. She takes up space, my Victoria, and that is something, in a world where we women often do not. And she takes up space not by being the loudest, or the silliest, or the most aggressive, but just by her presence, which is calm and knowing. Victoria is also beautiful, with her long, wavy hair and clear skin and tiger eyes, brown, with yellow flecks. I have known her in the past to show off her cleavage, but today she does not, for understandable reasons.

"You . . . ?" My eyes search hers. Then I gaze around. Darcy has wandered off to greet Sylvie.

Victoria nods.

Good. I feel a breath release from me that I didn't know I was holding.

"We will meet tonight, after dinner. You will come to my room."

"Of course."

"And don't tell the girls," I say quietly.

"Of course not."

"Don't tell the girls what?" That's Jade, coming over with a cheer I know is false, at least insofar as it is directed at me. As always, her eyes are the first thing I notice of her. The right one like a glacial lake, translucent and brilliantly blue. The left shifty—sometimes green, sometimes blue. Both eyes deboning me. Or trying to.

"To try to convince Séraphine that she really shouldn't be walking up and down stairs," Victoria says quickly.

"*Oui, oui*, I am old," I say, relieved at the easy way Victoria changed the subject. "Tell me something I do not know."

Jade meets my eyes with no fear, and also no reverence. I remember this. It is unusual to face a person who reacts to me like this. She is lean in a way that makes one wince, her muscle tone thoroughly American. In France, we take things far softer, including our muscles.

I remember twenty years ago that Jade told the girls how she'd tamed her relationship with food. I found this hilarious, inconceivable. I still do. French people don't have a relationship with food. I have no emotion for food; it is merely something I use to stay alive. I enjoy it to be presented well, and I often take pleasure in it, but food is not a person. I neither love it nor hate it.

But I digress. Jade is wearing some workout attire with so many straps and fasteners I imagine it must take her a while to get into the thing. The outfit is burgundy, an improvement in color from her outfits I remember, all of which had in common an allergy to anything that was not black. It was black denim paired with black leather. Black spandex with what was essentially a black bra.

If I were to offer my opinion, which Jade certainly does not want, she makes the French *faux pas* of wearing too tight a bottom and too tight a top, where going looser in one or the other would serve her. Another rule I stand by: If you are revealing your legs, cover your arms, and vice versa. But I am an old lady; clearly there is no longer anything tight, or revealing. Whereas Jade is my opposite, all skin, every curve on display. She could do with a little French style infusion. For instance, I love a *broche*. The jaunty little hat would provide some flair to her outfits, without resorting to skin. But then, no one much wears *broches* anymore. Strangely, this more than most things, makes me momentarily very sad. But perhaps Jade's way serves her just fine. The older I've gotten, the more uncertain I've felt, that the ways I've done things have been the right ones.

Jade adjusts her top, perhaps realizing that her cleavage is spilling out so thoroughly that a nipple might slip by. I remember quite well her black lace dress with spectacular cleavage at Darcy's wedding on that small island in Michigan, where there are no cars and they are known for their fudge, which is cloyingly sweet. Mackinac Island, that's what it's called. Where Oliver is from. The weekend my diamond necklace was stolen.

My eyes flit to Jade's beautiful, tanned flesh, and the necklace with a single diamond at her throat. I have to admit, Jade, as opposed to my granddaughter, looks quite young and radiant. Still, she has a hard, almost masculine, energy—evident in how she molds her body, and in how calculated I know her to be.

"Hello, Séraphine," says Jade.

"Hello, Jade."

"Thank you for inviting me."

"You are most welcome."

Jade nods. "I'm sure it will be an interesting week." I focus on her word choice. *Interesting*. She's almost baiting me. Or maybe I am imagining it.

"I think that it shall." I clear my throat. I see Sylvie off to the side, ready to busy me upstairs. She will insist I take a nap. And I will not object.

"Well, my darlings, I am happy that you are here." I meet their eyes, one by one, landing at last upon Arabelle, whom of course I have already greeted. "I am certain it will be a week of fun, and a week of truth."

"Truth?" asks Jade.

"Truth," I repeat. "Truth is a good thing, *n'est-ce pas?*"

I watch Jade search my eyes for clues. I wonder how much she already suspects. What she thinks that she knows. "Truth is always a good thing," she finally says.

I nod at Jade, then to Sylvie, and make my way back toward the stairs. It occurs to me that it is funny, that I made all this effort with my makeup and hair and outfit only to descend my stairs for a few minutes and then ascend them once again.

"Okay, ladies. I will see you at seven for *apéro* on the *terrasse*. Then eight for dinner."

"Seven sharp on the terrace," echoes Darcy, for the benefit of her friends. Darcy is never late, but this is what she's done all her life—go to battle for my comfort. For my happiness. And now I will battle for her, in a way I should have done a long time ago.

"Enjoy." I mount the stairs and decline Sylvie's proffered elbow. "For now, my darlings, just enjoy."

CHAPTER SEVEN

Jade

My appointed room is at the back of the chateau on the first floor. I arrived to my name in careful script on a wooden placard, strung on the antique silver doorknob of the same room I always occupied every time we came here when we studied abroad. But then Arabelle asked me to switch to her room just across the hall—giving me the larger, nicer room with the bathtub. Her allergies are acting up, and the larger room has windows that open up to trees which, during the height of ragweed season, isn't optimal. I said yes, of course, twist my arm. I have fond memories of taking baths in Arabelle's bathroom, with her flipping through a magazine on the chaise while I bathed. My original room abuts the stairwell and is cozy and cute, but smaller. Anyway, it doesn't matter much where we stay. We won't be in our rooms a lot, mostly together, out in the main spaces of the chateau and bopping around Provence.

Now I'm sitting on the bed made up in crisp white linens, with a thin cream velvet blanket, happy for some moments alone, as my bath fills in the ensuite. I told Arabelle she was welcome to come in and hang out during my bath. It's our tradition from my study abroad, how we'd catch up and further bond all those weekends Darcy would bring Vix and me to the chateau. But for now, I savor my alone time, even on girls' trips, and even when I'm with my family. It's not anything against any of them. It's just me. I need quiet in order to discern what's in my mind. Otherwise it's a giant messy swirl. And I need that quiet especially now, back at Séraphine's.

The first time Darcy brought us here, I remember Arabelle showing me her room. She lived at the chateau while in culinary school, so it had her things, but still, it had Séraphine's touch all over it. I used to call it the Blue Room, because while just as fancy-pants as the rest of the place, it was like a chateau in a storybook, where every room had a theme, and this one was blue, with a whole lot of faded chinoiserie and vintage cookbooks piled in corners. Now, with the restoration, the room is far more serene, and all of Arabelle's childhood artifacts are gone. The blue bedding has been replaced with the neutral linens, and hazy light drifts in from the windows. And unlike the main areas with gray stone floors, here there are hexagonal tiles all varying Sedona-red shades, imperfect, some of them higher than others.

My bath is ready. I have a sense for these things. Seb would call it flirting with danger, because I can putter around the house, jump down to the kitchen, check on the kids, while the bathwater runs. But I always go in right before the water spills off the edge. Seb's argument is that if I get distracted, the water will overflow. But I am never distracted. So why watch and wait, twiddling my thumbs?

My bath is ready now, but I don't go in and turn off the water just yet. Séraphine will never know. I'll wipe up any overflow. But I have to admit, it gives me small pleasure to spoil Séraphine's perfect floors for even a few moments.

⸺

"So, how's Seb?" Arabelle is sprawled on the cream chaise lounge, facing me as I luxuriate in the slate gray tub. She wandered in when she heard the bathwater running, and we danced around a bit before I submerged, both of us an almost childlike giddy to be reunited here and to relive such a simple tradition of our earlier years. The window behind Arabelle opens onto the terrace, where herbs brim in earthenware pots, their leaves spackled in dew. If I didn't know it was real, the view would seem an almost cartoonlike juxtaposition of fluorescent green against dazzling cloudless sky.

"Seb's good." I use a loofah on my arm, rubbing in my woody-scented body wash. "Same. Workaholic. Hardly see him lately, which sometimes is great for my marriage." I shrug, think about it. "We love each other, you know that. But I've always been kind of a loner. Besides you girls. Our marriage works for me. And I'm busy with the kids. . . ." I think about that sentence, and its truth, or lack thereof. The kids are older now. They disappear into their rooms the second I click the garage door shut, after shuttling them to and from their activities. Soon they'll be driving, or taking the subway on their own, and I won't even have those rides together. Truthfully, I won't mind it. It's nice to have some space. Do I miss the sweet newborn phase? The sticky toddler hands? No, unpopular opinion: I like them wiping their own butts, thank you very much.

"And anyway, I'm busy with—"

"Spinning."

"Spinning," I echo, even though it makes what I do sound simple, trite, when at the core, I am striving to make people's lives better. In the dark candlelit space that I intentionally curated to be both peaceful and enlivening, people shout out the things that they want to sweat out, out of their bodies and out of their lives. And then at the end, I ask them to call out what they are welcoming into their lives. Because often, someone who can provide pitch-perfect help is spinning on the next bike over. In my spin classes, we've matched an entrepreneur with an angel investor. A matchmaker with a single gal. Many, many connections, that have enriched both the helper and the helpee. *Women's Health* has called me the Oprah of fitness. It's important to me, to help people. Even if it hasn't worked for the one person whom I've wanted all my life to help.

But there is a nagging inside me, something that I've been pushing aside for a while. That maybe there are other, deeper ways to help people. Ways besides spinning. I have no idea what that would even be, and aren't I too old to follow some new whim besides? There's a reason you don't hear about forty-year-olds who switched from law partner to nuclear physicist. At some point you have to pick a path, and follow it to your death.

And trying something new would feel like everything I've done to build my career was for nothing. Wouldn't it?

But somehow, in this lead-up to my fortieth birthday, I keep dreaming about myself as a child, when I heard someone at school mention how they were playing the piccolo. The piccolo! I didn't even know what that was. But it just sounded cool, the word. When I went home, I told my father I wanted to play the piccolo and instead of telling me how expensive that would be, how impractical, that there were simpler things to choose if I wanted to be musical, like the guitar, or the flute, he indulged my spontaneous desire. And so for three years, I played the piccolo with a teacher we found an hour away. Papa took me on the subway every week. Frankly, I was terrible. But it was fun. I followed a whim. I don't know if you're allowed to follow whims after forty, when everything feels so intractable—husband, career, private school, stuff. So much stuff.

God, where did that all come from? Arabelle is sifting through her magazine, oblivious to my inner turmoil. I think about sharing it, but nothing is articulated enough inside of me to even express. This must be some sort of middle-age crisis, I tell myself firmly. It will pass.

"You and Giancarlo are different, huh?" I ask Arabelle. "Together twenty-four-seven?"

"More. Twenty-five-seven." Arabelle laughs. She leans closer, sniffing. "Is that Seb's soap?"

"Mine. I like to smell like a man."

"I like to smell like flowers." Arabelle laughs again. Her teeth aren't perfect, and neither is her nose, a bit on the bulbous side. Her skin isn't as flawless as mine, and that's not being critical, just accurate. She hasn't done Botox or fillers, just the creams you get at the pharmacy. Her nails aren't glossy perfect—they are buffed, that's it. And her long dirty blond hair is perfectly imperfect in a way I know is natural. She didn't blow dry, then curl, then flick through a straightener to add different kinds of curls, like I do. I once told her she should film an IGTV on her hair routine and she looked at me all confused. She said the video would be exceedingly short, because all she does is shampoo, add a bit of conditioner (sometimes, not always), and then brush it and let it air dry. To add insult to injury, she's never at the gym; hell, I don't think she believes in it, on principle. She runs—very fast, not very long. Not to lose weight, or to tone her arms or legs, things we Americans aspire to. She says it's to get out her energy. Can you imagine? I don't want to admit, mostly to myself, how much grit it takes me, how much pep-talking I need to do, to get to my spin class every morning. And I own the studio!

What it would be to just pop out of bed with too much energy that you need to run to get it out!

But Arabelle's workout continues into her day. The girl is never not moving. Where most people are deskbound, she is in the kitchen, stirring things, and walking to the market. Her spray tan is luxuriating outdoors, selecting the best cucumbers. All the while putting together outfits that could leap out of *Vogue* that she wears to deliver the short snappy videos and now reels she is famous for. In them she appears beside her farmhouse sink, with *just a little* astuce *to get your chef on*. Like whisking and salting your eggs fifteen minutes before you put them on the stove because the interaction with the salt and protein makes them creamier. I tried her tip, in fact. My family noticed nothing. But perhaps it's difficult to notice eggs that are a smidge creamier when you're riveted to the market fluctuations, or to the latest viral TikTok.

Now Arabelle looks just as unintentionally chic as in one of her Instagram lives, wearing an oversize white blouse with the sleeves pushed up to her elbows, tucked into a short cream skirt with an asymmetrical teardrop panel hanging down over one thigh. She's the kind of gorgeous that takes me massive effort to attain. I apply that massive effort, so I turn out well, I think. But it's the effort that people take note of, and subtract marks from your result.

"Hey." I sit up, displacing water to the floor. "What happened to the painting?"

"What painting?" Arabelle tosses down a towel, lest the water creep to the wooden feet of the lounge.

"The moody black one, with the flowers." I point to the empty spot above the sunken stone sink, between the two mini chandeliers that resemble small crystal shrubs. I squint. "Look, there's still the hook."

"Oh. I don't know."

"You remember it, though?"

"Sure." Arabelle shrugs. "Maybe they changed it in the renovation."

"And left the hook?"

"Mmm. Not sure. You liked the painting?"

"I guess." There was something about it, was all. It was just flowers, nothing special, really.

Arabelle checks her watch, a Rolex. Our girl isn't one for the dermatologist's office, but she does get swayed by pretty things. It's a drop in the bucket for her. Although she grew up with nothing, she's rolling in money now, entirely self-made. Her 1.7 million Instagram followers flock to @arabelleinnice for her French country food, aspirational Côte d'Azur lifestyle, posh, charming inn and cooking school, and the most naturally chic outfits ever paired with her Rolex, or an Hermès bag, or something Zara, because her philosophy is mixing high and low.

Darcy has 14,000 followers (@thefertilitywarrior). Whereas I have 115,000 myself (@churchofspinning). Not too shabby. But sometimes, on a low day, I can't help but feel like my followers are my most pertinent descriptor. The measure of my worth. Jade Assouline: 115,000.

And no, I didn't change my surname when I married. I couldn't. Not after what my father and his family endured in the Holocaust to retain it.

"Belle, why do you think Séraphine invited us here? Now?" I give a final rinse to my hair and stand up in the bath. Arabelle doesn't avert her eyes, like an American would. And I don't hasten into a towel. I'm proud of my body. I like showing it off. Even to a woman. Even to my friend. Maybe especially to my friend.

"I don't have a clue." Arabelle folds the magazine closed. "I assume we'll find out soon enough. She looks well, doesn't she?"

"She always does. That woman is a battle axe."

"She's a survivor," Arabelle agrees.

"Yes." That word always infuses my mouth with a metallic taste.

"Oh, Jade." Arabelle realizes. "*Désolée*. Your family . . ."

"My grandparents." I make my voice light, wrapping myself in the white waffle robe that was draped on a wooden stool at the foot of the bath.

"They were French, right? That's why you decided to study abroad in Avignon? Revisit your roots?"

"Yes. You know, my father refused to speak French at home when I was growing up. I wanted to learn it. My mom tried to convince him, but he refused. He was all about being an American, assimilating. Trying to forget the past. Which I get, but whenever I'm here, I feel sad I don't speak French nearly as well as you, or even Darcy. . . ."

It's my roots I'm thinking of, but also my children, and their precarious place in this world amid the recent dramatic rise in anti-Semitism. I've barely confided in my friends. Only Darcy. I suppose it's felt too heavy, too shattering. I didn't mean to hide it from Belle, it just never seemed the appropriate time to insert it into conversation.

I am transported to a couple of months before, when Lux lumbered across the courtyard at school pickup. My eyes immediately locked on the gash at his lower lip.

"Lux, what happened to your lip?" They should tell you in parenting manuals how your blood freezes up when you suspect someone has done something to your child. It makes running from a tiger sound like a leisurely country stroll.

"They took my necklace," he said quietly, the lifeblood sapped from my gregarious nine-year-old.

"Took it?" The Star of David necklace he requested for his birthday. Suddenly I felt incapable of drawing breath.

We are secular Jews, but I make a challah every Friday night. We say the prayers and bless the kids and Seb never works on Shabbat—

if you know him, a major concession toward us keeping the traditions. I remembered how I clasped the necklace around Lux's neck and we both smiled at his reflection in the mirror. Lux Jacob, my sweet boy, his middle name an homage to the grandfather I never got to meet. I did have a twinge of a thought then—is it safe to send my child out into the world wearing a Jewish bull's-eye? But I buried the fear, because living free and outright as Jews is an act of defiance to all those who would repeat or deny the Holocaust.

"Yeah. At recess." Lux hung his head so I could see the sweet tip-top crown, his light hair swooped into a side part, like his dad's. "They pushed me to the ground and grabbed it off my neck. They said Jews control the world."

"Did you tell the teachers?" I tried to keep my fury at bay, but I knew I wasn't succeeding. "They'll . . . suspend them! Kick them out of school. How dare they . . . How . . ."

Lux shrugged, looked down. "It's okay, Mom. I didn't want it to be a thing."

"It's not okay! It's a hate crime. That's what it is. Who did it?"

Lux didn't answer, just peered toward the school and then back at me. "Mom, can we just go?"

So we did, with me white-knuckling my handbag. And everything flew at me—what my father endured, but also the horrible boy who used to hate-whisper "Jew" at me in high school every time he passed me in the halls.

After, Seb and I debated enrolling the kids in Jewish school in the fall. We still haven't come to a decision. The kids like their friends and teachers. And Jewish school carries other hefty price tags—four armed guards at every entrance; frequent active shooter drills.

We bought Lux a new Star of David necklace, but he doesn't want to wear it out of the house anymore. I understand. Of course I do. But my heart breaks for my children who live in a world that will at times reject them for being Jewish. Now, every Friday night as we sing the ancient prayers, it feels like the joy has been sucked out of my family a little bit. If this can happen to us, in seemingly progressive New York City, then what has truly changed since the horrors my father endured? Contemplating that of late has become my own special purgatory.

"You've never told me the story of your family," Arabelle says now, looking at me curiously.

"Really?" But my heart has clenched, stopping me from offering it up. My mind drifts from Lux on over to my dad, to his nightmares. It's more than genetics that connect Papa and me. We are bound by this chateau, and the past, and certain loose ends. When I received the invitation from Séraphine, I found it eerily opportune. Because after what those kids did to Lux, I am determined to leave loose ends no longer.

Arabelle stands. She smiles at me sadly. I know she won't probe. An American might, but not a Frenchwoman. "This place is good for burying things, *n'est-ce pas?*"

I'm not sure if she's talking about this country, or this house. But it doesn't really matter. Because the truth is that, with enough effort, everything buried can be dug up.

But I don't say so. "Yes," I agree. "This place is good for burying things."

CHAPTER EIGHT

Vix

My clothes are all in my carry-on, and I place them one-by-one in the walnut armoire. Séraphine once told me this armoire used to belong to Rainier's mother, and with a wink she said she was sorry for saddling me with that wretched woman's energy. I don't mind; I don't believe in curses, or things like that. And I appreciate how all the furniture in this house has a personality, a story. Even the new stuff, I'm told by Arabelle, was sourced at antiques markets. *Sourced.* Just that word epitomizes the chateau, and Séraphine's sheer wealth. Other people pick up trinkets at markets; she sources things. It's ironic, though, I think, how my appreciation for the weathered, the nicked, the imperfect, doesn't extend to myself.

My eyes trip over the Degas hung casually beside the armoire. That's the thing about this place—it's all very cool, unpretentious almost, in its spacious restraint, until you catch on to the astounding wealth and genius encapsulated in these walls. The ballerina shimmers off the canvas, almost in flight, swathed in a costume of fluttery blue. I peer closer at the bold brushstrokes and vivid colors for which Degas was renowned later in his life. At once, the familiar shame barrels at me: that I am, most definitively, *not* Degas. That I have not created anything close to this scale and luminosity that Degas replicated again and again—and I likely never will. When I first saw the Degas, Séraphine was contemplating a renovation that would strip the chateau of *all the noise*. That would refresh her home, revert it to

47

a blank canvas, so she *could breathe again*. I asked if she would keep the Degas, though, despite its bold color—wouldn't she? She smiled and said she was a woman who could compromise on her preferences, if in the guise of a Degas. Or a Renoir. (There is a resplendent Renoir in Séraphine's bedroom from his lesser-known scenes in Algeria.)

I laughed, the response the moment demanded, but inside, I felt the knot tighten in my chest, that I would never be worthy of, or paid, such a compliment. Séraphine, always astute, said, "Victoria, I see so much promise in you." She was referring to my sketches, the charcoals I did out by the pool, of the girls, of Séraphine herself. And the landscape paintings I was attempting, of this land that had woven its way so completely into my soul. "Otherwise I wouldn't have asked you to . . ."

I nodded quickly. And I internalized the praise, let it settle in my core. Maybe I never fully believed in myself, but *Séraphine* believed in me. And that was enough then. But now I wonder, twenty years later, if she still sees all that promise. Or are her encouraging words empty these days—just the things she finds kindly to say?

I shake my head, try to shake away my thoughts, and I resume unpacking my carry-on, all the things that Arabelle helped me pick out. When she was in town after my most recent surgery, she took me shopping at Barneys. She insisted it was on her. A new wardrobe for a new cancer-free me.

I hang a white flowy dress on a silk padded hanger. Bronze leather pants. Slouchy boots—rich amber leather with silver studs. The boots are the nicest, most sumptuous shoes I've ever owned.

In a flash I find myself stripping my bike shorts, stripping my oversize tee. I slip out of my sandals and into the boots and stand in front of the mirror, naked. This is my new hobby—inspecting the new me. Trying to get accustomed to her. I look like a naked cowgirl. I turn this way and that. I always liked my body, is the thing. I was the biggest child in kindergarten, a chubby high school graduate. But my parents always told me I was the most beautiful girl in the world, and I believed them. It's a cringey story to retell, but my dad used to lull me to sleep with a bedtime story about the fairest, smartest princess in all the land, Victoria the Brilliant Beauty. To this day my parents still call me BB. I'm the biggest of my friends, but it never bothered me. I was voluptuous, sensual. But now, without my boobs, it all feels different. Like I'm wearing someone else's skin. I cup my frankenboobs in my hands, then let them droop. They are half moons, half suns—halves. It hurts to look at myself right now, in this body that isn't mine. I don't know how to dress it, how to walk it, how to move it. Nothing about it feels familiar, or home.

But these boots. I fix my eyes on my feet. When I came back to our East Village place after shopping, I modeled the boots for Juliet. Even though they're stunning, I wasn't sure about them. For one, the exorbitant price tag that Arabelle insisted on treating me to. Second, whether they are really my style. Pre-mastectomy I was called sultry, sassy, sensual. Sexy. My nickname was Vixen. The girls are trying hard not to call me that anymore, and it pisses me off, to be honest. Like without my permission, everyone has conspired to subtract a piece of my identity.

I used to like balconette bras, and satin tops that feel like water on your skin, slip dresses with tie backs. Dressing rooms were my favorite place, alone. Looking at myself in the mirror. It sounds shallow maybe, but it wasn't, not really. Maybe I loved myself too much.

Well, nothing about breast cancer says sexy. I don't want to be sexy anymore. Full stop. So I bought new things, covered things, edgy things, boho things, and God knows if they are me. Juliet did the whole nice, nice, about my wardrobe haul, and then she asked me who paid for it. I know she thought I was going to say Séraphine, but I told her the truth. I said Arabelle. And then Juliet proceeded to say some very cruel things.

As I stare at myself now in the mirror, I know that she was right. Cruel as it was, she spoke the truth. Did I see something wrong with Arabelle plying me with money? Considering Séraphine has been bankrolling my life ever since I was twenty-one. To this day, I'm still not sure why. She said she saw herself in me, from the very moment we met. That she believed in my art. That she didn't want me to ever have to depend on a man.

She comes from a different world. A different generation.

What would you do if a stranger offered you five thousand euros a month, until forever? Would you say no?

For fuck's sake, you would say yes.

I said yes.

Juliet only found out about this arrangement when Séraphine invited us for the reunion. She called me and asked me for one final favor, to be completed at the chateau. I did something for her when I was twenty-one, when Darcy first brought me here. And now she needed me to finish it. Juliet overheard me with Séraphine on the phone. She had always wondered how I could support myself, when I sell just a few paintings a year, for small amounts. *Small amounts.* Now, the pieces slipped in place for her. I've always felt ashamed, is the thing. Because deep down I think I could be doing more with my life. And I feel guilty, too, because I'm pretty sure Séraphine doesn't have the same financial arrangement with her own granddaughter. My best friend.

Juliet demanded to know what favor Séraphine had asked of me. What I'd sold myself for.

That riled me up. *I wouldn't sell myself to anyone, for anything!*

But didn't I? When you accept money you didn't earn, there is always a price.

In hindsight I think I was just angry at myself. Because I have sold myself, in ways that are like sawdust splinters in my skin, burrowed so deep at this point that they are impossible to pry out.

Then Juliet twisted the knife. She grimaced and said it made sense. But then she didn't expand. I know I shouldn't have asked. I know it. But of course I did. I asked her what that meant, and she said that she understood more than just my sources of my money. She understood why I approached painting almost passion-free. Those are the exact words she used. You don't forget words as cutting as those, far more painful than my post-surgery physique. *Passion-free.* It was like she dug right into my brain and pulled up my deepest vulnerability. I responded hotly that I had passion in spades, and she just said, *You might have it, somewhere, but it's buried under all the money. And I can't do this anymore.*

She meant me. She couldn't do me anymore. Passion-free, boob-less me.

All of this will be over soon, I promise myself, staring into my foreign, naked reflection. And then what?

Then there is a knock, and before I can say enter, or not, Darcy has slipped inside the room. My hands go reflexively across my chest.

"You're naked." She averts her eyes.

"Yep."

"Except for . . ." Her eyes travel to my feet. "Those are some really hot boots."

"Thanks." I smile weakly and check myself out in them again.

"Do you want privacy?" Darcy asks.

"What? No," I say, and then I catch a glimpse of my massive suit-case, still sitting packed and zipped shut by the painted canvas para-vent. I hesitate. Maybe I should say yes. Shuttle her out. Shove the suitcase out of sight.

"Okay, well . . ." Darcy is looking at me strangely.

"Well what?"

"Do you want to put some clothes on?"

"Oh." I laugh a jittery laugh. I pull a dress over my head.

When I look at myself in the mirror, clothed, I grimace. In this flowing dress, I look like Darcy. Not that she isn't beautiful, because she is, very much so, petite and feminine, with her billowing dresses. But I don't want to look like her. My style used to be revealing, body-skimming. And I don't know what it is to look like me anymore.

I sit on the bed and avoid looking at myself.

"You have *more* clothes in there?" Darcy indicates the suitcase that doesn't contain clothes.

"I didn't know what would look good on me," I hear myself snap.

"Oh, God. I'm so sorry, Vix." Darcy nods, blushes. "That makes sense."

So many lies. And too many of them to myself.

"How is it to be back here again?" I ask her.

"Oh." She goes to the window that overlooks the pool. "I always forget this room has the same view as my grandmother's suite."

Darcy is across the hall, in a grander suite than mine. Beside her, closer to Séraphine, is Sylvie's room. Darcy's and Sylvie's rooms overlook the front of the house.

I join her at the window. "I can never get over this view."

"Yeah." She presses a hand to the pane. "You know my grandmother saw him fall. Watched him die."

She's talking about her grandfather. I know how traumatic his death was for Darcy. Even though her father died when she was young, too, her grandfather's death was visceral. It happened feet from her, in a gruesome way. It makes sense that coming back here triggers it anew.

"It's horrible." I don't know what else to say.

"She's had such a hard life, my grandmother. A privileged life, but hard."

"She never remarried. . . ."

"No. She never wanted to. She's always said she had the great love of her life, and she didn't need anyone else."

I consider that, how just two weeks ago I thought I had the great love of my life, too.

"Do you think if Oliver died, you'd remarry?" I ask. Once it's out, I regret the morbid question. But I find myself thinking about death a lot these days. Death, and also its opposite. What it means to be really alive.

Darcy smiles a strange smile, and at first, I think she will laugh off the question. But then she says, "I think the better question is, if Oliver is dead, did I kill him?"

A laugh blurts out of me, unwittingly.

But Darcy doesn't laugh. Instead she slaps her hands on her thighs. It is her typical punctuation on a sentence, her unspoken transition to the next.

Sure enough, Darcy says, "I'm going to take a walk before dinner. Wanna join?"

"Sure!" But then my eyes land on my other suitcase. I need to unpack it, figure out where to hide things. "Actually no, that's okay. I'll just chill here for a bit, and see you at dinner."

"Okay, love ya!" she says.

I smile. "Love you."

"And don't be late, 'kay?" she adds. "You know . . ." she trails off, catching my slightly peeved look.

I was only late for dinner that one time, nearly twenty years ago. But clearly Darcy hasn't forgotten it.

Darcy shrugs as she waltzes off. "Grand-mère just hates it when anyone is late."

CHAPTER NINE

Raph

I am up in a tree, picking cherries, when I see a figure wander across the meadow from the main house. I throw a hand to my brow to deflect the waning sun.

It's one of the ladies, the one that sat up front with me on the ride from the airport, wearing the dress that looks like a nightgown. She's just spotted me, now a few feet away, and her darting eyes communicate that she's trying to decide if it would be rude if she passes without stopping to chat.

I add some cherries to my basket, trying to give off the impression that it would be quite fine if she moseys along without pleasantries.

But no such luck. She stops at the foot of the tree, in a chorus of birdsong that is so fitting to her that I almost laugh. *"Bonsoir,"* she says.

"Bonsoir," I reply.

"Hi!" She waves. "Darcy."

"Yes, I remember." Of course I do. Not only did she just sit beside me on the ride from the airport, but Séraphine has often spoken of her. I've been intrigued to meet the famous granddaughter. Once, when we were playing *pétanque*, and Séraphine had told me about her cancer, she leaned on her cane and said, "Watch out for Darcy when I'm gone, will you? Make sure she is safe." She said it in this very serious way, like Darcy was in danger, somehow. Like I could possibly watch over a woman I didn't know, who lives in New York.

But I said, *"Bien sûr*, I promise that I will," and we went back to playing *pétanque*. And I did mean it when I said it. I always mean the things that I say.

"I'm Raph."

She nods. "Yes, I remember, too." Something in the way she says it makes me want to salute her. Not in a mean way. Just, she seems like a formal person. Or maybe she is just very sad. I don't say it disparagingly, rather as an observation only we sad people can really make of each other.

There is nothing to do but amble down my ladder.

"Would you like a cherry?" I offer her the basket.

"Sure. Thanks." She reaches inside, selects a cherry, places it in her mouth. Her eyes flutter closed. When she opens them, she says, "*Coeur de pigeon.*"

"What?"

"It's the name of the cherry."

"Oh, yes. Right. How is it, then?"

"Well, to be honest, I think you picked them one week late." She nods ruefully in the direction of the fruit flies, now zipping around my basket. "See, if you'd picked them almost ripe, the flies wouldn't flock."

She's right, I immediately apprehend. I turn my head, so she won't see my reaction. I am irritated with myself. I've talked to the guy at the market many times about what to do. I had him come out here, show me some things. Some of it is intuitive. I thought it would be easy. How much knowledge does it take, to weed and pick and grow? I'm not in charge of the winery—I'm the pool boy. The cherry picker. I also must tend to the blasted herb garden, with thyme, rosemary, bay, and oregano. The *terroir* is my terrain—the earth, the soil. And God, I need to figure out when to clip the *courgettes* off the vines.

"How do you know so much about cherries?" I finally ask.

"My grandfather used to pick cherries, from this very tree. He taught me."

"Ah." It is likely she would be a better groundskeeper than I.

The mistral gusts in suddenly, whipping through the poppies and sunflowers that only in the past few weeks have spawned children and grandchildren and great-grandchildren in the meadow. "I suppose there is no longer a point of picking."

"I saw that Arabelle got cherries from the market." Her lips peep with a smile. "Yours will be fantastic for jam."

"At least they will be good for something." I fold up my ladder and tuck it under my armpit. Then, with my basket in hand, I start back toward the chateau. I look back. "Are you coming?"

"I think I'll wander a bit longer before dinner," Darcy says.

I nod, and begin to walk again, but then she continues alongside me after all. "I haven't been to the chateau in a couple of years," she says. "Gosh, it brings back so many memories."

"I can imagine."

"And I have two kids. It's not often that I have silence." I didn't ask these things; she offered them up. She wants to talk, I understand. She is lonely, maybe, even with her grandmother and all of her friends.

"Two kids," I repeat.

"A boy and a girl."

"Me too," I say, before I can stop myself.

"Oh really? How sweet. Are you married?"

"Not married. *Non.*"

"And your kids? They live here, with you?" She looks around, as if two kids might suddenly come singing down from the mountains, like in that movie *The Sound of Music*, with the actress whose voice sounds like honey and whose hair is short like a man's.

"No." My hand fumbles in my pocket instinctually, before I even have the thought that *man, I need a cigarette*. I rest the ladder against my side and then light up, exhale. Sometimes I have the sense that cigarettes have become my prop, a thing to do in a scene to avoid a conversational cliff. We continue on, passing evergreens that are planted along the border of the garden, farther from the house for fear that they will block the winter sun. I only know this because Séraphine told me. She has told me a lot of things.

Eventually we are back by the pool. My little cabin is a few steps away, with my laundry strung on the porch. Sylvie offers to do it for me, but I prefer to do things myself.

"Are you coming to dinner?" Darcy asks.

"What? Oh, no." Little in the world sounds worse. "I'll leave you ladies to it."

She nods, doesn't attempt to convince me. If she did, we both know it would be an invite of obligation. "Dinner of mushy cherries, then?"

"Suppose so."

She smiles a bit, amused. She is cute when she smiles. Less sad Victorian chambermaid, more mysterious woman. I suddenly realize that she's walked me back to the chateau, when she intended to stay out. As she gazes around and her smile fades, I can tell that she's realized it, too.

"I'll . . ." She points back toward the meadow. The sun is distinctive now, fiery orange.

"Have a nice evening," I tell her.

"Thanks." Her lips curve into a smile again, this time without teeth. "Have a nice evening as well." Then she pivots and strolls off, her nightgown dress billowing behind her.

An inclination washes over me for a moment, to go after her. To protect her. I shake my head. Shake off that strange instinct.

I remind myself that I'm here, at this chateau, for one reason and one reason only. Money.

CHAPTER TEN

Darcy

We have filed out from *apéro*—wine from our vineyard on the terrace, and noshing on wooden boards of olives and tapenade, small cheese pastries, cold escargots, shrimp *hors d'oeuvres*, and *saucisson*. And now we are convened around the dinner table. Dinner is outdoors, overlooking the vineyard and the rustic planters with giant topiaries shaped into cones, with fat bees buzzing hitherto, and a table that looks sprung from a photoshoot. The heady aromas of pine and juniper waft toward me, the crisp evening air playing against my bare arms. Over the table hovers the two-hundred-fifty-year-old plane tree that is the bedrock of the chateau and the thing that christened its name, Chateau du' Platane. My grandfather once told me that we have the largest plane tree in Provence. I used to sit under the plane tree with Grand-père, at a table long gone, and play Monopoly.

The whispers of the past are louder now in my ears. I readjust my headband so it's not squeezing my ears, and I take in the table. The tablecloth is a pleasing blue-and-white print with artful scribbles. Atop it are bronze trays with small terra-cotta planters holding yellow and white flowers, and little silver cups with lavender bunches. The rest of the table is all in keeping with the blue-and-white theme: a blue floral design on white china edged in gold; starched linen napkins that match the tablecloth; and gold cutlery. The chairs are large, comfy beige wicker with white cushions embroidered with a design of trees, done in blue. Everything has been thought out; Grand-mère leaves nothing to randomness. And tonight, as in all dinners at the chateau, wine will be refilled from jugs when you still have inches left in your glass, so you are never sure just how much you drank.

We sit. The wine begins, or begins again, for those of us who only ceased drinking a couple hours back. My mind is humming, with so many things. Things like, the groundskeeper who doesn't know the most basic facts about local cherries. What's that about?

Food begins to arrive. Arabelle sets down her bouillabaisse, describing how it's made of rockfish, sea robin, and European conger, in a tomato broth with orange zest, fennel, and saffron. I love hearing Belle introduce her dishes. There's something about her recitation, her tone, that's inordinately peaceful, one of the rare times this week my nervous system has unclenched.

"Remember when we rolled up in Paris, all clueless?" Vix asks, helping herself to a piece of *fougasse* flatbread stuffed with olives and herbs de Provence.

I dig my spoon into the bouillabaisse, and after I swallow, I make a chef's kiss at Arabelle. "Divine, Belle."

"Divine," the other girls echo.

"Okay, let me set the scene," Vix says, back to rehashing things we did twenty years ago. Whenever all four of us are together, this inevitably happens.

"It was the early aughts. We didn't have smartphones. We had Nokias. Off we were to Paris, with those, you know—what guides did we have?"

"*Lonely Planet.*" I laugh, then groan. "They were like bricks in my backpack."

"Yes! I had begged my parents for years for this trip." Vix stops, and I know the guilt is trickling through her again. Her parents didn't have the money, but Vix is their precious only child. Let's be real, no one needs to study abroad in order to succeed in life. It's a luxury for those of us privileged enough to receive it. Heck, Grand-mère fully paid for my semester in Avignon. I offered to contribute my savings from all my part-time jobs since I was a kid, and I even wrote out a whole sales pitch, about all the culture I'd experience, and the quality time we'd get. But ultimately Grand-mère's return fax just said, *Of course*. And she refused my offer to add my own funds.

It was the most excited I'd ever been in my life, embarking upon that semester. I'd morphed into an adult the day my father died, and I aged even more when my grandfather did, too. I lived at home in college and spent my nights studying, not partying. I was such a serious kid, not a typical New Yorker who springs first to every trend, and I stayed fairly insular, fumbling with friendships, never quite figuring out how to cement them. Maybe my keep-to-myself-ness was even a rebellion of sorts against my mother, who was constantly out on the town, frittering away money we didn't have on furs and lipsticks and spa excursions with her girlfriends, and always collecting a new suitor to wine and dine her. But then I came across a brochure for study abroad programs tacked to a library corkboard. Suddenly our apartment felt like it was closing in on me, and the last of my youth beckoned from the pictures of kids my age laughing, dwarfed by magnificent French ruins, then navigating the streets of Paris with clunky cameras.

In the end, it was a life-changing semester, lots of quality time with Grand-mère and meeting Jade and Vix. It was only after I came to like them, then in quick succession love them, and after we added Arabelle to our fold, too, that I realized how desperately lonely I'd been. Because unlike Jade, who requires endless alone time to recharge, who loves nothing more than an afternoon spent luxuriating with herself—I need people. I *love* being with people. In hindsight I think it was those early deaths with which I had to cope—in my mind, people you loved died, so why even bother? With the girls, it was finally worth it to bother.

"Remember how we found the cool stuff to do?" I say, all the lovely memories from that semester collecting in my belly like a warm hearth. "We just looked at the list of recommendations from the girls who had studied abroad the year before and followed along blindly."

"You made us stay in the Latin Quarter in Paris!" Jade says.

"That wasn't me," I say.

"It wasn't me!" Vix says.

"Well, it *absolument* was not me." Arabelle laughs.

"No," agrees Vix. "The next time we went to Paris, this time with Arabelle, she whipped us into shape."

"Yes, but before Belle, we were in trouble." Jade laughs. "Remember that bar we went to, just because they hung out there on *Real World: Paris*?"

"The Long Hop!" Vix squeals.

"Oh God." I laugh and drink more wine. My head is starting to feel woozy. Good. I drink more. I know this isn't the French way. French don't overserve, or get overserved. Look at Arabelle, sipping casually. She will finish a glass, maybe two. Never more. But we Americans drink for that rosy-glow cliff, after which we blessedly drop out of our lives, for a bit.

I watch Grand-mère eat her bouillabaisse. She stirs, and then lifts a spoon to her mouth, then puts it back in the soup without swallowing.

Strange. Even in my tipsy haze, it occurs to me that is strange.

"We went to Moulin Rouge, remember?" Vix says. "And we thought the Champs-Élysées was the height of cool."

Arabelle frowns. "It's the equivalent of Times Square."

"We were lost without you," Vix says. "When we went back to Paris with Belle, we stepped up in coolness. You took us to the Orangerie, with the floor-to-ceiling Monets. And Rodin, with all the sculptures. And the Marais!"

"The Marais is more commercial now," Arabelle says. "Now it's the ninth arrondissement that's hot, the eleventh, the second. But I wouldn't have taken you to those places twenty years ago."

"And St. Germain, yeah?" I'm thinking about my forthcoming Paris trip with Oliver and the kids. What spots we should hit. Even though it is difficult, borderline impossible, to conceive of life after this week. Of carefree Paris with my family.

Arabelle shrugs. She's removed her apron to reveal a taupe half-zip cashmere sweater tucked loosely into silver sequin wide-legged pants. "Americans idolize the Left Bank, but the Right Bank is the cooler area, with all the hot neighborhoods."

I flush, but I'm not sure if it's the wine or my not knowing the cool neighborhoods in Paris. Although why would I? I haven't been there in years.

"I wish I could go once more to Paris," Grand-mère says, and everyone falls quiet.

"I'll take you," says Sylvie. "All this talk of Paris has me hankering."

"If you both want to go, I can come," says Arabelle doubtfully, echoing my own thoughts, that they are too old to make the trip alone.

"*Non, merci,*" says Grand-mère sharply. "We will not go. I will not go."

"But Grand-mère," I say, "if you want to, go. You're welcome to come with us next week, too. We'd love it, in fact."

"*Non,*" says Grand-mère, and no one says anything more on the topic.

Other conversation resumes, but my ears are ringing, and I can hear only my own voice, echoing in my head. All of my fears, all of the promises I have made. Promises I don't want to break, because they are to myself. Everything is wrong, and everything is mine alone to bear. Grand-mère is the only one with whom I've confided about my problems—one of them at least: the money.

We are hemorrhaging money.

The Fertility Warrior is going to fold if I don't get more of it fast. I had pride, but I swallowed it. I sent a fax to Grand-mère, asking for money. And she responded that yes, she would help. She deposited money for me. Ten thousand euros, the equivalent to a bit more in dollars. Included in that sum was money to pay for our trip. It's kind but also laughable, that she thinks such a measly figure will solve the problem. I need ten times that much to make a dent. I can't go back to her now, asking for more. On one hand, she is rolling in money. Money she will never use herself. She hardly knows the difference between ten euros and ten thousand. If she knew I needed more, she would give it to me. And I haven't told her the extent of my troubles. I suppose I've felt ashamed.

I watch Grand-mère swirl her spoon in her soup, and I know I can't ask her for more. It's my pride, the pride I inherited from her. Once, I could ask. Not again. Although she did say she wanted to talk about her Will. That little line she wrote on the invitation. Perhaps that will be my *entrée*. It intrigues me to no end, why she wrote it.

Later, after laughs and more wine and *navettes*, orange blossom biscuits, Arabelle's special recipe, Grand-mère clears her throat, and the table falls silent.

"Tomorrow," Grand-mère announces, "is Jade's birthday."

All eyes swivel to Jade. Her lips turn up in a smidge of a smile. However complicated, or not, feelings are her toward Grand-mère, I can tell she is surprised, pleased, maybe, that Grand-mère remembers.

"And so tomorrow, we will celebrate. You ladies are going to the market and then the winery, yes?"

"Yes," Jade says.

"And then at night, something special," I say. Something special, indeed.

"You guys," says Jade. "You don't have to . . ." But her eyes are gleaming, saying *please do*.

"Forty!" Arabelle says. "God, forty is so young, compared to forty-two." She laughs. "Oh, I'm so happy we're all together for it. We're going to blow out!"

"And then after Jade's birthday, I will tell you why I've invited you here," Grand-mère says.

"Because you love them," says Sylvie. "Because we've missed them!"

She wraps an arm around Arabelle, and Arabelle leans onto her grandmother's shoulder. I've always envied their simple, pure love. The way they show it. Declare it. Like a stamp on some paper that is formal and irrevocable, and then framed for all to see.

"Not just because of those reasons," Grand-mère says. "There are some things I must tell you all. Things I have not shared. This is, after all, why I invited you here."

There is now only the sound of the *cigales*, those buzzing cicadas that form the backdrop of June.

"The things I have to say are things that will be painful to hear, for some of you." She looks around the table, goes face to face, and does not shrink from meeting anyone's eyes. "Things you may not want me to say. But I will no longer be silent, and soon you will know everything."

What is she talking about? *Who* is she talking about? Jade? Vix? *Me*?

I have been in the world of my own troubles, a vast world indeed. And now there is an ominous tenor to this week that I didn't foresee.

Yes, of course, I thought it mysterious that Grand-mère convened us all, twenty years later. I wondered. But Grand-mère likes grand gestures. She likes a grand entrance, and exit. She is old and lonely. Why not invite us all back, for some kicks? But apparently it was not just for kicks. Or not any kicks that I was predicting.

"How intriguing." Arabelle is the one to break the spell of silence, all of us stunned into our own heads. She has a hint of a smile on her face, like Grand-mère is exaggerating the whole thing. Perhaps that is it.

But I don't think so. Grand-mère is many things, but overdramatic, no.

"All these *things* you have to tell us," Jade says. "Is that, like, a threat?"

"No threat. *Non*, this is about the truth. What remains of it, anyhow. You will know soon enough." Grand-mère stands. Sylvie stands, too, but Grand-mère sends her back to her seat with a slash of a veined arm.

"*Non*. I can walk myself to my room quite fine on my own, *merci*."

And then she trails into the chateau without a glance back at the people she has left behind, confused. And as I gaze around the table, in a stupor of wine and regret, it occurs to me that maybe we are not just confused, but also scared.

CHAPTER ELEVEN

Vix

My mouth feels like someone has stuffed it with wool. I venture open an eyelid, and the sun stabs me in the pupil. Then there's that weird crawly sensation across my chest. I close my eyes and squirm in bed to make it stop, but I still feel it, like ants marching across my sternum. They call it phantom pain. Phantom, like something is inside me, that I didn't consent to, that I want to send packing, but can't.

I open my eyes, and the sun floods further in, cycling phantom boob pain with a different kind of pain. I grapple for my phone, resting on the floor, charging in the outlet that is hidden by the bedframe. The bedframe has a Spanish vibe, smooth rich brown leather, and the linens are purple-red, textured and faded. But also expensive-feeling, and new. This is Séraphine's chateau, after all. Everything has dollar signs and intention behind it. I have been placed in the only room with a twin bed—the rest have queens. Which says a lot, doesn't it? I am the only single lady. I suppose twin beds are in my future forevermore.

I scoot down the bed to push my feet against the footboard. My therapist says it's grounding, to feel your feet in the morning. I put my attention inside my feet, like she always encourages me to do. The leather is cool on my soles. Still, my chest throbs, this new me built on the ashes of the old me. I feel the opposite of grounded, like a balloon a child releases into the sky, floating aimlessly until striking a chimney or a satellite dish.

I flick through my emails, my texts. Nothing from Juliet.

Then I do something that feels horrible, yet inevitable. I go to Instagram to see if Juliet has followed anyone new, or if anyone new is following her. If they are, I will go to their Instagram page, then look them up on Facebook, then on Google, after on Twitter, but definitely not on LinkedIn (in case they subscribe to the paid feature that shows profile views). Based on my investigation, I will assign a probability figure as to whether they are sleeping together.

But before I can get to Juliet, I see a follow request. It's from @imwatchingyou88. Immediately I am struck by the handle's menacing tenor. But probably just a creepy rando. I click on the profile. There are no followers and no profile description, nor a profile picture, but it's a public account. Just one picture in the feed, and when I pull it up, my heart migrates to my throat.

It's a picture of feet, and two of them are mine, in my thick black sandals with silver studded straps. It is a shot of all our feet, I realize, under the table at dinner last night. Jade, in her new, It Girl sandals that look like the edgy cousin of Cinderella's glass slippers. Arabelle, in her cool white sneakers. Darcy, in her quilted heeled mules. Séraphine, in her navy ballet flats. Sylvie, in her sweet cream-colored pumps with a low heel.

The caption reads: *You can't hide.*

I scramble up out of bed and it hurts, as my reconstructed boobs bob braless in my race next door to Darcy's room. When I burst in, she's on her phone, too. She glances up, and I make out something primal and afraid.

"You saw it, too?"

I nod. I glance at the post again and feel chills traverse my arms. Darcy's eyes are blazing. "What the actual fuck?"

—

There is an unspoken acknowledgment not to alarm the older ladies, so nothing is said about @imwatchingyou88 over breakfast. Instead we butter croissants and down coffees and sing a halfhearted first

"Happy Birthday" to Jade. Then Arabelle arrives with damp hair, fresh off her morning run. If I know her, and I do, she ran a quick three miles, a distance she refers to with a flick of a hand as *rien*. Nothing. She sips her coffee and flakes off a croissant, but I discern in one curt nod that she gives me that she saw the account, too. Still we continue eating and chattering, too much chattering, when all the while we are simply biding time until Raph takes us to town for the market and we can talk about what the actual fuck is going on.

Still, as I sing another chorus of *happy birthday to you*, I try to process things. It had to be one of us, who took that picture, who set up this account. Why? Who? And they're watching *who*?

Ten minutes later we are in the car, after goodbyes to the older ladies and a paper bag of pastries foisted on us by Sylvie. Darcy is up front again. When the doors click closed and Raph starts the engine, we all start talking at once.

"Who started that horrible account?" Darcy says. "Guys? I'm seriously creeped out. Can someone please fess up now?"

"I didn't!" I say. "But like—"

"Well, I hope you don't think it was possibly me," says Arabelle.

"I didn't start a weird anonymous Instagram account!" Jade says. "It's my birthday, you think I'm gonna go creepster on my birthday?" Her contoured cheekbones become even more chiseled when she's irate. "This is very strange," she adds. "Very . . . scary."

"It *is* scary," I confirm. "Could it have been Sylvie? Or I mean . . . Séraphine?"

Darcy laughs, slightly psychotically. "No, I don't think my ninety-four-year-old grandmother has a handle on Instagram."

"Nor mine," says Arabelle.

"Maybe it was one of the waitstaff," I say, breathing a little easier when I consider it. "There was the chef who helped Arabelle, and the servers. Any of them could have taken the photo."

"But why?" Jade asks. "Why would anyone do that?"

"I know the chef well," Arabelle says doubtfully. "She's a class act. I can't imagine she would ever do anything like that. And the servers are locals, too. I know both of them. But . . . I guess anything is possible."

"But why would any of *us* do it?" I say.

"What are you talking about?" Raph finally asks, and we all chime in, explaining.

As he digests it, and I mean, it is a fucking lot to digest, I wonder if *he* could have done it. But what do I even mean by that? Crawl commando from his cabin, to snap a look up our skirts? Is that even realistic? And why?

"Sounds like you're being punked," he finally says, shaking his head. "Sort of a cheesy name they picked, too."

"Yeah." Jade frowns. "Maybe we, like, all show our Instagram accounts, and let each other poke around, and prove we didn't do it? Because one of us did."

"Fine by me," Darcy says.

"And me," Arabelle and I say in unison.

"But don't you think whoever did it would be smart enough to erase the evidence?" I ask.

"Still, we should do it," Darcy says. "Just to ease our minds."

So we all hand around our phones, but then there are passcodes to type in, and the car rolling to a stop. "We're here," Raph says.

We all gaze sheepishly around at each other. In the bright light of day, with people bustling outside in the familiar market, the shock value wears off a bit.

"Look guys," I finally say, reaching for my phone from Darcy. "I don't know who started the account, or why, but there's gotta be a reasonable explanation. It's Jade's birthday. Let's not spiral on Jade's birthday. Why don't we postpone the Sherlock Holmes-ing?"

Jade shoots me a grateful look. I get it; not the most epic start to a big birthday. She's wearing the flower crown Arabelle got from a florist in Nice, paired with a cutout midi dress, not in her usual black but in its cousin beige. She looks glowy, my dear friend. I give her shoulder an impromptu squeeze. "We all want you to have the best birthday!"

"Have fun. You don't look a day over thirty," Raph says as we spill out of the car, which causes Jade to look even glowier. He's smooth. Because I mean, let's be honest. We all look some days over thirty. Except Arabelle maybe, the oldest of us all.

"So forget the Insta-creep for the day?" Arabelle says.

"Forget the Insta-creep for the day," I say hopefully, and Jade and Darcy are quiet.

———

"Oh my God, we're here!" I say, in spite of the morning's weirdness. I step out of the car by the gates from the Middle Ages that lead into Saint-Rémy.

"We're here!" Arabelle dances my arm around, while Jade and Darcy are sulky and silent, both with massive sunglasses on.

I smile at Arabelle and lean my head on her shoulder. I adore Belle. She's the most uncomplicated of my friends, the least complaining. And she's the most thoughtful, always with a gift basket she arranges herself, with the best assortment of goodies, when you're going through something, like a breakup, or breast cancer. There have been lots of gift baskets of late. But she's not just about throwing money at things. She came in town especially for my big surgery, and then again for her book launch, so I've seen her a good amount lately. And last year we stayed at the Hotel du Cap together. That was when we got coined the Rihannas. Which I think is just the Mamas being a little jealous. Arabelle and I are childless, her by choice, me by circumstance. So why not live it up, when we can, as much as we can?

Darcy checks her phone. "Oliver and the kids are wandering the market now, too. The kids have been up since two, apparently, from the jet lag." She removes her sunglasses and rubs her eyes. "They're gonna say hi."

"Oh good," I say, which is the thing I know I'm supposed to say. And I mean, I love the kids. But this is our girls' trip, the one time I am not forced to confront other people's kids and contemplate how I may never get to have my own.

"Yay," Arabelle says, sounding genuine. "I can't wait to see the kids."

Darcy smiles. "Me too."

As we wander past the Church of Saint Martin, with its imposing bell tower, Jade stops. People in backpacks and a mélange of accents are already streaming around us, down through the pedestrian lanes that converge in the plaza, where a cluster of vendors always set up.

"You know, Jews lived in this area from at least the fourteenth century," she says.

It's not at all what I expected her to say. "No, I didn't know that." I know Jade's family is French, that most of them didn't survive the Holocaust. She never really talks about it, though. And she speaks even worse French than I do.

"Yes," she says. "The Jews in town lived right around here. They called the area La Jutarié." She pauses, gazes around.

I wonder if she will say more. I want to hear more, but I don't want to probe, especially not on her birthday. Then Jade walks quickly ahead, so I have to trot after her to keep up. By the time I do, she's in a different mood altogether, a shopping mood, scrutinizing some handmade yellow pottery outside a shop. I remember that yellow and green are the theme colors in Provence.

"It's different here now." Jade twirls a jug around on her palm. "Doesn't everything feel different?"

"It's not so different," Darcy says. "It's just that we're different."

I think about that. Are we so different? I mean, we are and we're not. Sometimes I feel like, without a partner or kids, life hasn't changed as much for me as for my friends.

"New paving," I say, then spot a familiar tree with its green leafy leaves. "I swear I remember this guy." I stop to put a hand on its trunk. This is it, the stuff of France that inspired me in college. That made me sketch and paint the best I ever did in my life, the semester I studied abroad here. That prompted Séraphine to believe in me so much, she asked me for a favor that would change the course of my life. I feel my fingertips prickle, enlivened. If only that old inspiration will strike again.

"Really?" Darcy asks. "You remember this random tree?"

I shrug. "Hello, tree." I lower my voice to a whisper. "I love you." I dart my eyes at Darcy, and by the smile on her face, I can tell she heard. "I do love it!" I say defensively.

"I didn't say anything!" But Darcy is laughing.

I say a tiny apology to the tree, that my love for it has been laughed at. It's just a thing I have to do, with trees that I notice. Tell them I love them, that I acknowledge them. Often, I put a hand on their trunk, or a branch, to let the import sink in. I think trees and most earthly things get way less love than they deserve. Certainly, the ocean and mountains and trees deserve more love than some people. And trees respond to our love, they really do! Like those experiments with plants being watered by canisters infused with loving messages or with hateful ones. Also, there is a huge oak tree in my apartment's courtyard, and obviously I tell the tree I love it on a daily basis. And wouldn't you know? I'd swear that in the five years of my residency, the tree has gradually grown directly toward my apartment. Its branches nearly brush my windows.

The tradition of expressing my love to trees started when I was eight and my parents took me hiking in the Catskills. It was the first and last time we ever went hiking. My mom couldn't stop complaining about the mosquitoes. My dad was too out-of-shape to manage, so there were a lot of fits and starts and huffing breaths and commentary about his out-of-shape-ness from my mom. All of that was a hum in the backdrop, though. I was an only-child city kid unleashed in the wilderness. The only parks I'd known were urban ones, with needles strewn by benches. *I love you*, I said to each tree we passed. Eventually my mom said, *Vix, stop it*, but I didn't stop it. I couldn't. Maybe I come by it naturally, as an artist. If you are an artist who doesn't like plants, then in my opinion, a world of suspicion descends upon you.

An older couple streams by with their yappy dog. We duck into a tiny *brocante* with the cutest antiques, then buy lime basil tartes at the same *boulangerie* we all fondly remember from two decades ago. The same old man in likely the same threadbare navy cap is still working the till. (He doesn't remember us, even though we keep trying to jog his memory by tossing out dates and memories to his curt *non*.) I notice how Jade declines the tarte, as usual, even though she eyes it like an eager dog. Her willpower to deprive herself is something I will never understand.

Then we pass a wine store doing impressive business in the early morning, followed by a cheese shop with gooey French cheeses that we all sample, and then a man selling his olives, homemade tapenade, and olive oil. I realize that I will have substantial space in my luggage on the return trip, so I load up with some olive oil. I don't cook, but Juliet does. She's always in the kitchen, making a frittata, or breading something. It's only when I've handed over my credit card that I remember that Juliet has left me.

"We used to take the bus here from Avignon," Jade says, as people stream off a bus in the plaza.

"The fifty-four." I tuck my credit card back in my handbag and slip the olive oil in there, too.

It doesn't feel like how I thought it would feel to be back here. Back then we were young and free, and the world was ours. Mistakes were something you were supposed to make, you were *entitled* to make. Now the world doesn't feel mine, and I've used up my quota of mistakes. I'm not usually so bleak, especially not on a trip, and especially not with the girls. Maybe it's our ominous new Instagram friend. And other things, too. My head is swimming with thoughts of Juliet, and my breasts, and my meeting scheduled with Séraphine. She postponed it last night. Said she was too tired, which surprised me. This morning, we were supposed to meet again, but again, she canceled, this time without explanation. I was in a state about the Insta-creep, and I suppose I didn't overthink it, but now I'm curious. Very curious, and a bit concerned. I have a suitcase full of supplies, and while I am roughly aware of what she'd like me to do, we haven't spoken of specifics, or how much time I'll have. Or why she is asking this of me, now. I have no clue, to be honest, where our meeting will lead. All I know is it is rescheduled in ink, as Séraphine said, for tomorrow morning. Today is Jade's birthday, and tipsy is the theme of our day. I told Séraphine I could maintain my faculties, that I wasn't about to get wasted. By her frown, I'm not sure *wasted* was the right word to use. Nonetheless, she said our meeting could wait. Tomorrow morning at six, before anyone else in the house awakens, I am to go to her bedroom and knock. She has assured me I won't disturb her. That she will already be long awake.

In the plaza, we meander through the food aisles, looking for the tomato stall next to the sausage stall with the best tomatoes any of us remember eating, ever. We don't find it, so eventually we wander to a vendor selling cotton textiles in printed Provincial patterns—lavender, lemons. Everyone is friendly. *"Bonjour, bonjour!"* I remember that you have to say *bonjour* when you greet anyone, before getting down to business, otherwise they will think you are rude.

We tinker around booths selling antiques, art, furniture. Jade considers purchasing antique hedge trimmers. We give her grief, wondering what hedges exactly she will be trimming, and she protests that they will look good on her mantel at the Hamptons home. Something about antiques juxtaposed with modern. So Arabelle distracts Jade with the promise of more coffee, and Darcy and I buy the hedge trimmers to give to Jade later. If the girl wants hedge trimmers for her fortieth, give her hedge trimmers. As Darcy bargains with the kind gentleman in a beige cap, flexing her French, I think that it's pretty ironic. Your twenties are for buying pretty baubles you will wear once. Your thirties are for prettier baubles, more expensive ones. Now it seems that our forties are for impractical knickknacks for the home. At least that's the theme I've observed in my friend group. I am the exception; there is not a real diamond that adorns me, nor a mantel I possess on which to place hedge trimmers.

"Trente." The vendor finally provokes a smile of acquiescence in Darcy. I forgot how she loves to bargain.

In Cambodia, Darcy positively killed me. She could spend forty-five minutes seeking out an elusive tuk tuk driver who'd charge one dollar instead of two. *We're being ripped off!* she would protest.

I miss being ripped off, I remember saying morosely to Jade and

Arabelle as we waited on a curb for Darcy to find a suitable driver, as sweat pooled inside my elephant-printed pants.

Now, Darcy hands over the bills. I tell her I'll Venmo her, and she waves a hand dismissively. Then she says, "Sure, Venmo is good."

I'm slightly taken aback, because I offered just to be nice. We usually only Venmo each other for big things. Fifteen dollars here, fifteen dollars there, it all evens out. But I get out my phone and make a note in my calendar, to remember to Venmo her.

"Mama!" Suddenly Chase and Mila swoop in, trailed by Oliver.

At the same time, Jade and Arabelle return with their coffees (an *expresso double* for Jade, and a *noisette* for Arabelle, which is espresso with a dash of cream and proof that everything sounds cuter in French). I bury the hedge trimmers in my tote. There are hellos and kisses and much exclamation over Chase's new toy, a wooden frog musical instrument with grates on top that can be played with a wooden wand. Chase proudly demonstrates the toy for each of us, over and over. And over. The wand against the grates makes a fairly earsplitting croaking noise. I feel sorry for Oliver, who will have to endure the hours and days until Chase tires of it. But still, he's too cute playing it now, with ferocious concentration, his lips pursed, a baseball cap with puppy dog ears askew on his little head.

"Ice cream after breakfast?" I hear Darcy hiss to Oliver, pointing to the empty cups in the stroller tray. "You know I don't like them having sugar this early."

Poor Oliver. His face falls, and he rakes a hand through his dark hair. He's generally good-natured, Oliver, the rainbow to Darcy's occasional wound-too-tightly storm. Poor Darcy, too. I sneak a look; her misery is oozing from her pores. I wonder what is going on with her. She's the kindest, best friend, in her quiet, dedicated way. She is the one in the background, taking care of shit. All of my friends are amazing, of course, especially this past year. Like Arabelle with her visits and gift baskets after my surgery. And Jade doing what she excels at: whirling around with all her get-shit-done energy. She made me personalized Spotify playlists, and brought me food she cooked with her mom's recipes, delicious Moroccan dishes. Jade even volunteered for the dreaded task of wrangling with my insurance people. But after Arabelle returned to Nice and Jade refocused on her spinning studio, and even Juliet went back to work, too, Darcy sat with me, day in, day out. I told her I didn't want to see people and she said, "I'm in your living room. If you don't want to see me, then no worries. Don't." And mostly, I didn't, but she still arranged me hotel-like trays of food and brought me ice packs and my pain medicine. She was there, physically, firmly. Even though she has a demanding start-up and kids. Even though I hate asking people to do stuff for me. And she didn't make me feel like I was a burden. She just calmly, quite determinedly, refused to leave. That's Darcy—fierce Mama Bear, taking care of everyone, usually before herself. It makes me teary just thinking about it.

Now Mila runs over, leaps into my arms, and asks to sing Ishka-pishka with me. Ishka-pishka is our thing. It's a cheer Jade learned at summer camp, that she taught us girls one very debaucherous night during our study abroad semester. I randomly pulled it out of the bag when I once babysat Mila, and now she asks if we can sing it at any opportunity. We start belting it out—*Ishka pishka hit 'em in the kishka, hocus pokus dominokus!* The lyrics are quite catchy, but we do garner some looks from the locals. The looks communicate that we are irritating Americans living up to our stereotypes, but Mila is the cutest ever, with her strawberry curls and colorful Band-Aids all over her arms that she adorns herself with as if they are stickers.

She stops after our third rendition. "Mama, can I have another Band-Aid?"

Darcy counts, then shakes her head. "Four is the limit, angel. You know that."

"But I want *five*!" Mila says, and I can tell we are close to breakdown city.

Darcy says something to Oliver that I can't make out, and then he lifts Chase up and deposits him in their stroller. He grabs hold of Mila's hand. "All right, say goodbye to the ladies," he instructs the kids.

Darcy kisses both her children on their cheeks, kisses that are somehow hard to watch, because I can tell she is inhaling them, that she needs them, more than usual. I wonder why. Then we all give hugs and kisses, too, but Chase is oblivious, still striking on his frog. Mila has fended off all hugs, including Darcy's, and is now refusing Oliver's proffered hand, a look of rebellion in her eyes. I can tell she is nearing the point of scorching earth for the fifth Band-Aid.

Oliver grips her hand and pulls her along. I can hear her pleading, "Just one more, Daddy. I promise!"

"They're so cute, Darcy," Arabelle says, a bit perfunctorily, as they disappear around the corner. It is the thing to say, after all, about children.

"Thanks," Darcy says, staring after them. Finally, she seems to come to. She brushes a tear from her eye, and I squeeze her hand, even though the reaction seems disproportionate, although what do I know? It's just, her kids are only heading out miles away. She can, and will, see them every day on this trip, if she desires. "But you don't want any, Belle?" Darcy asks. "Kids are so fun. They really are. A lot of work, but just so much . . ." She trails off, catching my gaze.

"No. Definitely not. I don't want them." Arabelle's face softens. "Just I mean . . . *alors*, no."

I stray off from them a bit, because no one ever asks me if I want children, and this conversation is triggering, in myriad ways. I'm the lesbian, without a partner any longer. The thing is, I do want kids. I don't know if my friends even know that I do. They've never really asked. Maybe because by and large I've been the single lesbian, regaling them with my dating stories. Perhaps I wasn't with Juliet long enough for them to wonder, even though we were serious. At least I thought we were. But having kids was something I began to mourn when I turned forty, and then even more so when my breasts were chopped off of me. I will never be able to breastfeed. It felt like some new invisible shove toward childlessness.

I can't express this to my friends, because they wouldn't get it. Arabelle, because she very emphatically doesn't want kids. And Jade and Darcy, because they have wanted, and had, kids in the way that most people do. With a hetero partner. Darcy's infertility—it was heartbreaking, yes, but normative in our culture. She got her warrior on and achieved what she wanted, and there are legions of women behind her and with her. But The Fertility Warrior is very clearly for married hetero women. Women who have a partner to support them, to endure fertility treatments with. To contribute their sperm. I have no partner, and no sperm. I'm so far below them in the trenches that the other warriors can't even glimpse me down here.

I am pretending to be on my phone, but now I slip a look back at my friends. They're sitting on a curb now, drinking their coffees.

"Okay," I say, walking over to them, putting up a wall so my thoughts don't darken further and bleed out over into this day. "I know what we need. Wine. And a lot of it. Yeah?"

"God, yes," Darcy says. "*A lot* a lot."

CHAPTER TWELVE

Arabelle

We are tipsy, all of us except the birthday girl, who restrained herself to the tasting sips. Jade makes a show about wanting to drink hard, but then she controls herself, fiercely so. I am always in control of myself, too, more quietly so.

We are at Château La Coste, about an hour from Saint-Rémy, up the road from Aix-en-Provence. It would be the perfect opportunity to dine in Aix tonight, at Côté Cour. It's quite up Jade's alley, like a hot West Village spot. But it wouldn't be kind to exclude Mamie and Séraphine, so we will return to the chateau for dinner.

The sommelier, a girl of about nineteen in a red flowered wrap dress, tops off our glasses of Le Blanc, the chateau's house white. I swirl mine around and sniff, then drink. Jade swirls, sniffs, and doesn't drink. Vix just drinks. Darcy is buried in her phone.

"Darcy." She looks up. "More wine," I say, indicating her glass.

She gives a sheepish smile. Then she stabs at her phone again. "Just posting a photo from Valensole."

We stopped at the Valensole lavender fields on the way here, and the girls took pictures there like good tourists do. It's not that I'm above it, more that as a Frenchwoman, I've been to quite my share of lavender fields. And I've been preoccupied with things, like @imwatchingyou88. It's strange, this Instagram account. I've been trying to figure it out in my head, who could have started it. I have a guess as to who did, but I'm not positive.

Darcy turns her phone over. "So." She looks at all of us, in better spirits than earlier. Her cheeks are flushed the same color pink as her puffy headband. She conjures a vision of bubble gum, from her headband to the cloying pink of her dress. The puffy headband trend perplexes me—I think they evoke the aura of a kindergartner, setting off bravely on the first day of school, her backpack just about the same size as herself. And I don't get these twee nightgowns that masquerade as dresses, that Darcy is fond of wearing. Frenchwomen prefer boning and zippers to elastics.

"So *salut* to Jade!" I raise my glass, then savor a sip.

"*Salut!*" everyone echoes, Jade with her Perrier. During the tasting, she asked if it was organic wine. (It is.) Biodynamic? (Yes.) But still there is natural grape sugar, she told us. She switched fairly quickly to mineral water.

"Any resolutions for the next decade?" I ask.

Jade scratches an oval white fingernail against her chin. "To have more sex." She smiles.

I smile, too.

"A-freaking-men," Vix says.

Darcy is quiet, her mouth set in a frown. She looks quite like someone not having a lot of sex. I recall her vibe at the market with Oliver and her kids. Something was decidedly off.

"I have another resolution, about my family," Jade says, then stops, and blinks her eyes up at the sky.

I follow her gaze. The blue sky is smeared with clouds, like child's paint. It is a perfect summer day, the way most of them are in the South of France. I lean back on the white-cushioned chaise. "Tell us."

"You know, my father is from this area," Jade says.

"Right," I say, but I don't know much beyond that, although it's interesting that this topic has come up a couple of times now on this trip. Jade is the least French person I know, and her French skills are nil. She says *bonjour* in as cheerful, New Yorker of an accent as can be. I've never met Jade's father; she doesn't talk about him much, at least not to me. I know he's older, in his mideighties maybe. And he was a tailor. Maybe he still is. I suspect that some people subconsciously refrain from talk of their parents when they know how I lost mine. "Your father grew up where, Jade?"

"An orphanage, after age ten, but he was born in Saint-Rémy. He was saved, but his parents—my grandparents—were murdered in the Holocaust."

The word *murdered* crackles among us like lightning.

"How was your father saved?" I ask, realizing I'm the only one asking. Vix and Darcy must already know the story, which makes me feel simultaneously like a bad friend, and also a little like I've been excluded.

Jade's eyes focus the way I've seen when she leads those cultlike spin classes. But only now she's in some other place that I can't make out. "By the people who betrayed the rest of my dad's family. My grandparents gave these people their life savings, their most precious possessions, in exchange for their safety. But later, instead of continuing to hide my dad's family, these people forced them to leave. The one thing they did do was take my dad to an orphanage. He was ten."

"Wow. That's crazy, and also appalling." I'm surprised I didn't know any of this. It's a horrible story. I look at Darcy, but her face is the wrenched of recycled secondhand pain, not fresh secondhand pain, like mine, or deep pain in your bones, like Jade's. Vix's face is placid; I'm not sure whether this is new information or old.

Jade nods. "I just . . . My dad doesn't sleep. The doctors have ruled out every reason. He has nightmares. Wakes up screaming, sweating. My mom says it's gotten even worse lately."

"You think it's because of his childhood?"

"Childhood trauma," Jade replies. "No question."

I nod. I know something of it. But I was four, and her father was ten. There is a world of memories that exist in that span, memories I never had.

"I just . . . He never got justice for what happened to his family. And look what's happening in the world now. We think the Holocaust could never happen again, but anti-Semitism is spiraling. It's . . ."

She swirls her wine and stares at it blankly. "Very scary," she finally whispers.

I process the conversation. I agree with it all, of course. But what does Jade's fortieth have to do with any of this? Probably nothing, I decide. If I've learned anything running an inn, it's that when people have something they want to talk about, they can turn a conversation about the rain into socialism to make their point.

"So you're looking for justice on your father's behalf?" I ask, then realize something. "Is that why you studied abroad in Avignon in the first place?"

"Yeah. The lure of my family's past." Jade grimaces. "Sorry, Belle."

I shrug. "This doesn't have to do with me."

"I know. But—your parents—I don't want to—"

"Pour salt in my wounds? You're not. It's a totally different situation. My dad was the one driving. The one who veered off the road. No drugs in his system. Nothing. Just a horrible accident. No one to blame." I quote the party line Mamie has told me all my life. "Anyway, I don't remember them. I don't remember anything."

Is that true? I do have one complete memory, and otherwise there are lights, voices. Maybe I pretend them away. We all do, in some respects, with some voices, don't we?

"I just don't . . ." Darcy starts, and I turn to her, surprised. "No, about Jade, I mean. I think you should leave it, J."

Then Darcy gives Jade a look I can't quite put my finger upon—a warning is what comes to me. But a warning about what? Darcy's hands are twisting, twining. With a start, her wineglass drops to the ground, skids in fragments across the gravel. "Shit." She reaches down for a shard of glass, and then another. Like collecting them will help, or matter. She stops, puts the glass on the table. "I didn't mean to do that. Shit."

"It's just a glass," Vix says quietly.

Darcy runs her thumb over the edge of one of the glass pieces. "Just, I think some things should be left where they belong. In the past."

I'm surprised at the callousness of her words.

"But Darce," says Vix, "if Jade being back here has triggered something, has made her want to seek justice for her dad—"

"Justice, and answers," Jade says, angrily. "I want answers, too. I deserve them, Darce. You know that I do."

The two stare at each other, communicating something in silence that I feel completely outside of. It's strange, because they are very close. I've almost never heard them fight. And their husbands are best friends, too; Seb and Oliver go rock climbing together at Chelsea Piers every week. Their families vacation together, with the older kids doting on the younger ones in photos that could be used as the stock ones for frames. They call themselves *framily*—a friends/family mashup.

"I need answers," Jade repeats, her eyes fixed on Darcy.

"Answers," Vix echoes, sounding confused, as the girl in the flowered dress returns with a broom and begins sweeping up the glass. Another girl swoops in with a fresh glass for Darcy. Wine sloshes into the glass, then into Darcy's mouth. I think I should cut Darcy off. Off the wine, and off this conversation.

"I want answers, too," Darcy says, with bite to her tone. "You think I don't want answers, J?"

"What do you want answers about?" Vix asks.

I'm curious about that, too. Darcy's face scrunches up like she is mulling something over. Finally, she just says, "Maybe looking for answers is like picking at a scab. It's picking and picking, and you know what happens when you pick?"

Some of us, especially Darcy, are too drunk for metaphors. I'm about to say so when Darcy says, in a weird, sad voice, "You don't see me trying to go back and relive the day my grandfather died."

Just the chirping of birds now. I've hardly ever heard Darcy talk about that awful day.

"He died accidentally, Darce," Jade says sharply. "My dad's family didn't die accidentally."

Darcy is quiet, then she gives a visible exhale that blows her baby hairs up toward her headband. "Yeah, I know. Sorry. I don't know why I brought it up."

Jade softens, I can tell. That's how Jade is. Hard and tough until you show the first sign of vulnerability, and then she is putty in your hands. "I've never heard you talk about it, Darce. It's good to talk about things."

"Is it?" Darcy looks at us all, strangely. "I think I blacked out. One minute I was handstanding in the pool, showing off for my grandfather. I would surface and he would clap and say, *Bravo, bravo.* The next minute I'm gulping for air, shoving my hair off my face, and when my eyes open, there's blood. His body floating. I ran out of the pool to that hidden room under the stairs, you know the one, Belle? I used to go there and read sometimes, to be with myself. You did, too— I remember you with all those cookbooks. Everything felt so big and much after he died. In there, it was small and cozy. I felt contained or something. I remember I was shaking and shaking and cold—" Darcy bites her lip. "I wonder if that room is still there."

"It's not," I say slowly. "They got rid of it during the renovation when they expanded the kitchen."

Darcy nods. No one speaks. I push my wine away from me a couple of inches.

"Sorry, Darce," Jade says, breaking the quiet.

Darcy nods but doesn't look up.

"So . . . new subject?" Jade asks.

"New subject," I agree.

"Well, okay, happy birthday to me." Jade laughs, a forced laugh, but an effort nonetheless. "We still don't know what the deal is with that Instagram account, by the way."

The account hasn't posted anything new, but its existence sits in disquiet among us.

"Let's go home and get ready for dinner," Darcy says abruptly, standing, pushing in her chair. "It's Jade's birthday. Tonight, it's still Jade's birthday."

"Tonight it's Jade's birthday," I agree, rising. "Tomorrow we can deal with everything else. All these heads have a lot going on inside them, it appears." I make a circle with my pointer finger, encapsulating all four of us.

Laughs, strained ones.

"Your head seems pretty happy," Vix says to me as we gather our bags.

"Oh?"

"Yeah, you just seem happy, Belle. Less on edge than the rest of us."

I smile but don't answer, because those statements are true, and not true, both for reasons she wouldn't suspect.

CHAPTER THIRTEEN

Séraphine

It is dinner again, and I struggled to join. Now my days revolve around meals, and there are so blasted many of them. I was supposed to speak to Victoria earlier—I must speak to Victoria—but another conversation, a surprising, unpleasant conversation, diverted me. When was that again? I've always been sharp as a tack, but the hours, the minutes, are blurring and whirling. I do know I went to nap after breakfast and awoke bleary-eyed at four in the afternoon to Sylvie's gentle touch. She was asking me questions, and soon I will be forced to provide answers.

But there is a saying that is appropriate here. *Petit à petit l'oiseau fait son nid.*

Little by little, the bird makes his nest.

I have gathered them here, after all, have I not? Jade, at the opposite end of the table, wearing red, not black. Her dress is cleavage-bearing, but an appropriate length for once. She is smiling, chatting with Darcy beside her, and Victoria on her other side. For now, I watch Jade and Darcy. They don't see it, but I do. I have, from the moment Jade entered my house.

There is much to make right, and the pieces are nearly in place. Tonight, we will celebrate Jade's birthday. Tomorrow morning, I will meet at last with Victoria. And then I will gather them. It will be difficult, but I will tell them every last bit.

Arabelle is here, too, of course, with her grandmother. Sylvie. A lump catches in my throat. Perhaps until this moment, I didn't realize how many people I still love. I am ready to leave, though. At ninety-four, I have lived a life both full and empty. A life of pride, and a life of shame. My body is failing me. In some ways, I am surprised it has brought me this far.

The waitstaff begin to bring out our next course—*le plat principal*, the *confit de canard*. Duck, at Darcy's suggestion, although I did think Jade was vegan. I bristle as a woman whose name I do not know sets down my plate. They neglected to bring out the lime sorbet to cleanse the palate after the fish course. I would normally say something, pause the meal for a recalibration with sorbet, because there are correct ways of doing things. Rules that must be followed. But just as I open my mouth, Sylvie's crinkled blue eyes catch mine, and she smiles, a smile just for me. So I refrain from berating my waitstaff.

Sylvie has the most beautiful smile. I have always thought so. Her teeth are crowded but white. She goes to my dentist, a talkative man in Aix, who convinced her to whiten them. None of that matters. It's the glitter to her smile. The kindness that shimmers from her face. Sylvie is the kindest person I have ever met. Occasionally I think her kindness has rubbed off on me. More often, I think it has not.

The *mistral* blows in from the vineyard, and I rub my arms and reach for my shawl. Sylvie notices. She always notices my littlest movements. She scoots her chair over and helps me arrange it over my shoulders. Fear prickles at my neck, or maybe it's just the wind. There is chatter, American English chatter, that plays in my ears like an orchestra of notes without language. Perhaps I shouldn't have gathered them all, or perhaps I should have told them already why I have.

I open my mouth, to just come out with it, but then I press my lips tightly together. What I will say will have many repercussions, and it is Jade's birthday, after all. We are civilized people, at a civilized table, even if what I must talk about are not civilized things. There is no need for an outburst now. It can wait, I assure myself. I feel how I want, need, to believe it. It can wait.

"Tomorrow," I announce. "I will need to see you all after breakfast."

The chatter stops. I see the confusion, then the heads eventually nodding *okay*. Anyone else who would make such a statement would invite questions. But I am not a woman to be questioned.

Still, Darcy, in particular, looks very small and unsure.

"Grand-mère?" she asks in a tentative, childlike voice, and I am reminded of that horrible morning when she discovered her grandfather dead. After, she ran off, I'm not sure where to, and then she finally turned up in my bedroom, shivering uncontrollably in her yellow bathing suit with purple appliqued stars.

"*Comme il faut,*" I say. The way it must be done. I am trying to convince her that it is okay, even though it is not.

She nods, because there is nothing else to do. She rearranges her face into something palatable. The Demargelasse way.

Then she whispers, "You said you wanted to talk about your Will."

"My Will?"

She nods, lowers her voice even more. "You wrote it to me, on the invitation."

Of course I remember. I am old and sick, not an *imbécile*. "We will talk," I say firmly. "We will talk about everything. But only tomorrow, when the time is right. You will understand. After tomorrow."

Darcy nods reluctantly; what else can she do? It is I who make the rules. It has always been so. Ever since Rainier's mother died, and then Rainier, and I became the lady who presided over all of this.

The olive groves are whispering in the wind. The scent of rosemary floats in from the bushes. My gaze takes me to the potters on the side of the terrace, then to the vista onto my small corner of the world. I remember when I was first seeing Rainier, how he took me to his family's chateau. My family was well-to-do, but his family's wealth blew mine's out of the water. We met through our fathers; I understood the match would be pleasing to mine, and after my mother died, pleasing my father was my first and only job. But I liked Rainier immediately. He wasn't a person who talked excessively, or boasted. He was quiet, calm, or at least he appeared as such then. Handsome and tall, with a shock of dark hair that always caught in his left eye, that over time I came to brush tenderly away. His mother was the key to our moving forward. I understood that from the start, and he prepped me, about how to impress her (discuss books I'd read, especially by her favorite author, Proust), and how to disgust her (leave food on my plate).

That first time at the chateau, we sat on the terrace as the servants brought us *apéritifs*, followed by dinner, and I was acutely aware of her gaze not straying from me. Only when I'd cleaned my plate and set my cutlery down did she nod curtly at Rainier. Then she and her husband departed, and Rainier and I stood on the terrace, as he pointed out things, the vineyard, the cherry trees, the mountains, and then we danced. I don't even recall if there was music. Just the pleasant feeling of being in his arms, of how things were solid, and made sense. When we were happy, we used to dance. Our time for dancing didn't last long.

Chatter resumes at the table without me. Tomorrow after breakfast cannot come fast enough. Perhaps I shouldn't have done this, invite them all here, put them at risk. Because I have to admit, that tickle in my heart, that uncomfortable jiggle, is a feeling I recognize.

It is fear. And not just for myself.

CHAPTER FOURTEEN

Jade

The older ladies go to bed, and the party continues. Darcy makes me wait outside the living room with my champagne, and then when I enter, there are black balloons, streamers, kazoos. The lights are low, and a fire is roaring. The music is decidedly untz untz. Something is plopped on my head—I think it's another flower crown. I lift it off to look. Black flowers. Fresh ones, dyed? There is a sign that says *Happy birthday, Jade* in gothic script. Darcy went all out. I know it's her. This doesn't have Arabelle's touch, and Vix may be an artist, but she isn't an entertainer. I feel a slight pang, that I didn't do the same for Darcy. I was frazzled the week of her birthday—Sea and I were fighting. Sea, oozing tween angst, was furious at me because I wouldn't let her get a fourth piercing in her daith. When someone close to me is mad at me, I can't function. It's not just that—when someone close to me is mad, or sad, period, I need to solve it before I can rest. But my reluctance to splash out for Darcy's birthday went deeper, too. It was about Lux, and the replacement Star of David necklace sitting in its velvet cushion case in his dresser drawer. I told Darcy about what happened. In fact, I called her right away. And while she was appropriately horrified, and said all the right things, I couldn't help but feel resentful, that I've kept her family's despicable deeds secret—and to what end?

"Tequila shots!" Darcy announces, and I sink down to the couch, suddenly sad. Maybe it's the darkness, the spacious living room with its taupe couches piled in cream cushions, soft beneath my hard-exercised body, but in this calm, forty is like a train barreling at me.

Alcohol. I need more alcohol. I've been drinking more than usual, but still not a ton. Not as much as Darcy, certainly, or even Vix. But I worked out twice a day the week before coming here, so that I wouldn't feel guilty about the inevitable indulgences. I deserve another drink. I deserve whatever I want.

Forty. It's just so hefty, the number seemingly tossed into every conversation this past year like a grenade. Or forty-one, really, as Darcy informed me walking over from dinner that I have already lived forty years, and now I am technically onto my forty-first. I was just wrapping my head around forty, and now forty-one is in the mix? On the outside I've been pretending this doesn't matter. *It's just a number. Forty is the new twenty.* Pretending it to myself, too.

Forty isn't the new twenty. Forty is forty. Or forty-one. Closer to facelifts and mammograms. All that is exterior, though, which matters, but what really gnaws at me is what happens lately in the middle of the night, when Seb is sleeping and I awake sensing an intruder. I bolt up. There is no intruder, at least not one outside of myself. I am the intruder, and in my nightmares, I am closing a door on myself. Slamming it, really. It's like all those carefree moments, all those mistakes I made that didn't seem to matter, because I had a lifetime stretched out to rectify them, and you were *supposed* to make mistakes when you were young, besides—all that is over. There is a reason there is no Fifty under Fifty. Those accolade-type lists stop with forty. Our thirties are the buffer zone. The world says we should have some things figured out but it's okay if we haven't gotten them all just so. But by your forties, all your ducks should be in a row. My ducks are ostensibly all lined up, neat and prim. Husband, check. Kids, check. Thriving career, check.

But it just feels like everything I do now has to matter, has to be right. The stakes seem higher, the mistakes potentially bigger and more shameful. And fixing them must be a grim and swift affair. But it's like instead of the shiny car that I borrowed from my parents at age sixteen, now I'm in some clunker with the windows smeared with rain. I can't see out clearly. And I'm veering into some abyss.

There's another thing about forty. It means parents getting older. I love my father perhaps more than anyone on earth. Maybe I love him that way because that's how he loves me. Ferociously, with need. And it is good to be needed. But my kryptonite has always been pleasing him. And that is difficult, when someone is fundamentally un-pleasable. I don't begrudge him it; his past is a minefield of trauma, and you never know when you will happen across one. He works out like crazy, still, in his eighties—ten-mile walks; weights. He would hike Everest if he could. It's how he controls himself, tames his beast, however little it works. He's passed those neuroses onto me, I know. When I was young, I was pudgy, always dipping into the breadbasket, taking three sprinkle cookies at kiddush after synagogue, my weekly OREO Mc-Flurry at the McDonald's around the corner. Normal kid stuff. God, I lived for that McFlurry. I can still taste the OREO crumbles.

But Papa always spoke of his mother—how *thin* she was; how she moved so gracefully with her body. Those were his few memories, trailed before me like breadcrumbs. I stopped it with the bread, the sweets. I realized how good it felt, not just to be thin, but to be the object of my father's praise. My father's moods always dipped and spiked; I couldn't control that completely. But once I reined in my food, hardly a day passed when he didn't praise me for my weight, my beauty. I haven't had a sweet treat—not a one, not a bite of cake at my wedding—since I was twelve.

Can that be? I sift through my memories. Yes, twelve. I remember that final McFlurry, and something inside me feels desolately sad.

It's not just me, I suppose. All of us inherit from our parents, and not just their genetics. Their little neuroses. Like, my mother is OCD about her granite countertops. She won't just chop vegetables on a cutting board; she has to put a towel underneath. And if I'm cooking in their kitchen, forget it. For me, she puts down two towels. And wouldn't you know it, when Sea tries to make all her gluten-free baked goods, she's groaning when I'm placing towels down, too. The

91

towel thing kills Seb. But he has his own shticks. Like how he insists we don't run the washing machine if we're leaving the house. This is the source of many arguments, given how much I love doing laundry. I just do. I love all my clothes clean and in my closet. I love that I can pick anything to wear on any given day. But his mom had some phobia about the whole house flooding in their absence, with some hypothetical washing machine mishap.

My father likes clean clothes, too. He only had two outfits, in those years in an orphanage during the war.

How does my mind cycle round and round, always landing on my father? I suppose it's just this birthday, and being here with Séra-phine. Just the thought of her, the whiff of her Guerlain Shalimar still clinging to the air, sears my insides. Sizzles. Then turns my stomach. I'm on edge. We all are, it feels.

"You're taking a shot, right J?" Darcy's hair is mussed, her head-band askew. She shoves a shot glass in my hand. Her dress brushes my face, this one green with white polka dots.

"Yeah. To forty or forty-one, whichever it is!" I say as cheerfully as I can muster, downing the shot, then blanching as the alcohol streams harshly down my tubes.

"Midlife, as Séraphine says." Arabelle laughs.

Talk turns to what we still want to do on our vacation—perhaps a day trip to Baux, or Aix. I say I want to visit the sanitorium where Van Gogh spent the end of his life. The olive groves at the sanitorium inspired him to create one hundred fifty of his best paintings in his final year. I never went on any prior visit, and this time I have prom-ised myself I will.

"A sanitorium on a girls' trip?" Vix asks with a laugh.

I shrug. "You guys don't need to come. But I want to go."

She puts a hand on my forearm. "If you want to go, I'll come. We have nothing else on tap."

"Other than Grand-mère's mysterious meeting tomorrow," Darcy says.

"Yeah, what's that about, Darce?" asks Arabelle.

"No clue."

"Really?" Arabelle looks surprised. "Your grandmother hasn't said anything?"

Darcy shrugs. "You know Grand-mère. She keeps everything close to her vest."

My head is buzzy, and I lean back on the cushions, so cozy I feel like I am flying, or sinking. The meeting tomorrow. I mull it over for the thousandth time. There is another round of shots, this time *pastis*. I am all-in at this point. The flavor is anise, which I hate. But food and drink aren't for enjoyment in my world. People might pity that, but I find it freeing. I eat and drink for the fuel. Because in restricting myself, I feel light in my body, light with my father. And today I am drinking because life is generally good, and I deserve good. I do.

I try to savor this blurry moment. It blends, though, with other times, the most carefree of my life, with these girls. Ducking out of class to wander the Gothic fortress of the Palais des Papes, me with a coffee and Darcy and Vix munching on nougat. Putting on our cutest tankinis to go to the aqueduct at Pont du Gard. A giggle launches out of me when I remember how Darcy was suddenly in desperate need of going to the bathroom, and I don't mean number one. But there was no restroom in sight. She went in the bushes, with swarms of tourists around her. I don't think I've ever laughed that hard, before or since.

"Hey, remember Pont du Gard, Darce?" I'm already laughing.

She frowns. "Do you have to bring that up?"

Vix claps a hand over her mouth as she giggles. "Oh wow, I forgot about that. The sound—"

"Can we not? Guys . . . oof." Darcy buries her head in her lap.

"Right in the middle . . ." I'm gasping for breath at this point.

I double over in hysterics, but just before that, I see Arabelle give a slight grimace. Well, she wasn't there with us that day, and I suspect it bristles her a bit. She didn't study abroad with us, she lives across the world, and she's a couple years older, although that matters for nil now that we are in our forties. I cringe—God, our forties. But Arabelle's part of us. Whatever alchemy was at work when we all met our first weekend at this chateau, it needed her to cement us. There is some magic to us as a foursome that dissipates when we're only two or three. She knows that, doesn't she? I make a mental note to remind her. And then I make a mental note to remember this mental note.

I check my phone as another birthday message flits in, this one from a lady at the spin studio, who writes that I'm the hottest forty-year-old she's ever seen. The messages are increasing now, the time difference no longer an impediment, as America emerges from its sleep. I already FaceTimed with Seb, and the kids even called from camp. People are tagging me in Instagram Story tributes. I open the app again, appraised of yet more tags. I am happy, but not the happy where there is nothing wrong. Is there even such a kind of happy, where you have lost every last desire? If there is, I haven't found it. I've allowed myself a birthday reprieve, but tonight, when everyone is sleeping, I must do it. There is no more time to waste.

I click on my tags, and immediately, I see it. @imwatchingyou88. I gasp. The anonymous account has posted a photo of a coffee table strewn with wineglasses and shot glasses.

This room. Our drinks.

Another caption: *I know what you did. You won't get away with it.*

———

They must see it on my face, because everyone reaches for their phones. But this time I am scrutinizing their eyes, their faces, their reactions. One of them posted it, so who is the liar?

My skull feels like someone is at it with a hammer. The alcohol, the photo, what I am planning to do. I flick to the photo again. It's an aerial shot. We've all been drinking, taking photos, the whole night. There have been trips to the bathroom, trips for a cigarette outside. Anyone could have done it. And what is the chance the evidence would still remain? Photos can be deleted from camera rolls. Accounts can be signed out of, and back into again.

"What the fuck?" Arabelle says angrily. But now I wonder, is she pretending? And if so, who is she trying to expose? Who is the person she is watching?

"This is hugely fucked up." Vix is staring at her phone, like someone in shock. But is she acting? Vix just endured cancer, then a breakup. It can't be her, can it?

"Okay, guys, time to fess up. Who is doing this?" That's Darcy, my best friend of them all. Her eyes are wild; she is pissed. Or is she? "Seriously, *who*?" she demands. "This is my grandmother's home. It's fucked up to do whatever this is, at my grandmother's home."

I stand up, but the dizziness overwhelms me. "I'm . . . oh God." I rush outside and throw up right on the terrace, on the cold stone ground. Moments later, I feel hands on my back, rubbing it, pulling back my hair.

"Are you okay?" It's Darcy.

"Yeah." But then I feel it rise up, and I throw up some more.

"Let's get you to bed."

"But the . . . Instagram person . . ."

"Forget it. Let's get you to bed."

I allow myself to be led, tucked in. There's a garbage pail beside my bed, with a new plastic bag, Darcy says. There's water on the nightstand. I roll over, chug.

This is forty. Forty feels like shit.

I forgot how much I hate being drunk. How horrible it feels, to lose control.

I'm not drunk enough, though, to forget what I planned. I roll over and set a quick alarm on my phone. *I will never drink again*, is what I think as my eyes flutter shut.

I'm not sure why, but I blink open my eyes again and see Darcy, still standing over my bed, staring at me with a strange look, a look I cannot decipher. Then sleep comes for me, hard and fast.

CHAPTER FIFTEEN

Darcy

I can't sleep. Maybe it's the alcohol, but I don't think so. I am petite, but I hold my liquor well. It's something Oliver marveled at when we first met, how I could match him drink for drink, even finish off with a whiskey nightcap when he was already way past his limit.

Every time I close my eyes, I am in the Hamptons again, back early from my day trip to Amagansett, only a week ago. Oliver is on the terrace of his best buddy's place, who is out of town and has graciously invited us up for a midweek stay in his stead. Oliver's with one of the neighbor dads, the type who talks incessantly about golf and wears pink swim trunks that end at his mid-thigh, covered with little red lobsters.

"It's not so cut and dry, man," Oliver says, his voice deep and scratchy. He has a sore throat again. I'll remind him to take elderberry syrup. "It's one of her best friends."

That stops me dry in the path. I do sentence mathematics. I am the her. I am always his her, aren't I? A few strands of eucalyptus from my bundle scatter to the gravel. I bought them to tie to the shower head, because Oliver says it makes him feel like he's in a spa.

As I gather up the eucalyptus, my mind unwittingly goes to a few weeks prior, when I was doing our millionth load of weekend laundry. What I found in his pocket, because I always empty out pockets. It's a thing you learn to do, when your son slips in mini race cars and your daughter hoards sidewalk chalk. Oliver wasn't a typical pocket culprit, but that day I turned out his pockets and found one of those real silk hair scrunchies they sell for an exorbitant price. It was black. I asked him about it, and he gave a convincing shrug. *Mila?* he posited. I resisted the urge to say our daughter hadn't become a billionaire with her own charge card at Sephora last I checked. I chalked it up to a mistake. I even started using it—my ponytails were bouncier and less squeezy on my scalp. The scrunchie-in-the-husband's-pocket was a mistake that was hard to reconcile, but I was determined to reconcile it. Because no way, no how, was my mind going to go to an affair. We were happy. We were so happy. We still had sex! A fair amount of it, at least. So, maybe the scrunchie was resting on some ledge at Starbucks and Oliver pocketed it absentmindedly, like he claimed. Perhaps . . . Okay, I couldn't think of any other plausible scenario. But the scrunchie had to have a reasonable explanation. That's a mantra I live by, in fact. Everything has a reasonable explanation.

You have to believe that in this crazy world, don't you? Otherwise you'd just hop inside a hole and never come out.

But now a horrible sentence is ringing in my ears as I eavesdrop on my husband and the douchey neighbor: *It's one of her best friends.*

"One of her best friends? Shit, dude. You're either a bastard, or a bastard who's in love."

Silence. The import of this conversation is now irrevocable. I have no thoughts—thoughts will come later. I only have a heart that has ceased beating, awaiting my husband's answer.

"Unfortunately the latter," Oliver finally says, and there is no nervous laughter.

The words ricochet through me. Now the whole of the eucalyptus tumbles to the ground. My husband is in love. With one of my best friends.

But I'm not one of those girls with different groups, many friends. I am an extrovert, yes, but I am a one-on-one girl. All that time other people sprinkle among ten or twenty, I devote to three. I have only three best friends, and two of them live in New York, close by. Vix and Jade. But Vix is a lesbian. She doesn't like men. She has never liked men. Jade is my best friend. My *best* best friend, of the three.

Unfortunately the latter.

———

So yes, my family has collapsed, my business is on the threshold of ruin. But I am a warrior. Underestimated, yes, made a fool of, surely. But a warrior fights.

I suppose I have always been a warrior, in a variety of ways. When my dad died of a heart attack when I was six, and months later, my mom went out to dinner with her friends and told me to stop crying or the babysitter wouldn't like me, I dried those tears right up. I was a warrior after my grandfather died in front of me. Grand-mère said we had to move on, and she shushed me whenever I spoke of him, so I stopped and shoved the memories down. I was a warrior through fertility treatments and miscarriages. I've been a warrior in motherhood, when Chase had open-heart surgery as a newborn. I think all mothers are warriors, when our babies are inside us and even more, when they live outside us, even less in our control. I was a warrior even with Oliver. *Especially* with Oliver. When I met him, the world froze around us. For me, everything else ceased to exist. It felt like he disarmed me of all thought and sense. He was a musician, a vocalist, and not even a struggling one. His star was ascending, playing at all sorts of venues around the city and even in Europe. We went on a few dates, and he told me he felt our connection but wasn't looking for anything serious. It took two years of playing the cool-girl, don't-care, pulling back when he finally wanted more, enduring months of no contact. I knew he'd come around. And I suppose I willed it, because eventually he did, waxing poetic about how perfectly we fit together, how right we were as a team. I remember at our wedding, the satisfaction I felt, that I had achieved him. Made him mine.

Until now, when it appears that he isn't.

I am a warrior, though. I will make them both pay. But not before saving myself, and my children. Not before securing our future.

I stare at the ceiling, watching the shadows dance.

———

In the early shreds of morning I hear a knock on the door. I am awake. Haven't really slept, other than nightmares. I glance at the bedside clock. 6:03. I am almost unsurprised at the knock.

But the person who appears in my doorframe does surprise me. It's Vix, whose entire face is warped in a scream. "Darce, ohmygod, Darce, you have to come." When I don't instantly react, she shouts, "Come *now*!"

I spring out of bed. "Vix, wha . . . what is it?"

"I just . . ." She shakes her head, then turns so her face is shrouded in a column of night. "You have to come to your grandmother's room," she whispers.

My grandmother's room. Why has Vix been inside my grandmother's room at 6:03 in the morning?

Doubtfully, I throw off the covers and follow after her, my heart slamming against my chest. Vix is wearing nineties-style baggy jeans and one of those oversize T-shirts she now favors. Jeans and a T-shirt at six in the morning?

My toes curl in the doorframe like brakes.

"Vix," I whisper, but she's already disappeared down the little hall that leads to Grand-mère's room. I make myself walk. One foot in front of the other, although it doesn't feel like me walking. It feels like someone else, someone foreign, has slipped into my place, and I have exited this life. Pulled the cord, initiated the parachute.

"Darce, I'm so . . . I'm . . ."

Then I see it—red, like my grandfather. But different. And I realize I'm not in the parachute. I'm still here, and my grandmother is very, very dead.

CHAPTER SIXTEEN

Vix

It is gruesome, Séraphine lying in her bed, a knife plunged in her heart. The sheets are in a tangle, like perhaps there was a struggle. Tears collect in my eyes—I don't want to think of the struggle. Poor old Séraphine, murdered in her sleep, or perhaps awakened just before the moment of her death. Aware that someone—who?—was about to plunge a knife right into her.

And then again, and again. Her chest, the glimpses I am willing to take before nausea bursts in my throat, is a chest plundered. Destroyed. Whoever did this didn't strike once, but over and over. Viciously.

The who part of it dances among us, but for now we are distracted by our horror, by our grief. Our grief, but mostly Darcy's. It is she who we must support. She who is throwing up in the black marble trash can in the corner, with Jade rubbing her back.

I feel a presence behind me, a hand on my shoulder. I flinch, turn. Oh. It's Arabelle.

"Sorry, Belle. It's just . . . who did this?"

"I know." She shakes her head. "We shouldn't touch anything. The police are going to want to take apart the crime scene."

"Right. The police. God." I notice the antique silver bedside clock on the tile floor. It's facing up, but its glass face is smashed. I crouch down, but don't touch it so my fingerprints don't skew the evidence. The clock has shattered at 3:16.

100

Jade crouches down beside me. "Must be the time of the murder. Whoever did this probably knocked the clock over. Maybe it's a clue. Maybe there are fingerprints. On the knife, too." She gestures at Séraphine, but I don't follow with my eyes. I can't look at her again like this. A sob wracks my body.

"I need to wake my grandmother up before she hears us and wanders into this hell." Arabelle gestures toward the bed.

"Oh, shit." I bite my lip thinking of poor Sylvie, finding the woman for whom she has worked for a lifetime in this horrific condition.

Arabelle is with Darcy now, having swapped out with Jade. Darcy's sobs are ferocious. Suddenly I feel like a caged animal. We need to get out of this room.

"This is insane." Jade taps her long nails on the dresser. "I can't believe it. I really can't believe it."

I nod. "Me too. I hope it's a nightmare, and we're going to wake up from it any moment."

"It's not a nightmare, Vixen," Jade says grimly.

I am looking at Séraphine again; I can't help myself. I want to cover her with the sheets. Yank out the knife. But she's dead. Zero question of that. And if I disturb the knife, I could ruin evidence. God, was it a break-in? Is there a serial killer on the loose? It can't have been one of us. I know these girls. I know them better than I even know myself.

Raph, the groundskeeper. Maybe he did it. I shiver. We've spent time with him. We've spent time with a murderer?

"I'm so confused," Jade says. "Who found her in the first place?"

I clear my throat. Even in the chaos, in the shock of finding Séraphine like this, I've had the wherewithal to think about how I will answer this question. "Well actually . . . I did."

"You?" Jade's breath streams right at me; it's sour and stale. Morning breath, mingled with death. I back away, but the death stench is still here, potent. They can't depict that in the movies. How a body smells in the hours after life has been snuffed out of it.

"Yes. Vix found Grand-mère." At Darcy's voice, her first words since she reluctantly followed me in here, I swivel. She emerges from the trash can, separating the curtain of strawberry strands from her eyes. "What were you doing in here at six in the morning, Vix?"

"I don't know. . . ." Well, I do know. But I'm not ready to say so yet. Not before I think through things. Figure out what's what.

"You don't know?" Darcy isn't accusing me per say; her voice is childlike, frail.

"Séraphine wanted to meet with me. We were supposed to meet the first day, then yesterday, but she kept canceling on me. She told me to come to her room before everyone else woke up. Six in the morning. I knocked, but she didn't answer. I waited a minute, then decided to go in." I gasp involuntarily. It was horrible. They can't understand how horrible, to be the one to discover it. To see the woman I loved and admired, maybe idolized, lying so helplessly in her nightgown, brutally done apart.

"You have no clue why she wanted to meet with you?" Arabelle asks.

It sounds fishy. I get it. But at the moment, there is nothing else I can say. I made a vow to Séraphine, and now I am even more determined to keep it.

"No clue at all." I pray it sounds genuine. My eyes flicker to the fireplace mantel, on which an iconic Marcel Duchamp sculpture is perched. In it, an arm thrusts out of the chessboard-adorned plinth, its hand cradling the head of a weathered old man. The man's eyes are closed—unclear whether he's sleeping, or dead. Séraphine once told me it was one of her favorite pieces, which says a lot, given the prestige and value of her collection. I'll never forget when she showed it to me. She winked and said, "My favorite sort of man." I smiled, somewhat uneasily. I have always wondered what she meant.

Now I hear footsteps at the door.

"Oosh," Arabelle says, and hastens to the little hallway. I hear murmurs in French. Footsteps retreating out of the room. A shriek. I put my pointer fingers in my ears, instinctually. When I finally release them, I hear a door closing shut.

"I need to get out of here," Darcy suddenly says, and stands.

"Yes, let's." Jade props Darcy up, almost hustling her out.

I follow them. Just outside the door, Darcy plops down in the hallway, like going farther to her room would be an effort she cannot bear. "It's my fault," she says to herself. "This is entirely my fault."

"Darce, no way," I say. "Why would this be your fault?"

She doesn't answer or look at me, just closes her eyes tight. With her eyes closed, she says, "I don't get it. Who would do this? Who would do this to my grandmother? Did one of you . . . ?" Her eyes are even greener, purer, when she cries. Then her tears suddenly stall, and her eyes widen. "Did one of you . . . ?"

"Of course not," Jade immediately says, loudly. "Darcy, of course not."

"Of course not," I whisper.

Now Arabelle comes to slide down beside us. "Darce, I loved your grandmother like my own." She pulls Darcy into her arms and hugs her fiercely. Those two have a bond unlike the rest of us. They grew up together, with their grandmothers, like a family. "I called the police by the way," Arabelle says. "They will be here soon."

Darcy's chin trembles in their embrace. "How is Sylvie?"

"She's devastated," Arabelle says quietly, pulling back to dab at her eyes with her sleeve. "Disbelieving. I'm just glad she didn't have to see what we saw. She wants to, you know. But I convinced her not to. I gave her a Xanax."

I take in this information. I don't ask why Arabelle had a Xanax in the first place. There are so many questions stacking up in my mind. Suddenly I desperately want to be alone and sift through the facts and questions before the police arrive.

A memory visits me, from one of my many phone conversations with Séraphine over the years. After Darcy's explosion in the car on the way over, and her revelation that she doesn't talk on the phone to her grandmother, I didn't want to admit it, but Séraphine and I have spoken often. She is—was, God, *was*—always interested in my life. She wanted to know about my art, what paintings I was working on, all the people who were clamoring to buy. I never wanted to let her down, so I embellished buyers. I didn't want her to know how much I needed her monthly support payments; how much I felt like a failure, when galleries turned me away. Maybe likewise I didn't want to disappoint her when Juliet and I broke up, because Séraphine supported our relationship so much. She said Juliet sounded like my perfect counterpart. But the memory that pops up now is a lighter one. I don't remember what upset me, but suddenly on the phone with her once, I shouted, *Fuckety fuck!* It just blurted out, a knee-jerk reaction to something that probably ceded in importance an hour later. Probably I saw a cockroach or a credit card bill. And then I realized to whom I was speaking.

"Victoria, it isn't ladylike to curse like that." I swear, I could see her frown through the phone.

"Sorry," I mumbled.

"If you're going to swear, at least say *putain*."

"*Putain*?" I asked uncertainly.

"It means something similar. But it sounds more ladylike in French."

We both laughed. And then she told me, for the thousandth millionth time, that I really should go by Victoria and not Vix.

"Victoria is so refined. Vix sounds like a candy bar!"

I bite the inside of my cheek, hard. I'll never laugh with her, or hear her opinions, again.

"I'm afraid. . . ." Now Arabelle kneads her fingers together. "What if Mamie can't recover from this? I don't quite know how she'll get on."

"She was devoted to Séraphine," I say. "For how many years?"

"Sixty," Darcy says. "She's been my grandmother's housekeeper for at least sixty years, I'd say."

"Housekeeper?" Arabelle's face takes on a peculiar look. "Yes, she was Séraphine's housekeeper, but surely you know how it turned?"

Now Darcy glances up with tear-stained cheeks. She looks wrecked. My heart absolutely breaks for my friend. We should get her something—a Xanax from Arabelle?—before the police come.

"What do you mean?" Darcy asks.

"Well I . . ." Arabelle looks around at us, like we might chime in, but I have no idea what she's talking about. "They were lovers, your grandmother and mine. They've been lovers, in secret, more or less, for decades."

Darcy looks as startled as I feel. "Love . . . wha . . . lovers? What . . . you can't mean like *actual* lovers?" When Arabelle nods, Darcy says, "No, that's not possible. . . ."

"They were in love." Arabelle's eyes cast down toward the foyer, where day is breaking through the windows. I try to absorb this, slot it into place. All those conversations with Séraphine about Juliet take on new, murky meaning. Is this why Séraphine took such an interest in me? Because . . . why? She saw something hopeful in my path, that her generation couldn't have? Or something more, or different? My head is spinning.

"Lovers . . . in love . . . partners," Arabelle says. "I always wondered why your grandmother didn't tell you, but they came from another generation. I felt like it was her news to share. I thought you might have suspected it, though. To me, it was obvious. In any case, it's the truth. Mamie will tell you herself.

"Your grandmother meant everything in the world to mine. And mine meant everything to yours."

CHAPTER SEVENTEEN

Arabelle

They've sent us two officers, a male and female from the gendarmerie. Mamie is sleeping upstairs, and the officers have agreed not to disturb her for now, until they're ready to question her. Which leaves the rest of us situated in the living room where we partied just hours before: the four of us girls and Raph, the groundskeeper, too. The room is back to its pristine state. Before we went to bed, Darcy and I cleaned up. Jade had passed out, and I wasn't surprised that Vix disappeared when it was cleaning time. Vix is wonderful at a lot of things, but she tends to drift away when cleaning is involved.

Not that cleaning matters now. I glance around at my friends, all in various states of stunned. My hands are still trembling, my brain whirling. I watch Darcy, and wish I could know what she is thinking. I can tell that the girls are shocked, too, by my revelation about Mamie and Séraphine. I'm surprised that none of them suspected it all these years, especially Darcy.

The male officer has disappeared upstairs, and the female officer is seated on a chaise, surveying us. She has introduced herself as Officer Darmanin. She has long, dark hair wrapped in a low chignon, and sultry brown eyes. She is in her thirties, early thirties I guess, and is quite pretty, with her pale blue shirt and navy pants tailored nicely to her figure, which is frankly bombshell.

I'm not under any illusions, though. The gendarmerie in small-town France has a certain reputation, of being incompetents. Although her English is rather exceptional, maybe even better than mine. I wonder if she's spent time abroad, or has an Anglo parent.

"My partner is investigating upstairs. Gathering evidence. Dealing with the body." At the word *body*, I see Darcy flinch. I reach over to take her hand and stroke her skin. Her skin is unbearably soft. Like a child's. I don't think I ever knew that. Her hand feels slack in mine, though, like she's not even aware I'm holding it.

But then Darcy retracts her hand. "What will they do with my grandmother's . . . body? We'll need to . . . oh God, we'll have to bury her. A funeral . . ."

"There will be an autopsy, yes? You will have to wait for the results before you can do anything."

"An autopsy," Darcy repeats.

"And, of course, we will need to speak with each of you. Figure out what you saw, and if you had an alibi."

"Alibi?" Jade asks. "Like . . . you think we . . . you think I might have—"

"You are all suspects," Officer Darmanin says curtly. "Unless you have an alibi that clears you. We suspect the murder took place at a quarter past three, given the clock that appears to have been smashed by the killer in the course of the murder. But at a quarter past three in the night, you would claim you were sleeping, no?"

Nods all around. Except for me.

Oh heavens. Do I say it? Or hide it? Hiding it would be no doubt the kinder route, but it's bound to come out now. Do I just come out with it? Or wait until I'm alone with the officer? They're all going to find out now, in the end.

"Well . . ." My heart is pounding like a techno rave. I feel all eyes boring into me. I force myself to keep going even though I want to crawl under the blanket in my lap and hide like a child. "I do have an alibi, in fact."

"You *do*?" Jade asks. "What, you were with one of us? Or with Sylvie?"

Thank heavens Mamie isn't here right now for this. Although she will hear of it soon enough. The thought squeezes my heart.

"Not with any of you, no." I pause, trying to think how to say this. But there is no good way. "I had a man with me," I finally admit.

The room is the terrifying sort of silent.

"Raph?" asks Vix. "You were with the *groundskeeper?*"

"*Non!*" says a horrified male voice. I swivel, to see Raph, standing behind the couch, his arms square across his broad chest. I'd almost forgotten he was here. "I did not have sex with her." He stabs a finger in my direction.

"Not Raph," I say. "Someone . . . well, someone else. He came over after the girls went to bed. We went right to sleep—it was late— but we woke up and we . . ."

Shit. I can't do this. "Can we?" I whisper, gesturing Officer Darmanin toward a vacant corner.

"You woke up and had sex?" Officer Darmanin stays looking at me with a placid expression.

Slowly I nod, stare at my lap. "We had sex, and when we finished, he handed me a glass of water, and I asked him the time. The clock was on his side of the bed. He said 3:19. We went back to sleep after that."

Officer Darmanin doesn't say anything, just cocks her head, appraising me. The tension in the room is suffocating me. I need to get out. Séraphine dead, telling them about my night. Now, the girls' reactions. I pull my sleep shirt from where it's strangling my neck.

"So he left after the scream?" Jade asks. I can tell by her face she heard something outside her door. Footsteps, maybe. We knew something was going on at Darcy's first scream. It wasn't a question—he needed to skedaddle.

"Yes. He parked beyond the main road. I never in a million years thought anyone would find out. My room is close to the door. We planned on him leaving early, but not exactly at six. But after we heard Darcy scream, it felt . . . *prudent* that he go. Immediately."

"I heard a car engine," Raph says. "It woke me up, and I went out to see."

"I saw you outside," Jade says, looking thoughtful. "I thought it was strange you were wandering around. You didn't hear the scream. . . ."

"I heard the engine," he says again, defensively.

"He parked far though," I say. "I wouldn't expect you'd be able to hear."

"I heard it," Raph repeats, frowning at me.

I shrug.

"We'll need to talk to this man you had over," Officer Darmanin says. "Confirm your story."

I nod. I bite my lip.

"Who is he?" Darcy asks. She's been quiet, but now her eyes bore into mine.

I should have done this in a private, more compassionate way. But what I must say is now a ball of yarn skidding across the floor—an unstoppable unravel. I force my eyes to meet Darcy's. I don't move my gaze. I owe her that much.

"Your husband," I say, at last. "I'm so sorry, Darce. It's Ollie, who was here."

I realize too late I've called him by my nickname. He's Oliver to everyone else, even Darcy. It always sounded kind of formal to me, for his wife. Oliver this, Oliver that. A pang of remorse washes over me. I've taken her husband and made him into an Ollie. This isn't how I ever saw it going down. Trust me, I have reckoned with what I have done. I have known the consequences that were coming. But I'm in love with him, more than I've ever loved another man, including Giancarlo.

It's funny, but I married Giancarlo because the sex was the best in my life. A good enough reason as any, I felt. I was thirty-four. I didn't want kids, but it seemed time. He was kind, charming, but talked a lot—still does. A chatterbox. Politics mostly, complaints about the local government, things I don't care a fig about. But the sex was so good that it didn't matter, until it did. I once heard Jade describe her relationship with Seb as having a baseline attraction that could surpass anything. He could floss his teeth and show her the string of meat that came out, he could fart too often—nothing diminished her attraction. This didn't happen for me. I loved Giancarlo. I think I did, at least. I can't pinpoint the exact moment the love left, but maybe it's when the sex died down. Died out. That was our bridge, and our frequency went to fumes. I started coming to New York more often with my cookbooks, which led to me and Ollie. To there finally being a me and Ollie.

But you have to understand, I met him first, before Darcy. I'm the one who introduced Ollie to Darcy, in the first instance. I met him at one of his shows, when he was playing at this dive bar in Paris. I had a boyfriend at the time, but there was an undeniable spark, and we texted a bit after, forming a casual sort of friendship. Then when I was in New York not long after visiting the girls, he invited me to a gig, and I brought Darcy along. They hit it off immediately. Darcy fell head over heels, even though it took him a long while to commit. I was at their wedding, of course, a bridesmaid. Typically, no good friend, or good wife, looks at her friend's husband properly. But I had always looked at Ollie *properly*, from the start. But once I finally broke up with that boyfriend, Ollie wasn't an option anymore. For so long I tried to shove my attraction down. Even though the way he looked at me sometimes, many times, made me suspect the attraction wasn't one-sided.

One night, though, not so long ago, when we were all on Jade's deck in the Hamptons for a dinner, and Ollie was passing me a jar of olives, our fingertips brushed together. *Coup de foudre*, we call it. A lightning bolt. And nothing could be the same after that. I knew he felt it, too, the jolt. It was only days later, when I extended my trip, that we quite literally devoured each other.

At first it felt impossible—not only was Ollie my best friend's husband, but we lived across the world from each other. But my cookbooks were giving me more excuses to jet to New York, and our web became tighter, more interconnected. Ollie came to Saint-Rémy this week for me. It wasn't Darcy's idea; it was his, hidden behind the rationale of a family vacation. We knew we wouldn't have much time, but we'd sneak some. And for that little time, it would be worth it.

My explanation for this betrayal is rather simple, even though I know how it sounds, how awful a person I am. But I fell in love. Hard, deep, once-in-a-lifetime love. He's unhappy with her. They aren't going to make it in any event. He's only staying because of the kids, and even that won't sustain them. He's told me so many times, when my doubts and shame threaten to flatten me. And how can something that feels so right, to both of us, be wrong? But maybe that's just what I tell myself so I can live with myself.

"Who was with my children last night?" Darcy asks, a reaction I hadn't expected. Her eyes are blazing like a dragon's, spitting fire. But I suppose it makes sense. Darcy is a mother. The whereabouts of her children should, and would, be her first thought.

"He got a babysitter, a woman from town," I say quietly. "You know her. You trust her." I see her face, as I am inadvertently informing her of whom she knows. Whom she trusts. "Coralie," I say quickly. "Ollie said she babysits for you guys whenever you come to town. She's as trustworthy as it gets, he said."

I realize immediately how that sounds, coming from me. Jade's face puckers, like she's sucked on something sour. I deserve it. I am prepared to take my punishment. Besides, in the face of Séraphine's horrific murder, maybe a little infidelity won't seem quite as egregious.

No, it's egregious. I hang my head. I can hardly breathe.

"He planned to be back before the kids woke up," I say, still trying for some reason to defend him. It's a strange, convoluted thing, to defend a man to my best friend, who happens to be his wife. "Before they knew any different."

"Before they knew any different," Darcy echoes, still staring into my eyes defiantly. Strangely, she seems surprised, but also not.

"I'm sorry, Darce, I'm truly so sorry." I wonder if I should say more and then I just do. "I love him. If that counts for anything."

"It doesn't, it really fucking doesn't," she says, and finally looks away, out the window onto the vineyard.

Everyone is avoiding my gaze, I notice, except for Officer Darmanin, her pretty, small features trained on me without a glimmer of reaction.

CHAPTER EIGHTEEN

Raph

It is a soap opera I have found myself in, in these early morning hours. Just like the ones Margaret used to watch, with sister betraying sister, son murdering father. She used to call them *meurtres heureux*. Happy murders, because you could watch without a hand clamped to your eyes, like in those scary horror movies. Happy murders were suited to popcorn and sweet dreams. It really says so much about her, doesn't it?

I am inside a horror soap opera. On another day at this time, I would be doing my calisthenics workout on the lawn. Perhaps it is not the life of a typical groundskeeper, but I am not a typical groundskeeper.

Darcy stood and went to the window after Arabelle's big confession. I am still quite appalled by the whole thing. I think everyone else in the room is, too. Sleeping with your best friend's husband? In her grandmother's chateau? It's a cruel sort of ballsy. Darcy is wearing a long pink nightgown with flowers that I assume is for sleep but looks like her other dresses. Her dresses swallow her whole. It is impossible to infer what her legs might look like beneath. I have a strange compulsion to go over to her and put an arm around her tiny shoulders. But I don't think that would be welcomed, so I refrain. She has girlfriends to do it, two remaining, at least. Sure enough, Jade goes to her friend at the window. There are tears and whispers and a long embrace.

I look away. Overt displays of emotion have often left me uncomfortable. Not because I resent them, or don't understand them, but because I understand them too well.

Séraphine is dead. Murdered. I twine my hands together, thinking, remembering. There is one *pétanque* game in particular that sticks to me. The one where she asked me to look after Darcy. I summon it back, rewind, fast forward. The look on her face. Steely, but also maybe scared.

The male officer returns from upstairs, holding a plastic bag in his gloved hands. The bag looks like it has a slip of paper inside. He summons Officer Darmanin. The two whisper things I cannot hear, although I strain to. He hands her the bag.

And suddenly Officer Darmanin is staring straight at me, the bag concealed in her hand behind her back. I am overcome with impulse, to know what is inside that bag.

Slowly she reveals it. Then steps closer to us.

"My partner found this piece of paper in Séraphine's sheets. It seems she tried to write something, perhaps while the murderer was distracted."

Darcy comes over from the window. "She wrote something. What?"

I squint, trying to make out the writing. The paper is small, and it's been torn across the top. I step closer. It is cream notepaper, I can see now. Expensive paper.

Merde alors. I can now see what is written on the notepaper.

"What does it say?" Jade asks. "I don't know what it says."

"It is the beginning of a sentence," Officer Darmanin says. "Or at least, that is what it appears to be. We aren't sure how she was able to write this without detection by the murderer. We have a preliminary theory, though."

"Which is . . . ?" Darcy asks.

Officer Darmanin and her partner make eyes at each other. Finally, she says, "We think the murderer may have had a gun, in addition to the knife. Perhaps the murderer wanted something from Séraphine. Something from the safe perhaps, that was in the bedroom? Because the door of the safe was flung open."

"So there will be fingerprints," Arabelle says. "That's good."

"*Non*. There are none. We assume the killer used gloves. Or wiped the fingerprints clean. Perhaps the motive for the murder lies inside the safe. We will need an inventory from the estates' attorney, to determine what, if anything, is missing. This is why we wonder if a gun was involved. If, for instance, the killer focused his attention to open the safe, what would have motivated Séraphine not to scream and rouse the whole house? Only a gun that he trained upon her."

With a shiver, I note the use of the pronoun *he*. I am the only *he* here.

"But why would the murderer kill with the knife then?" Arabelle asks. "If he had a gun."

Officer Darmanin shrugs. "We don't know yet. Fury, perhaps. The knife matches the set in the kitchen. Anyone could have taken it. No fingerprints, again. A gun would provide more clues. Even without fingerprints, a gun leaves a trail. If our theory pans out, we will find the gun. And hopefully the gloves, if there were any. The killer can't have hidden things far."

"But the grounds are massive," Darcy says. "And I can't imagine how any of us would have gotten a gun. Wouldn't that make it . . . like . . . premeditated?"

Officer Darmanin nods. "A vicious murder in the middle of the night while the victim is sleeping. It is the definition of premeditated."

A gun. This is so much worse than I thought. *Merde*. I am still staring at the notepaper, my heart battering my chest. Now Darcy seems to remember the note exists. She steps closer, appraises the bag with the paper inside. She reads, her face blank.

"*Assassiné R*," Darcy says slowly.

"What does that mean?" Vix asks.

"*Assassiné* translates to murdered. I guess she didn't get to finish writing the rest." Darcy's face crumples in.

"R," Vix says. "But whose name here starts with an R?"

Merde. Merde.

All eyes in the room train on me.

CHAPTER NINETEEN

Jade

Raph, the groundskeeper and murderer apparent, has gone to the station for questioning by Officer Darmanin. The note isn't the only evidence, although it is the most persuasive piece. Darcy also informed the officers that she found it strange how ignorant Raph was as to when to pick a certain type of cherry off its tree. Though perhaps not the most incriminating of observations, Sylvie then confirmed that Raph was the least exceptional groundskeeper ever employed at the chateau. And if he wasn't actually a legitimate groundskeeper, then why was he posing as one? These questions, coupled with my seeing Raph wandering outdoors in the early morning hours, have cast a long shadow of suspicion.

Now other officers have arrived, to remove the body. The body. It's still very surreal. Others are searching the chateau, the grounds, Raph's cabin, for the gun they suppose Raph had. They've placed tape around the bedroom crime scene and ordered us not to disturb it. They've also done preliminary interviews with each of us, gathering what little we know. We've been instructed to stay close to the chateau. In any event, not to leave Saint-Rémy.

"Darce, let's get you upstairs," I say finally, after we've both finished our interviews.

No reply. Darcy is on the couch, her hand fanning her face. I try to coax her up, but she feels like deadweight. "Come on, you need to lie down."

"I don't know. . . ." Darcy rubs her eyes and gazes around list-lessly. She reminds me of a doll, lifeless. Just stuffing. She needs to sleep. It's like I told the kids when they were little and having a tantrum: Sleep cures all. You wake up with new energy after a nap. Although in this case, sleep will not cure all. It will only postpone the breakdown. Nothing will bring Séraphine back, or change the fact that Arabelle's been having an affair with Oliver—seriously, I could murder that girl.

Wrong word choice.

"Come on, sweetie. One foot in front of the other. Your bed is calling your name."

Arabelle wisely says nothing. Vix chimes in, though, stands up. "Here, let me come, too."

"No," Darcy whispers. I almost have to strain to hear her. "Just Jade. Okay? Sorry, Vix. I just . . . it's too . . . just Jade." She leans her head on my shoulder.

I have to admit, I feel good to hear it. There's been some weird-ness between Darcy and me this trip, weirdness that I can't put my finger upon. This feels like confirmation that we're okay, even though nothing else is okay.

Vix sinks back down to the couch. I can tell that she's hurt, but also that she understands, that she is willing to put our friend ahead of her ego.

"You'll be okay down here, Vix?" I don't look at Arabelle. I can't. I'm so angry. But I am mindful that a murder has taken place. It seems like Raph did it, that we are safe with him now gone, escorted by the police. Right? Who knows. My mind is a blender soup of mush.

"Yeah. I'm good."

Darcy and I walk to the door. Something occurs to me, and I turn back.

"Guys?" I say.

"Yeah?" says Vix.

"If you go to your room, lock your door. You know? To be safe."

It echoes in the silence, what I haven't said. To be safe . . . from one of us? Raph is gone now, yes. He's very, very likely the one who did it. But still.

"Yeah," Vix says. "I think that's smart."

This isn't what I expected. This isn't what I expected of today at all.

———

I wind up carrying Darcy to bed when she falters in the foyer. She's so small, it's like carrying Sea when she was younger and fell asleep on the couch. I tuck Darcy into her bed. Her eyes are closed, her porcelain cheeks crusty with tears. I stroke her cheek for a moment, then pull the quilt up to her chest. And I am reminded of the girl I met nearly twenty years before. I remember her exact outfit when we collided in the lobby of our dormitory—a black tank top paired with flared red pants and chunky black platforms. She fiddled with her top as we spoke, smoothing it over her stomach in a way that made me think she wasn't aware just how gorgeous she was. Her red pants with her red hair had me conjuring fire. But I quickly learned she wasn't fire at all. She was the girl down the hall with the sweet, cozy energy, with whom I always felt like I was home. And then I learned her full name. Darcy Demargelasse. Could it really be, a descendant served up to me on a silver platter?

I probed, asking her why she, too, chose Avignon for her study abroad instead of Paris, and about her family, and she spoke of Saint-Rémy, and I saw a letter from her grandmother, with the crest my father had sketched out for me many times.

Yes, it was luck, or it was God. Or it was the devil himself.

Still, the luck, or lack thereof, of Darcy's genetics aside, we've been real, true friends, from the very start. I never had a sister, and Darcy slotted easily into that place. We've endured so much together. We've held each other's hands in the best times and the worst ones. We've hardly ever fought, but perhaps things have been simmering below the surface of late, warranting a fight. I've sacrificed a lot by keeping her grandmother's deeds quiet.

"Jade?" Darcy murmurs.

"Yeah, honey. I'm here."

"Do you think Grand-mère suffered?"

I consider the question. The image is seared in my brain—the knife lodged in her heart. "I think it was quick. I'm sure the first stab hit . . ." What I was going to say is the right spot.

"Her heart. It went right into her heart."

"I know, honey. I'm so sorry. But she was old. She . . ." I was about to say she had a good life. But I can't bring myself to say it.

Darcy's eyes are closed, though, and she doesn't respond. The shades are still drawn, but day blurts into the room nonetheless. Things will be better after she sleeps. Or maybe that's just something I—we—need to tell ourselves, to keep moving through life.

I stand. The truth is, things will be worse for Darcy, before they get better. But things will be clearer, maybe.

"J?" Darcy whispers, after I've walked to the door.

"Yeah?" I turn. Her face looks slack, wrung out. It stuns me, this shadow of my friend. She is typically the warrior—sweet and shy, but beneath it ferociously going after what she wants, until the object of her hunt falls obligingly at her feet.

"Did you kill my grandmother?" she whispers.

My breath skids. "Darce, you've gotta be kidding. Of course I didn't. I *didn't* kill Séraphine, Darce."

Her eyes are still closed. "You hated her."

"I do, yes. I mean, I did. But I didn't kill her." Darcy is quiet. I'm not sure if she's fallen asleep. Somehow I think she has not. "I had every reason to hate her, Darce. You know what she did to my family. And I've waited this long—decades—in silence. My father has, too. For you. We could have confronted Séraphine. We could have even gone to the press, filed a lawsuit. . . ." I wonder if I've gone too far, letting my hate and pain bleed out today, of all days.

Darcy turns suddenly on her side, away from me. I'm not sure if she's fallen asleep, or if she just doesn't want to talk about all this now.

"Love you, Darce. Sleep tight." I slip out of her room. Her question reminded me, there is something urgent I need to do.

I am in Séraphine's large, glamorous closet when I hear a rustle outside. I spin from where I am rifling behind Séraphine's collection of designer bags.

Footsteps. Shit.

What is my story? My story is . . . I am looking for clues.

But ostensibly Raph did it. So . . . I am looking for . . .

I hear Séraphine's dresser creak open, then the scrape of the dresser against the floor, pulling it flush from the wall. I know these sounds, because I just did the dresser search myself. Who is out there? I consider hiding here until whoever it is leaves, but there isn't really anywhere to conceal myself. The closet is as sparse as the rest of the chateau—more space than stuff. Each item is immaculate, though, expensive and stunning. Séraphine KonMari'd her stuff far before the term entered the zeitgeist. But I know it is here. The Van Gogh that belongs to my family.

I've only been in this room once before, when I snuck inside the summer we studied abroad. Darcy was my lookout, but it was an effort that bore no fruit. I found nothing. Only this time, I'm not leaving without it.

Footsteps now approach the closet. I step toward the entry. Best be unapologetic, like I've done nothing wrong, than be found skulking about.

"Hello?" I call.

Vix appears in the doorframe. She looks surprised to see me. And I am surprised to see her.

"Hi." I give an awkward wave.

"Fancy meeting you here." She cocks her head at me, in the same way I suspect I am appraising her.

"What are you doing in here?" I ask. "Does it have to do with your meeting with Séraphine?"

Vix's cheeks flush pink. "I really don't want to talk about it yet."

"Did you tell the police about it?"

She nods. "But I'm not ready to tell you. Anyway, they have a suspect. What do they need with my meeting with Séraphine? It has nothing to do with anything. So . . . what are you doing here?"

I've never heard Vix so defensive. What was this meeting about? Why is she bent on protecting it at all costs? I turn so she can't see my face and stroke the pebbled leather of a navy Chanel bag. I suppose all this designer loot is Darcy's now.

"Séraphine has something of mine," I finally tell Vix. "And I'd like it back." The whoosh of honesty feels refreshing.

"Séraphine has something of yours? What does that even mean?"

I trust Vix—or at least I think I do. But contrary to her, I haven't told the police about what I am looking for. Besides, Vix isn't telling me everything, either. And I have no idea why.

"We're not enemies," Vix finally says, wearily. "If Raph murdered Séraphine, we need to band together. Especially me and you, after what Arabelle confessed."

"I know. You're right."

But still I can't eject the words. This is too important, too raw. Something I have been dreaming of my entire life. It involves my family, our past, our future. Part of me thought—hoped—it might in fact comprise Séraphine's big revelation. That after all this time, she would try to make things right. Acknowledge what she did to my family.

How she—herself, with her faculties intact—sent my grandparents straight to their graves.

"I'm right," Vix says with a catch to her voice, "but still, there's a part of you that wonders if Raph actually did it, right? That suspects it could be one of us, instead."

"I don't know," I finally say. "Maybe we should get some rest, then reconvene."

"Yeah." But she makes no move to leave. I realize now that Vix could be looking for the same thing I am. But that makes no sense. How would she know about the painting? And why? My brain is playing tricks on me. It's inventing suspicions out of thin air.

"Shall we leave together?" Vix asks, almost like she doesn't trust me. I realize in that moment, I don't exactly trust her.

Anyway, the painting isn't here. I considered the safe in the bedroom, which has been cleared by the police. But it's too small. It has to be somewhere else then. I'm not giving up.

"Let's go," I say, and quicken my pace when I catch a glimpse of the Renoir. In it, a woman is adorned in a scarf and bejeweled headpiece, and her knowing, suspicious eyes strike me almost as Séraphine's proxies, chasing us out of the room.

CHAPTER TWENTY

Darcy

When I awake from my nap, I am disoriented, gaze around to place myself. I'm at the chateau. What time is it? From the light I think two or three. Immediately, I bolt up—am I late for something? I imagine Grand-mère tapping at her watch, her face crimped in disapproval. And then I remember she is gone.

My tears come, hot, fat—a waterfall. I remember this from when my grandfather died, and my father before him, even though I was so little, not much older than Mila, I realize. It hurts now again, the pain gnawing at all my edges, but I remember how the tears are almost a reprieve. It's the time after, when you walk around like a robot, feeling all dead inside, that is the worst part of grieving. Because everyone else eventually goes on with life, and you're still a robot.

Then there is Oliver. Oliver and Arabelle. It still strikes me on such a surface level, so bizarre it can't possibly be real. Even their names sound odd together, like sardines and maple syrup. How is there an Oliver and Arabelle? In fact, I met him through her, so I always knew the we of Oliver and me began with some kernel of connection between them. But I have to believe both of them love me enough that they wouldn't do this just for sex. Sex. God. My stomach constricts. She's beautiful, certainly, and svelte. I stare down at my stomach, wobbly even at rest. I've let myself go. Is that it? I shake my head, try to shake out all the futile self-hate. I may not be exactly gung-ho about this new body, may be mightily struggling to love it and be positive about it, but I've resolved not to do all those self-punishing things I used to—strict diets and cutting carbs and the like. I want so much more than that for Mila, want her to feel like more than a body, more than parts that must be chiseled and maintained for the pleasure of others. I have been trying so hard to like the me that I have become, and now the project is made even more difficult, what with supermodel Arabelle and my husband.

But come on, what do they even have in common? They both like rehashing strange stories they read in the news—the diver who was swallowed and spit out by a humpback whale; how football play-ers caught a cat who fell onto the field mid-play. Once we were all at Jade's house, and Vix made the observation that Oliver and Arabelle like one-in-a-million stories because it makes them feel like they can have one-in-a-million lives. And something about that bristled me. Like Oliver wasn't happy in his nice and ordinary life, in his hundred-in-a-million life. Sometimes I could see it, in his anger when his cover song didn't make a particular ranking, in his disappointment when after our wedding, I totaled all the checks we'd received and told him the figure. (Although the next morning, Grand-mère gave us her check—a boatload. He wasn't disappointed about that.) I wanted to shake him—*Wake up, we have so much!* But you can't ever make someone happy with what they have.

I think about how hard I fought for him, and how the chase made him more enticing. I made up lots of stories in my head about the years he couldn't commit—he was a masculine man, and he needed to reach a certain pinnacle of success before settling down; he had scars from his last relationship and was afraid to get close. But he loved me! I knew that he did deep down, in the way he looked at me, the way he touched me. He just needed to realize it. Eventually I made myself indispensable, in a calculated way. I realize so much of my life has been calculated, aimed at achieving those milestones other people make look so easy. All I wanted was the storybook life, but maybe the storybook life has never wanted me. Is that why every-thing feels so hard? You can push the boulder up over the hill, sure, but don't be surprised if when you're done, your back is broken and every last thing that was good inside you is gone.

I imagine Oliver and Arabelle having sex and reciting their ridiculous stories to each other. *Darcy rolls her eyes when I make her read something outlandish on my phone. You and me . . . it's different.*

It's always different, isn't it, when it's not the wife?

We made promises. I don't want to go back there, but my mind takes me all the same. Standing under the altar at that lavish wedding in Traverse City. My mother said I could have a wedding or the money. She'd set aside something from my father's life insurance payout; it surprised me, the uncharacteristic thoughtfulness of that gesture. Of course, I chose the grand affair. But it was more than childish fancy, or wanting the Hollywood ending, even though it was those things, too. But I wanted everyone watching, witnessing, when we made our vows. I wanted our promises etched in stone in their eyes. Only now do I understand. Every time we make promises we tell lies at the same time. We don't mean to, no, but by definition, promises are a future endeavor. How easy to say you will take the garbage out tomorrow, when you are lying comfortably in your bed tonight. Promises are things you say on behalf of your future self. But future selves are inherently unpredictable, messy, human.

I think, too, about those qualities I was confident I would possess as a mother. Not just patient and loving and all those blah blah blahs, but also, how I would never be that person who only talks about her kids. Who flips out the photo album at any opportune moment. Then two humans came out of my womb, and all those little promises to myself about who I would be flew out the window.

So can I blame Oliver? I mean, I do. I wholeheartedly fucking do. For so many things, not least of which is that for a week now, I thought it was *Jade*. I was planning to . . . well, I won't go there now. Now isn't about my marriage. I need to stop these ruminations, or I am going to spin out of control, more than even before. Now is about Grand-mère. I need to talk to the police. Find out about the autopsy, and Raph.

But what I really want to do is curl up in a ball, and never emerge from this bed. But I can't. I am a grown-up, a *mother*, with responsibilities. *But I'm a human beneath!* I hear myself screaming, as the boulder comes rolling back on its easy descent, flattening me.

Okay, fine. I dust myself off. I stand. I become Darcy Robot. I am good at this character, I realize. Darcy Robot walks, opens the door, heads down the stairs. When she reaches the bottom, Oliver is standing by the entry.

———

Immediately, Mila rushes at me, buries herself in my legs. I look at my husband with the question that has immediately arisen. He shakes his head. Then he opens his mouth, and I nestle my head down, into my daughter's hair. She doesn't know about Grand-mère. Good. Oliver did one thing right, at least. She barely knew Grand-mère. We don't need to tell her. How do you even explain death to a four-year-old?

I remember what my mother told me, about Papa. *He's gone to the place where wizards go.* Maybe because I'd been on a *Wizard of Oz* kick. Or maybe she just said it offhand, like she says most things, without thinking them through. But for a year after, I dressed up in my Dorothy costume, got really obsessed with the weather channel. I was the only kid on the planet on hopeful tornado watch, praying it would blast in and take me to my father.

I lift Mila into my arms. "Mama, Mama." She rubs her eyes.

I brush her hair with my fingers, the sweaty part at her scalp. "Did you just wake up from a nap?"

Mila nods. "And when I woke up, I was very sad, and I don't know why."

I bite my lip. "I feel that way sometimes, too, angel. It's okay to be sad."

Mila strokes my cheek, then she jiggles. I set her down. "Let's play hide-and-seek!" She dashes away, toward the living room.

I look at Oliver. I can't summon anything to my face, good or bad. "Where's Chase?"

"With the nanny." He coughs, looks away. He is wearing his outfit that I have always joked makes him look like a blueberry—pale blue shorts with sky blue top with navy blue eyes. "He was still sleeping. And Mila wanted to come. I wanted to come, too."

Of course. The nanny. The same one who watched the kids so he could come here to my grandmother's chateau and have sex with my best friend, while I slept upstairs.

I turn, follow after Mila. Oliver follows me.

Where is everyone? My heart jabs at my chest when I think about seeing Oliver and Arabelle together. I can't. Please God, spare me something.

Mila has crouched down beneath the coffee table, her pink saddle shoes jutting out obviously.

"Don't tell Daddy where I'm hiding," she whispers.

Oliver smiles at me sadly. I don't smile back.

"Darce, I'm so sorry. I'm so, *so* sorry." He makes a move to come closer. I thrust out a hand.

I hear footsteps, and my heart wriggles.

Thankfully, it's Jade who appears in the doorway. She takes us in, three-quarters of my family. What is left of us. I wanted to keep us together at all costs. I never had a family unit, not really. And the two men I loved died when I was a child. I wanted the white picket fence, the whole shebang. So I fought for Oliver. Then I fought for each of our kids. And now I just wonder, what for?

"I found you!" I hear Jade exclaim, and Mila collapses in giggles in her arms.

I crouch down beside them. I exchange a glance with Jade. "Angel." I kiss Mila's soft cheek, relishing her sweaty, powdery scent. "Auntie Jade is going to take you to the kitchen and get you a treat."

"*Pain au chocolat!*" Jade says.

"Yippie!" Mila scrambles up and darts out of the room without a backward glance. Jade squeezes my hand, then follows after my daughter.

Slowly I stand up. Suddenly the room is spinning, and I falter.

Something catches me. When I come to, I am on the couch, in Oliver's arms.

⸺

Immediately I spring back. His touch is prickly on my skin. No matter how much I still long for my husband, how much I want him to hug me, after what happened to Grand-mère—my body isn't having it. Every molecule in me is screaming, *Danger, he will hurt you. He has already hurt you.*

"I'm so sorry about Séraphine," Oliver finally says. "It's crazy."

"Yeah." I stare at my hands, for lack of anywhere else to look. They look older, I realize. Veiny, and the pores distinct.

"They think they found the guy?"

"The groundskeeper." I nod. "They have him in for questioning, but they found a note Grand-mère wrote that implicates him."

He nods. I realize he already knows.

"Oh, you . . . right. Okay, then."

His cheeks redden. "She just . . . because I left so . . ."

"I get the full picture, Oliver." I feel myself stiffen.

"But you don't, I haven't—"

"You were *here*, having sex with my best friend, while I slept upstairs. Is there something I've missed?"

He bites his lip, smiles at me sheepishly, like he does when he apologizes, but about something small, like not showering before he gets in bed after a show, smelling like cigarette smoke. I don't smile back. This is not cigarette smoke. "I mean, that *is* what happened, but you don't have to . . . like . . . you make it sound worse than it was."

"I don't think I could make it sound any worse. You love her."

"How do . . . did she tell you that?"

"No." I take a deep breath. Part of me—a deep, stupid part—hoped his initial reaction would be a fierce denial. "I heard you say it to that awful dad in the pink shorts in Amagansett."

I watch his mind work, his eyes roll around as he sifts and recalls and ultimately remembers. His eyes widen. "Shit."

I nod dully. "In France, they say *merde*."

"*Merde*." He attempts another smile, and this time it just pisses me off. "It doesn't mean I don't love *you*, Darce."

"I'm not a sister-wife. I'm your *wife* wife." It's a strange anger and desperation I feel now, tempered by my loss. It's all of these adult things, when now more than ever, I feel like the child who used to spend summers at this chateau. It's all blurring together, the tragedies, the person I was and am, the question marks descending like an avalanche.

I'm furious at Oliver, but above all, I'm scared. We have babies together, and they're still so young. We're deep in the trenches, surviving the outbursts, marveling at their moments of genius, of staggering humor. He's my companion in this strange, difficult, consuming parenting journey. For some reason I think of Elf on the Shelf—that blasted elf who arrives every Christmas season to torture moms. Some moms love Elf on the Shelf, making him little props, knitting him costumes. That's not my thing, but Oliver and I tag-team the elf, and it's even fun sometimes, to figure out what the elf is going to do the next day. Last year, we had the elf put Mila's underwear on the tree—that was a big hit. And he also crepe-papered the kids' room. Chase didn't get it, but Mila loved it, running through all the crepe paper to bust out. But then I think about the single mom I met at the playground last year who confessed that she bandaged up her elf's leg and wrote her kids a note saying he was out of commission that Christmas season because he'd tried to climb a tree and fell. I remember giggling but quickly turning somber, because I registered the look on her face. She said it was too hard to do it alone. That all her joy had gone. And now I get it. That very well may be the future I'm in for, our poor elf with his leg in a cast, hanging out on some sad shelf.

"Of course you're not a sister-wife," Oliver says. "I just . . . it sort of just happened, Darce."

"Okay, so what do you want, Oliver? Who do you want?" I'm surprised, a little awed in fact, at my bluntness. At my ability to ask a question whose answer I dread.

He hangs his head, and I know. Suddenly I know.

"Forget it," I say, feeling sick. "Sleeping with her here, beneath my nose. I know the answer." Suddenly I need to get away from him. From this. I need to walk outside, smell the rosemary, feel the sun on my skin. I think of all the times we've hugged on the couch, me on top of his lap. The best kind of hug, because he is very tall, and I am very short, so hugging standing up has its limitations. He is sitting on the couch. I could climb on top. My body sags a bit, anticipating the hit of oxytocin.

But no. Hugging him would be like buying a fake designer bag from one of those street vendors in Midtown. Totally unsatisfying. Breaks the second you wear it.

"I just need some time, Darce. Just a little time, to figure out what I really want."

"You have to go." It comes out more forceful than I even intended. "Out." I point toward the door.

"But Darce, with Séraphine . . . I want to be here for you now."

"No." I am struggling to put words to the storm inside me. "What you can do for me is take care of the kids. Be a father right now, while I deal with all of this."

Slowly Oliver nods. He's a good dad, is the thing. Even if his poor choices indicate otherwise. "You should come with us. It's not safe here. There's a murderer on the loose."

"He's not on the loose. He's with the police. And I'm not leaving this place." I think about our apartment in New York, how perfectly I styled it, finding the best stuff at TJ Maxx and Home Goods. The kids' room that I made so cozy and warm, with little stuffed rainbows and pithy sayings that ring false, now that I know what was happening between the cracks. That was my home, but it was my home with Oliver. I don't have a home anymore. Despite all that has happened here—and it's a lot—the chateau is the only home I really have.

"There are things to take care of, with Grand-mère gone."

"Oh." I see it on his face, even though he doesn't speak it aloud. Money. All of this. To whom will it go, but to me?

"When will we talk?" Oliver asks.

"I don't know." I get up. "We'll talk when I know what I want to say. When you figure out who you want." I look pointedly at him, and he avoids my gaze. "Just . . . tell Mila I love her. I don't want her to see me this way. Take care of my babies this week, okay?" I hear my voice crack. Part of me wants to gather Mila in my arms and wake a sleeping Chase and never let them go. But the broken person I am isn't the mom they need right now.

"Of course. Hey, Darce." I turn. He is looking at me with that Oliver look, his I'm-sorry-but-admit-it-you-can't-resist-this-face expression. And normally I can't. Normally I cave. Normally I make myself smaller and smaller, until I fit right back inside his arms. I haven't been a warrior, I realize. That's just the false thing I've been calling myself. I've been a shell of something I wanted to be, and I can't even put a real finger on who that person is.

"I love you," he says. "I still really love you. Two things can be true, you know, at the same time?"

I dig my fingernails into my thigh. "Then please don't come back here again and fuck my former best friend. If you love me, then that's the very least you can do."

I know this is my cue to leave. I've teed it up nicely. But I'm not ready to yet. There are so many things we have left to say. I can see it in his eyes—words and sentences are bubbling up in his throat, too. For a few moments our eyes flicker at each other, and I can see it all so clearly. The grief, the love, the sadness. The relief.

Yes, relief, too.

Like a nightmare, it floods back at me. The electronic notifications. How Oliver screamed at the bank representative and then sat with his head cradled in his hands. The word *foreclosure* like a constant noose on our necks, as Mila swirled her spoon around her cereal bowl and chattered obliviously about how crazy it was that the milk changed colors from red to purple.

You can't speak these things aloud—the vast silver lining of my grandmother's death. Death isn't supposed to leave silver linings for the people left behind. Oliver's face shades in shame, because he knows I have seen it, in the relax of his jaw, that I haven't seen relaxed in months. He's not proud, I can see, and neither am I, not whatsoever, even in the smallest measure, to find some happiness in my beloved grandmother's death.

But nonetheless, the sentiments have passed between Oliver and me, partners, as we have been, in children and careers and the banalities of marriage, and the spiral of our finances.

Now, in the span of a day, our family has been destroyed. But yes, our eyes communicate to each other: Our home, and livelihood, has been saved.

CHAPTER TWENTY-ONE

Arabelle

I am standing by the living room door. I suppose you could say I've been eavesdropping. It's my best friend in there, my sister, and I've devastated her. But it's my love in there, too. I have the sense of making my way through fog, unable to see to the other side, to the way it's going to go.

On her rush out, she sees me. She stops, crosses her arms over her chest. Her cheeks are strawberry pink, her hair spiky from the static of sleep, not firmed down with her usual headband. She gestures back inside. "Well . . . he's all yours."

It's not what she just told him, but I don't say that. "Darce, I'm so sorry. Truly I am."

"What are you sorry for?" When I meet her eyes, her chin is square, defiant. She is going to make me say it.

"For falling for Ollie. And of course, for what happened to Séraphine."

"And . . . ?"

I know what she means. "And for betraying you. I'm so sorry about that, Darce. I wish you could see inside me to realize how truly sorry I am."

She snaps her fingers together. "That makes everything okay then, huh? One sorry, and it's erased. I thought we were best friends, Belle. You always called us sisters."

"We *are* sisters. We *are*!"

"We're not." Darcy shakes her head. Suddenly she isn't angry, or sad, but very still and sure. "We were never really sisters, to be honest, and we never will be again."

I feel something old and tired whoosh out of me, and another sensation replace it, colder, more honest. It's like I've sunk down to the depths of the ocean, where everything is clear. I am impressed with her, to be honest. She is a true warrior, not backing down. As she should not. That's her husband, the father of her children. I knew she would fight. I just didn't know if I would. And what exactly I would be fighting for. But I can see it, coming toward me through the fog, this new life with Ollie and their kids. Being a stepmom. I never wanted children of my own, but they are wonderful in doses. We would hurt Giancarlo, Darcy. We would hurt them badly. We already have. That part stings terribly. But perhaps this new life is possible. I have plenty of money for us, even though Ollie doesn't. I know of their money troubles, although Darcy has never confided them in me.

I open my mouth, trying to summon something that is going to patch up the whole thing, but then suddenly Darcy shakes her head hard and a strangled noise emerges from her, like a horse's bray. She doesn't look at me, just dashes off toward the front door. She is barefoot, in a yellow dress.

"Darce, be careful, there are . . ."

She doesn't turn, and I watch her go, out the door.

There are prickly things on the ground, fallen from the trees, is what I was going to tell her. It's quite painful, when you get one stuck in your skin.

———

I linger as Oliver retrieves Mila from Jade. We exchange glances when he returns to the foyer, a sleepy bundle in his arms.

"Auntie Jade wore her out," says Jade, from the kitchen, her voice getting louder as she nears. "Don't tell Mama, but there was sugar involved, and I'm not talking natural date sugar."

"Oh." She stops when she sees me. Her eyes dart to Ollie. Her face falls. "You two . . . you can't do . . . whatever this is, here."

"I know," Oliver says quickly. "Anyway, I need to get this little lady home . . . back."

I shuffle my feet on the stone. I know we can't talk now, but we need to talk.

He nods at me, like he knows. But Mila, and Jade.

I nod back at him. We'll talk later. There is time, so much time now.

"Bye." Ollie waves, awkwardly, but his eyes are warm.

"Bye." My eyes follow him out.

When my eyes return to Jade, she is glaring at me. The scarlet letter is certainly real.

I clear my throat. "I think I'll go to the market. Get some things for dinner. We need to eat, don't you think? Mamie will be awake soon, and I want to be able to feed her."

Jade softens at the mention of my grandmother. "What about the chef who comes in from town?"

"She's heard about the murder." I shrug. "Would you want to work somewhere the day of a murder?"

"No. I hardly want to be here myself." Jade gives me a half smile, then seems to remember to whom she is giving that smile.

"Do you want to come with me? Get some fresh air?"

"No. I think . . . in case Darcy needs me, or your grandmother wakes up . . ."

"Yes. Okay, that's a good idea."

"I'll come," says a voice, descending the staircase. It's Vix, in the white flowy midi dress and studded booties we picked out when I took her shopping.

"You look nice." I smile, realizing how good it feels to smile after this day.

"The boots perk me up." Vix lands at the bottom of the steps and smiles, directly at me. I feel such enormous relief at that smile, that at least one of my friends doesn't ostensibly despise me. "I needed to be perked up. Anyway, you don't look too shabby yourself."

I glance down at myself. I am wearing pale bleached denim, a silk button-down, suede boots, and a Brixton hat. I suppose Vix is right. I don't like to look shabby. Even with a gruesome murder and my affair unwittingly exposed, I feel better when I look better. Most French-women do, although their closets are generally a bit more pared down than mine. Maybe my love for fashion is shallow, or else there are deeper reasons. Clothes are my armor. How I suit up for battle.

Vix is still meeting my eyes, unlike Jade. Perhaps Vix doesn't hate me. My heart leaps a bit in hope. Please don't let Vix hate me.

"Well you're dressed perfectly for a supermarket outing, Vixie. Let's go. Jade, what do you feel like? It's still your birthday week." I realize how ridiculously normal that sounds. Am I trivializing things? Maybe. I've always preferred to smooth things over, get on with it. I am an entertainer, a chef. Is it wrong to appreciate festivity, food, good fun? Is it wrong to want life to straighten out, after the inevitable bumps?

"I could go for pasta," Vix says.

"I could go for anything but pasta." Jade isn't smiling now, but she's not not smiling.

"So pasta and not pasta. Got it." I make my tone bright. "Be back in a bit. You'll take care of Mamie, if she wakes, right?"

Jade softens. "Of course."

"Thanks. Don't get into trouble without us."

I realize how that sounds only after it is out. No one laughs. Jade turns abruptly and walks back toward her room.

"Let's get outta here," Vix says softly.

"Yes. Let's."

My car is parked past the front walk, in the gravelly lot around the side of the chateau. I drive a silver Porsche Carrera. I know it's a bit flashy, especially in the countryside, although in Nice a car this posh is par for the course. But I bought it myself a few months ago when I hit a big business goal. I felt so proud of myself, when I signed all the paperwork. I imagined my parents watching over me, beaming, too, at the person I've worked so hard to become. People see overnight successes and think we were handed things. But I wasn't—I worked a chef job and bartended in my spare time, starting an Instagram account in my spare spare time.

As a kid, I wore hand-me-downs—Séraphine's, even Darcy's. But my arms are longer than both of theirs, so I was rocking the three-quarter length sleeve trend for decades, long after it lapsed. I bought my first non–hand-me-down coat, with sleeves that actually hit my wrist, at age twenty-five. I'm not complaining, though. In some ways, I think I fit into the David and Goliath mold—coming from nothing is an excellent motivator.

Ever since I was a kid, I've brainstormed recipes, orchestrated photoshoots of the meals I created, catered events, starting small and gradually, by word of mouth, growing. I was a chef, a food and fashion stylist, a photographer—everything. Giancarlo helped, of course, in the later part of my career, but I built it. I did it. With my sweat and tears and many, many long days and nights and years, and in the face of nasty trolls and a thousand other obstacles. And when I click the car opener that feels so smooth and exclusive in my palm, and hear that distinctive ping, unlocking the door, there is something in me that feels I have made it. Not just made it—it feels like I don't have to worry anymore, that I am secure in this world. It is said that money can't buy happiness, but I disagree. There is a certain amount of money that does indeed buy happiness. I now have far more than that amount, but I once had far less. I was a poor, pitied orphan—those are the facts. All my life I've been the girl without parents. The granddaughter of the help. The ones the kids whispered about, looked down upon. Even Darcy, to some extent, before we became close. *No prospects* was practically stamped on my forehead. But I am smart, and Mamie loves me. Those two aspects of my life irrevocably changed it.

I click the opener. The dopamine hits. I round the side of the chateau where I pulled up two days before. Two days before—I shake my head. Whiplash. In that span, everything has changed.

The leather is scorching when we enter. Immediately I blast the air. As I do, my eyes catch on the thermos of coffee in the tray.

Giancarlo prepared it for me before I got on the road. Like he does every morning, he ground fresh beans by hand (better than the electric grinders, something about the high heat on the beans); then he put them through our fancy espresso maker; then he added his homemade frothed cashew milk. Even though I digest cow's milk just fine. It's our little joke, though, that I am the chef, and he is the vegan barista.

He knows the most about me in the world, my husband, but not about Ollie. And not about some other things, too. Like the cat I tussle with every time I go to the market. The cat is gray with green eyes and he doesn't flee when I approach, like other cats. He is my nemesis. Giancarlo has no clue how much I hate that cat. Or, here's another thing: Every morning before I run, I do tai chi by the waterfront. And when I walk down the last alley before the sea, I pass by a woman sitting in a wheelchair, staring out at the vista. She is young-ish, fifties, probably. I always say *Bonjour*, because that is what you say in France when you cross someone's territory. She says *Bonjour* back. But we never say anything further. I wonder briefly about her, and I'm sure she wonders briefly about me. She is a regular in my life, and yet, I forget about her every morning after we part, until she crosses my path again.

These are minor things, yes, but things that are just mine. You don't share everything—you just don't. There are things we keep secret, inadvertently or intentionally, even from the people closest to us. That is the nature of being a distinct person with boundaries and borders. We aren't meant to bleed into each other. We are meant to have places to hide things, skin to fold them up in, brains to tuck them away in corners.

I think the world is better for secrets. Everyone should have some privacy. But I don't think my husband would agree, at least not about Ollie.

I wonder what will happen. The future feels like a giant open field in front of me, with so many permutations it makes me dizzy to conceive.

"Ready?" Vix says.

I realize I have just been sitting, staring at the thermos.

"Ready." I rev the engine.

———

My favorite thing in the world, besides cooking, is driving. Despite—or maybe even because of—that formative car accident that dictated the course of my life.

I suppose I could have shied away entirely from driving—or felt some trauma response every time I slid the key into the ignition. Yes, you can tiptoe through the world, try to walk the safe line. But to really live means taking risks. And as the sole survivor of the car crash that killed my parents, I feel like it's my gift, and also my duty, to really live. Besides, are you truly less likely to die walking down the street than say, skydiving? Well, not if you're the person standing beneath the scaffolding when it collapses right on top of you.

Anyway, my point is that when I'm driving, some would say like a maniac, I feel fully alive.

"Sheesh." Vix is clutching the handle with a death grip, her hair whipping in the wind.

"Isn't it good?" I say, or maybe I scream it. I like when the windows are open, full blast. There is something about air-conditioning that feels suffocating. At our place in Nice, Giancarlo and I always have the screen doors open, the windows pushed out to let in the sea air. I don't care if insects meander in. Let them; it's their world, too. I'm not the squeal-at-a-spider type. And too much air-conditioning gives me a rash on my skin. Darcy loves air-conditioning.

"You drive like a maniac." Vix rolls her window up.

"You know that. You love it."

She laughs. "In a weird way a psychologist should analyze, I do."

We pass fields of wheat, and others populated by wildflowers, *coquelicots*. We pass the ruins of the ancient stone city of Glanum at the flanks of the Alpilles mountains.

"Oh my God." Vix has her nose pressed to the window. I refrain from asking her not to. Smudges, and such. "Remember when—"

"Oh God." I laugh.

"She was so—"

"So."

The wind is making us its whipping boy. Is that the right way to say it? I start in with the Americans, and occasionally I mix up their idioms. Anyway it's impossible to talk with all the wind. No matter— we don't need full sentences to rehash Glanum. We went there, the four of us, all those decades ago. Jade, as ever dressed in something skimpy, got pegged by a few German tourists as someone famous. They kept following us around and snapping clandestine photos of her. Jade pretended like she was annoyed, but she loved the attention, of course. Even the modest ones, like Darcy, like attention.

"I can't believe about Séraphine," Vix says. "It still doesn't feel real."

"I know. It's insane."

"The knife. It was so savage."

Yes. It really did look that way. "Like someone who hated her," I say.

"Huh?"

I close the windows halfway. "Like someone who hated her," I shout.

"Oh." Vix nods. "Why do you think Raph hated her?"

"I don't know. We still don't know hate is the motive anyway." I remember something I saw on one of those crime shows Giancarlo likes. "I once heard there are three different motivations for murder. Money, revenge, and concealment."

"Concealment?" Vix asks.

"Like, to cover something up. And don't you think it's strange?"

"What is?"

"How Séraphine wanted to tell us all something this morning? Right? She made a point of it at dinner last night."

"Right . . ."

"Well, what do you think she wanted to tell us? Don't you think it might have something to do with why she was killed?"

"That's . . . that's . . . I don't know, Belle."

"Yeah. Me either."

We drive in silence for a bit.

"How does Raph fit into it then?" Vix finally says.

"Barely spoke two words to him." I shrug, make the turn toward town, catching a pleasing whiff of lavender from a nearby field. I could drive this route in my sleep. It is my favorite route in the world, both because it leads to the chateau, and also away from it. There are some places in life—people, too—that are double-edged swords. The best and the worst of things, all wrapped maddeningly into one.

"This is all just so insane." I rake a hand through my hair, now unruly. I may have a more abundant closet than most minimalist Frenchwomen, but I do appreciate things undone—hair mussed, buttons open, eyeliner smudged.

"If I had to guess, Raph's motive was twofold. Concealment, and money. Maybe she left him something in the Will. Maybe she threatened to cut him out, or . . ."

"The Will. Ohmygod." Vix claps a hand over her mouth. "You think she left Raph something? But why? He's just a random person to her, right? A stranger. She wouldn't have."

"I don't know." I shrug. "I suppose we'll find out soon enough. The cops will be digging into him good. At least, I hope they will. You never know with the gendarmerie. They aren't known for being the quickest, or most thorough."

"I didn't even think about the Will." I can see Vix doing mental arithmetic. "Séraphine's gotta be worth a fortune, Belle."

"A fortune," I agree. "I'm sure we'll hear from her estate agent soon. Darcy is about to be a very rich woman, I'd expect."

"Wow. I mean . . . Darcy could use the money, I know that much."

"Really? Is she having money problems?" I know some from Ollie, but I wonder what else Vix has heard.

Vix flushes. "I'm not sure. Just . . . I think. Look, I'll let her tell you herself."

"Right." I laugh sadly.

"Oh, yeah." Vix pauses. I can see she is weighing it, whether to start in about Ollie, or wait. "Well, if she did have money problems, they're probably moot now. But what about Sylvie? Could Séraphine have left the chateau to her?"

"No." I shake my head. "The chateau was in Rainier's family, so by French inheritance law, it goes to the wife only for life, then to the heirs. And Antoine is long gone."

"Antoine?"

"Darcy's father. He died of a heart attack when she was young. Not as young as I was. . . ." God, why did I bring that up? "But young. Six, I think."

"Right." Vix pauses. "I'd forgotten his name. You guys have so much in common. I never put it together."

I pause. "Yes, I suppose we do."

"Oh, shit." She sighs.

"So Darcy is the only heir," I say quickly. "But Séraphine had significant other assets of her own. She has to leave a certain proportion to Darcy, by law, but I'm sure she made ample provisions for my grandmother. I hope so, at least."

"My head is spinning," Vix says.

"I know." I place one hand over my chest, where it throbs. Ollie— I think of Ollie, how he held me just hours ago. It's a crazy thing to think of, his embrace, after everything. Or else it's the sanest thing to think of.

"Do you think that Instagram account has anything to do with it?" Vix asks.

"The creepy one? @imwatchingyou88? Maybe. I mean, probably? What are the chances it's a coincidence? I told the officers about it."

"You did?" Vix sounds surprised. "I forgot to mention it."

"We haven't heard from our internet friend today. Strange, eh?"

"Strange," echoes Vix.

Finally, we navigate through town, down the quaint boulevard Victor Hugo, lined in cypresses and poplars, that featured daily in my childhood. I pull into my favorite market. In my opinion, it's the most beautiful grocery store in the world. Plus, I know the owner, and we always talk about the leeks, or the herbs (which are arranged in a pretty stone fountain—tell me another market that does that!). They have an exceptional home goods section you can peruse, and the best local flowers, and yes, I could spend my whole life in this market. We humans would die without food. Wilt. Perhaps that is why I love it so much. It is so basic, and yet it shapes our whole lives. Or perhaps it is just that my grandmother is a cook, and so I became one. Sometimes things are really that simple.

"Belle?" says Vix, once I've parked and switched off the engine.

"Yes?"

"Are we going to talk about your affair with Oliver?"

"Yes." I open the door. "But only when we're back in the car. First, we are going to shop for food. And we won't spoil that."

CHAPTER TWENTY-TWO

Vix

French supermarkets are the indisputable cutest, like shiny, pretend markets made for a movie set. We enter in the veggie area, with endless rows of the most stunning, glossy produce, above which is a row of glass bottles of *velouté de tomates*. I don't even love tomatoes, but I want one, just for its cuteness factor. I grab a bottle and hold it up. "Do we need this?"

"Sure." Arabelle grabs it and puts it in the cart. "For the pasta sauce."

She picks out leeks, then potatoes, then eggplants, the latter of which she rolls around her palm, inspecting for God knows what before deeming them suitable. We make our way to the pasta area. Even the way the pasta is set up is so pleasing—in stacked rustic crates, all the different varietals, each declaring from which area of France or Italy it hails. We select a fettuccine that Arabelle promises is fantastic. Then we get a dozen brown eggs divided into two blue crates. I make a face, which Arabelle catches.

"Feathers in your eggs?" I touch one gingerly.

"In America, you bleach your eggs." Arabelle clucks her tongue. "Feathers attached to eggs is exceedingly normal. Okay." She claps her hands. "You get us wine. I'll get the chickens."

"Chickens?"

"For a simple chicken *francese*."

Of course. Leave it to Arabelle to cook us an extravagant meal on this horrible, no good, very bad day. I realize that sounds callous, even in my head. Cooking is Arabelle's therapy, and feeding people is her way of loving them. And we could all use a good meal, even after everything that happened. *Especially* after what happened. And especially Darcy and Sylvie. You're supposed to cook for the bereaved, I remember.

I wander over to the chilled beverage section and take a while selecting two bottles of rosé by a brand called Barbebelle. Each bottle has a tab with an artsy sketch of a guy, his beard composed of flowers.

"You know this wine?" Arabelle asks, when I add them to our cart.

"The branding is cute. In my experience, that's a good barometer."

Arabelle smiles indulgently at me.

We stop at the cheese counter to buy butter by weight. Arabelle gets half a kilo, which feels excessive, but she is the chef, and I am just the happy eater.

God, I love it here, I think, as a man in a jaunty beret scoops fresh butter from the mound. I've always felt this way, some strong sense of home in France, which is strange, considering my mastery of the language is poor, and I always get the cultural norms wrong. Like, at what point in the day is it more appropriate to say *bonsoir* than *bonjour*? New York is the everyman's home, streets crushed with people. I love that, in a way, but growing up I felt other. That's the only word to describe, how my parents were the typical straight-edge parents, and I knew early on that I was not. Avignon is where I met the people who I consider home, the ones in whom I first confided that I was a lesbian—and they didn't blink an eye. And in Provence, the landscapes drove me into an artistic sort of frenzy, where all I could do for weeks was sketch and paint. Those works were the best I ever created, before or since. They had life. Verve. Zest. They cemented my desire to go all-in on my artist aspirations. And they prompted Séraphine to take note of my artistic talent, which changed everything, really, for me.

And Saint-Rémy has always felt like home, as well. Séraphine was a big part of that, in encouraging my art career. But there was more to the interest she took in me, I now think, still shaken by Arabelle's revelation that Sylvie and Séraphine were long-time loves. I understand

Séraphine more now, I think—why she saw herself in me. She once told me she loved to paint, but when she married, her painting days were over. It's like in me she saw the things she had to repress, that through me she could support, in some obtuse way. And I have been the benefactor of her support, all these years.

I think about what Arabelle said, the motives for murder. Money. I think about what will happen if Séraphine's support of me comes to light to the others.

And I can't help but wonder if her support for me will stop now, or if it will continue in some way.

"Do you think Sylvie will be okay?" I ask Arabelle softly, as we wait for the butter.

"No." Arabelle closes her eyes and I can see her pain, acute, re-flected in the scrunch of her faint "eleven" lines. "I don't think Mamie will be okay. Not for a long time. Maybe not ever. My grandmother . . . she loved Séraphine. She loved her more than anyone, except for me. The way she looked at Séraphine . . . it was obvious. I'm surprised none of you girls noticed."

Arabelle frowns. She flutters her eyes open but looks away, and I wonder if she is crying. She is very good at concealing her emotion, my friend, but this must be so taxing on her. However at fault she is for this thing with Oliver, she clearly loves him. She wouldn't betray Darcy and Giancarlo for anything less than love. And she grew up with Séraphine. And poor Sylvie, who is Arabelle's de facto mother. More than a mother, even. She is Arabelle's world, plain as day.

"You've known about them for a long time?" I ask. "You never said."

"It wasn't my place," Arabelle says. "I'm good at keeping secrets. You know that."

She is. She is the person to confide in, if you don't want anything leaked to the others. Anytime I told her something private, she always said she wouldn't even tell Giancarlo, which I believed, although now I find it a bit suspect. It's like with me and Juliet—can a relationship ever be real and true, when you are hiding something, however small, in the cracks?

We grab Ancienne macarons. And then while Arabelle goes on to chatter with someone or another, I cross the honey and tea nook, then the shelves with nougat and caramels and *pâte de fruit*, and stop to linger in the home section. I browse and want and consider all the gorgeous *toile de Jouy* patterned cottons, especially mustard yellow dish towels with a quaint pastoral scene that would regretfully clash with my urban, plant-filled, black and white, elder millennial apartment. Instead I select white ceramic cups that say Little Marcel on them, with blue and red stripey designs. An image pops into my head, of me and Juliet in the morning, drinking matcha from these cups.

I shake my head and tuck the cups under my arm and check my messages, my Instagram. Mom checking in, and a meme from my cousin Arnie. I haven't talked to anyone about what happened to Séraphine, only my friends who have lived it alongside me. The only person I want to confide in is Juliet.

I scroll her page. The last picture she posted is her with a dog, a shaggy, black, ugly mutt who often stayed at my apartment. Juliet is laughing into his fur. I zoom in on her glittery smile. The pain is a cliff-top, and I am falling. I am always falling, right into a patch of cactus needles. But have you ever fallen into cactus needles? I have, and you don't forget it. The thing about cactus needles is that one by one, you can remove them. They're gone, but the sting remains.

When I meet up with Arabelle back by the checkout, I hand her a greeting card I selected from one of the stands. It has a dog with a party blower in its mouth, done in watercolors. *"Bon anniversaire de mariage!"* it reads.

She turns it over, perplexed. *"Bonjour!"* she greets the checkout woman. She hands the card back to me.

"Happy anniversary. To you and Giancarlo, I mean," I say pointedly. "You know I remember every date. This time eight years ago, we were in Saint-Tropez at the vine—"

"Yes, yes." She unloads the cart. "What's your point?"

"My point is, I thought about buying you this card, but I don't know if I should be congratulating you on your marriage, or its demise. So I'll wait until you fill me in."

Arabelle grimaces as she places the eggplants on the counter. "*Bon*, in the car, I'll fill you in."

———

"What do you want to know?" she asks, as she revs the engine, and puts her index finger on the window lever.

"No," I say, as we maneuver through town back toward the countryside. "Don't roll the windows down. I want to hear you. And slow down. I also want to live to remember what you say."

She smiles, halfway. Retracts her finger from the lever. "Give me your worst."

"My worst. Oye. I'm not trying to interrogate you here. Belle, like . . . I want to know what's going on. I mean . . . look, you know you're my best friend. . . ."

"But," she says.

We're on the route toward Glanum now, rich gold wheat fields whizzing past.

"But." I think how to say this. "Darcy is my best friend, too. And I just don't get how you could do this to her. With Oliver. In her grandmother's home."

"It's my home, too," Arabelle says softly.

That stops me in my tracks. I suppose I've never thought of the chateau as Belle's. But it's as much her home as Darcy's, I suppose. More so, maybe, in some ways. She grew up there, while Darcy had her primary home in New York with her mom, however imperfect that life was.

"I know it's your home. But Belle, it's Oliver. *Darcy's* Oliver."

"You think I don't know? You think I did it on purpose?" Arabelle slips on her aviators, but not before I see a tear slide down her cheek, which surprises me. Arabelle isn't a crier. "Darcy is a sister to me, Vix. Our foursome may have really brought us together, but we grew up like sisters. I adore Darcy. I really do. I know you may not believe me, but the thing with Ollie, it just happened."

"How does something like that just happen?"

"I don't know. It's like, sometimes life zigs, and you zig with it, *t'sais*? I don't mean to sound heartless about it, because trust me, some days lately I can barely function for all the guilt and shame I feel. Still. *C'est la vie,* I suppose."

"So Oliver zigged?" I ask. "Or *you* zigged?"

"I don't know." Arabelle heaves a sigh. "It was just . . . we connected at a dinner. Our fingers brushed. There was . . . okay, I know this will sound bad. But there was electricity. Things have been bad with me and Giancarlo for a while, and suddenly, I noticed Ollie. I just noticed him. I could tell he felt the same."

"How could you tell?"

"I just could."

I nod. I get it, how some things just are, even before physical evidence. I had a massive crush on Juliet from the start, when I met her at an expo for creatives. And I was certain I intrigued her, too, even before she reached out with some half-baked work rationale.

"After one of my book events, Darcy was tired. She went home to relieve the babysitter, and Ollie stayed out with us, and then all of a sudden everyone was gone, and we were a little tipsy, maybe, but I think, we just looked at each other. . . ."

I can tell she is reliving it, with some kind of nostalgia. Not intentionally, no. I know Belle at her core; she has a heart of gold. Look how she was there for me through my cancer, how she's been there for all of us, over the years. But there it is—love blurs morals. Money does, too.

I think about Séraphine, and how she's made it possible for me to be a non-starving artist all these years. Handing over her money, with no real strings, until now. That's the thing. At some point there are always strings.

"You had sex with him in the chateau, with Darcy upstairs," I say quietly.

"You're not going to get over that one, are you? No one will, I suppose. Don't you think I'm punishing myself more than you ever could? I never thought Darcy would find out. It seemed so innocuous to me. I couldn't go to him, clearly, with the kids. What if one of them woke up in the middle of the night or something? I figured everyone was wasted here, passed out. He came over when I was sure Darcy was in her room and asleep, and I figured he'd leave soon after sunrise, with no risk of anyone figuring it out. But then . . ."

"Then," I say.

"I loved Séraphine, too, *t'sais*?" The way she says it is haunting, desolate. "It's Darcy who is getting the brunt of all of this, of course. I want to be there for her, but I can't. But still, Séraphine was as much a mother to me as Mamie. I didn't have parents. I grew up with them, and Rainier. Believe it or not, Séraphine taught me how to swim. She taught me *pétanque*. My grandmother was often working, but Séraphine was a woman of leisure. She had more time than my grandmother, to spend with me. She always encouraged my cooking. She . . . I owed her a lot. And I'm devastated, Vix. I'm absolutely *dévastée* that she's gone."

Arabelle's voice warbles, and she dabs at the corners of her eyes. I have never seen her lose her composure this way, and it rocks me a bit.

We make the familiar right into the long, picturesque road that leads to the chateau. Then suddenly, Arabelle kills the engine. She cradles her head in her arms on the steering wheel.

"Belle . . ." I pat her back, rubbing circles with my thumb, something my mother used to do for me when I was sad, or scared.

"I don't need you to feel sorry for me," she says, her voice muffled. "I brought the Oliver thing on myself."

"Will you give him up?" It's awkward to probe, but I have to know.

Arabelle's silence is my answer. But I knew it, didn't I?

Then she says something unexpected. "You're judging me. I know you are, Vix. And you have every right to. But what about you and Juliet?"

I stop stroking her back, no longer feeling so generous. "What about Juliet? There was no affair with us. No cheating. Just two people who couldn't make it work."

"Because you were keeping secrets."

"What do you mean?" I ask, trying to keep the anger from my tone.

"I don't know the full extent." Arabelle lifts her head off the steering wheel. She peels off her sunglasses to reveal big, brown eyes, red and raw. "But Juliet and I have talked a few times."

"You have?" I'm not sure what my feelings are about this—whether I want to press Belle for every last morsel of how Juliet is doing, or whether I am angry that my best friend has gone behind my back with this.

Arabelle sighs. "She wanted to make sure you were okay."

"Did she talk to Darcy and Jade, too?"

"I don't know. I don't think so. She knows you and I . . ."

"You're my closest friend in the world," I whisper. And it's true. The Mamas and the Rihannas. We are a foursome, but two twosomes within. It's why relationships sprout, I suppose. We don't want to be one of three or four or five, but a half of something. The most special one, to one other person.

"And you are mine," Arabelle says. "I only talked to Juliet out of love for you. With the . . ."

I nod. I can't bring myself to say the c-word, either.

"And then you and Juliet broke up so suddenly. You haven't talked about it."

"I have."

"Not really. Not the juice. You gave me the version you'd tell your grocer."

I don't answer, just play with the pleats of my dress.

"And what were you doing in Séraphine's room this morning?" Arabelle asks. "Why were you the one who found her?"

"I don't feel well," I finally say, because otherwise it's all going to come out. How my entire life is a lie. "I think I need to lie down."

Arabelle starts up the engine again. "Sure, Vixie."

"I'm sorry," I say, as we rumble down the road. "I don't want to keep things from you."

"And I from you," Arabelle says. "But sometimes secrets have good reasons behind them."

She is referring to her and Oliver, and I don't have the strength anymore to disagree. To claim that it's different from what I've kept, what I've done. All secrets burn through everything good.

"Darcy will probably never be my friend again," Arabelle says as we pull into the chateau's gravelly drive. She parks swiftly and everything goes silent again. The sun is setting over the vineyard. It is a ghost of a sunset, an albino sun—eerily suitable for the day. The sky is a wash of ombré, very on trend. Muted blue at top, fading into yellow, then pink, then a lavender gray. And near the horizon, hovering over the vines, is a barely there, blink-and-you-miss-it orb. A nothing sun that you could hardly believe capable of lighting a single room, let alone the entire earth. I watch as the nothingness collapses into the horizon.

"Darcy may not forgive you," I finally say. "Especially if you and Oliver . . . if you . . ." God, I can't imagine it, much less say it. It's not just Darcy and Oliver, it's Mila and Chase, too. Arabelle would be splintering a family—taking parents from their children. It's not the same as the way hers were yanked from her. But still, I would think that of anyone, Arabelle would have compassion for that.

As if reading my mind, Arabelle says, "I don't want to break up their family, Vix. Trust me on that. It's the last thing I want."

"Okay . . ."

"Say you believe me." She grabs for my arm with surprising strength. "Please, Vix. Say you believe me. That you don't think I'm some horrible person, not intentionally."

"Of course I believe you." I sigh. "You're not a horrible person. Even if I think what you did was horrible. And I'm always your friend, Belle. But I'm Darcy's, too."

"Of course." She looks a bit mollified. "Okay, should we go inside? I expect Mamie is up from her nap, and I want to see how she is."

She closes her eyes briefly. "It's going to be excruciating for my grandmother, to face what happened."

"I know." But do I know? No. I can only imagine how I'd feel if it were Juliet who'd been murdered so savagely. Just the thought feels like the whole earth has collapsed on my chest.

"Mamie is too old for this. She should have been able to live out her last days in peace and happiness." Arabelle's gaze is fixed out the window, and I know she is thinking about her and Oliver, too. I know it, because I'm still thinking about Juliet. Other people's love stories, especially ones ripped apart so viciously, always have you thinking about your own. It's who we humans are, at the bottom of things— concerned most with ourselves.

I put a gentle hand on her wrist. "Let's go inside."

"Yes." But she makes no motion to open her door.

I get it. Part of me, a big part, wants to tell her to turn the car back down the drive and take us somewhere else, anywhere else. Even though the killer has been apprehended, the chateau has a newly bleak aura. It's unfortunate how something you once loved can turn in an instant.

Just then, the front door of the chateau opens, and out pokes Jade's head. She shouts something that I can't hear. I open the door.

"Sorry, what?" I call.

Jade is irritated; I can make that out plainly from afar. Her stilted voice only reinforces it. "I said, where have you been for so long? Sylvie is up, and she wants to see us all."

Arabelle opens her door, too, and rushes out. I follow after her, but she is already running down the path between the pines, toward her grandmother. Arabelle bursts through the front door and swiftly disappears. I go back for the bags, feeling Jade's gaze following me. I manage them all, then heft them up the drive, under Jade's penetrating stare. I drop the bags in the entrance. Jade just stares at the bags, then again at me.

"How is Sylvie?" I ask.

"Not good. Not good at all. But she wants to see us."

"Us? She must want Arabelle. I'm sorry we were late, we were just—"

"All of us," Jade interrupts. "Sylvie says there are things we don't know. And she wants to tell us everything. Over dinner."

"At last," I say. "Someone in this house who wants to talk straight."

"Please." Jade puts a hand up to block me from walking forward. "Is that a jab at me?"

"No . . . I just—"

"Because why were you in Séraphine's room this morning? And then later, too?"

"I thought we played this game already. Why were *you*?" I counter.

We both just stare at each other. If I didn't know that Raph was the murderer . . .

No, that's a crazy thought. Stop. Stop before things get even darker than they already are.

"I thought so," Jade says, as if she got the last word, as if I didn't find her rooting around Séraphine's closet this morning.

"Just because you have kids and a husband and money and a house in the Hamptons, doesn't mean you get to make me feel small. Not this time!"

I find myself storming toward the living room. God, where did that come from? Did I mean it? I suppose, in some way, I did.

Interesting how the things that live beneath, unseen, like tectonic plates, can unexpectedly cause little earthquakes.

CHAPTER TWENTY-THREE

Jade

We are back on the terrace, with the empty chair at the head of the table. Before me is a plate of *pasta pistou*. As Arabelle explained, it's linguine with mushrooms in the French version of a pesto sauce, with parsley and chives in addition to basil, and *crème fraîche*, too. She informed us she was going to do something with a tomato *velouté*, but then she decided to go heartier, and then she broke off, because no one was much paying attention anyhow.

I have eaten a few token bites of my pasta, but that's enough carbs for me. If I could, if I let myself go wild, I would slurp up every last bite. Thank goodness Séraphine isn't around to eye me with that judge stare, her all-knowing tally of what I have eaten and what I have not.

I gaze again toward the empty chair. Beside it is poor Sylvie, stoically eating her pasta. Actually, as I watch for a few moments, I see she isn't eating anything, just twirling pieces and slowly disentangling her fork.

"Mamie?" Arabelle puts a hand on her grandmother's arm.

Sylvie's fork slips out of her fingers. *"Je n'arrive toujours pas à y croire."*

I don't know what it means but it sounds utterly desolate. I look away as Arabelle folds her grandmother in her arms. Soon come muffled weeps. I feel my ribs squeezed, like a dry towel trying to wring itself of phantom damp. The sound of someone in pain is excruciating to my ears. Maybe it's because of my dad, the trauma he endured. I didn't just inherit the heterochromia of his eyes, but also the cries of my ancestors. My brother is happy-go-lucky, unscathed by our childhood. Somehow my brother never tabulated Papa's footsteps on his return home from work, like I did. Just by the way he shut the front door, or the strength of his tread, did I calculate whether to go say hello, or hide a while longer out of sight, dreading the unfurling of his moods that always felt like mine alone to steer. Perhaps I've simply sat in too many dark rooms with my father, listened to too many chilling tales, quieted him when he awakens screaming at night and my mother shuts down, tasking him to me. I've tried all my life to fix him, to make him happy enough to live in the present instead of the past. And nothing has worked. Not so far, at least.

I fiddle with my necklace, pressing the diamond into my skin.

"You girls didn't know about me and Séraphine?" Abruptly, Sylvie pulls back from Arabelle. Her eyes are swollen red, her wispy gray hair not its usual fluffed, but thin, stringy. I realize now she wore a hairpiece, and she looks older without it.

"I had no idea. At all." Darcy is seated across from Sylvie, just to my left. Both she and Sylvie are still in their rightful places, sandwiching Séraphine's empty chair.

"To be honest, Sylvie," Darcy continues, "it makes me wonder if I even knew my grandmother at all."

Sylvie pushes away her pasta and rests her elbows on the table. "Your grandmother was a difficult person to come to know. She had many little corners. . . ."

"Corners?" Darcy asks.

"Corners. To tuck away little pieces of yourself. I think I was the person in the world with the most access to Séraphine's corners, but still, I didn't know everything. . . ."

"Sylvie, what do you think she was going to tell us this morning?" I ask. "Did she tell you?"

"*Non.* She didn't. I am as confused as all of you. I asked her, of course. But she merely said that all would be revealed in time."

"But why did she have us here, Sylvie?" Darcy asks. "Why now? Why all of my friends? Why twenty years later?"

Sylvie frowns. "I don't know, *ma petit chou*."

"But you must have . . . I mean, did you at least probe?" Darcy asks.

"*Bien sûr*. I asked her. She was just so insistent on it, that the four of you come at once. I thought she was a little lonely, a little bored. That she wanted some nice, young spice in the house. You four . . ." Sylvie passes her eyes over each of us with her tender grandmotherly stare, and I feel myself arch toward her, like a flower striving for sun. "You four were special to her."

"All of us?" I ask lightly.

"All of you," Sylvie says firmly.

I know otherwise, but I keep that to myself.

"There was obviously more to it," Darcy says. "But how will we ever know now?"

"Séraphine liked keeping us on our toes." Vix smiles.

Sylvie smiles, too, a little bit. "She did. Oh, she did." Then her smile fades. "My goodness. She did. It is impossible, that I am speaking of her in the past tense. Just yesterday . . ." She stares at Séraphine's chair. "And the knife. The *knife*. So brutal. How painful, her last minutes . . . How could he do it, to my beloved? *How?*"

"How much do you know about the groundskeeper, Sylvie?" I ask. "Why would he do this?"

"I don't know much. He came to us a year ago, I believe." Her forehead scrunches, dragging up a memory. "I think he has some relation to a person Séraphine knew. A friend, perhaps. I am not certain. He needed work, money. And . . ." Sylvie gestures around. "This is a pleasant place in which to work. Most of the time, at least."

"The police are unraveling it, I'm sure," Vix says. "Maybe as we speak."

I realize I haven't told them. "They were back here, in fact. While you and Belle were at the market. Officer Darmanin and the male, too. He's called Officer Valliere."

"Oh?" Arabelle asks. "What did they want? Or did they have some break in the case?"

"No break," I say. "Obviously Raph is still the prime suspect. They're holding him now. But the only concrete evidence so far is the note Séraphine wrote. They've confirmed it's her handwriting; it wasn't forged. But as of yet, they have no motive for the crime. They're talking to the attorney, to get the Will. Maybe that will answer the motive piece. He's coming tomorrow, right, Darce?"

"The attorney?" Vix asks.

Darcy nods. "He contacted me today. I don't know how he even got my information. Grand-mère left it, I guess. He'll be here tomorrow after breakfast. He knew I was here on a trip with my friends. That we all met studying abroad. Well, except for Arabelle."

The way she says the last part is laced in bitterness. I love Arabelle, but I have to admit, I can barely look at her myself. She and Oliver—it's an incomprehensible betrayal. In some ways, it feels like she has betrayed all of us, not just Darcy.

"What else did the police say?" Vix asks.

"They still think Raph had a gun, though why he wouldn't use the gun is beyond me," I say. "They've been searching—they've torn apart Raph's cabin, and nothing. They've looked inside the house, too, and on the grounds."

"The grounds are massive," Darcy says quietly. "You could hide a gun anywhere."

"I know." I nod. "They also figured out that the murderer washed up in the sink in the kitchen."

Arabelle grimaces. "I know. I used the chef's kitchen tonight, not the family one. The whole area was cordoned off, like the bedroom."

I pause, thinking of how earlier today I disregarded the bedroom's protective tape. For good reason.

"They took samples this morning," I say. "Apparently there was blood that matches Séraphine's. And Arabelle's fingerprints, and Sylvie's. And a few of the servers, and the chef, who've been working here this week."

Arabelle nods. "The chef typically uses the other kitchen, but because I was cooking in the family one the first night, and she was helping . . ."

"But no other fingerprints," I say. "It's possible Raph was wearing gloves and hid them somewhere, probably with the gun."

"Wild," Vix says.

"Wild," echoes Arabelle. "Might blood have splashed on . . . his clothes or something . . . when . . . ?"

I nod. "That's what they suspect, too. They've looked in all our rooms, in Raph's, too. . . ."

"They have?" Vix asks. "They've looked in our *rooms*?"

I nod. "Yes, in all our stuff. This morning, and now again. But they didn't find anything of note. That's what they said, at least."

"Why wouldn't Raph have washed off in his cottage?" Darcy asks.

"Yeah, why in the sink in the main house?" Arabelle frowns, and I get it. The kitchen is her domain, and now it's been sullied.

"To throw the blame on one of us?" I wonder aloud. "Anyway, if he'd left blood in his cottage, he'd have made himself a fairly obvious suspect. And he didn't bet on Séraphine implicating him, perhaps. Thought he'd get off scot-free."

"But if there are gloves, clothes . . . where are they?" Arabelle asks.

"You know I saw him in the morning, outside. He said it was because he heard Oliver's car, but they think he might have hidden things—"

"Buried them," Darcy says slowly. "But they could be anywhere."

I shrug. "They're police. They have their ways."

"Don't be too sure," Arabelle says. "Crimes are known to take forever to be solved in the countryside. Many times, not."

Sylvie nods. "The police are incompetents. Especially the gendarmerie."

There is some uncomfortable shifting in our chairs at that lackluster pronouncement. But Raph is in jail, at least for now.

"They did say they can only hold him for so long," I say.

"What, and he would rightly come back here?" Vix says. "We'd have to stay with him on the grounds?"

"Well, I'm sure it won't come to that," I say. "More evidence will accrue. It has to. But anyway, if not, ultimately we could kick him out. I mean, Darcy can. Presuming she's the one who inherits all this."

Thick silence ensues. I know we are all thinking the same awful thing: What a horrible thing to have your grandmother murdered so brutally, but what an incredible thing to become filthy rich because of it.

Arabelle brings out the next course, assisted by Vix. Chicken cutlets, resting in buttery lemon sauce. There is even a vegan option with soy cutlets, but my appetite is nil.

When all of us have our plates, Sylvie says, "You know, I first met Séraphine on this very *terrasse*. Right by the plane tree." She gestures to the massive tree, the bedrock of the estate.

Darcy leans forward. "Really? I've never heard this story."

"Yes." Sylvie's eyes flutter shut. "I wanted to gather you girls. I wanted to tell you about what it was like back then, with me and Séraphine."

"And Rainier," Arabelle adds.

"Yes." Sylvie's eyes open, and I notice the slight clench of her jaw. "Rainier, too."

It's the first time I realize—it can't have been easy for Sylvie to watch Séraphine with her husband. I wonder when their romance started, if it, too, began as an affair, a betrayal. If so, this won't be easy for Darcy to hear. There will be too many parallels, between grandmother and granddaughter.

"It was after the war that you came to work at the chateau, right?" I've already deduced as much. Sylvie is too young to have been working for them during the war. And my father didn't mention her. He was young when his entanglement with this family, with this chateau, came to pass. Only ten. But his memories from that time are sharp, sharper I think than from any subsequent period of his life.

I grew up on the bedtime stories of this place. This family. Of my friends, only Darcy knows the true, dark story, albeit not the latest chapter. But I went to Avignon to study abroad with a purpose. And only now, two decades later, are my ends finally in sight.

159

"I was eighteen, newly married," Sylvie says. "It was 1953. The war was well over, but our country was ravaged. The Jews—" Her face grays. My heart does something familiar, turns over itself.

"The Jews of our country had suffered, the ones who survived, at least. So many didn't. So many. Our men had gone off to fight. Luc, too. I knew him as a child, and he returned a man. A hardened, wrecked man. Our parents were friends. One minute he was just Luc, their Luc, and then all of a sudden, he was mine. My Luc. That's how things happened back then. You girls have love. We had duty. *Pfff*, love."

Sylvie throws out a hand, a hand against love, but then her features soften. "Well, I had love, too. But that story comes later."

"Did you love Grand-papa?" Arabelle asks, and I think what a funny question it is, how never once did I think to consider if my grandparents were in love. Especially my dad's parents—the ones I never met. My mom's parents were okay; they could take me or leave me, and that's how I felt about them, too. They died when I was young, anyhow. So I romanticized my lost grandparents, the ones who were taken from me. I imagined them to be madly in love, before everything was stolen from them, before the horrors they endured. It pings my heart now to imagine they weren't, to think they had other problems like the ones we all carry. To think they went to their graves troubled, not holding hands.

I took it for granted, I suppose—love, as the base reason we marry. It's the reason I did, after all, or one of them, at least. Although Seb was doing well by then, moving up the ranks at Goldman Sachs, and he had the right education. I knew we'd be financially fine. It sounds callous, maybe, that such a thing was a consideration, but my father always told me I needed a man who could provide for me. And in choosing a man, I listened to my father, as I always do.

Besides, I am a realist. Money can buy you many things, sometimes even your life.

Sylvie shakes her head. "I didn't love your grandfather. *Désolée*. I tried. But truly, if there could be a medal given for how hard I tried to love him, I would be first place. We had a small apartment in those days, on Rue Nostradamus. Your grandfather made textiles, and I came to work for Séraphine and Rainier. We had very little money. Often during winter, we didn't even have heat. At least if you have love, you are okay. But without money or love . . ."

"It's a cold existence," Arabelle says quietly.

"Cold," Sylvie affirms. "Even in the middle of summer, cold. But I had your mother, Arabelle, my Delphine, and then later, I had Arabelle. They made my life very warm." Sylvie squeezes her granddaughter's hand, and I experience a pang of envy. It's funny how you always want what you don't have. I have so much, arguably so many things that Arabelle doesn't. Parents who are alive and generally wonderful; children who are wonderful, too. But she has a grandmother who adores her. I always wondered what such an unconditional love like that would feel like. A grandparent loves differently than a parent, after all, without expectations, with the blessing of an interceding generation that comprises the sieve for the trauma that collects and thins before dripping down.

"Did you . . . I mean, you and my grandmother . . ." Darcy blushes. "Did you . . . while my grandfather was alive?"

"*Non*," Sylvie says, aghast. "*Absolument pas*. We made vows, to our husbands. Those vows meant something. They have to mean something, or it all falls apart."

I look at Arabelle. I notice Vix does, too. Darcy is staring at the trunk of the towering plane tree, not speaking. She is amazing, my friend. I am in awe, to be honest. If it were me, and Belle had taken Seb, or tried to, I'd unleash it all. I'd tell Sylvie who Belle really is. But I suppose today isn't the day. And Darcy is in a sea of grief, besides.

"So when, then?" Vix asks. "When did you and Séraphine . . . ?"

"Well you know, Rainier died here, in the pool." Our eyes travel southward just a bit, to the pool edged in pale stone, with the family crest statue towering above. Darcy once told me that when her grandfather's head hit the statute, it left blood that remained the entire summer. No amount of scrubbing would remove it, until winter. So strange, how husband and wife both died violently on these grounds.

161

Part of me wants to get on the first plane back to New York. Hug Seb fiercely, pull the kids out of camp and hug them, too. But another, bigger part needs to finish what I started here.

"And then Luc died a few years later. Lung cancer. He picked up smoking in the war. They didn't know it was bad for you back then, but even if they did, who cared? He barely made it out of Normandy. He never thought he'd live to marry, or have a daughter. He lost his friends, his right eye."

"His eye?" Vix asks. Her hand goes to hers. So does mine, I realize. It's instinctual, how we try to protect what others could not.

"*Oui.*" Sylvie's lips form a grim line. "He was handsome, Luc, even without an eye. But I was never a beauty."

"Mamie, you are the most beautiful," Arabelle says.

"*Pfff.* I *certainement* am not, nor was I ever. I was a worker. That was my strength. And I am funny. I have a humor. I always joked Luc chose me because he could only see half of me." Sylvie's eyes get a faraway glint. "And it was true. In more ways than one."

Arabelle's face is white, even in candlelight. Though I'm angry at her right now, so angry, I feel for her. I have a soft spot, a wound, you could say, for grandparents.

"Séraphine, you ask?" A tear inches down Sylvie's cheek and she makes no effort to brush it away. "I loved her from the moment I met her. Of course, there were a thousand reasons we couldn't be. We were married to other people. Men. Strong men. And besides, our world didn't allow a union like ours. Even now, when things have become progressive, and our husbands are long gone, Séraphine never wanted to be public with our love. She always said it was no one's business, that other people would sully it. And I don't know . . . maybe she was right. But I would have liked to sit in a restaurant one day and hold her hand. To stand at the Eiffel Tower and kiss her cheek."

"Sylvie, can I ask you? Was Grand-mère always so . . . " I can see Darcy thinking how to put it. A bitch, is how I'd label her, even though one shouldn't speak ill of the dead.

"A ballbuster," Darcy finally says.

"Ballbuster?" Sylvie dabs at her eyes with a handkerchief.

"Strong. Demanding. Umm . . ."

"*Oui, oui*. Always. But she had to be, because Rainier was . . . a strong man himself."

"Really? I always thought of Grand-père like a teddy bear."

"A teddy bear?" Sylvie clucks her tongue. "I wouldn't say that. No. A teddy bear, like something sweet and cuddly?" Darcy nods. "No, I wouldn't say that at all. Your grandfather was a proud man. He had a lot of opinions, and he wasn't shy about sharing them, especially those concerning your grandmother."

Sylvie bites her lip. Suddenly she looks around like she is a child stranded at a department store, searching futilely for her mother.

"Mamie, why don't I give you another of those little pills?" Arabelle says. "And help you to bed?"

"Yes, that would probably be best." Sylvie presses her hands on the table and pushes herself up to a stand.

"I'm sorry if we asked you questions that were too painful to think about," Vix says softly.

"Oh, *ma chérie*, you didn't! I need to talk about Séraphine. Please. I want to talk about her. I don't want to forget her. I don't want any of you to forget her. How special she was. How . . ." Her voice is brittle. It squeaks to a stop.

"Come, Mamie." Arabelle stands, and links her elbow through her grandmother's.

"Sylvie, before you go, what was your favorite memory with Séraphine?" Vix asks.

Everyone stills. Sylvie smiles. "At the beginning of our courtship, we used to exchange letters. We had a secret place for them, and every morning I would rush to the place to see if I had a new one. We couldn't date, you understand. It wasn't the times, and there were others working at the chateau. Even though Séraphine was in charge here, we had to be discreet. Every time I got a letter, I would sit at my desk in my room with a cup of tea, and open it to read. I can still remember how the paper felt on my fingers, how her curt handwriting softened when directed to me. We haven't sent each other letters in decades, not since I moved into the room upstairs, and it became easier to do as we please. But still . . ."

Vix is wiping away tears. We all are, even me. No matter how I felt about Séraphine, I love Sylvie. She is just innately lovable. Some people are. It's not a thing you can change, or affect. I wonder briefly whether I am innately lovable. It is an uncomfortable question, without a comfortable answer. I have always felt like I was lovable, as long as I did certain things correctly.

"That's such an incredible story," Vix says. "So where did you hide your letters, Sylvie? Like, on the grounds somewhere? Or in the house?" She looks around, as if a letter is going to come dropping any moment from a tree.

"*Non*." Sylvie shakes her head. "Where we put our letters is a secret between me and my beloved."

And then she shuffles off with Arabelle toward the house.

"So many secrets," Vix murmurs. "And we haven't even gotten to Raph's."

Something dark crosses Darcy's face. She doesn't say anything, though.

And I am lost in my own thoughts. Yes, Raph is the murderer—it is a neat, easy solution to what happened this morning. But I suspect we are all thinking the same thing: There are still far more questions than answers.

CHAPTER TWENTY-FOUR

Darcy

Monsieur Deveaux is the *avocat*, sitting with us as we breakfast on the terrace. He is younger than I expected, in his late forties, with a tall, rakish build and a neat gray-black beard. Not unattractive. The type of man who probably pulls better women as he gets older, with the distinguished looks and career trajectory that women of a certain age favor. I realize with an unfortunate start that I am a woman of that certain age. He isn't wearing a wedding ring, I happen to notice. Funny, how my eyes never used to linger on other men's wedding fingers. It's like my subconscious is prodding me along, with an arrow to my future. Perhaps this is the type of man I could hope to snag, if I am single.

Am I single? My scrambled eggs sit like an anchor in my stomach.

The table is strewn with coffee cups, and I reach for mine as a stapled photocopy slides across the table before me. *Le testament de Séraphine Demargelasse.*

The coffee that a few sips before was velvety deliciousness turns to sludge in my mouth. I push my chair back from the table and lean over, with a view onto my feet, trying to beat back the nausea that has burst forth. My toes are painted Big Bird–yellow because I spent money I didn't have on a pedicure before this trip. Oliver gave me a look as I was going that said everything, and I gave him a look back that didn't say enough. I just hustled out the door with Mila, and as my daughter's reward for waiting so patiently in the nail salon, I let her pick my color. What a waste of money, I thought morosely, after the technician had finished. I tried to convince myself it would look better in the Provençal sun, but now, in that very sun, my toes still look positively sickly. Is this why Oliver has fallen in love with someone else? Because I have grown wrinkled and tired and paunchy in the stomach, because my beauty has been suctioned out by the years and the children and the struggles? I can't even see Arabelle in my current vantage point, but just her beautiful, radiant, flat-stomach energy across the table upsets me. Actually, is *upset* the word, when your best friend has slept with your husband? Is *in love* with your husband?

Monsieur Deveaux asked for our meeting to include just me, Sylvie, and Vix. God knows why Vix. Maybe Grand-mère left Vix a small piece of art. I haven't much dwelled upon it, my mind having an endless parade of subjects upon which to dwell. But I said all of my friends could join. Why not? They will all know the contents of the Will soon enough. Arabelle, through Jade or Vix, or Oliver. It's not like I can keep my finances from my husband, however long he still holds that title.

Jade rubs a hand against my back, and I have to admit, I feel guilty for suspecting her of sleeping with Oliver, even though she doesn't know that I did. I think of the secrets Jade and I share, the things I promised her many, many years ago. Promises I will uphold now, if I can.

We have all made our introductions, and Monsieur Deveaux appears up-to-date on each one of us. He asks about Vix's health, in a way that implies he knows the extent of it. He comments upon Arabelle's fashion, and asks if her outfit will be featured in her Instagram. Barf. I do note with satisfaction, though, a flicker of disappointment on Arabelle's face. She gets put out when people talk about her fashion and not her culinary success. Her *business acumen*.

Men don't like talking about a woman's business acumen. They'd prefer to talk about their looks, and fashions. That's what Arabelle would say now, guaranteed, if Monsieur Deveaux departed and the circumstances were different. She means it, but sometimes I think she is just reminding us that she does indeed have it all.

Then, of course, Monsieur Deveaux inquires about The Fertility Warrior. Says how many women he is sure I am helping. Like I am Mother freaking Teresa, instead of a fledgling entrepreneur, emphasis on the fledgling.

I mutter something about it going well. His eyebrows raise just a little at that, and I wonder what Grand-mère told him. Everything, I'd expect. You are supposed to tell your *avocat* everything. So he knows about my financial problems, the small amount I shared with Grand-mère, at least. How embarrassing. And now, if I am to inherit what I suspect I will, he will know that it isn't me who will bail myself out, who will succeed on my own merit. I look around at the sheer size of this place, the land, the vineyard, the chateau. I will succeed because of her, because of all of this.

"So let's get down to it, yes?" begins Monsieur Deveaux. "Darcy, you are sure you want to include all of your friends in this private matter?"

I pause, second-guess my decision to include Arabelle. She was once my ally, and now I wonder if she is clocking everything to bend to her benefit later. But what can she bend here? The Will is what it is.

"It's fine," I finally say.

Monsieur Deveaux clucks his tongue, disapprovingly or approvingly, I'm not sure. He is wearing a brown tweed jacket with a starched white shirt and dark blue jeans, and the sun is a spotlight onto his face, which is turning tomato red. He doesn't seem to mind. He is a lawyer—he sits in the chair to which the client points. Maybe that's an unfair supposition, but I've always thought lawyers are a bit like hamsters running at full speed on their wheels to please.

"Well, this is awkward to say, but I think it's how I must start. You see, Séraphine came to see me just last month, wanting to make some changes to her Will."

For the very first time, I wonder if Grand-mère did something crazy, like cut me out. What if she just left it all to Sylvie? I know there is some French inheritance law that says children, or grandchildren in their stead, must inherit a certain percentage. So you can't disinherit your progeny, not completely. But what if Grand-mère found a work-around for some reason? She did say she wanted to discuss her Will with me. It's a horrible possibility to ponder because—oh gosh, even admitting this to myself feels intolerable. But Grand-mère's murder has felt like a solution to a massive, gnawing problem.

How can something so terrible, also be so good? Only what if now it's not?

"Darcy, Sylvie, to you especially I am sorry to tell you something to which I do not think you have been privy. You did not know that Séraphine had cancer, did you? A blood cancer, very rare. Very lethal."

Cancer. What?

"No," I say slowly. "I did not."

I see on Sylvie's face the shock that must be written on mine. "*Non*," she says. "Séraphine . . . cancer? It's not possible. I would have known."

"I thought not." He nods delicately. "Some clients choose to keep this information private, to spare their loved ones pain."

To spare us pain. I fan my face, suddenly smoldering. Grand-mère had cancer, and didn't tell me? Her granddaughter! Why not at least tell *me*?

Because I would have treated her differently, I realize dully. Because our last time together wouldn't have been normal, but with a sticky layer of sickness. Because I would have convinced her to do treatments—to fight—and at her age, her fight was probably gone. And just the word *cancer* blackens things, overtakes all other conversations and moments.

"Séraphine told me at our last meeting that she had invited you all here. Darcy, Arabelle, Jade, and Vix. You thought . . . what did you all think about this meeting?"

No one speaks. Finally, Jade arches an eyebrow. "Fun and games?"

"Yes. She hoped you would." He nods. "But she had reason for inviting you here. That's what she told me. Things she needed to tell you. She was worried. I saw it in her eyes."

"Worried?" I ask, my heartbeat quickening.

"*Oui*. Worried you wouldn't take it so well, what she had to tell you. Worried it might cause . . . problems."

"Problems?" I ask. "Did she tell you anything more?"

"Unfortunately, no," he says. "This is also what I told to the gendarmes. They were very interested, you can imagine, in the Will. In my last conversation with Séraphine. Especially given what happened to her. I feel terrorized, myself, to be frank, that she came to me, an old, worried woman, and I didn't . . . well, I don't know what I might have done. But it seems she had cause to be worried. I wish I knew more. Had any suspicions. But I don't."

"The police already know about the Will?" Arabelle asks.

"*Oui*." He nods. "So let's get to it, yes? Now the document is before Darcy, Sylvie, and Vix, but I will sum it up quite easily. It is not complicated, though its thickness might indicate otherwise. Most of it is complex language to deal with taxes and such. As for the pertinent provisions, now the bulk of the estate comes from Séraphine's husband, Rainier. Darcy's grandfather. And that property passes as Rainier provided in his Will. But Séraphine had her own assets, as well. Income from Rainier's estate, invested over the years, has done quite well. For purposes of this conversation, we will act as if the estates are combined, because practically, it doesn't matter if the money is coming from one or the other. Okay?"

The words are disintegrating in my ears, turned to dust. How did both my grandparents meet such brutal endings on this land? It all feels so raw, with the swimming pool in its turquoise stillness only feet away.

I realize Monsieur Deveaux is looking at me, waiting for something. "Uh huh." I nod. I've forgotten what question I'm supposed to be answering.

"Right. So off the top, I would like to say that, Darcy, as the sole heir of your grandparents, your father having predeceased you, you are a very, very rich woman."

I feel a breath I quite knew I was holding finally release.

"Well, that's . . . fine." I can feel all eyes on me, and I think they know I want to squeal. Wouldn't you? I've won the lottery, however the circumstances. Money doesn't buy happiness, is the saying. A rich person must have said it.

"The chateau is yours, along with a healthy portfolio, some in trust, in appropriate investments, some outright. We can go through all of the details at a later time, or after this meeting, in private, if you wish."

I look at my hands in lieu of looking at any of them. "Yes, we can cover the details in private."

Monsieur Deveaux nods briskly. "Now, Darcy, you have what we call the residue of the estate. All of what is leftover, after the payment of taxes and expenses and also, after a series of specific gifts. I would like to list those gifts for you all now. First, to Madame Sylvie. Séraphine left you the sum of five million euros, in trust for your life, and at your death, to Darcy."

"Five million . . . euros?" Sylvie looks poleaxed with shock. "But what do I need, with five million euros?"

I think to tell her five million euros isn't even a crazy lot. By the time she gets a place of her own, in this real estate market. A nest egg, in case she is sick, maybe a caretaker eventually, which in her mid-eighties, is a probability.

Apparently, I am now a person who thinks five million euros isn't a crazy lot of money.

In the movies people breathe into paper bags. I think I would like a paper bag.

"Séraphine wanted you to be supported in a wonderful manner for the rest of your life," says Monsieur Deveaux. "And so you shall."

"It's too much . . . it's just too . . ." Sylvie is dazed, staring off at the gigantic plane tree. The one that is supposedly the largest in Provence. I realize with a start that the plane tree, too, is now mine.

"And now we arrive at Madame Victoria," says Monsieur Deveaux.

I watch Vix wring her hands nervously in her lap. Her meeting with my grandmother—the one she refuses to talk about—now drifts up into my head. She spoke to my grandmother on the phone, even, before this trip. They had a clandestine meeting planned, hours after she was murdered.

But there must be a reasonable explanation for Vix's inclusion in the Will. Grand-mère always had a soft spot for Vix. Most people do. There is something supremely likable about Vix, which I suppose can't be said for the rest of us. Arabelle has that fashion model gloss and is uber successful, the envy of everyone—the women who want to be her, and the men who want to have her. Jade is too skinny. It's hard to feel sorry for someone so skinny. I suppose I have never related likable to pity but maybe they are indeed correlated a bit. And as for me? I fight for the big things I want, that is true. But as for the minutia, I've always felt I could take it or leave it. Sure, bring me a chai latte, bring me a cinnamon muffin. I've never had strong preferences, besides my husband and my children. A person without strong preferences fades into the backdrop, too vanilla to be noticed, the necessary precursor, after all, to likability. Vix has very strong preferences. Her Starbucks order takes forty seconds to rattle off—I've timed it.

Perhaps Grand-mère is giving Vix a token of her admiration. A piece of jewelry, or a dish Vix has said she liked. Vix is always complimenting people on things—it's another one of her likable qualities.

"To Madame Victoria, Séraphine has left another five million euros in trust, for her life."

There is an audible intake of breath that dominoes across the table.

Five million euros to Vix? But . . . *why!?*

Vix has that stunned, waxy look of elderly plastic surgery patients. When she finally speaks, she says, "That can't be," in her likable, whispery voice.

"It is, I assure you. You will see it right there in the Will." Monsieur Deveaux flips through the pages, points. "Séraphine was clear on it to me. She said Victoria would be surprised, but also wouldn't be surprised." He winks at Vix, like she is in on something.

What the hell is she in on? Why would Vix not be surprised that my grandmother, whom she hasn't seen in nearly two decades, would leave her five million euros in her Will?

Jade chuckles in an acerbic way. "If Raph wasn't the murderer, this wouldn't look great for you, Vixen."

171

Then Jade grimaces. We're not supposed to call her Vixen now. Yeah, yeah.

"So there you have it," Monsieur Deveaux says. "There are a few smaller bequests that you can read about on page—"

"Was there anything to the groundskeeper?" Arabelle asks. "I think I'm not the only one wondering it."

Monsieur Deveaux glances at me, and I don't understand why, until I do. He is looking for my approval, to share. It's a strange measure of respect and courtesy he's showing to me, that makes me feel like I've aged fifty years and slid into my grandmother's place. It makes sense, I realize dully. He is a businessman. If he wants to continue with this account, he will have to work with me.

I nod. It is bizarre, for my nod to now wield power.

"The groundskeeper in custody." Monsieur Deveaux nods. "Raphael Archambeau."

Oh, what a good name. I can't help it, that's what I immediately think. I've always thought Oliver's last name was a bit . . . plain. One-note. Personality-less. Oliver Bell. Darcy Bell. Ring the bell for the Bells! (That's the placard below our buzzer. I couldn't help myself.)

Dermargelasse. Archambeau. Those are names with provenance. Those are names that make you feel like they have roots, like the plane tree before me. Maybe that's why Oliver took up with Arabelle. Bell has no roots.

Monsieur Deveaux clears his throat, interrupting my love affair with the groundskeeper's last name. It's like he was deferentially waiting for my reverie to pass. "I've told the gendarmes this, and they were quite interested. To Monsieur Archambeau, Séraphine left an outright gift of five hundred thousand euros."

Five hundred thousand euros to the groundskeeper who picked those awful cherries?

I can't help my indignance. I think about the ten thousand euros deposited into my account that Grand-mère expected to solve my financial difficulties. Did she have no concept of money? Assuming that such a relatively small amount would be significant for me, and

172

yet that Vix and the groundskeeper would be entitled to such large amounts? Nothing makes sense. My head feels like it's one of those whirling teacup rides at the fair, the ones I'm fearful will at any moment splinter apart, because you always hear things like that at shady local fairs.

"In France, we have a slayer rule, like in America, too. A murderer cannot inherit from the estate of the person he killed," says Monsieur Deveaux. "So if Monsieur Archambeau is guilty—"

"If?" says Arabelle. "It seems even clearer now that he is. Money is a fantastic motive for murder."

Monsieur Deveaux shrugs. "I am not up-to-date on the investigation. I only relay to you the facts of which I am aware."

"Do you know why my grandmother left such a large amount to a relatively new employee?" I ask quietly.

"It is not my responsibility as the *avocat* to probe. But I think Séraphine mentioned something about a grandmother."

"A grandmother?"

Monsieur Deveaux nods. "A grandmother of Monsieur Archambeau, whom Séraphine knew. That's all I remember. She didn't say anything else."

I file that information away. His grandmother knew mine? Still, even if that is so, why did she leave him so much money in her Will?

A zealous bird who has been trying to pick at our breadbasket arrives once again to forage.

"Shoo. Shoo, bird," Vix says, attempting to flick away the brilliant blue bird who matches our tablescape. Of course. Everything here is picturesque, even the animals.

My head is throbbing. "I need to lie down," I say with a start. I stand, push in my chair.

"*Bien sûr.*" Monsieur Deveaux nods. "One more thing, though."

I freeze.

"It doesn't have to do with you, Darcy. You can go now if you want."

But of course, I want to hear this.

From his leather portfolio, Monsieur Deveaux slips out a letter.

"Séraphine gave this to me. She said if something were to happen to her, I should give it to her Sylvie."

"To me?" Sylvie practically lurches for the letter. I am envious, but happy for her, too. I think about what she told us, how she and Grand-mère used to write letters to each other. And now she gets one from beyond the grave. It is touching, for sure.

"Is there a letter for me?" I can't help but ask.

Monsieur Deveaux shakes his head, not unsympathetically. "I'm afraid only for Madame Sylvie."

"What did she mean, if something were to happen to her?" asks Arabelle.

"Yeah," I say. "That's strange. She said it just like that?"

"It's peculiar, *n'est-ce pas?*" Monsieur Deveaux says. "At the time, I thought she was referring to her cancer. But now I'm not so sure, if she didn't know she were in danger."

"You told the police?" Jade asks.

"*Oui.* I did."

"I think I'll take my tea upstairs," Sylvie says. "Have a rest myself."

There is a question nagging me now. If Grand-mère was indeed afraid of Raph, afraid for her life, then why did she leave him five hundred euros in her Will?

I watch Sylvie stand, collect the teapot and her cup, and tuck the envelope under her armpit. Arabelle tries to take the teapot from her, but Sylvie swats her arm away. "*Allez!* I am quite capable of walking upstairs by myself. I've done so for far longer than you have all been walking this earth." She turns and nods curtly at the *avocat*. "*Bonne journée*, Monsieur Deveaux."

Then she drifts away, back toward the house.

I remember what she said—how she used to have her tea and read Grand-mère's letters.

"I am going to rest, too," I announce, then realize that I've said it already, that my second announcement dilutes it somehow.

"I didn't sleep well last night. I'm going to rest, too," Arabelle says.

Why didn't she sleep well? I resist the urge to ask. Was it because she was in my husband's bed? No. Oliver wouldn't. Not at the apartment, with the kids around.

Or would he? I feel like I don't know my husband, or anyone close to me, at all.

"I'm going to lie down, too," Jade says. No surprise. She's always itching to be alone at any opportunity.

"Well if everyone's going . . ." Vix says, never much one for a solo party, like me. She takes a croissant from the basket. I'm quite sure the beautiful bird was just nibbling on it, but I don't say so. It would require too many words, too much passion, that I don't currently have. Besides, I feel a sudden and very acute anger toward Vix, who has siphoned off a piece of my grandmother's affection. Five million euros of affection, to be precise. It's not the money I'm upset about. If my suspicion of the ballpark value of Grand-mère's estate is in even the range of accurate, Vix's gift makes little dent in mine. It's the secrecy of it that bothers me, the relationship they've knitted and maintained without me. And it's the secrets Vix is still keeping, about their meeting, about their phone call.

She is lucky Raph is the killer. She is lucky indeed, because otherwise I would have suspicions. I think anyone rational would.

"Let's rest and reconvene later," Jade says assertively. She likes a plan.

I can't be bothered to respond. I can't even be bothered to say goodbye to Monsieur Deveaux, who hasn't done anything to me per say, but make me a very rich woman. But I have a perhaps irrational dislike of him now that he didn't press my grandmother on why she made gifts to Vix and Raph. On why she wrote a letter to Sylvie and not me. As the last person with intimate knowledge of her, he shared a whole lot of nothing.

Impulsively, I grab a roll from the breadbasket, at the same moment as the bird swoops back to have at it. We tussle for a moment, and I win, yanking it from his greedy, little beak. At first a feeling suffuses me—victory! Then I realize, I am excited about winning a bread roll from a bird.

I feel eyes on me. Eyes I don't want to meet with my own. The bread roll is still in my hand. I'm not going to give anyone the satisfaction of putting it down.

Instead, before I walk inside, I force myself to take a big bite out of it. "Mmm," I say, defiantly, although I'm not sure to whom.

Don't worry, I didn't take a bite out of the part the bird pecked. I'm not a complete savage.

CHAPTER TWENTY-FIVE

Vix

I awaken with a start, to five million euro signs. Darcy is a rich woman, but so, it appears, am I. I rub my eyes, orient myself back to the room. Did I sleep? Or just drift? My time navigating The Big-C felt dreadfully similar—the lines blurred between awake and not, as I was told to rest. Ordered to rest. It's not very restful when you are lying in a hospital bed, or in your own bed, with gauze and needling pain, desperate to yank foreign material out of your breasts.

My eyes catch the armoire that Séraphine so despised. Her mother-in-law's. I think of Juliet's mother, who is very thin, and always cold. Every time I've met her, she is wrapped in some woolly blanket, her apartment hot like a sauna. She is a complainer, one of those people who can make a gray sky seem like a personal affront. Juliet hated going to visit her, but they had a ritual of Saturday lunches. I joined a couple of times. We would sit at the kitchen table and eat her mother's Niçoise salad. Always a Niçoise salad, with exactly three olives per plate. Three olives!? I always restrained myself after, when Juliet would play-by-play in the car, from the comment I really wanted to say, which is that people who choose odd numbers over even numbers for things are serial killers. Juliet may have complicated feelings about her mother, but no one wants their mother called a serial killer.

My mind drifts into a memory of Juliet and me eating our Niçoise salads, and how at a certain point in the meal, when Juliet's mother said something I thought was irritating but also innocuous, and Juliet clearly thought was outrageous, Juliet's hand would snake into mine and squeeze hard. I'd let her squeeze me for a bit, like a stress ball, and then her hand would relax in mine, and we'd continue eating. It worked somehow—I am left-handed, and she is right-handed, so when I sat on the left, we could hold hands while we ate.

I stare at the armoire and can't help but think how unfair it is that I don't even get a wretched mother-in-law. But on the plus side, I do have five million euros. That number keeps going round and round my head.

I didn't sleep well last night. I can't imagine any of us did.

I am hungry. I weigh the pros and cons of leaving this room. Pro: I will find food, preferably vegetable soup. I really, really want vegetable soup. People often think when you are fat, you eat mountains of carbs. I do eat carbs, in reasonable amounts, but this is just my body. It does what it wants. You think I asked it to create cancer? I wish people understood this, the ones who treat their bodies like a thing that is to be whipped if it falls out of line. Bodies just do what they please, without consulting the people who live inside them.

I used to be so nice to my body, so loving. I run a hand down my chest and wince.

Vegetable soup. Ooh, gazpacho. Wouldn't it be nice if Arabelle would make me some? I bet she would, if I ask nicely.

Cons on leaving this room: I will face questions, about the five million euros. About why Séraphine wanted to meet with me the morning after she was murdered.

I pull the covers up to my eyes. Gazpacho, questions. Gazpacho, questions.

In the end, my hunger wins. Somehow, I'll dodge the questions, I decide. After all, I have a twenty-year track record proving I'm an expert at that.

———

I walk down the hallway, past Sylvie's room. I near the stairs, but then I turn back. Sylvie's door is open, which is odd. Ever since I arrived, her door is always shut. I walk slowly back.

"Sylvie," I call. I don't want to intrude on her privacy, but there is something decidedly strange about the wide-open door.

"Sylvie?" Her bed is perfectly made, the duvet and pillows in various shades of luxurious ochre red. I step closer and take a quick mental snapshot; the color scheme feels prime for a painting. The red conjures something. Blood? I shiver, then my vision zooms back out. Everything in the room appears neat and fine. Sylvie must have left her room and forgotten to close the door.

But just as I am readying to keep walking, my foot nudges on something by the desk onto the window. My eyes cast down to the tile to absorb a crumpled shape, gray tendrils framing a placid face, eyes closed.

"Sylvie!" I dive down beside her. I feel for her pulse, but damnit, where does her pulse live? I always got confused by it in a safety class I never finished, trying to become a lifeguard during a short-lived *Baywatch* phase.

"Someone help!" I still can't figure out her pulse, and it feels weird and like I'm hurting her even more, pressing all over her neck in a futile effort to find it. As I do, I nudge upon something hard—a copper cooking pot turned upside down, beside one of the table legs.

"Can anyone hear me? Sylvie's hurt! *Help!*"

———

We are all sitting in the living room, with the officers again. Sylvie is okay, thank God, or she seems to be, at least. She is sitting beside Arabelle, and Arabelle has one hand applying an ice pack to her grandmother's head, and the other arm wrapped protectively around Sylvie's shoulders, eyes darting around at each of us, like someone might strike at any moment.

My heart still quickens, rewinding and replaying the moment I stumbled upon Sylvie unconscious on the ground. My luck that this week I am the one who happened upon two unconscious old ladies.

At least, this one survived.

Thank God I came across Sylvie when I did. Thank God. She's

refused to go to the hospital, but Arabelle phoned a local doctor who used to call on Séraphine. The doctor took all her vitals and such and said she'll have a nasty bruise, but that she appears to be fine. She knows the year, I checked that much, when she finally came to on the bedroom floor. And I held up four fingers and she said, *Quatre*. I wasn't sure if that was French for four or five, but then Darcy told me it was four, and I could relax a bit.

I'm lying. I'm not relaxed at all. Not in the least. Why would someone hurt Sylvie? But beyond that question, a horrible one has risen to the top. Who did it? Because . . . it couldn't have been Raph. Raph is still in custody, as far as I know. Which means . . .

I shake my head violently, to banish that thought. There has to be another explanation. There *must*.

After I found Sylvie, one of the girls called the police, and the doctor arrived, and there was a flurry of activity. It wasn't just our two officers, but more again, as a troop of them dispersed across the house. I'm not sure what they are all doing, but we've been advised they have a warrant again. I suspect they are cordoning off Sylvie's things. The house is becoming awash in police tape, more rooms added with each passing day.

Now our two main officers are speaking by the door in hushed voices. The woman is consulting her notepad. Officer Darmanin. She has long chestnut hair that falls in ringlets past her boobs. Last time it was up, so she looked a little less beauty queen, but now locks tumbling down, she is like the gorgeous, intimidating policewoman on an unrealistic cop show that you watch more for her relationship travails than her detective skills. These judgments are un-feminist, and probably unfair. Hopefully, her detective skills are good. Otherwise we are screwed.

"Madame Carnot." Officer Darmanin comes over to the sofa and perches on the armrest, by Sylvie. "Can you tell us what happened?"

Sylvie nods. "But first, can you tell me?"

Officer Darmanin's eyes flicker with uncertainty. "Tell you what?"

"My note," whispers Sylvie. "Is my note from Séraphine gone?"

The officers exchange glances and Officer Valliere, the lackey, slips out to check. When he returns, I can tell by his staid face that yes, the note is gone. Sylvie is distraught. There are more tears that I attempt to drown out by fixing my gaze out the window.

"Why don't you tell us what happened, Madame Carnot," says Officer Valliere, his gaze flitting to Officer Darmanin. She nods, leaving no doubt; she is in charge. I like a woman in charge. Juliet was like that. Her opinions always floated above mine a bit. Not even for her necessarily, but for me. I let them float above mine, even though, generally, I am quite opinionated. I suppose Séraphine was like that, too, for me, in some way. I feel myself squirm, contending with what that says about me. Why don't I want to be in charge of my own life?

"I was exhausted when I came upstairs, after the *avocat*," Sylvie says. "My heart was beating so fast. I couldn't believe I had a letter from Séraphine in my hands. It felt important, whatever she would say to me. I wanted to be alert when I read it, so I had a quick rest. Not more than twenty minutes. I closed my eyes, but I didn't get to dreams. I awoke, clutching my letter. I went downstairs to refresh my teapot. I like it scalding."

A tiny smile escapes her lips.

"When I got back, I sat at my desk, with its view onto the front yard. It's barren out there. The color is brown. The pines, yes, but it's very severe. I told Séraphine we should soften it, but she would have none of it. It's different out back, with the view onto the pool and the vineyard and all the green. Séraphine offered me every room in the house." Her cheeks turn rosy. "Sometimes I slept with her, of course, but I needed my own quarters, too. We were older ladies when we got together, set in our ways. . . ."

"Yes, yes," says Officer Valliere impatiently. I shoot him eyes. Let an old lady reminisce, why don't you?

"Anyway." Sylvie fiddles with her hands in her lap. "You didn't find the letter. You are certain?"

"It wasn't anywhere in your room," he says. "And we've searched the other girls' rooms—"

"You searched our rooms already?" Darcy has a funny, almost guilty look on her face. I wonder if my face reveals the same. They searched our rooms before, but this feels different. Before, it was quickly evident that Raph was the probable killer. And now, even though no one has said it, I think everyone in the room is questioning that, at least a little bit.

"*Oui*. We will do what we need to. And presently we are operating under the theory that the person who battered Madame Carnot could have a connection to the person who murdered Madame Demargelasse."

"Could be the same person, you mean," Arabelle says.

"*Oui*. Madame Carnot, can you please finish your story?"

Sylvie suddenly shoves off Arabelle's ice pack and squirms out of her embrace. She scoots over on the couch.

"Sorry, *ma petite*. I just need a bit of room to breathe. And I felt like in . . . what is one of those things in Russia, or Iceland? An ice room with your ice box." She indicates the ice pack, and rubs her head. "Although you are very sweet. Anyway. There is not much to tell. I was sitting at my table, trying to encourage myself to open the letter. There was so much running through my mind. Séraphine's writing was leaping out at me, so many memories, of our notes."

"You read the note, then?" Arabelle asks. "What did it say, Mamie?"

"*Non*. I didn't read the note." Sylvie's voice cracks. "Just the envelope. She had such pretty calligraphy. She learned from Rainier's mother, she once told me. It said: *A l'amour de ma vie, Sylvie.*"

"To the love of my life, Sylvie," murmurs Darcy, although I'd gleaned as much.

"And then I just remember something hard on my head, and pain, and blackness. That's all. Everything went dark."

"Something hard on her head. The pot, then, yes?" Arabelle's face wrenches in fury. "Someone hit my grandmother on the head, and stole the note. Is that what you suspect?" She is looking at Officer

Darmanin, and it occurs to me that people—men and women alike—find it easier to take their anger out on a woman.

"That is our working theory, yes," says Officer Darmanin, calmly.

"Can you find fingerprints on the pot, then? Something to indicate who did this . . . gruesome thing?" Arabelle asks.

Fingerprints. Now that's a good idea.

"There are no fingerprints," says Officer Valliere. "Whoever did this wore gloves, or brushed off their prints."

"So . . . ?" says Arabelle.

"So . . . ?" echoes Officer Darmanin, in the same tone and tempo, which I'm sure will irritate Arabelle, because it irritates me.

"What now? What are you going to do?" Arabelle is speaking to the officer a bit condescendingly, like she is a sous-chef who has messed up her *beurre blanc*, and not the officer in charge of figuring out which of us in this room is lying. Because isn't that the crux of things? Raph is in custody. So one of us banged sweet Sylvie over the head with a pot and stole her letter. I was never good at mathematics, but here, the calculations are pretty simple.

"What I am going to do is first off, ask you if any of you heard anything? Ask where you were when this crime happened?"

"We were resting," Jade says. "I mean . . ." She looks around at us, galvanizing support. "We all went to rest after the meeting with the attorney."

I nod. So does Darcy, and Arabelle.

"I see," Officer Darmanin says, but she says it in a way that she sees something beyond what we have said. "So your story is . . . you were all resting. None of you heard anything."

"It's not a story," Arabelle says icily. "It's the truth. At least in my case it is."

"I may have heard something," Darcy ventures. "Now that I think about it."

"Yes?" asks Officer Darmanin. "What?"

"I don't know." Darcy reddens. "I felt feverish, almost, in bed. Maybe I dreamed it. But I thought I heard footsteps in the hall. And if everyone else was resting, then that would be the person who knocked out Sylvie, right?"

"Oh, that's convenient. Eliminating yourself as a suspect." Arabelle mutters it so softly that I think only I, who am closest to her, catch it. It rouses two things in me—first, her resentment toward Darcy. It's blazingly obvious. But second, it occurs to me that Arabelle is right. If Darcy claims she heard something, she casts suspicion away from herself. But Darcy couldn't have hurt Sylvie. She wouldn't. Except . . . what if there was something in the letter that for some important reason Darcy couldn't have anyone see?

"Do any of you know what was in that letter?" Officer Darmanin asks, echoing my thoughts. "Sylvie, do you have any suspicion about what Séraphine wanted to tell you?"

Sylvie shakes her head desolately. "Not a one."

"How is it possible you haven't found the letter?" Arabelle asks. "If someone here took it, then it would be on the grounds. It couldn't have gone far."

"From growing up here, you would know the grounds are enormous," Officer Darmanin says pointedly. "There are many places to hide things. But I will assure you, I will assure all of you. We will find whatever there is to be found. As we speak, there are more officers searching outside. And meanwhile, I will instruct you all again not to leave the area. That includes your husband." Officer Darmanin looks at Darcy.

"I'm not currently speaking to him," Darcy says. "But I'm sure Arabelle can pass that along." The last part she says with a hint of a smile. This makes me very uneasy. Suddenly I am afraid for my friend, that everything that has happened—that *is* happening—is driving her over some cliff none of us can yet see.

For a few moments, no one speaks. I glance over at Sylvie, to see if she has noted that subtext, but her face is its same pained as previously, and I gather that Darcy's comment has blessedly passed her over.

"Does this mean you are ruling Raph out as a suspect?" Jade asks.

"Monsieur Archambeau remains a suspect in the murder, as do you all. And Monsieur Bell."

"I am the only one with an alibi," Arabelle says. "In case you've forgotten. Well, Ollie, too," she says softly, although Sylvie has closed her eyes by now, her head tilted upon a throw pillow, and it is clear she has checked out entirely from this conversation.

"I have not forgotten," Officer Darmanin says with an edge to her voice. "But you could have planned the crime together. You could have both been in on it. And then, forgive my profanity, your alibi would be shit. And moreover, what happened to Sylvie casts some doubt on the note implicating Monsieur Archambeau. Was the note a forgery, for instance—"

"I thought you said Séraphine's handwriting was substantiated," Arabelle says.

"It was, yes. But perhaps the killer placed it there to be read out of context. We don't know."

I hadn't thought of that. "So Raph is going to be released?" I ask.

Officer Darmanin nods. "As we are speaking. We didn't have enough evidence to hold him any longer as it is, but especially with today's assault, he is no longer our prime suspect."

My rib cage feels squished, breath elusive. "Then who is your prime suspect?"

The officers exchange glances that I can't analyze. "All of you." Officer Darmanin smiles, for the first time, a smile that is not taking joy in our circumstances, I can tell, but a sad sort of smile. "I'm afraid all of you are still suspects."

"Even me?" asks Sylvie, coming to. "You think I banged my own head?" She laughs almost hysterically. I have to admit the possibility hadn't even occurred to me. Is that even plausible? To what has this week descended?

Again, the officers communicate in some coded way with their eyes. "The investigation continues," Officer Darmanin says. "In the meantime, I do have some advice."

"Yes?" Jade asks. "What do you advise?" She says it almost sarcastically, but I can make out the hysteria behind her voice, because it's the same hysteria bubbling in me. We can't leave the country, so we are locked here together—and someone is a murderer?

"Lock your doors when you sleep, just in case. That is my advice. Although now that the letter is gone, we don't suspect Sylvie is in any further danger. Nor any of you. Whatever the motive for the murder, we think it to have been achieved with Séraphine's death. And the assault of Sylvie seems incontrovertibly connected, and the aim of it achieved with the stealing of the note. So you can all rest easier now."

"Oh yes, when you leave, we will slip into our bathing suits and go lay out by the pool with fruity cocktails." Arabelle's wide eyes have gone to angry slits. "Is that the rest easier you contemplate? Just lock our flimsy doors. Some wonderful advice."

"What do you care?" Darcy says. "You can go sleep at my husband's. The rest of us have nowhere to go."

"Yes, poor little rich girl," Arabelle says, in a voice so hateful that my heart stills. "You have nowhere to go, but everywhere."

Everything seems to freeze, even the breeze from the open windows. I glance at Sylvie again but she is out of it, missing all the nuance, intentionally or unintentionally, in her own aching world.

Then the anger gusts out of Arabelle's face so fast I feel a little whiplashed. "Darcy, I'm so sorry. I didn't mean that. I just . . . my grandmother—"

"How about *my* grandmother? How about *my* husband?"

No one speaks.

Finally, Jade says, "Are we adjourned?"

"Yes, that is all for now." Officer Darmanin stands.

"I'll help Mamie upstairs." Arabelle stands, too. "And then I'm going out for the afternoon. I need some fresh air."

"Mamie." Arabelle strokes her grandmother's cheek.

"I can walk upstairs by myself, Arabelle." Sylvie comes to, rubbing her eyes. "I am quite capable."

"But . . ." Arabelle stands there, arm extended, and I can see her vacillating. "But Mamie . . ."

"*Oui, oui.*" Sylvie swats Arabelle away, puts her hands against the couch cushions to prop herself up. "I am fine. I am absolutely fine. I can manage myself now, thank you very much. Now I get a glimpse into how Séraphine felt, with all my babying."

"You'll lock your door?" Arabelle asks.

"*Oui.*" Sylvie disappears into the foyer without a backward glance.

"I just want to clarify for everyone still present," Darcy says in a distant voice, once Sylvie has gone. "When Arabelle says she's going out for fresh air, she means she's going to see my husband."

Arabelle's face falls a bit. "Darce," she starts, with a tone that is sad and apologetic and helpless. But then her mouth closes, because what more is there to say?

Right. Arabelle is going to see Oliver. And everything is fucked.

CHAPTER TWENTY-SIX

Arabelle

I take Ollie to Gordes, the cutest town in Provence. We don't speak much on the drive, but we hold hands, and that speaks enough for me, for now. I'm still processing everything that happened with Mamie. I haven't told Ollie yet. I'm not ready to. It changes everything, and I'm scared. And right now, I just want some quiet with Ollie, before we have to talk about things. A lot of things.

I take the hairpin turns fast. Ollie lets go of my hand, as if I need it to keep us alive, but I reclaim my grip on his. His other hand is holding tight to the side handle. I can drive with one hand. I am good with this car.

My phone rings, and I retract my hand from Ollie's. I can drive with one hand, but not neither. My heart starts to jitter, and it's not the increase in altitude, or my driving. What if something else happened to Mamie? The shock of the attack has finally absorbed. Maybe I shouldn't have left her. It was selfish to leave her. I'm about to make a U-turn, to go back, but then I turn over my phone to see who it is. Giancarlo. I stare at the screen for a few moments, while speeding up to pass a gargantuan truck.

"Jesus." Ollie looks like he's sweating.

I put my phone on silent. I spoke to Giancarlo, of course, yesterday. But he doesn't know the latest development, nor does he know about Ollie.

If Ollie saw who was calling me, he doesn't let on. "Where are we going?" Ollie asks. "We could have just stayed in Saint-Rémy." He pauses. "Oh."

Yes. Saint-Rémy is filled with memories of his family, of his wife. I want to take him somewhere new, somewhere different. Somewhere that, for an hour at least, we can be different people other than Darcy's husband and Darcy's best friend. Other than two people in this web of horrible crimes, horrible violence.

"I still can't believe she knows," Ollie says.

Darcy. "I know."

"I don't understand why you had to tell her."

"It was our alibi. . . ."

"But we didn't need one! We have no motive! And—"

"Raph heard your car. Jade heard footsteps. It was going to come out. And if it didn't come from me, it was going to make us look guilty."

Quiet, then, "You know she found something in my pocket." It's a statement, not a question.

"What do you mean? No. I don't know." My eyes flick over at him.

"Before we left. She found one of your . . ." He gestures toward me vaguely, in no way explanatory of the object he's indicating.

"One of my *what*?"

"Those thingies you use to tie your hair."

"*Merde*."

"Yeah."

"What did you say?" I ask.

He shrugs. "Something about how I must have picked it up from somewhere and stuck it in my pocket absentmindedly."

"*Merde*," I say again. I mull it over. "What color was it?"

"Black."

"So . . . you could have said it was for your man bun." I say it with a hint of humor, because he's grown the top part of his hair shaggy of late.

"Black *silk*," he says, very much without humor. "And I don't have a man bun."

"Okay," I mutter.

Ollie draws a deep breath. You can always tell when he's hesitating to ask something. It's one of his least attractive qualities. "Why was it in my pocket, out of curiosity?"

I feel anger pulse at my throat. "You think I put that hair tie in your pocket *on purpose?*"

"I didn't say that. It's just weird is all."

I'm irate. I want to leap out of my seat and strangle him, is how I feel. "I don't even wear *perfume* when we're together, Ollie. And I always wear perfume! But I don't want you to smell like me. Darcy is one of my best friends! She's my *family.* I've known her far longer than you have, to be frank. I'm not trying to hurt her. Hurting Darcy is the last thing I'm trying to do!"

I am so furious I see my spit land on my steering wheel, which isn't the most attractive of things, but fuck it. Fuck him!

"I'm sorry, Ar," he says softly. He puts a hand on mine, and instantly my body responds, like Jell-O. Traitor. "This is just . . ."

"Yeah." My heart is still thrashing in my chest. "It is."

The village approaches, white stone houses baked into the cliff, with green trees interspersed that from this distance look like heads of broccoli. I pull over at the iconic vista. However upset I am, I want him to experience this. We look at each other, exchange a silent conversation about *are we going to let this rest, please let's end this conversation.*

"Come on." Ollie's face twists into his crooked, disarming smile. "Let's take a photo."

We scramble out and stand windblown by the side of the road, looking out on the Luberon. We're here early enough that dark shadows haven't yet descended on the lower half of the village. The village is quaint; you imagine happy families and that kind of thing, living in the little houses, looking out on the farmland, saying happy family things. It is a romantic village, if I ever saw one. I think of that old movie with Grace Kelly and Cary Grant, all those hairpin turns as they drove above Monaco, in one long game of seduction. This place conjures something similar in me, a Hollywood moment made for poignancy. So far, Ollie and I have only traveled within New York, to hotels in the city, when I've visited with increasing frequency for book stuff, and him stuff. The Four Seasons, so not slumming it, and not long ago we escaped up to the Berkshires for a few days when I told the girls I was returning home and Ollie told Darcy he had work upstate. What work did a (struggling) musician have upstate? He finagled something, a story about visiting venues and interviewing a drummer. He's good at lines, Ollie, that's the thing.

We take a selfie, with Ollie's long arm. But he's not kissing my cheek, and I don't feel like kissing his at the moment. I scrutinize the picture. We look happy and windswept. But Ollie says, "What a traumatic week. For everyone."

"Ollie . . ." I gather up the courage. "Which of us are you more worried about?" I ask, before I can stop myself. "Like you said, it's been a traumatic week for everyone."

"For Godsakes, Ar." He looks angry, or something else I can't decipher. Even though I'm on the edge of the cliff awaiting his answer, the *Ar* always pings my heart. He pronounces it with his Michigan *a* so it sounds like *air*. Everyone else, including Giancarlo, calls me Belle. But Oliver's last name is Bell, so we share a nickname. He has always said, ever since I met him, that it's too weird to call me by the name he associates with himself. Thus the *Ar*. I used to think us sharing a nickname was a sign. "Belle Bell," he said recently, offhanded. He laughed. "Can you imagine?"

Indeed, I could. But instead of saying so, I smiled in a way I knew was mysterious.

I'm not mysterious anymore. I'm pushing us to the edges, maybe pushing too hard. He looks at me wearily now, with that killer two-day stubble, like hoping I will retract the question about which of me and Darcy he is more worried about—but I don't.

Suddenly I long for some Hollywood lines in this Hollywood place. I don't expect Ollie to say he is only worried about me. Of course not. This is the mother of his children we're talking about. And she's just lost her grandmother, in a horrendous way. Hell, I love Darcy, too, however much it seems that I don't, by virtue of this thing with Ollie.

I just need something to reassure me, in this very fraught, scary time. Something to reaffirm how much I mean to him. Because this thing with us—and we both know it—it was as unstoppable as the ocean.

My one memory with my father is swimming with him in the Golfe du Lion. I remember standing in the harsh current and no matter how I tried, the ocean swept me in the direction it pleased. But still, it was the most fun I'd ever had! At one point I paused, shouting, "Papa, the sun is sprinkling confetti on the ocean like at my birthday party!" I don't remember my birthday party itself, but I remember that I remembered it. That my parents loved me so much they threw me a birthday party with confetti. Just after I squealed with delight, and the ocean swallowed me again.

My father eventually caught me, flailing, coughing salt water. He shouted at me, for swimming away from him. "You think you can move the sea? Tell it to do what you want?" Then he saw I was scared, so he softened a bit. "The ocean is big and mighty, Arabelle. You can't swim against it. One day it's fierce and choppy, like today, and you have to be careful. Even though the next day will be calm, the stillest waters you couldn't have conceived."

This has stuck with me all these years. The only memory of my father, of either of my parents, that I've played back a million times. Frozen in time, the anger, and then the love—seawater glistening on his caramel skin, his eyes brown, or even black? Mamie doesn't know. My mother is her daughter, so she never studied my father's eyes, and photos don't answer the question. My parents are both only children. The only answer to any question about their looks or personality is me. Still, so many unanswered questions that I've always put in a box, because what is the use of asking things that will never be resolved? Just, I've always felt that memory meant something. Or to put it another way, I've always tried to shape it to mean something. And when I met Ollie I finally understood. We couldn't move the sea. We might have tried, allowed others to intervene. But ultimately, we couldn't make it do anything other than what happened when we both fell inside it.

Now I'm just hoping, waiting, for the day after. Calm seas.

"Both of you," Ollie finally says quietly, not meeting my eyes. "I'm worried about both you and Darcy, Ar."

The Hollywood luster goes and it's just a rocky promontory in the midst of the Vaucluse. It's just a cloudless sky. It's just undulating lavender fields. It's just a spectacular vista, of which there are thousands in France, in the world.

We walk back to the car.

———

In Gordes, Ollie wants to visit the castle. I know this about him, how he doesn't believe in going somewhere new without ticking off something on the list of top things to do. In the Berkshires, we went to some obscure concert at Tanglewood. It was fun—when you're with the right person you could make fun out of sitting in a cardboard box—but I could have opted for a romantic dinner in town instead. In Gordes, I would have been content to wander the cobblestone streets, but no. First to the castle.

I've been before, but I like seeing things anew through Ollie's eyes. After a quick wander, we head over to the antiques market that's operating specially for today.

"Let's pick stuff out to decorate our place!" I suggest.

"Our place?" he asks hesitantly.

"We can pretend it's for our place." I find myself bristling, and try to calm. "I know we haven't exactly decided things," I say, even though after the Berkshires, I thought we had indeed decided things.

He nods but still looks unsure.

"I can always use the stuff for the inn."

He brightens. "Okay!"

We both like antiques markets. Antique things. It's how I decorated the inn. Antiques have a story; that's why I'm drawn to them. I don't necessarily know the particular background of, say, my copper dog-shaped salt and pepper shakers, but I can imagine it, and then so it is. I tell guests that the shakers belonged to one of the Louis's.

That always garners a laugh. It's not true, but what is truth? Malleable. Something that once was not, but then manifests. Maybe it *was* one of the Louis's! Anyway, antiques give character to things, patina. Whereas Darcy's apartment (with Ollie, yes I know) is beautiful, but modern. She always says clean lines, but in my non-uttered opinion, all that gray and cream and empty shelving is sterile. And it certainly doesn't represent all her feminine, Victorian dresses. But isn't that like all of us? We are made up of so many different parts, different preferences, different memories, different traumas, and thus we become conundrums. Not predictable. Surprising people from left field, at times, with actions or choices that seem contrary to our core persona, but if you look closely, if you look deep, deep, deep, you'll tease out the root.

I'm not sure about Darcy's root for modern, minimalist living, but in any event, Ollie is a maximalist at heart. Take one look at his man-cave-slash-study overflowing with gadgets and trophies from when he was ten, and you'll know.

"Look at the grain on these." Ollie is admiring some olive-wood something or another. It's not even antique. They make them in town. But the childlike glee on his face isn't something I'll spoil.

"Do you need a cheeseboard?" I ask.

He turns it over. "Aren't we shopping for you?"

"Oh yeah." I grin. "I can't resist a good cheeseboard."

We buy the cheeseboard, and the blue and white teacups with two mismatched saucers. Then Ollie has a particularly fraught haggling session for a hefty pair of stone Dobermans.

"They're massive. How will they even fit in the car?"

"They'll look great on your porch."

"You've never been to the inn," I remind him, somewhat icily.

"I've seen pictures."

I nod. That's not what I wanted him to say.

"I'll come, Ar. Of course I'll come. And when I do, these guys will greet me." He surveys them in satisfaction. We've told Pierre we'll be back for them in an hour.

"Okay. Are we done?" Ollie is starting to say yes, but then I spot a spectacular antique champagne bucket. I go over to have a look.

"See, you're into this." He comes behind me and wraps his arms around my waist.

"I'm into this," I confirm. "*Combien?*" I ask the woman in a yellow headscarf.

"*Cinquante,*" she says.

I count out the euros. Perhaps I could bargain, but I don't find the whole back-and-forth game to chip off a couple of euros a satisfying one. Darcy and Ollie are negotiators. Me? I know what I want, and I am willing to pay full price to have it.

"This was fun," I say, as we walk off with my bucket.

"This *was* fun." Ollie smiles down at me. He's taller than me, a lot taller, which is rare for a man, because I am five foot, ten inches. But he is six foot, four inches. Giancarlo is taller than me, too, but just a touch. Ollie sails far above. It's protective, in a way I've never experienced with a man, and didn't think I could. It's like, he's higher up in the atmosphere, scoping things out, ready to swoop down if anything falls from the sky. Without him, I'm on full swooping alert. And I have to admit, it feels nice to let go, to unclench on occasion, and leave the swooping to Ollie. Or maybe it's just nice to believe that he will.

"Hey, want to hear something good?" I ask. We're always telling each other crazy true stories, the crazier the better. "I read . . . can't remember where, but there's this woman who likes to sleep on her stomach, but she doesn't want wrinkles, right?"

"Right." We pass a small alley with a restaurant, where people are having leisurely *prix fixe* lunches. I peer down, to see if I should make any mental notes. *Pâté de fois gras.* Ravioli with prawns. Braised ribs in red wine. Chocolate mousse. Nah, fairly straightforward.

"So what does she do?" I ask Ollie. "Guess?"

His face scrunches in thought. "Gets one of those silk pillows?"

"Nope!"

"Gets Botox?"

I laugh. "Well probably that, too. But nope."

"I give up."

"Hires someone to cut out a circle in her mattress so it's like a massage table. She sleeps with her head right smack in the mattress."

He laughs, a good, hearty laugh, and I feel proud. "That's nutty," he says.

We stop at another vista. God, I forgot how many there are here.

"So different from New York." Ollie presses his hands into the banister, tips himself forward a bit to see down.

"Yeah." I stop at the rail. I don't need to see down.

"I always think . . ." He returns, his back straight again.

"Yeah?"

"Like, you're not getting out your phone to photograph this."

I don't know what he's getting at. "I'm not big with my phone. You know that. And photographing can take away the magic of actually living the moment. I just want to live this moment with you, you know?"

He smiles. He wraps an arm around me. "It's like, she doesn't know if she lives something unless it's online." Oh, I get it now. We're talking about Darcy. "It doesn't mean something unless it's photographed. You live a quieter life."

"Welllll," I say, feeling the desire to defend my friend, however warped the scenario. And to defend myself, and my work ethic. "I have Instagram, too. I work a lot, too."

"You made it, though. Your follower count is insane, Ar. And you spend so much less time on your phone than Darcy."

I feel myself churn with a familiar storm. "I made it," I say coolly, "not just because of Instagram, but because of my cooking workshops. My inn. My books. It took a lot of work, Ollie. A lot of years. I didn't have any help."

He nods. "I admire what you built. You're amazing, Ar. Really, it inspires me, how much you've achieved."

I nod. I need him to acknowledge it, because while I grew up in the chateau, I was the de facto help. This was long before Séraphine and Mamie got together, long before Darcy and I became close. Perhaps those later facts ingratiated me more, gave me a place at the chateau that I never really felt prior. But I worked at the chateau as a kid, doing odd jobs in the evenings and on weekends for Séraphine and Rainier, and I worked two jobs while in culinary school. I earned every last thing that belongs to me.

"You know," I say, "Darcy is building something now. It's very hard to be in the building stage. It's grittier, far more wrenching than where I am now, but it doesn't mean I didn't go through it, too. I was in that stage for many years. There were many moments I didn't think I'd make it. I had boyfriends who didn't understand the late nights, the times I disappeared into the work. You of anyone knows . . ." I stop. It's a delicate subject, the implication that he, too, is still in the building stage, of the musician career he's been trying for his whole life. Darcy never complains when he goes on tour opening for a band, or plays until four in the morning at a venue across town. He is too minor still to call the shots, with anything. She supports him because he loves it. I want him to do the same thing for her because it shows what kind of man he is.

"I know," Ollie finally says bitterly. "I know all about the building stage."

Right. Sometimes I forget momentarily about the male ego, and how gently it must be handled in areas related to career and sexual performance. Change of topic then.

"And by the way, Darcy is on her phone because she has cute kids to photograph," I remind him. I know I am defending her in a way that could detract from myself. There is not infinite pie. There is one pie—the Ollie pie, and he is not divisible. Winner takes all. Still. Sometimes he has a fifties-housewife mentality with Darcy that I find I cannot quietly withstand.

"I'm not talking about pictures of the kids!" He bursts out with that in a way that makes me think he's been sitting with this unspoken grievance. But that's how it is when you are married. Giancarlo and I could write novels about it, I'm sure, each of which would surprise the other. "Darce takes the most inane shots, like thousands of them,"

Ollie says. "Whereas you post pictures of food. It's different. In her captions, she talks about the most intimate things in our family."

Oh. So this is about her last post. I thought it was great that Darcy had gotten so vulnerable on Instagram, but I didn't think how Ollie would feel. He went through the fertility journey, too. He's told me how grueling it was, on them both, how he felt he needed to bury all his feelings to support Darcy, because she was the one getting the injections and operations and enduring two difficult, high-risk pregnancies.

"Do you still love her?" I hear myself asking. Immediately, I wonder if I'm pushing it, if I shouldn't ask a question to which I maybe don't want the answer. He's told me he loves me, but we haven't talked about this most crucial piece. The ranking.

"I love her," Ollie says slowly, "but it's a different love than I feel for you."

That clunks through the sieve of my mind. I open my mouth, but then I shut it. With Giancarlo, I'm used to sparring over everything. We don't need to agree to love; in fact, sometimes a particularly impassioned fight, with poignant arguments on either side, can leave us in some mid-place of agony, a common valley of grudging admirations toward the other's well-formed case, so we nearly forget what we were fighting over in the first instance. That is to say, our differences can unite us, or they could, before our flame whittled down to embers. With Ollie, it's different. He likes harmony. He would rather bury things than study them. He prefers smiles to scathing rebuttals. So now, I'm afraid to ask more. To parse through Ollie's love for me, on the one hand, and his love for Darcy, on the other. I feel a rush of hate, not for Ollie, but toward myself. I may be many things, but I never thought a coward was one of them.

We don't speak for a bit. "Another selfie?" Ollie asks. "You can throw it on Instagram, and I'll even caption it."

He smiles, and I know he's trying. Trying to do what, I'm not exactly sure, but it's some sort of bandage, some glue, piecing us back together.

I shake my head slowly. "This means something." I point to him, then back to me. "I don't need us photographed to know how much it means."

He smiles and is quiet as we walk along, and I wonder if I was wrong. If I need a photo and his caption after all.

We have a saying in French—*avoir un coeur d'artichaut*. Literally it means, to have an artichoke heart. Artichokes have layers, but by the time you peel them back and get to the heart, there are many leaves on your plate that can be given to anyone. The phrase is used to describe people who fall in love often and aren't satisfied in relationships. People who share their affections often.

I really, really hope I haven't fixed the whole of my affections on a man with an artichoke heart.

When Oliver says he loves Darcy but it's a different love, I want to understand. Is it the love that is the way you love your foot, or your arm? Because those things are intractable; they're never coming off. Or is it a driftier love, the love I still have for ex-boyfriends? It's like, I don't love them at all now, I never think of any of them, but if you mention one of their names, I can remember how hard I loved, how big my feelings once were. The memory of the love is still there.

So what is Darcy: the arm, or the memory?

CHAPTER TWENTY-SEVEN

Darcy

The local police station is a stone building off the main boulevard in town, with a typically French green awning and flowerpots brimming with purple bougainvillea. I pull in, already a bundle of nerves, and accidentally burst over a speed bump. Shit. I break hard, too hard, but I'm in a foreign car, Grand-mère's Mercedes in fact, that she hasn't driven in years, but still somehow works perfectly fine.

I glance around. Did Officer Darmanin see me clearly ignore the purple sign with the triangular design of a speed bump? I've already broken a law, in the police parking lot, no less. This doesn't feel like a good omen.

I pull into a spot, kill the ignition, and try to breathe. Breath feels like a stretch right now, though, like something I've forgotten how to do, and will need to enroll in a course to refamiliarize myself.

Why am I even here? Well, just after Arabelle departed to meet my husband, Jade, Vix, and I debated whether we should leave the chateau for the remainder of the investigation, in light of Sylvie's assault and the inherent risk—however seemingly ludicrous—that one of us posed the rest of us danger. But the only option that we identified to solve the issue, given the police's order to remain local, was to each book into a separate hotel in town. But what a shitty option—each of us isolated and alone, and perhaps even more at risk, without the others as a veil of protection. And if we all booked into the *same* hotel, we might as well just remain at the chateau. So all I did was call Officer

Darmanin, with a perfectly reasonable request for an officer to guard the chateau until the murderer is apprehended. There was silence on the other end, and then the clearing of a throat. Unsurprisingly, Officer Darmanin's clearing of her throat sounded like honeybees, not like a hacking woodpecker, à la me. (I know this, because Oliver has used that exact description. I may be small and feminine, but in my sneezes and throat clearing I am unfortunately not.)

"I think you should come in," she said, which took me entirely aback.

"Come in? Why? Do you want to see the other girls, too?"

"Just you," she said. "As soon as possible, *oui*?"

Leaving no doubt that I am not only a suspect, but the prime suspect. Right?

Still, I'm feeling calm, relatively so, as I leave the car and walk the ten steps inside, through the glass door, fully anticipating the interior to match the quaint exterior, perhaps magazines fanned out on side tables, like at the dermatologist. Alas, no such room greets me. The box of a waiting room is as intimidating and sterile as you see in the movies, only they couldn't portray in film how the antiseptic scent overcomes you. It's all I can do to keep down the leftover pasta I ate an hour ago.

I sign in and soon I am escorted down a grim corridor by an unsmiling man with gray hair.

I try to make conversation—*comment ça va?* He ignores me, walks vigorously ahead. I want him to know I am like him, seeking justice—and half French even. Not in any way a criminal. He seems to give two fucks. He seems to assume I am a criminal. *You are in a police station*, I remind myself, *called in for questioning. So what else would he think?*

I am shown to one of those rooms you see in the movies. I know I keep relating back to the movies, but you always think they are overblown, exaggerated. But no. The fluorescent lights are so fierce I half expect to emerge with a burn. Looking too directly at one of the lights is like looking at the sun, perhaps some preliminary sort of torture. I drum my fingers on the metal table that is no doubt fastened to the ground. I register the camera in the upper right corner by the ceiling. They are watching me. I realize I am frowning. Do guilty people frown? I affect a look I think is calm. I even smile. Wait. Do guilty people smile?

Finally, Officer Darmanin walks in, lifting me from this purgatory. Her male colleague is absent—I keep forgetting his name. He has the unforgettable features and manners of someone subservient, although he is older than her. She's young, I think again. Early thirties even, but no wedding ring. She is wearing a black dress and a nice plain belt with a simple gold buckle. It's the kind I always covet, when I see people in their interlocking Gucci's Gs and Grand-mère's voice wafts through my head—*People with money don't need labels, rather something fine and well made.* But I've never had the money to spend on a fine, well-made belt. The cheapo one from Target has had to suffice.

Now, however, I can buy a thousand fine, well-made belts, if I want.

"Do I need a lawyer?" I blurt, realizing I have inadvertently omitted the requisite *bonjour.* In certain parts of France, and with certain people, such a transgression could cause lifelong repercussions.

Officer Darmanin sits and opens a yellow notepad. I strain to see if anything is on it, to clue me in on what is about to go down. Empty. Figures. Up close her forehead is wrinkle-free. Not even those smidgen lines you start to get in your early thirties, that dissipate with a vigorous rub of moisturizer.

"So," Officer Darmanin says.

She hasn't answered my question about the lawyer. Is she evading me? "Do I need a lawyer?" I ask pointedly.

"I shouldn't say so." She meets my eyes. "Probably not at this stage."

I feel myself whither under her gaze. *Probably not.* Not at all reassuring.

"So I am a suspect? Your prime suspect? Because I inherit? I'm not the only one, you know, who benefits from my grandmother's death."

She leans back, relaxed. Her arms cross her chest. "No, but you inherit by far the most. And you are the one with money problems, no?"

I feel myself teeter in the chair. I'd been bouncing back and forth on the front legs unknowingly, and now I realize it when I nearly buckle to the ground. How does she know about my money problems?

I open my mouth to defend myself, but she cuts bluntly in. "Let's just clear a few things up, shall we?" Officer Darmanin leans forward, poises her pen over her pad. "Your grandmother sent invitations to this reunion weekend with your friends, correct?"

That takes me aback. "You looked in our things."

She nods, but doesn't offer an apology. "We have searched the house several times. You are aware of this."

It's one thing to be aware of it theoretically. It's another to imagine foreign hands in my lingerie. In my private notebook that I use to journal both the most banal and deep thoughts I possess. Oh my gosh. Did they look in that notebook?

"Yes, she sent us invitations. She is old-school like that."

"And on yours, she wrote that she wanted to talk to you about her Will."

"Well, yessss." Immediately I apprehend that my s is too drawn out—a guilty person's s.

"And did you?"

"No," I admit. "She was very tired. Now I know she was sick. At dinner, the last . . . at Jade's party, she said we would talk the next day. The next . . ." I feel positively sick.

"I see." Officer Darmanin makes notations in her notepad, but angled away from me, so I can't see.

"You see what exactly?"

She flicks the end of the pen against her chin. "I just see. It's an American expression, no?"

"Oh."

"And your story is . . . you were asleep the entire night? You heard nothing?"

"I've already said that," I say, with more bite than I intended. "It's the truth."

"Mmmm. Now tell me about your friends. Jade, she is Jewish, no?"

"What does that have to do with anything?" I ask, suddenly angry on Jade's behalf at the question that rings of some sort of bias or hate.

"Her last name is Assouline."

"Yes. But why do you ask?"

"I ask, because I understand that Jade's family has a connection to yours."

My heart nearly stops beating. Does she know about the necklace? Does she know about my *part* in the necklace? What else does she know? I pause, thinking how to frame things. Thinking what part of the story to reveal.

"How do you know that?" I finally settle upon.

Officer Darmanin shrugs. "Sources. You know, this town is small. I've heard whispers, far before this case, that a Jewish family was betrayed by your grandmother, left to perish during the war."

My veins feel flooded with ice. How does she know this? How could she possibly know this?

"You're wrong," I finally say. "That's not what happened."

"Why don't you tell me what happened then?"

"I . . . I'm not sure," I finally admit. "I've never discussed it with my grandmother. But I just know it didn't happen as cruelly as you portray it."

"But Jade knew? Jade knew your grandmother was the one who betrayed her father's family? Who sent them to perish at Auschwitz?"

I close my eyes. "Yes," I whisper.

"That's why she studied abroad in Avignon in the first place, to avenge her family? Finding you was just a bonus? That's why she befriended you at school?"

Pain ricochets through me. I'll admit it's always been a bit of a sore point. I know Jade and I have a real relationship—I *know* we do. But some deep-rooted part of me always wonders if our friendship originated in a lie.

"I wouldn't say she was trying to avenge anything," I finally say. "She knew her family had roots here. She knew bits and pieces of her father's painful past. When she saw my family crest, that her dad had sketched out for her many times, and heard my last name, she knew she had to pursue it."

"Pursue what exactly?" Officer Darmanin asks.

"Justice, I suppose," I finally settle upon.

"And could it be that she has finally achieved her aim? With the murder of your grandmother?"

"If you think all this, then why isn't Jade your prime suspect? Why *me*?"

Officer Darmanin leans back in her chair, ticks her pen back and forth between her fingers. "Because if Jade had wanted to murder your grandmother, she had twenty years to do it. Why now? Sure, we could be looking at a crime of passion, or of spontaneous opportunity, but certainly Jade had many opportunities the semester you all studied abroad. And Jade has never made public what your grandmother did. She could have easily done so. Those don't seem the qualities of a woman playing a long game of revenge."

I am quiet. So she doesn't know about the necklace. And she doesn't know about the painting. She doesn't know that Jade has kept quiet all this time for me, to spare my family's reputation, and my grandmother's pride, while she was still alive. Jade has told me the whole story, as much as she knows. And it's indisputable: What Grand-mère did was reprehensible. That's why I helped Jade steal the necklace.

And this elusive Van Gogh painting that Jade claims Van Gogh gave to his favorite nurse at the sanitorium in his last year of life? Supposedly it's an improved *Starry Night*. An even more hypnotic one. And the nurse? Jade's great-great-grandmother.

It's hard to know what is truth and lore. I've never seen this painting, but if it exists, I've promised it to Jade at my grandmother's death.

I could tell all this to Officer Darmanin, but parts would implicate me. And beyond that, even though I am a prime suspect, I'm not about to throw my best friend under the bus merely to spare myself.

"And Vix?" I ask. I wonder if it is clear, how much I want to change the subject. "What about Vix, who in a shocking turn of events inherits five million euros from my grandmother?"

I realize I am now throwing Vix under the bus a bit, to disentangle from this conversation about Jade. But I'm not saying anything about Vix the officer doesn't already know.

"We don't find Victoria to have much of a compelling reason for murder," the officer says.

"Five million euros aren't compelling enough?"

"Not when your grandmother has been giving her five thousand euros every month for twenty years."

I hear myself gasp.

"You didn't know. I wondered if you knew."

"Say that again?" I whisper.

"You heard right," she says, with even some sympathy. "Neither of them ever told you?"

"No," I say, my voice steely. I think of all my money troubles, all the times I wanted to ask Grand-mère for help, but resisted out of pride. Ten thousand euros. That's what she gave me, outside of my study abroad semester, my wedding gift, and birthday and Christmas gifts. I never thought she wasn't generous. She was! But I can't help now but compare it all with what Grand-mère gave her precious Victoria . . . *her precious Victoria.* . . .

It's too much. It's all too much.

No wonder. So many things now slot into place. How Vix creates three paintings a year—three nice paintings, I'll give her that. She is often able to sell each for a good amount, six or seven thousand dollars, maybe. But no one lives in Manhattan on twenty thousand dollars a year, unless they have a wealthy benefactor. I used to think Vix must have done odd jobs, or maybe she was supported in part by her girlfriends. Maybe even she had some wealthy great-uncle who left her an inheritance, but didn't want to cop to not being entirely self-sustained. It's not polite to talk about money; I of anyone have adopted this maxim. Yes, sometimes I think it a bit indulgent, how much time in her day Vix allots for creative meanderings, as she calls it. As far as I have understood, the times I've joined, creative meanderings means shopping through the West Village, lunching at the best places on Greenwich, and occasionally sketching something in a notebook. There has seemed little time devoted to actual painting.

Who am I to comment on her work habits, though? I thought she'd created a life that worked for her, that supported her. Not everyone needs to strive for billionaire status. Vix's is a life that has seemed to include little work, but I thought I was just jealous. Little did I know she could indulge little work because my grandmother was supporting her.

Why? It feels entirely self-pitying, resentful, to ask, but *why*? Why didn't Grand-mère support me, her actual grandchild?

"I'm curious though," says Officer Darmanin. "Do you know what she brought all those supplies for?"

"What supplies?" I ask, still reeling. I now remember Vix's massive suitcase that she claimed had clothes inside.

"So you don't know," the officer says. "And you are sure you are best friends, the four of you?" I bristle at her accusation, but I have to admit, I understand the sentiment behind it.

"We are, but everyone has secrets," I say quietly. "Even from ourselves."

"You wouldn't call Arabelle your best friend any longer, would you?" The officer doesn't say it cruelly, more out of curiosity.

"No. That would be a definitive no. But you didn't answer my question. What supplies did Vix bring?"

"Painting supplies. A lot of them."

"Well, she is an artist. . . ."

"I should rephrase. Not painting supplies to paint something, but rather supplies that would more likely be used to restore something."

My mind goes topsy-turvy at that. "Like . . . a painting that was damaged?"

"Maybe. In any event, it probably doesn't have to do with the case."

Right. Or does it? Fear prickles the back of my neck, or maybe it's the heavy blast of air-conditioning from the wall unit directly behind me. I wonder if they've done studies—the exact degree of freezing to catapult a suspect into a confession. I sit with it all in quiet. It can't be a coincidence, the missing Van Gogh and the restoration supplies? They could be for a painting that was covered over. . . . I think about Vix's meeting with Grand-mère, the one that supposedly never happened. Is this what it was meant to be about?

My mind is garbage soup. I can't reconcile any of it.

"And Arabelle?" I finally ask in a quiet voice. "Any secrets there? Besides fucking my husband?" I feel immediately ashamed at my vulgar language. But is there a more polite, flowery descriptor that I am obligated to use? At this juncture, let's just call a spade a spade.

"No. Not that I know of." The officer shrugs. "She has a solid alibi, unlike the rest of you. No motive. And she stands to inherit nothing. Besides, she is very wealthy."

Yes. I know how wealthy she is. Self-made. Successful. Beautiful.

"Well, then. If you aren't holding me, I'll go." I stand but my legs wobble, buckle. I lower myself back down, embarrassed. But it would be more embarrassing to collapse.

"You're free to go." Officer Darmanin regards me not in a cruel way. I don't get the sense she is taking pleasure in my pain. She is neutral, like a camel coat. But she thinks I did it.

"And about the guard? Someone to protect us?" I ask, although I can already tell it's futile.

Her shoulders budge upward. Her lips curve into an almost apologetic smile. "We think the murderer has achieved his aim. The note has been stolen. There shouldn't be any further . . . what do you Americans call them? Shenanigans."

Shenanigans. It sounds almost like she is making a joke of my grandmother's murder. Of the collapse of my life. Of the unraveling of my friendships, my marriage. I know she didn't intentionally use a word to trivialize these things. She simply doesn't know the specific tone of the word she selected. We make little errors like this, when we speak a language that is not our mother tongue.

Still, I find irrational hatred bubble up in me, toward this beautiful, seemingly perfect officer, whose grandmother wasn't just murdered, whose husband didn't betray her in the worst way, whose life isn't in shambles.

"I'll show myself out," I say, and hurry past her without an *au revoir*.

CHAPTER TWENTY-EIGHT

Vix

I find Darcy on the lawn beyond the terrace, lying atop a Turkish towel, her legs vertical resting against a tree trunk. I plop onto the grass beside her.

"If you focus on a cloud, you can watch it change," she says without looking at me. "Did you know that?"

"What are you doing out here, Darce?"

She doesn't answer, so I follow her gaze up to the piercing blue sky smattered in clouds. Clouds that have been immortalized by iconic artists who painted this part of the world into life. Into history. Perhaps from this very vantage point.

"But really," she says, "have you ever noticed that clouds are always slightly moving?"

"Um. Well, it's not the same sky every day, so I guess that makes sense."

"But like, have you ever watched the clouds move?" She sounds manic. I wonder if she is losing it. I mean, I am, too. But not in a cloud-obsessing way.

"Come watch the clouds with me, Vixen. Oh, I forget, I'm not supposed to call you that."

Is it just me, or did her tone have an edge? "You can call me Vixen. I don't know why you guys think you can't call me that."

"Oh?" Darcy turns to me with an unreadable expression. Her

210

strawberry hair is wild, frizzy, the opposite of its typical glossy and tamed. "It's fascinating, isn't it? What they do."

"What *what* do?"

"The clouds." She sounds exasperated. "They're utterly fascinating."

I stare at the sky again, but then avert my eyes. Strange the things that can make me feel inadequate, but here I go again, thinking of all the great artists who have spun genius out of these ordinary feats of nature. "I have Netflix to fascinate me." I try another tactic. "Do you know a murderer is on the loose?"

Darcy laughs, a startling, unhinged sound. "Oh yes, I've heard. But here's a riddle for ya. What if the murderer is you? What if it's me?"

I don't quite have an answer for that.

"Being outside is safer," she adds. "More places to run."

"More places for the murderer to hide," I say.

Silence, then: "You're distracting me. I'm missing stuff my cloud is doing."

"You're a nut. But a nut whom I love." I'm clearly not going to get anywhere with her right now. Not that I'm even sure where I want to get. "I'm gonna get a move on."

"Places to go? Places to be?"

I smile. "Look, when you're done communing with your cloud, lock yourself in your room, okay?"

"In case the murderer gets me." Darcy laughs her psychotic laugh again. I half expect her to stick a flashlight up her chin at a campfire and regale me with some ghost story.

"In case your clouds mess up your brain, which I think has already happened."

At that, she springs up to a seat, her face suddenly solemn. I find myself retreating backward on the grass, crab style. Her face is more than solemn, I realize. It's angry.

"Vix, when were you going to tell me that my grandmother has been giving you money every month since we were kids?"

Oh, shit.

"Who told you?" I ask quietly. "Jade?"

"*Jade* knew?"

Fucking idiot, Vix.

"I'm sorry. Darce, I'm so sorry. I wanted to tell you, so many times I did, but Séraphine asked me not to."

"Right. *My* grandmother asked you not to. That's my grandmother, Vix. And I knew nothing. Nothing about her. Nothing about any of you, it seems."

Darcy shifts to a cross-legged seat in the grass. She doesn't look at me, just digs up a clump of grass, then watches it sprinkle through her fingers.

"You know how much she loved you," I say quietly.

"Oh, really? Do I?"

We sit in excruciating silence for a while. I think about all the things I need to tell her, but all the missing pieces. Will it make things harder for her if I admit the truth? What even *is* the truth?

"The police told me about your painting supplies, too."

My breath catches, leaps, falls. "You spoke to them?" I ask carefully. *Do not admit, or deny,* just pops into my brain.

"I went to the station. I'm their prime suspect." A weird smile crosses Darcy's face. "Can you imagine it?"

I shake my head, watching a flock of birds taking flight in their coordinated *V*. I really can't imagine it. This whole week has spiraled so unbelievably.

"What are you doing with a suitcase of painting supplies?" Darcy asks. "Restoration supplies, is what the officer informed me. Does this have anything to do with the Van Gogh?"

My head whips back toward her. "How do you know about the Van Gogh?"

She tips her head at me curiously. "Have you spoken to Jade?"

"No." I shake my head slowly. Again I remember how Jade and I came across each other, in Séraphine's room, right after the murder. "But I did tell Jade I'd go with her to the sanitorium tomorrow morning. You know, where Van Gogh painted his most famous paintings in the last year of his life?"

"I know about the sanitorium."

"Right." So Jade has something to do with this painting? I said I'd join her for my own reasons, but now I'm curious. More than curious. "Well . . . do you want to come with us?"

"Come with you to the sanitorium?" Darcy is still weeding up grass with vigor. "No. I'll pass."

"Okay." I take a deep breath. "Well, listen, after the sanitorium tomorrow, I'll tell you everything you want to know. I just need to gather my thoughts. Try to piece things together."

"You and me both, *sister*." The way she says it feels laced with irony. Like we once were sisters, our bonds iron-clad, and now we are something else entirely. But we *need* to be sisters, still. I need it, at least. The rest of them have partners, children. I have my parents, but no one else I truly care about but them. And if I don't have them anymore, then who am I, really, in this world?

"Maybe you want to see Mila and Chase tomorrow morning?" I finally ask, pushing down my distress. "Maybe seeing the kids will help things?"

"No." She says it decisively, but oozing pain. "I don't want them to see me like this."

I look at my friend, properly. She's come totally undone—from the strap of her dress dangling off her shoulder to the grass in her hair and smudge of mud on her cheek.

"I'm worried about you," I finally say.

"Well, don't be. I'm a warrior." I can't tell by her toneless voice if she means it facetiously, or not.

"Right." I summon some wisdom, something, but my well of wisdom, if it ever existed, feels very utterly dry. "This will pass, Darce. Somehow this will pass, and things will make sense again."

"Maybe," she says, "or maybe things will never make sense again."

She's right. It's something I had to face when I was told I had breast cancer. It could have gone either way. It still could, really. The future is always opaque.

"I asked the police for protection, you know? They said no."

"Protection?"

"Someone to guard this house. There is a murderer on the loose. A murderer among us, I should say."

"Not on the loose," I say. "It's that guy. The groundskeeper. It has to be him. Raph, right? I wonder where he went after the police released him."

"Where he went?" Darcy looks puzzled. She seems totally out of it. "Well, here, of course. I saw him go back to his cabin just a little bit ago."

"You let a *murderer* back on the property?" My mouth hangs agape. Has she completely lost it?

"He didn't bash Sylvie on the head," Darcy says. "So he can't be the murderer."

"Maybe someone wanted the note for a different reason, though! What about the paper with his initial in Séraphine's bed? How can you dismiss that evidence?"

Darcy shrugs. "I don't think he did it. Not anymore. Things are always connected. It feels totally unlikely that two different people, for two different reasons, attacked my grandmother and Sylvie. Anyway, don't worry. I'll talk to him. See what my instincts are." She says it decisively, like her instincts are a superior source of wisdom than the rest of our instincts.

"Our instincts have been terrible, Darce. Did our instincts point to Séraphine's murder, or to Sylvie's assault?"

Darcy is quiet.

"You just feel better with a man on the property," I finally say.

"Maybe I do! Maybe I don't know if I can trust my friends anymore. So maybe it's not so crazy to trust a stranger instead."

"You're telling me that you trust . . . the groundskeeper over *me*?"

"Maybe I do," she says defensively, and I regret pushing it. Darcy is a Taurus through and through. Stubborn like hell, in unexpected ways. Sometimes she wants something just because you don't want her to get it.

I get up. I can't listen to this anymore. "I'm going inside," I say quietly.

Darcy waves a hand dismissively. She doesn't look up, just mumbles something that I'm not quite sure are words.

I hurry across the lawn, even though I'm not sure what I'm hurrying away from, or to. Truth is, I have my own things to cope with, a queue to my brain. There's the cancer, and my creative blocks, and the murder, and Sylvie's assault, and the painting, and my meeting with Séraphine that never was. My brain is taxed. Fried. Spent. It needs a couple weeks on a beach in the Maldives to recoup.

And worst of all, there is one thing that has jumped the queue. That occupies most of my attention.

Last night, I sent Juliet a text. First, I wrote, *I need you.* But then I deleted that and substituted, *I miss you.*

It's early afternoon in New York, and still no response.

Take that, brain. Figure that out, brain.

Suddenly it whooshes at me, how her hair always smelled like watermelon. Juliet has thin, fluffy blond hair, the type you typically find in women half a century older. We used to joke about that, how her hair was one part senior citizen, one part six-year-old. Her shampoo bottle was smattered in watermelon wedges, and I was always teasing her about the globs of pink goo around the shower.

I hear a sob burst out in the wind, and it takes a beat before I realize it came from me.

CHAPTER TWENTY-NINE

Raph

It is difficult to know what to do when you are a suspect in a murder. Hide in your cabin to avoid the judgments? Or walk around like you belong, as if you've done nothing wrong?

I choose the latter, and it is on my return to Chateau du Platane after that brief, unpleasant stay in custody, on my walk around my grounds—what used to be my grounds—that I come upon the new madame of the chateau. She is quite unlike the prior madame, in that she is lying on her back in the grass with her feet vertical in the air, resting against a tree. Her red hair is wild in the wind, punctured by short grass clippings from when I cut it (quite terribly) a few days prior.

The day is coming to a close; the sun is on its exit, remarkable or unremarkable, depending on whether you're one of those people who go wild over a sunset. I am a person who finds the sunset unremarkable. Perhaps I sound like a cold person to say so. How dare I not whip myself into a frenzy over the clouds, the sky, the purples, the reds? To this I reply: I have seen many sunsets. If I am granted the chance, I will see many again. I make it a point, to pay attention to these things, to the natural world. So many people escape to their screens; they might as well climb right into their devices for that is where their attention lies. For them, sunsets are relegated to vacations, used as backdrops for photoshoots. I am an outdoorsman; when I was not on a job, in my previous career, my day would spurt alive at sunrise, wind down at sunset. We are meant to live to the rhythm of the world. This is what I think. If you ask my prior employer, she would have said I am a go-with-the-flow person. Chill. Easy. I am indeed those things. (Although she would not say so anymore.) But sometimes, when you are an easy person, there are a few things you aren't easy about, that you discover you are in fact quite rigid in insisting upon. For this you might be labeled archaic. Backward.

Dangerous.

Is it dangerous to want my twins to feel sun on their skin? To toddle barefoot across the grass? To see their mother or their father in bottle feedings at dusk, instead of a night nurse? Their mother favors designer baby sunglasses and impossibly soft leather baby shoes. And night nurses.

How did I land again on the subject of her?

I shake my head, hovering over Darcy, my shadow long behind me. Her eyes are closed. She looks shockingly still, like a painting.

Or a dead person.

I have an urge to dive down, to verify that she is alive. Her chest moves with her breath. I find mine once again.

She is very small, and I feel my heart quickening at the sight of her, so plainly vulnerable. Perhaps it explains why I went into the career I did, but I have always felt strongly about protecting those with the piddliest shields. There is an instinct so deep in me that only my children have awakened it of late. I thought it had gone, in regards to women, and now I realize it has not.

I am unique, everything about me, including my instincts. I've known this since I was a young child. Perhaps most people think they are unique, but I've always felt like an outsider. I've always preferred simplicity, and thought many trappings of this new century to be easily discarded because of their needless complication. But all these guidelines are nice in theory. It's only when your life becomes complicated that you understand you don't always have control to steer things back to simple.

It's been nice, to be a groundskeeper for a little while. I could pretend things were as simple as I prefer them.

"Um, hello?" Sleeping Beauty has awoken. She comes to a seat. I wonder—am curious, to tell the truth—if she is going to banish me from here.

"*Bonsoir.*"

She cocks her chin, stares at me, says nothing more. I shift uncomfortably. I am at home in silence, but only when the silence is peaceful. Hers doesn't feel peaceful; it is concealing little darts. To bide the silence, I stare defiantly into those green eyes.

Mine are blue, so I am used to the compliments, as I'm sure she is, as well. Conventional wisdom says that light eyes are prettier, but I've always preferred brown on a woman. There is something heartier about brown eyes, more earthy. More genuine. But somehow, I am turned on my head; her green eyes are shockingly delightful. It's funny how the mere sight of a person's eyes can remind you that your convictions are ever-changing.

"Back from the slammer?" she finally asks.

I can't help it, I spurt out laughing. "The slammer. That's good."

She smiles, too. "Hot shower yet?"

"Two. Once, and then straight back in again."

Her smile fades. "But you're okay?"

It takes a moment for me to formulate a response, to contend with her care, however minute. I didn't expect this. I know that a horrible assault took place this afternoon on Sylvie, which helped facilitate my release. I am still trying to piece that together. But nonetheless, the note in the bed implicates me. If I didn't do it, then one of the girls did. Right? So why is Darcy being kind to me? Surely, she would rather pin me as the murderer, instead of one of her friends.

Unless she did it and knows it couldn't be me.

"I'm okay," I say carefully. "One day in jail won't break me. You can trust that."

She nods. "You seem like you're made of sturdy stock."

Sturdy stock? I'm not sure exactly what that means, but I get the gist. "How are you doing?" I realize it's a loaded question, and I'm not sure if I'm asking about her grandmother, or Sylvie, or her husband and Arabelle.

"Oh." I'm surprised at how she takes me into her gaze. Doesn't fidget. "I'm pretty shit." She squeals. "I've always wanted to say that! It's the Brits' expression, isn't it?"

For a moment, I fumble with what to say. I feel myself blushing, as the gap between her exclamation and my response balloons. I know exactly how I feel—it's a swirling purple gust of emotion that storms me, on her behalf, on every level. But what words describe such a thing? Eventually, I manage, "I'm really sorry."

To my surprise, she seems to get the enormity of what I mean. "Thanks. My grandmother is dead. Murdered. Brutally so. I still can't process that. And, my best friend is with my husband."

"Your best friend is with your husband, as in, *officially*?" I ask.

"Well, they aren't exactly with . . . I mean, he said . . ." She hangs her head. "Who the fuck knows. But they're together now. Off making out in lavender fields probably."

I nod. The purple ballooning thing returns to my stomach.

"I'm not sure if I'm just messed up, about my grandmother," she says, "or about everything. But you just asked how I am, and yes, I'm shit, but also, at the same time, it's like there's a little crack. A tiny—minuscule, really—crack in the window where there's some light and . . ."

I'm having a hard time keeping up with this conversation, but I find myself really wanting to keep up. A tiny crack? What does it mean? Why do women love to speak in metaphors? "And?"

"And there's a crack," she says, stronger now. "It's like . . . even if they're together, Arabelle and my husband, like, officially. Like, forever." She closes her eyes tightly, then flutters them open. God, so green. So very green. "Even if they ride off into the sunset, it will be fucking painful, *really* fucking painful, but I'm not sure anymore that she took everything from me."

"Oh." I nod. I get it.

"Fuck it." She laughs again, and it deflates my balloon. She has a really cute laugh, not too high-pitched, which was Margaret's problem. (One of them.)

"I thought it was Jade, you know?" she says.

Jade? Oh, yes. The girl who wears all those athletic outfits with straps. I don't know what Darcy is getting at. But I nod.

"I wanted to make her pay." Darcy's jaw tightens. "I thought she took everything from me."

Oh. I think I follow now. "You thought it was your friend Jade who was . . . with your husband?"

She nods. "I heard him telling someone he loved my best friend."
Merde. Bastard.

"And I found a scrunchie in his pocket."

"A scrunchie?"

"For ponytails." She motions to her hair.

"*Merde.*"

"I just . . . I wanted revenge."

I nod. I know that feeling well. But I don't know what she's getting at. "So you did something?" I guess.

She nods. "I did something. Something childish and dumb. I started this Instagram account, a private one. Oh, I can't believe I'm telling you this."

I'm very intrigued. "You started an account? Like, to do what?"

"I posted private pictures from this week, with threatening sayings. And I tagged all my friends. Tagged myself, too, as a decoy."

I process this. It rings a bell—something the girls were talking about in the car when I drove them into Saint-Rémy a few days ago. "What kind of threatening sayings?"

She reddens. "Like, *You won't get away with this. The truth will come out.* When I look back on it, it's severely dumb. I was just trying to make Jade scared. I was trying to expose her in a humiliating way. I knew the threatening fake account thing was relatively minor revenge, but I was just so angry. And I wanted to make sure it really *was* Jade, get her to confess. Or at least allow me to endure a weeklong vacation with her. I knew we'd have to have it out in a real way after the trip, but I was trying to communicate that she wasn't going to get away with it, that I was going to fight for my family. And then it turns out it was actually Arabelle, and it all came out sideways. . . ." She hangs her head. "You probably find me really pathetic."

"I don't."

She raises her head slightly. A front piece of her hair hangs over one eye. I feel an urge to brush it off her face.

"You don't?" she asks in a very small voice.

"No. I understand the want for revenge."

"Oh," she says, inching back, and I realize how that sounded.

"Not against your grandmother, nothing like that," I say quickly.

"Okay," she nods, but by her expression, I can tell she's now skeptical, that the trust we've built this afternoon is quickly disintegrating.

"I have two kids," I say. "Like you, but twins. A boy and a girl."

"Okay. . . ." She nods, but still with that dubious look to her.

"What I said about revenge, it's just . . . okay, in a prior life, I wasn't a groundskeeper."

"No shit, Sherlock!" She laughs.

"Shit . . . Sherlock?"

"After the whole cherry thing, I didn't really think you were an expert groundskeeper."

"Oh." I smile. "Right."

"My grandmother knew?" she asks.

"Your grandmother knew. Your grandmother was . . ." I take a deep breath. "A wonderful person. She saved me, you know?"

"Saved you? How?"

I pause. Am I really going to tell her everything? Or am I going to edit it, make it more palatable?

"See, I've always worked in security."

"Like protecting people?"

"Yes."

"With a gun?"

"Yes."

"Oh."

She nods, and I can't read the nod, can't see into which filing cabinets her brain is now slotting things. I debate not continuing, but something prompts me to forge on.

"I worked my way up, and eventually, when I had enough experience, your grandmother helped me get in with more high-level placements. Séraphine and my grandmother were friends in their girlhood, and Séraphine connected me to some prestigious employers where I'd be better paid. Diplomats, tech moguls, movie stars. And people with titles before their names. The cream of society. Three years ago, I took a job to protect Baroness Margaret von Uckerman of Denmark."

"A . . . real baroness?"

"Yes. From a noble, old-money Danish family. I was the head of her security detail."

"Hmm. Okay." She nods. But she doesn't see, not yet.

"I did something . . . dumb. Something . . . regrettable."

Her brow furrows. "Someone attacked her? And you missed?"

"No! Of course not." I find myself bristling at that inference. "I never miss. If I shoot, I never miss."

"Oh." She nods, scoots back from me again, and I realize how that sounded. *Merde.* This is a convoluted conversation.

"I didn't kill your grandmother," I say, but I hear it come off defensively.

"Okay."

"What I meant to say is, the regrettable action I took was . . . I became . . . I suppose you could say, entangled with her."

"Entangled . . . with the baroness?"

"Yes." I hope she will spare me further inquiry.

"Sex?"

"Yes."

"Oh." I can feel those green eyes on me, judging me.

"She wasn't married, or attached. Not to anyone. Still, you never get involved with the person you are protecting. That's a pillar of my work. I know this. And yet . . ."

"And yet you did." She doesn't say it meanly.

"Yes." I feel the familiar shame barrel at me. That in the end, I succumbed to the most basic of impulses.

"And . . . the baroness got pregnant?"

"Yes." I crunch down on my lip. "Her family was . . ."

"Upset about the development?"

"Upset is an understatement. In their eyes, I was swine. The lowest of the low. Their daughter was meant for royalty. Someone important. Not the poor nobody protecting her. I was supposed to be neither seen, nor heard. And now my DNA was raining down on them."

"Right. That sounds . . . horrible. So what happened? You said you have twins, so she had them, and then what?"

"Well, before she had them, she got engaged to a minor count. Of Liechtenstein. Loads of family money. A reformed playboy. That's not my description. It's what he calls himself."

"Oof." She grimaces. "That says everything, doesn't it?"

I have to restrain myself from going off on more tangents. I've been told by longtime friends that for the past couple of years, I've had the bad habit of arriving to drinks and monopolizing the conversation with a long list of complaints as to the count's lesser qualities. By which I mean, *all* of his qualities.

"It does say everything," I finally settle upon. "Without going into detail, he's really a vile person."

"Oh no." Her face shades, and I can see she now comprehends. "They decided the children would be his. The public would think they were born of their marriage?"

I wonder if she's seen the gossip rags. If she's put it together, with the headlines about their speedy marriage and the unending cuteness of *my* children.

"That they did," I say, hearing the bitterness that I've been unable to excise from my voice. "Because we weren't married, and because she is akin to Danish royalty, they prevented a DNA test for over a year. The count's name is on the birth certificate. I needed money to fight them. They have an army of lawyers, endless funds. Like I said, our grandmothers were once friends. On her deathbed, my grandmother told me that if I ever was stuck, if I ever needed anything, to come see Séraphine. My parents are wonderful, but they don't have the funds or connections to help. I felt lost, without any options. I wasn't going to let my children be taken from me. But I spoke to a lawyer—"

"You needed money."

"Lots of it," I say. "To fight their huge legal team. And when the story spread in certain security circles, I was a pariah. No one would hire me for the job for which I've been trained."

"Wow . . ."

I can see her process it. I feel myself blush, at the money I've been left in the Will, that I only just discovered today. The fact of it makes me feel like a leech, like the opposite of a man, who considers at the core of his desires the need to provide for himself and his children.

"I didn't know your grandmother left me money in her Will," I say. "I need you to know that. She gave me the groundskeeper position, yes, so that I could work for funds. She did advance me some money upfront, so I could fight Margaret and the count for access to my children. But I've been working it all off. We're in the midst of a court case. I've only met them once, you know. My children."

"Once? That's . . . that's just . . . inconceivable."

"With supervision. I've never even been alone with my children, Darcy." My voice has fallen to a whisper.

"God. I'm so sorry."

"Thanks." I nod.

We fall into a silence that is horrible, excruciating, but then, when it settles, strangely peaceful. I've told no one this story, other than my closest friends.

Darcy breaks the silence first. "We're really a bleak pair, huh?"

I don't know the word *bleak,* but I can guess what it means.

"Your turn now, to unload your misery." I feel my lips curve up.

"Oh, sure. I got misery in spades." She grins. "You know my revenge account on Instagram?"

"Yeah." I try to gather myself back, all the pieces of me that dispersed when I told my story.

"Well, it's just an illustration of how much I suck at Instagram."

"What do you mean?"

"No one even followed me! None of my friends whom I was trying to alarm. Like, I tried to do this great revenge thing, and it barely gave a blip. It's like The Fertility Warrior."

I don't know what The Fertility Warrior is, but I don't dare ask. She shoves her phone before my eyes. "Look."

I do look at her account. @imwatchingyou88. She is following four people, the four girls, including herself, and no one is following her. Well, that makes sense.

"Let me get this straight." I think of how to put it delicately. "You're upset no one is following your creepy account?"

"Not upset." She laughs. "It's just a metaphor."

"*Pfff.*"

"What?" She half laughs, her brows up, like little half triangles.

"Talking to you is sometimes what I imagine law entrance exams to be like." I'm not sure if I'll offend her. Sometimes I unintentionally do, with my honesty.

But she guffaws, and I find myself smiling.

"I'm not the lightest of people on the best of days, and you haven't caught me on my best," she admits.

"Well, I'll follow you," I say.

I pull up my own neglected Instagram on my ancient phone that I've been chided is only a tiny step up from the old flip phones.

"You'll follow me?"

"On your creepy account," I explain, typing into the search icon in the app. "I'll be your first follower."

"The account is over though," she says. "No more revenge. I don't even know what revenge exactly I was contemplating. Exposing Jade, I guess. Making her pay. It was a flop."

"Still, check your follows."

She smiles. Which was my goal. "Okay," she grumbles, but I can tell she's pleased. "My only follower in the past week, on either account."

"You're exaggerating," I say, which seems to be the right thing to say, even though I don't really get all the Instagram intricacies. I do, however, clock that my ten followers have now turned to eleven.

"Hardly."

She puts her phone back in the pocket of her dress. I'm surprised; I didn't realize dresses could have pockets. That seems like a nice invention, the kind my buddies and I would discuss over drinks, trying to come up with our moneymaker.

"But when the cops ask us to explain this account," Darcy says, "which they inevitably will, you do the explaining as to why you're following it."

"Sure. I survived their brutal interrogation, so I can survive a bit more."

"Was it brutal?" she asks, looking sincerely concerned, which touches me.

"No." I laugh. "It wasn't. And I'm innocent," I feel the need to clarify.

She nods. Her face falls serious. "So . . ."

"So. It's dark. We should go. There is a murderer somewhere, after all."

Her lips set together in a grim line. "I keep pushing that out of my mind. It's too outlandish to be real, when you cue up the short list of suspects. I have to admit, I feel a little safer knowing that you were in security. In defense. You have a key to the chateau, I'm assuming?"

I nod. I wonder if she's going to ask me to give it back.

"That makes me feel safer," she says, to which I feel relief.

"Good. Well, you have my number, and my Instagram name now, too. If something happens, if you're at all scared, I'm a quick sprint away."

"You're a fast sprinter?" Her eyes go to my legs, then look away quickly.

I pretend I didn't see. "I came in second in a grade four school race."

"Oh, great. Now I feel a lot better, thanks." But she is smiling. I am, too, I realize.

"Okay." She stands and brushes grass remnants off her arms, her legs.

"Your hair, too." I point.

"Oh." She blushes. "Okay, well good night."

"Good night."

She steps toward me like she might hug me goodbye, and then seems to think better of it. Instead, she walks hurriedly away and doesn't look back.

I watch her go, thinking, thinking, an awful lot. I'm thinking about trust, and how strange a thing that is. I told her my story and she believed it. It's funny how humans are, always wanting to believe the best. After all the lies she's been told, and the evidence against me, and my placement in her grandmother's last Will, her better judgment might compel her to oust me from this property. Instead she has let me keep my key, has made herself vulnerable to me.

Well, for the most part I've told her the truth. Some lies though— the worst kinds, often—aren't overt ones, but lies of omission. I didn't tell her where I went right after I was released from jail, before coming here. And she didn't ask.

But if she had, I wouldn't have told her. Because where I went was to retrieve my gun.

CHAPTER THIRTY

Arabelle

We stop at a small gelato stand in Gordes, and Ollie says, "Ice cream?" I nod. We wait for a couple with four children to pass. I get vanilla, which Ollie jokes is boring for a foodie. He gets some multiple-scoop concoction that is very American, although I don't say so. We make our way through an ancient gateway, over to a little square beside an imposing citadel-like church. Ollie plops down on a stone ledge encircling bushes of pink flowers. I lower down to sit beside him. As he eats his ice cream ravenously, I just stare at mine, melting in the still potent sun. I want to hug him, feel his arms around me tightly, locking me in place. But I don't know what I'm allowed anymore. Hugs used to pass so freely between us. I wonder if this is how Darcy felt, always wanting to pull him in closer as he slips away.

But where is he slipping to? Back to his wife? To his children? I'm not going to take him away from his children. My parents were stolen from me. I would never do that to Mila and Chase.

Maybe Ollie liked the secrecy of us, whereas I didn't. From the start, I longed for it to be more than just a little affair. Even though it's painful to admit, given my relationship with Darcy, I wanted me and Ollie to be everything. Maybe it's only when you register someone who feels like home that you realize how the home you've been living in has a crumbling foundation.

"So this groundskeeper," Ollie says. "Are the police any closer to charges?"

"Ah." I lick my ice cream, then in a split-second decision, toss it in the garbage.

"You had so much left!"

"I was done. I really only wanted a bite." I squelch a smile. Americans think just because they paid for it, it needs to land in their stomach.

Ollie shakes his head, like he doesn't get it. "Raph," he says, with a mouthful. "Isn't that the guy's name? What's going on with him?"

I pause. I should tell him about what's happened to Mamie. But somehow I can't force it out. It's too painful, too incomprehensible. It's a cloud hovering over me, and I know if I tell him, he'll wonder why I didn't sooner, and it will be a cloud hanging over us both. He'll find out eventually. I don't want to spoil the time we have left.

"I don't think they have enough evidence to hold Raph longer," I finally say.

Ollie shakes his head. "Imbecile cops."

"Yes . . ."

"I just . . . it feels like everything is insane right now."

"I know." I squeeze his hand, the one he's not licking of fallen ice cream. He squeezes back.

"We have a good alibi, the two of us," he says, a bit wickedly, and he smiles, which makes my heart surge.

Oh, how did this happen? I like him too much for my own good. I shake my head.

"Hey, Ol, what do you think. . . ." I retract my hand, twist it with my other one.

"About what?"

"There's a hotel I've stayed at, just across town. La Bastide de Gordes. We could . . . get a room? Just for a few hours?" I feel myself holding my breath. I don't need sex; he has to know that. I just want him to hold me, really hold me.

"You're tired?" He clearly doesn't get it.

"No. I just want to be together. Just hold each other," I clarify. "Decompress."

I see it immediately on his face. "Ar, no." He shakes his head. "I need to get back to the kids."

"Of course." I look away. What am I doing? Who have I become? The other woman. I can't be the other woman. No. Not anymore. "I'll take you back."

He doesn't meet my eyes. "I think that would be best."

At once, like a curtain closing at the end of a play, the sun slides beneath the horizon, drowning us in shadows. We don't look at each other, but we also don't go. There is still a thread between us, however frayed.

Suddenly a heron swoops down, landing on the ledge an inch from Ollie's arm.

"Oh my! Oh, hello!" Ollie's eyes are sparkling anew, in awe of this snowy white creature with green feet and green eyes. The heron is less common here, in Provence, where it is black crows that blanket the countryside.

"Hello, *héron*," I say.

We both stare for a while, beaming at the heron, then at each other. Ollie's hand weaves into mine. Solid. His fingers press against my palm with what feels like a thousand promises, and I return the same with mine. I am reminded that this is what animals do, what nature does—remind us of our bonds, to them and to each other.

The heron creeps along the banister but doesn't fly off again. We sit for a long time, watching him. Impossible to know what the heron is thinking, if he is thinking. Impossible to know what I am thinking, for Ollie, or what he is, for me. People and animals are impenetrable, to a point. But beyond that impenetrable part is this weird web that connects us. The magical part—like sparks of potential, of the greater, maybe impossible, thing that Ollie and I can be, if together. A darkness slips over me again for a moment, when I think of what awaits back at the chateau. But then I feel Ollie's hand in mine, firm and real. I find myself trusting in the sparks. Trusting in the impossible. I have to.

CHAPTER THIRTY-ONE

Sylvie

It is the middle of the night, and I cannot sleep. I used to sleep like the dead. That's what Séraphine would tell me. She was a tosser and a turner. Sometimes we'd share a bed, but mostly separate ones. There is a misconception that when you are in love, you have to share everything to proclaim it as real. We were real, as real as anything I've ever known. There was no proclamation needed. But for the most part, our love enjoyed separate bedrooms, separate walls.

The shadows are having a party on the walls. The room is saturated in moonlight because I deliberately didn't draw the curtains. I've locked my door, but darkness is too dark tonight. I need to remember that there is life outside this room. My phone is at my bedside, charging. Normally I forget, and then it dies, and Arabelle nags me that I haven't answered her call. But tonight, I've promised my granddaughter that I will keep my phone beside me, plugged into the little cord thingie, and ring her at the slightest hint of danger.

I am not frightened. When Séraphine left this world, a part of me—the biggest part—wanted to leave, too. I have had a long life, difficult in parts, softer in others. This last stretch was the best one. I love my granddaughter, but she will be okay. There is something stirring between her and the other girls, and I don't know what it is. This concerns me, but still, Arabelle is a fighter. If I know anything, I know she will land on her feet. She doesn't need my help to do so.

But I can't go just yet. There is something nagging at me, although I don't know what.

I sift through my brain. Nothing but cobwebs and old hurts, old memories. Little joys. Arabelle, as a child, making me concoctions in the kitchen—strawberry soup, of which she was so proud, dancing on the balls of her feet until I gave her my rave. Séraphine, and how detailed her steps were for tea service you would think the queen herself was expected. I would make the tea service perfect, but I would tease her still. She liked that I wasn't a pushover. Respected it, I think.

She wrote me so much once in one of her letters. We didn't say things to each other, face to face, especially not in the beginning. That wasn't our way. It was easier to write our deepest feelings. Maybe it was our generation, the secrets we had to keep in order to navigate a world hostile to different. But whenever I looked in the box buried beside the plane tree, Séraphine's deepest thoughts would splay out in paper, as my eyes greedily absorbed them.

Oh my. I bolt up in bed.

I know what is nagging me. The box where we hid our letters. What if there is another letter waiting for me? Séraphine was exacting, thoughtful, always anticipating three steps ahead. It's a long shot, but not out of bounds.

Tomorrow I will check. I know this letter she wrote me was important. I cannot rest until I find the one that was stolen, or discover one anew.

I slowly roll back down into bed, still on edge, but slightly less so, now that I have a plan.

Then I spring up again, at the sound of a scream.

CHAPTER THIRTY-TWO

Jade

It is 2:44 in the morning, and I am staring at the ceiling, the moldings, the insides of my eyeballs, willing them to shuttle me off to anywhere but where I am. They don't. They have other plans for me. *I* have other plans for me. Where is the painting? I haven't felt comfortable to hunt for it during daylight. Darcy has promised it to me, yes, but amid everything, we haven't yet had the awkward conversation of it.

I pad out of bed and creak open the door, careful to do it softly, so as not to wake Arabelle across the hall. The air is cool out here, and I rub my shoulders as I move along, reaching out to the wall occasionally when I can't see ahead.

My aim is Séraphine's bedroom. The painting has to be there, somewhere. I must have missed it. This time I won't.

I tiptoe upstairs, reach the landing. I pause. The only sounds are those of a resting house: the whisper of leaves against windowpanes, the subtle patter of my feet against stone. I am about to turn right, to Séraphine's room, when a blobby shadow morphs into human shape. It lunges toward me.

I scream.

—

Minutes later, we are all gathered in the hall, in varied states of undress. The lights are glaring. My eyes are very unhappy. All of us are unhappy, I'd venture.

"What were you doing?" Darcy asks, looking supremely aggrieved, wrapping her robe tighter around her waist. "Jade, *what* were you doing?"

"Nothing nefarious! I swear. I mean . . . nothing murder-y."

"Why were you skulking around like a criminal, then?"

Arabelle is standing there, too, in her pink silk nightgown with a matching robe. Vix in her cactus print pajama shirt and shorts. Sylvie in her pale blue cotton nightgown with rosebud flowers. I can't believe I've bothered Sylvie, the night after her assault. I feel like the scum of the earth.

"The painting," I finally say, staring only at Darcy. "I want the painting."

"The painting." Her mouth curls into a frown. "Jesus, Jade. Can't you let my grandmother rest a couple days before we talk about your painting? You're obsessed with the painting. If I didn't know better . . ."

"If you didn't know better, *what*?"

But she doesn't say anything, just stares at me defiantly.

"I'm not skirting around this anymore," I say, locking her down with my eyes. "Not after those kids attacked Lux. And if your grandparents had been sent to Auschwitz, you might be obsessed with their painting, too."

"Auschwitz?" Sylvie asks weakly.

I close my eyes. "Let's all go back to bed. We can talk about this in the morning."

———

In the morning, however, we don't talk about it, because Vix and I wake early and eat a quick breakfast before the others. Soon we are ensconced in an Uber that smells like a teenage boy's gym bag, so our windows are ratcheted down, and my hair is now textured like a Brillo pad. I didn't bring a scrunchie, but Vix did, so her hair is attractively piled up atop her head. Lucky her. She stares out the window as the fields whiz by.

"We're close to the sea," Vix says. "Weird we won't see the sea this trip."

I'm not sure why she's conjured the sea, when we're still pretty far, but I'm just glad her first instinct wasn't to complain about how I woke her up in the middle of the night—and to interrogate me about the painting. "We'll be lucky if we just get out of this country," I say. "Remember Amanda Knox?"

"Shit." Vix swivels toward me. "I didn't think of her."

"Years in a French prison could await us." I'm joking, but then I'm not. "Unless we can escape the Chateau-of-Horrors."

Quiet, then Vix says, "I'm excited to go to the sanitorium. Take our mind off of things."

I don't respond, because this excursion will only take my mind off of one horrible thing and supplant it with another.

"Juliet liked building sandcastles by the sea, did I ever tell you that? She once won an award. She could spend hours doing it. She'd love Nice, I bet." Vix blushes. "I don't know why I thought of that."

I know why. Love conjures memories at the slightest provocation. We are nowhere by the sea, and as far as I know, Juliet has never been to France. If it wasn't clear to me before, it is now, by Vix's mind drifting into something wholly unrelated to our task at hand: Vix isn't over Juliet. Hell, I'm not over Juliet. She was my favorite of Vix's girlfriends: interesting, kind, and funny. And clearly adored my friend.

"Where did you guys build sandcastles?" I shout over the wind gusting through the car.

"The Jersey Shore. Juliet's mom has a place there. It's crazy, she could just spend hours molding and carving." Vix smiles. "I never got it. She would spend so much time building something, only for a wave to take it out."

I nod. I don't get it, either. Neither Seb nor I are sandcastle building people. We're the couple that has a goal and must achieve it, with lasting effect. We're not really the couple who sits on a beach and builds things only for them to eventually disappear.

"Have you talked to her?" I ask. "Told Juliet what happened?" I realize for the first time how hard this must be for Vix, in particular. The rest of us are married, albeit with the Arabelle, Darcy, and Oliver triangle. Seb has been checking in, very concerned. He even spoke with the police officer in charge of the case. I have no clue how he even got through to Officer Darmanin, let alone commandeered her time, but that's Seb. Even if he didn't discover anything other than that they feel they are closing in on a prime suspect. Seb confided he thinks it's Darcy, which I find utterly outlandish. Darcy never would have killed Séraphine. But then, Seb doesn't know the contours of their relationship. Only we girls do.

"I texted her," Vix says, and it takes a moment for my brain to orient back to my question.

"And did Juliet respond?"

Vix shrugs. She forces a smile. "Nope."

"What happened with you guys? I still really don't get it."

"Juliet found out I've been accepting money from Séraphine all these years."

I'm quiet. I've known about the Séraphine benefactor thing. Vix told me once, because it never made sense to me how she afforded her lifestyle, and I probed. I don't want to pile on Vix now, but I am unsurprised that Juliet would find the arrangement . . . unpalatable.

"And I don't know, Arabelle took me shopping and paid for things, and I was in a bad way from the mastectomy. And then Séraphine called and wanted to meet with me here. And I couldn't tell Juliet why. So Juliet just felt like there were too many walls. Which I get. But . . ."

I wait for her *but* to continue, but nothing comes. "Yes." I gather hair from my face. "Well, you know what they say?"

"What do they say?" she asks, hopefully, like I'm going to give her some magic pill. I feel a wash of sympathy for my friend.

"They say it's not over 'til you're dead." I smile, but then I realize it's not so funny in the context of this week.

"It's not over 'til you're dead," she repeats, and then I realize the other implication. What a jerk I am. How have I said that to my friend who survived breast cancer?

"I didn't mean . . . oh shit, Vix, I totally didn't mean that."

"Yeah. It's meant to be encouraging."

I nod. "Vix, look, you're going to have to tell me about your meeting with Séraphine. You told the police, I'm assuming?"

"Yes, but it's just not fair," she says, and I realize she's talking about Juliet now, and not the painting, which irritates me. "I was such a good girlfriend! Remember how I got her tickets to Billy Joel at Madison Square Garden? Our seats were insane, and we had the best night. And I took her on a surprise weekend to Charleston for her birthday, and—"

"Those are all gifts," I put in softly, watching the cornfields and olive groves fly by.

"Huh? Yes, of course they are. Stellar gifts!"

"Well maybe gifts aren't how she feels loved," I say, trying to sound light. "Maybe honesty is."

Vix's lips clamp together and she returns her gaze out the window, twisting her body away from me.

"I'm not trying to hurt you." I put a hand on her knee. "Just show you another perspective maybe. Like, Seb loves extravagant gifts, too. But my love language is acts of service. So even though it's not his natural inclination, he always comes home from work and takes care of the garbage, or fixes the dishwasher if I text him to. Even if it's three in the morning."

"Mmm." She dabs at her eyes with her sleeve and slips on her sunglasses.

"Vix . . ." I say, my hand still rubbing her knee.

"Sometimes I just want to get off the ride." Her voice is barely audible in the roar of the wind.

"The ride? Like, this car?"

"No. The ride. You know? The ride of life, I guess. Sometimes I just want to stop and get off."

My throat feels riddled with lumps. Is it because I feel for my friend, and how heartbreaking a statement she has made? Or is it because deep down, the sentiment resonates inside of me, too?

"I do know," I finally tell her. "I think all of us want to get off the ride sometimes."

"Yeah?" she asks, with a note of hope, and I am reminded of how good it feels for someone to tell you your thoughts aren't crazy.

"Yeah." And then we are hugging, tentatively at first, and then so tight that I'm leaning forward, my seat belt strangling my neck. I'd forgotten how Vix smells—like jasmine. It's been that long since I've hugged her this hard.

"We should hug more often," she says, when we slip apart. Her body is still an imprint against mine.

"We should," I say. "We really should."

"*Nous sommes ici*," the driver says, pulling down a gravel road that bisects a lavender field. My stomach roils. I need to get out of this car.

"*Merci!*" I shout, bursting out the door as soon as he comes to a stop, and Vix adds a quick "*Merci,*" too, before scrambling out after me.

Then we both keel over our legs, panting, sucking in the fresh, steamy air. "That was brutal," I say.

"Brutal," she echoes, but grabs my hand, and I squeeze it back.

When we are upright again, our hands unravel, and I survey the sanitorium where Vincent van Gogh spent the last year of his life, producing one hundred fifty of his most acclaimed paintings. I've never been here before, never had the strength to come. It is a museum now, this massive stone building with moss growing on the sides, and tufts of trees interspersed. There are a series of arches out front pinned down by pillars and we start to walk toward them.

I consider not broaching the thing I want to broach, after the whole eject-from-the-ride bonding thing. My mind is still chewing on it—I could take her admission as something suicidal, but I'm choosing not to. This is a bonkers, shitty week, and Vix has had a bonkers, shitty year. But I just can't hold this in right now.

"Okay, V, tell me. The meeting. Come on. It was about a Van Gogh painting, wasn't it?"

She frowns, and for a moment I fear she's going to erupt on me, or dovetail back into tears. But then her face sags. "Yes. It was. At least, that's what Séraphine told me before we came to the chateau. On the phone, when we spoke."

"So there's a Van Gogh. There really, truly is. The one Séraphine stole from my family." I can hardly breathe. "I've never seen it, but it's true. I knew it was true, and yet I almost can't believe it."

"I didn't know it was stolen." Horror brands Vix's face. "I swear I didn't, Jade."

"What did she ask you to do?" I whisper. "I need you to tell me."

"I'll tell you everything. Of course. When we were kids, when we visited the chateau, and she discovered I was an artist . . ."

"What?" I say impatiently. We're almost at the entrance, where a gaggle of senior citizens with lanyard cords around their necks have slipped inside.

"She asked me to cover it up," Vix whispers.

"Cover it up," I say flatly.

"Well, cover it up so it could be restored if she wanted it down the line. Carefully, so as not to disturb any of the original. I had to research, how to do that kind of thing."

I take it all in, these surprising, but maybe also unsurprising, facts. "And you did?"

"I didn't know it belonged to your family. I swear to God, Jade."

"But you knew there was something hugely wrong with what she was asking you to do."

Vix looks away. "I wanted to do this for her. It seemed important. I trusted her. I didn't think she had evil intentions."

"And she gave you money for the rest of your life for doing it," I say, putting it all together. "Don't forget that part."

"That's not why I did it!" But Vix doesn't say it with much conviction.

"The painting in the bathroom," I say, more to myself. "The moody black, with the flowers. It was you."

"Wow, how . . . I mean, how did you possibly figure that out?"

"I always thought there was something odd about the painting. All the other art is abstract, textured. Creams or grays or nudes. Not stark, and nothing like the realism of it, unless we're talking about the Degas or Renoir."

Vix stares down at her hands. "No, Degas or Renoir I certainly am not."

"And the size," I hurry along. "It's roughly what my father described. But I didn't actually think . . . I didn't really believe. . . ." I change tactics, because otherwise I might scream, or something worse.

"And what did Séraphine want you to do this time? Why meet with you?"

Vix pauses a beat. "She wanted me to restore it. To the original."

Restore it? My God. But why now? Was she planning to give it to me? What other reason could there be? Or perhaps she wanted it to be included in Darcy's inheritance, not tossed inadvertently into some estate sale? For not the first time since Séraphine's death, I am inordinately angry. For twenty years, I suppressed my urge to confront her. Rally against her, for what she did to my family. And now, it's too late. I'll never be able to say everything I want to say, to ask the questions that despite likely eliciting painful answers, might also catalyze elusive closure. I wonder if Darcy truly appreciates the sacrifices my father and I made, to enable her precious grandmother to coast to her death, with hardly a consequence for her sickening actions.

"Where's the painting, Vix?" I finally ask.

"I have absolutely no idea."

We both stare at each other, stricken.

"I looked for it, you know?" I tell her.

"When I saw you, in Séraphine's room." Vix nods. "I was looking for it, too."

"Not just then," I say, stopping then, not sure I should confess this, not sure how it makes me appear. "After my birthday party."

Vix furrows her brow. "You looked for it. Where?"

"Everywhere. The storage closets. The pantries, in both kitchens. The guest bathrooms."

"Everywhere but her room?" Vix's face gets a peculiar look to it, that I can't read. "When?"

"Around five in the morning." It's cloying to my ears, when it emerges cheerfully from my lips. "After Séraphine was murdered, apparently. Eerie, huh?"

Vix doesn't reply. I wish I could dive inside her head, see what she is really thinking. If she even believes me. "I had no idea that this painting meant anything to you," Vix finally says. "If I had, I never would have covered it up for Séraphine. And I still don't understand, why a Van Gogh painting that Séraphine has belongs to your family."

"Come on," I say, feeling my feet nudge into the earth, feeling all my anger and uncertainty and fear swish and turn into something new, something different, not anything okay, but more eager. Eager for answers. To see and to understand.

I sigh. "Come on, and I'll show you."

CHAPTER THIRTY-THREE

Darcy

I awaken groggy, unsure where I am. Then my eyes catch the light through the blinds, and it hits me. The chateau. A place I now own, that I once loved but now has become the site of my nightmares. It's Groundhog Day here, with no end in sight. I haven't squeezed my kids in days, cupped their tiny shoulders in my palms, brushed my lips on their silky skin, wishing I could freeze the moment for eternity, when instead it is all too brief, snuffed by a jerky squirm away. I prop myself up on my elbows and catch a glimpse of myself in the mirror across. I look a fright, black eyeliner smeared on my cheeks. I forgot to wash my face last night. I am a person who was once religious about face washing. But now I am becoming something else. A new person. And I'm not sure I've even made her acquaintance as yet.

I grapple for my watch on the nightstand. 10:10. I don't think I've slept past 7:30 since before kids.

Well, I needed the sleep-in. Last night I couldn't get past that drifty phase after you lie down and pray to everything that exists to dissolve your thoughts and make sleep swift. Sleep wasn't anything close to swift. I started counting snails. That's what my grandfather taught me to do. He said sheep are too big, too fast. Snails go even slower. *Fa-la-la-la-la.* Somehow, his sound of a snail moving was a Christmas tune. *Fa-la-la-la-la.* That worked for a time, but not last night. I tried to conjure snails, but I'd forgotten what they looked like.

Like a shell? I googled it, and the glare from the phone expunged any trickle of melatonin. Then I heard a rustle outside. Jade.

Was she actually looking for the painting? Or trying to do something else?

I don't know what I'm getting at with that thought. Do I suspect Jade? I suppose I suspect everyone, including myself. My brain isn't working properly. I may be going a bit insane.

I know why I couldn't sleep, though. It's not my grandmother, or even the assault on Sylvie, or Jade creeping around, or the groundskeeper who makes me feel quite uncertain, lurking nearby. Friend, or foe? I think he is a friend, but as we can acknowledge, my judgment sucks.

No. What has kept me awake is that Arabelle and I haven't had it out. Not properly. Not decisively. To whom does Oliver belong? We need to settle this. We need to settle this now.

I stand, pull off my nightie, then survey the dresses hanging in my closet. One among the rainbow is black—unusual for me. I'm not even sure why I packed it. Perhaps subconsciously, I was anticipating a funeral.

Somehow it seems right to wear it now. This talk with Arabelle will be bleak, however it goes.

I shrug on the dress, avoid the mirror. Nothing good can come from seeing my sorry self again.

I pad down the hall, past Sylvie's room. Her door is shut. I consider checking on her, but think better of it. She locked her door at night. We all did. Vix's door, on the other hand, is open. I peek in. The bed is awry, covers tossed to the tile. She and Jade will have gone early to the sanitorium. All the better for a private confrontation with Arabelle.

I take the stairs in surprising leaps. It reminds me of being a child, before my grandfather died, every step in this place a gleeful one. I start toward Arabelle's room, but then I stop. I run my fingers over the paneled wood behind the stairs, now freshly painted, feeling for the old grooves. You used to be able to put your hand exactly so, and open up the secret passage to the hidden room. That's where I played as a child. Arabelle did, too.

Jade's family was hidden there, during the war, I learned. I showed her the room once, twenty years ago. Afterward, she agreed not to expose my family's horrible betrayal. I've always felt guilty about asking her to do so. It was my grandmother's name I was protecting, but it was also my own. What have I perpetuated, by keeping things a secret? Jade was right to search for the painting. I will tell her when she returns. Of course I will give it to her. There has never been a question about that. We will find it. It must be here somewhere. Grand-mère wouldn't have gotten rid of it. Maybe, even, it was the purpose of her calling us here. She said she wanted to make things right. Who more to make things right with than Jade?

Without thinking, my hand brushes those grooves. My fingers feel into the place where I used to push. It's a shame they got rid of the secret room in the renovation. When Arabelle said so, a sadness came over me that I tried to brush away. It's just, so much happened there in my early life, good and bad. My grandfather used to tell me stories inside, about the history of the house, and the people who lived in it. Of course I didn't know the sordid stories, not until Jade informed me. I try to think my grandparents were naïve. Not deliberate. But my brain doesn't always accommodate that graciousness. The room is also where I ran to when my grandfather died right before my eyes. I suppose it is cave-like, a bit of a hug, which can't be said for the rest of the ginormous chateau.

I push at the grooves, expecting nothing, but nothing is not what I get.

I am stunned—paralyzed momentarily—when the panel pops forward. And then in rote repetition of so many childhood times, I slip inside.

CHAPTER THIRTY-FOUR

Vix

"It is 1889, and a thirty-six-year-old artist named Vincent van Gogh checks himself into this sanitorium in Saint-Rémy. Only a little time before, Van Gogh, plagued by hallucinations, had cut off one of his ears with a razor blade. He feels discarded by society and abandoned by his beloved brother whose wedding day is approaching. In this asylum, Van Gogh spends what will be the final year of his life producing his most renowned, breathtaking paintings."

A grandmotherly lady in a pale pink tweed suit, named Faustine, walks briskly from the foyer up a set of stairs cloistered from the sun. We follow after. At the top of the stairs, down a dingy hall, she leads us to a cheerless room, with bars over the one small window. I take in the simple quarters that formed Van Gogh's final year and the most prolific of his life. It is the birthplace of genius. Hard to believe, that so many paintings I've studied and admired originated in this sad space.

"Where did the staff stay?" Jade asks Faustine.

"Not here," Faustine says. "These are the men's quarters. Besides, most of the staff stayed off property."

Jade nods. I try to pan her face but can't read it.

"You can look around, and I'll wait outside," Faustine says, and slips back into the hall.

Jade goes to the window that is beside a bare twin mattress in an iron frame. I walk over to stand beside her.

"You know what we're looking at," she says, and I am too transfixed to respond. Wheat fields spread out in the glow of the sun, with olive groves and vineyards, too.

I spot cypress trees—iconic Van Gogh. He said they constantly occupied his thoughts. But the cypresses are much smaller in scale to those he typically depicted. And beyond the cypresses lie the foothills of the Alpilles, a feature of all of Van Gogh's paintings that depict the view from this window.

"He had a studio downstairs," I say. "That's where he did his painting, according to Faustine. He didn't paint here."

Jade nods but her eyes stay gazing out. "He was only allowed to sketch up here. But still, the view from this window is represented in some form in twenty-one of his paintings."

I, too, know this. I, too, have done my research, both as an artist, and as the person with whom Séraphine shared her secret, or at least the fumes of her secret.

"Twenty-two," I say quietly, scarcely able to form the words. "The experts have it wrong. This view is actually represented in twenty-*two* of Van Gogh's paintings."

"Yes." Jade nods, almost proudly, like a schoolteacher whose pupil has said something clever. "That's exactly correct. Twenty-two. And if I've been accurately informed, the twenty-second painting is the most transcendent of them all."

I have to hold on to the window bars briefly for support. "You've been accurately informed," I finally say.

———

After Faustine shows us Van Gogh's first-floor studio, and the rest of the uninspiring facilities, Jade and I wander out to the garden. Faustine said the director of the sanitorium was a progressive, and believed exposure to art and music, and being surrounded by nature, to be good for troubled souls. The director ordered the planting of extensive gardens that remain today.

We wander through a series of stone arches and then a maze of manicured hedges, and sit on a bench by an almond tree. My mind is whirring. Sitting here is surreal; I can almost conjure Van Gogh's *Almond Blossom*. In a letter to a friend, he gave himself the seal of approval on that particular painting, painted, as with the rest of them, between episodes of hallucinations. There is a common belief that Van Gogh's paintings benefited from his mental illness. But in fact, from all the research I've done, and by my own artistic assessment, his paintings were fantastic despite his illness, not because of it.

Sometimes I wonder myself, are my paintings subpar because I haven't needed to rely upon them? Vincent dreamed of being an artist; painting and success drove him. But perhaps my drive to create is blunted—has always been blunted—by Séraphine's patronage. They aren't fun thoughts through which to parse.

I am three years older than Van Gogh was when he killed himself. And what do I have to show for it? One exhibition in a gallery in Chelsea, five years ago now. A few paintings sold for piddling amounts per year. Van Gogh painted hundreds of paintings in his year at this sanitorium. I manage a small fraction of that amount, each produced with grit and force. No flow. If I am to admit it, no joy, either. I hoped I'd be inspired returning to Provence, to the chateau. That goal seems utterly laughable now.

I fix my eyes back on the almond tree. Van Gogh was influenced by Japanese prints of the time, a fact most evident in his *Almond Blossom*. My mind darts between reality and the painting, the painting and reality. Above Van Gogh's almond tree was the most radiant and clear blue sky that he ever painted. He conceived of the painting as a christening present for his little nephew, named after Vincent.

"I love you," I whisper, to the tree, of course.

"Oh God," Jade says, but she doesn't laugh like usual.

I don't tell Jade that maybe I am saying *I love you* to the man, as well, whose painting has shaped my life, for better and for worse.

But I always think the best way to know God is to love many things. That's what he said.

Maybe my problem, Vincent, is I love too many things, too much. And like clockwork, my thoughts turn to Juliet. What a bore my thoughts are. I force them back to the painting that sits like an elephant between Jade and me.

As we absorb our surroundings in quiet, I can feel the specter of the man who occupies our thoughts. It is a quadrangle we find ourselves in—Jade and me, Séraphine, and the artist named Vincent van Gogh.

"Will you tell me about your family?" I finally say. Fear shivers through me, as I realize that we won't be able to go back to the Jade and Vix we were before this. Somehow I know, what we say here will change everything. Will she forgive me? I have absolutely no idea.

Jade is staring at the almond tree, too. I wonder if she is thinking the same things as me, about all the secrets and lies we've kept. And about Van Gogh and his sad life, and all the beautiful things he created.

But then she looks at me, her face ashen, and I know she is not thinking of Van Gogh's sad life, but of other sad lives. I know she is not thinking of our secrets, but of other, older ones.

"Yes. It's time we tell each other everything, don't you think?"

———

"My father grew up in a well-to-do family, in La Jutarié section of Saint-Rémy. His father was a businessman. His mother doted on him. He was born in 1932, so he was eight when the Nazis took control of France. Paris fell in 1940, on the fourteenth of June—his birthday. Papa remembered how his mother baked him a chocolate cake, but she was crying so much that day her tears kept falling into the frosting."

"Your grandparents knew what it meant for them?" I ask. It was sunny before, blindingly so, but now clouds have come to hover over us, appropriately dark. I rub my bare arms, now sprouting goose bumps.

"Papa says they tried to shield him from the fears. Plus, they were wealthy. They thought there was no way anything could happen to them. But they heard rumors, about deportations, camps. Especially when it all started in Paris. And then the Jews of the Vaucluse had to register."

"Register," I repeat, feeling sick.

"Yes. They thought about moving to Nice or Marseilles. Those places were in the Unoccupied Zone at the time, like Saint-Rémy, but on the coast, where perhaps they could board a boat and make a run for it. But they had a nice life in Saint-Rémy. They figured if need be, they could get quickly to the coast. And meanwhile, they thought the same as everyone at the time—this will pass."

"It didn't pass," I whisper.

"No." Jade closes her eyes. Her face looks placid enough, but I notice her fists balled at her sides. "No, it definitely did not.

"In 1942, the Germans occupied the south of France, and that is when my father's family finally sprang into action. There were rumors there was going to be a massive deportation. My father's parents had money, yes, but their greatest wealth was tied up in their two most prized possessions. One was a painting that hung in my grandfather's study. It was a special painting, come to the family in a special way. They didn't advertise they had it. They didn't even tell their closest friends. They never considered parting from it until fate forced their hand."

A lump forms in my throat, because of course I've seen this painting. I've handled this painting. I am guilty and shameful, for this painting. And never in a million years did I conceive that it once hung in the home of Jade's family.

"*Starry Night Two*," I whisper, and I am transported in my head, to that day in Séraphine's closet nearly twenty years ago, when she left me to my assigned task. It was both the best and worst day, to stand before that masterpiece. I had read that Van Gogh tried to kill himself by swallowing his paints and turpentine only a few weeks before painting *Starry Night*. In all probability, the paints he used were the remnants of that failed suicide attempt. And I was assigned to gaze at the thick impasto strokes only inches from my face, and cover over them up.

Well, no one forced me to. Decades after the fact, I feel it, my failed integrity. I felt it then, too, but it is easier to push such feelings away when you are in your early twenties. It is easier to be a bad person, a person with loose morals. You think, soon, I will become a person I am proud of. And then soon turns into years that stack atop each other like Jenga bricks. One little piece is snatched, and the whole sturdy tower you hoped you were topples down.

"Yes," Jade says. "That's right. The superior *Starry Night* that, outside of rumors, few people know exists. You see, my grandfather's grandmother—my great-great-grandmother—was a nurse at this very sanitorium."

"Oh, wow. Oh my God."

"Yes. Apparently, she was the kindest woman. She was the one who gave Van Gogh his twice-weekly baths. They would talk. She said he was smart. Exceedingly smart, and well-read, and articulate. The sanest patient at the sanitorium, she called him. All this was passed down. Family lore, I suppose. Papa remembers the stories, told in candlelight at night. Every time she bathed him, Van Gogh would tell Papa's great-grandmother what he was painting. He promised he would paint something for her."

I can scarcely draw a breath, let alone speak.

"Yes." Jade is almost triumphant, at the power of this story. "I've told so few people this, Vixen. Just Darcy, really, and Seb. It's crazy to tell you now. Van Gogh told my great-great-grandmother that he would paint something exceptional for her."

I finally find my voice. "He wrote in a letter that *Starry Night* was a failure. He thought he hadn't pursued the *real sentiment of things*. It wasn't his favorite painting, by any means."

"No," Jade agrees. "That's why he did a sketch, of how to improve it. The sketch was looted by a Red Army officer after World War Two. It's held by Russia in the vaults of the Hermitage now."

Of course, I know all about this sketch. After I first met Séraphine and she gave me the task of concealing a painting that she claimed belonged to her family, I did the research. How could I not?

"But for *Starry Night Two*," Jade says, her voice crackling with emotion, "Van Gogh fixed the problems he saw with the original. You know, he paved the way for modern artists with his *Starry Nights*. Usually he painted what he saw, but with the *Starry Nights*, he had to paint from his imagination. The view was from his bedroom here, but he imagined a little village in the valley that didn't actually exist. He gave each house in the village a bright gas light, to set off the stars. And Papa says *Starry Night Two* was even more electric than the first, if you can imagine."

"I can imagine," I say quietly.

She nods. "The stars and swirls in the sky, the galaxies, are pushed closer together in *Number Two*. Then comes the early morning mist, but the mountains are more convoluted—"

"And the roofs in the village houses are curved in *Two*. Not straight."

"Yes." Jade nods approvingly. "I'm glad the other girls didn't join today, Vixen. I knew it was just supposed to be the two of us."

Something about that sends a chill through me. It's as though I've forgotten there was a murder amid this. Not just a murder, but a *murderer*. None of us want to believe it could be one of us. It can't be. That would challenge everything we know to be true about the world. But this story is already challenging everything I know to be true about the world.

Whatever Séraphine did to Jade's family, she did it knowingly. She had me cover up her painting. And I idolized her. I took money from her all these years. I feel sick, realizing how that money came with blood. The blood of Jade's family.

"There was another expensive thing my father's family had to barter for their safety," Jade says, stealing me away from my spiraling thoughts. "A diamond necklace my grandfather inherited from his mother, and gifted to my grandmother. It was very unusual—a gold chain, with three evenly-spaced flowers made out of diamonds."

"Oh shit." I feel my hand go to my bare neck, as if I'm going to discover a necklace there. This story gets crazier. Just crazier and crazier.

It's a wild thing to be sitting in the sanitorium where Van Gogh went insane, and to feel like I'm going insane, too.

"You remember," Jade says flatly.

"Of course," I finally manage. "Séraphine was wearing it the first time we met her. All of the times, really, that semester we studied abroad."

"Yes. Exactly. And I always thought how telling it was. She may have squirreled away the painting, but my grandmother's necklace she had right around her neck. Blood against skin, let's be honest. She did what she did, and wore the spoils on her neck. There was no mistaking it. Maybe I would have thought differently of her, tried to ascribe her more benign intentions otherwise. But she was so blatant. Wearing the necklace . . . how much more evil can you get?"

I don't answer. I am absorbing it all. Or trying to, at least.

"And when Darcy got married, the necklace somehow disappeared."

I am still staring at the almond tree, my mind whirring, but then out of the corner of my eye, I see Jade's hand at her neck, fingering the necklace she always wears. It has one massive diamond, floating on a chain.

"Is that . . . ?"

"Yes," she says, almost proudly.

"I think you better continue the story."

"Sure. We're almost at the best part." Her face sags. "The best part is the most horrific part," she clarifies. "I'm sorry in advance."

"For what?"

"For how I'm about to put the last nail in the coffin on the image of your precious Séraphine."

———

"Papa was ten at this point in the story. What do you remember from when you were ten, Vixen?"

I flip back through the memories. "Bits and pieces, I guess. Nothing so discrete, unless something was particularly awful." I grimace at the memory of a huge dog who got off his leash and leapt at me, mauling my face. I had to have surgery, stitches. To this day, I am terrified of big dogs.

"Exactly." Jade nods. "It's the awful things we remember the best. I wonder why that is."

"Must be some psychological explanation. So your father remembers everything?"

"Everything. See, my grandfather and Rainier's father did business together. Papa never knew the contours of it, just that all of a sudden one day, he was ordered to pack a small suitcase and be ready to say goodbye to his home. He had a baby brother by now, not even a year old. His mother tried to make it sound like an adventure, but Papa wasn't fooled. There were whispers of a roundup and, suddenly, they were departing in the middle of the night. Papa remembers how his mother clapped a hand over the baby's mouth when he started to cry. Papa was afraid she was going to suffocate him to death, but she didn't lift her hand, not until he stopped whimpering. They walked miles by foot, finally arriving at a grand iron gate. Papa remembers the crest exactly."

My whole being tenses in dread. Of course, I already know. "Three lions pawing at a crown."

"Yes. They were shuttled into a room underneath the staircase. They were meant to stay there, not make a sound. Séraphine delivered them food."

"Séraphine?" I say, still having trouble conceiving of it.

"Yes. Papa knew her by name. They were allowed out a couple of times a day to the bathroom. To stretch. That was it. That was life."

"Like Anne Frank," I say, disbelieving. "All this happened in the chateau?"

"Yes." Jade nods. "Darcy showed me the room, where they hid. Under the stairs."

"Under the stairs." I remember vaguely, some conversation between Darcy and Arabelle about it, but I'd never heard of this room under the stairs previously. I am dreading it now, what more lies ahead in this story. What more I don't know, about Séraphine, about my friends.

"But one day a couple of months later, Séraphine came to the room. This my father remembers perfectly. She told them they had to go. That the family couldn't shelter them anymore. That Nazis were going door-to-door, to root out the Jews. It's not like the Nazis had specific intel—that *my* family was hidden at the chateau. But the Demargelasses just refused to hide my family any longer, not when it might mean actual danger for them."

"My God." I feel something rise up in my throat. I lean over the bench and gag. Nothing comes up. I gag again, and I feel Jade rub my back. "I should be consoling you, not you me," I say, when I finally sit upright again.

"I know this story, Vixen. I've had a lifetime with it. You haven't."

"So Séraphine betrayed them? Your father is sure. It wasn't Rainier's mother?"

"I've shown him pictures of Séraphine. Yes, it was her. No question. She was young then. Nineteen, something like that. Papa wouldn't have confused her with Rainier's mother."

I nod, not able to reconcile such a horrible act with the person I thought I knew.

"She did one thing, though. One redeeming thing."

"What?" I ask.

"She saved Papa. She took him to a couple who was saving Jewish children. They had a children's school of sorts, in Mausanne, and later he was transferred to Le Mas Blanc, between here and Taracson. There were a lot of children there whose parents had been deported or arrested. Conditions were horrible. There was no electricity or heating, and Papa was always afraid, of deportations and raids. Plus, he'd lost his family. He was ten years old, and everything he knew was taken from him in an instant. Séraphine hardly let him say goodbye to his parents, to his baby brother. She took his hand and said, *Come*."

I shake my head hard, wanting to shake all this out of me. "And what happened to your father's parents? To his baby brother?"

"They were all caught," Jade says simply. "Deported to Auschwitz."

I nod. I don't ask anymore. The word *Auschwitz* says it all.

We sit in quiet for a very long time in the shadow of the almond tree, until it begins to drizzle. But neither of us makes a move to go back inside.

"Any more questions?" Jade asks.

"Only a million," I whisper.

"Yes. I know that feeling. A million questions, and no answers. Not anymore. Not from a dead woman."

"Why didn't you expose her?" I ask, the question that has leapt ahead of the rest.

"I promised Darcy I wouldn't," Jade says simply. "Not while Séraphine was still alive. I saw the crest on a piece of stationery that Darcy had early on when I met her. It's not like I targeted her," she says, answering another question I have. I wonder if I believe it. "I swear I didn't target Darcy, Vix. I mean, I did want to study abroad here because of my family connection. Because of Papa's nightmares. He has always had nightmares, and they became my nightmares, too. And once I saw the crest, I wanted justice. Of course I did. And maybe I wanted revenge, too. You can understand that, can't you?"

Can I? I'm not sure of anything, let alone justice, and revenge. Where did it all start? Where did it end? Or has it?

"You stole the necklace, but . . . I mean, how?"

"Darcy helped," Jade says. "Once I got up the guts to tell her about the connection between our families, she wanted retribution for me, too. You remember, don't you? Every time we went to the chateau?"

I shiver. How could she have done it? I don't understand. But it's incontrovertible. That whole semester, every time I saw Séraphine, she was wearing that diamond necklace with the flowers, with the blood of Jade's family all over it.

"It was her wedding weekend, after all, when Darcy suggested it was the opportune time. It was so . . ." Jade breathes in, deep. "It was the most generous thing a person ever did for me. Here it was, her wedding, and for Darcy, that . . ."

She trails off, but I get it. Darcy has always been a fairy-tale princess wedding girl. You just knew when you first met her that she had a scrapbook under her bed, with magazine clippings from the whole of her life, dreaming of the entire affair.

"She got a duplicate key to Séraphine's room, made up some excuse. Séraphine didn't question it. We chose a time Séraphine had a spa treatment scheduled. Darcy suspected the code to the safe, and she was right. It was her father's birthday. And wouldn't you imagine it? The necklace was just lying there for the taking. It felt crazy, absolutely wild, to hold it in my hands."

"Your father must have been over the moon," I say. "To have it back."

Jade's jaw hardens. "Papa isn't over the moon about anything. The necklace was almost too much for him to contend with, and anyway, there were some financial things." She pauses. "Bad investments."

"Ah. So that's all that's left?" I point to her necklace, the one large, circular diamond.

"Yes." She drags the diamond back and forth on the chain, like she always does. Funny how things you've always noticed but never thought consequential are cast in a different light when you dig deeper.

"But the necklace wasn't enough, right? You wanted the painting. I mean, of course you did. It's yours. It's your father's. And that's what you were looking for, when I saw you in Séraphine's bedroom."

"Yes."

"Did . . ." I can't bring myself to finish the sentence.

"You can ask me, Vix. You can ask me what you want to ask."

"Did you kill Séraphine?" I finally say quietly.

Jade is quiet. Just twisting her diamond round and round in her fingers.

Am I sitting here with a murderer? I need to know.

Or do I?

Maybe that's my problem. Maybe I have always known, but pretended to myself that I didn't. That things weren't kosher, that what Séraphine has asked of me all these years hasn't been kosher. But I was complicit. There's no way around it.

And doesn't that make me just as bad a person—just as evil—as Séraphine?

CHAPTER THIRTY-FIVE

Darcy

My heart thwacks my chest as I creep through the hidden space under the stairwell. It's been twenty years since I've crept inside here, for no particular reason. It was a childish inclination, and after my grandfather died, I think I associated it with him. I came here, dripping wet in my swimsuit, after I saw him floating there. All that blood. His body, twisted in a way bodies shouldn't twist.

I walk farther in, down the narrow part. I could get out my phone, light the way, but I find I don't need to. It's seven steps, I remember, until I reach the string dangling at the mouth of the room. Six, seven—my hand clasps the string. I pull, and I'm startled almost, that the bulb still sparks, that all is illuminated. Well, not all. My brain is whirring, but it's like a fan, round and round, not catching on anything meaningful. Just creating a lot of air.

The place hasn't changed. Not in the least. It is about six feet by eight, barren, the walls rough, just foundation, the ceiling planked in wood, the whole expanse laden in dust. I slide a hand along the wooden bookcase—the only furniture the room has ever known. At least as long as I've lived. When I took Jade here, after she told me the story of her family, and the recognition that had dawned when she saw the crest on my stationery, she told me there had once been a mattress in here, where her father slept with his parents and baby brother. I asked her father's name then, but I already suspected its first letter.

M. She confirmed it. Maurice. And then I showed her, the carving in the wall, that I had always asked Grand-père about.

I run my fingers over it now, just beside the bookcase. *MA.* Maurice Assouline.

It's the only time I've ever been angry at my grandfather, when I stood there beside Jade, as she traced her father's initials with her fingers. Grand-père told me his best friend in boyhood had carved that in. I only learned the truth long after his death, when Jade told me. I've never been able to dwell on it much—of my grandparents' complicity in the betrayal that shuttled Jade's grandparents to their deaths. Jade's uncle, as well. An innocent baby.

It was a lot to process, Jade's tale of her family. What it meant about my own. It would have been easier, perhaps, to put a kibosh on our friendship. To question the accuracy of what her father said he remembered. To accuse her of using me to reclaim what she said was hers. For her to hate me, for my genetic part in things. But I will never forget what happened as we sat on that navy sofa in the common area of our dormitory. Tears—hers, despite her tough girl New Yorker persona. Nails digging into thigh—mine. Perhaps we said some strong things, things we might want to take back, but in the end was the fiercest hug I've ever known. Promises to each other, to be friends, true friends, to remove ourselves from the ugliness, because neither of us created it. It is the best aspect of our friendship, I always think, that despite our beginning, we can ascribe each other with benevolent intentions. I know Jade believes the best in me, and I in her. At least, I typically in her. I think about @imwatchingyou88, and wish I could travel back in time, never start that account. To add insult to injury, I planned to tank her at a time she needs me most. I need to delete the account, immediately. I don't want Jade to ever know I thought she'd betrayed me. She would never do that. Never. I know that now.

I sit on the floor, beside the bookcase. A milieu of nostalgia storms me. I used to read in here, with Arabelle, too. She was always poring over cookbooks, making notations, spines littered with Post-its. She was too old to find me interesting, or entertaining, even though I was the eager younger girl, trying to impress the confident older one. We used to read in silence. Sometimes I thought she might resent me, but whatever for? Then I thought I was making it up. She was simply older, cooler. That was before we became friends. Best of friends. Before she stole my husband, too.

Why did Arabelle lie to me about this place being covered over in the renovation?

Suddenly my eyes catch again on the bookcase. On the top shelf is a little rattan box that I've never seen before. And leaning against the bookcase is something wrapped in brown butcher paper. It is flat and square—a painting. No doubt.

I reach for the painting and am surprised when I feel something adhered to the outside of the butcher paper. When I turn the painting around, I can see it clearly. It is an envelope in expensive cardstock. On it is written *To: Jade, From: Séraphine.*

———

I flip the envelope over to its flap side. The flap is open. That strikes me as strange. Grand-mère didn't believe in merely tucking the lip inside an envelope. She believed in the seal of saliva. *You want to know if someone opened your letter, Darcy. You want to deter any prying eyes.*

I used to laugh it off as old-school paranoia. Now, I see what she meant. I am the prying eyes. And as I take in the congealed film on the seal, I understand there were other prying eyes, before mine. Of course, I wonder whose.

I put the letter aside for a moment and peel the butcher paper from the painting, surprised to see a canvas of flowers against a faded black backdrop—the painting that hung in one of the bathrooms, if I remember correctly. Arabelle's room, maybe.

What Officer Darmanin told me about Vix's restoring supplies is ringing in my ears. Is this possibly the Van Gogh? The Van Gogh Jade has always believed my grandparents stole from her family? I thought that aspect of her story a bit of a stretch. The necklace I fully bought into—Grand-mère wore it often, and Jade showed me a sketch her father made that depicted it perfectly. But this phantom painting? If my grandparents had a Van Gogh, wouldn't they have at least displayed it? Or sold it through some clandestine, illegal dealer, of which there must be scads? Or, if they felt themselves cursed by it, then perhaps burned the damn thing?

If this is the Van Gogh, it is a painting dripping in blood. But it must be the Van Gogh, because why else would it be here, propped against the bookcase, accompanied by a note to Jade?

Clearly Grand-mère wrote this note before she died. But why did she do so, when she could have just given it to Jade herself?

Did Jade murder Grand-mère? It's what I come back to, again. There have been far lesser motives for murder. And Jade's been struggling, I know, since the attack on Lux. The school ultimately suspended the kids responsible, but as Jade said, "Anti-Semitism isn't going to be solved by two happily suspended kids playing video games in their bedrooms while they would have been at school."

What would help solve it then? Murdering my grandmother?

The ethical dilemma pervades me for a moment—save Grand-mère's note for my friend, or read it first myself.

Fuck it, of course I'm going to look.

I unfold the note, my eyes lingering briefly on the crest. Sometimes I think if I see another lion in my life, another crown, I will throw up.

I begin to read Grand-mère's perfect script with my heart in my throat.

Dear Jade,

If you are reading this, I am dead. Murdered, most likely.

This may sound dramatic, but I am afraid. I am very truly afraid. Non, it doesn't matter, not for purposes of this letter.

I called you here to the chateau for a specific purpose. You and your friends. I intended to tell you my version of the story that you think you fully know. And I wanted to give you this. The painting that belongs to you.

Please know that I wanted to do this in person. I am not a coward—not at this stage, at least. I hope I will be able to do this in person, to look in your eyes as I tell you horrible things. To allow you to look inside mine. But this note is a failsafe. If I am gone, I don't want this to die with me. I need you to know.

Out with it then, yes?

There is history that has passed between us, since the moment we met. I don't know how exactly you landed in my chateau, with my granddaughter. You became friends, before or after you knew who she was? It doesn't matter at this point, does it? Somehow when you walked through the door, I knew you were always meant to.

I was always waiting for you. For your father or you. That is the God's honest truth.

I recognized you right away. You have your father's eyes. The strange combination, one so different than the other. Eyes that are not twins. Eyes that see into your soul. Well, that is what I've always felt. I knew it immediately, the moment I saw you.

You will want to hear my side of the story, won't you? If we are face-to-face, as I hope we will be, perhaps you will tell me that no, you don't want to hear my side. That my side is irrelevant. But I know that isn't true. That you, like me, have been waiting for this reckoning all your life.

I know the way you look at me. Perhaps you think me a stupid old woman, that I don't see it. That I have not always seen it.

But I know hate. Trust me, ma chérie, that I do.

In November 1942, the Germans took over. They'd had France for a while, but down here, we had the Italians. Or we were under the illusion that we did. But when the Italians fell, too, Rainier informed me that a Jewish family was coming to stay with us in the room under the stairs.

I didn't know we had a room under the stairs. He showed me then: a decrepit little space. Not fitting cattle, let alone humans. I asked him where they would sleep. He waved a hand. They would bring blankets.

No, I said, hardly able to believe he was suggesting that in good conscience. You must get them a mattress.

I had never spoken to my husband this way. I was half-terrified that he would slap me across the face. Thankfully he did not, not then. He smiled, like I was a woman with charitable inclinations toward street cats.

Okay, ma chérie.

I knew it immediately: If Rainier's parents had determined to shelter a Jewish family, it was not an act of charity. Soon I discovered there were two somethings in it. A necklace and a secret painting by Vincent van Gogh.

Rainier's mother was positively gleeful at breakfast. The Jews were in the room, she said, and the painting was stored beneath a blanket in Rainier's father's study. Rainier showed it to me. It was spectacular. Starry Night, but even more fantastic. I was an artist, or at least I fancied myself so. I was an artist but born at a time when all I was meant to be was a mother. I understood my place. But still, a woman can't exorcise her passions, no matter how she may try.

I was under strict orders not to discuss the painting with anyone. Yet right out there in the open, a new diamond necklace encircled my mother-in-law's neck. Diamonds don't need to be concealed, apparently. The Demargelasse family was certainly wealthy enough for diamonds, even if Rainier's father was too cheap to purchase them. I thought it immensely crude, to wear a persecuted woman's necklace. I tried not to look. How could Maman sit there, with property belonging to other people? Other people who were crammed into a dark, dank room, hiding from a ghastly fate.

But I was newly married, still tiptoeing around. My mother-in-law was a stern, strict, exacting woman. She spoke and you obeyed. Her husband was quieter. I thought him kind. But he didn't rule the house. She did. She assigned me the task of bringing food and water to the Jews. The maids weren't to know they were there. No one was to know.

Our reputation is everything, *she told me. Our good name is* of utmost importance.

I've had my whole life to reflect, and here is how I've come out. She thought she was above the law. Above the Germans, for some time, at least. She loved money. She loved things. She loved them better than her son or her husband, and absolument *better than me.*

Perhaps, Jade dear, you are thinking I am describing myself? I know you don't think highly of me, and I understand completely why. But I am nothing like my mother-in-law. Maybe this is how I sleep at night, telling myself so. But if you just read along, I hope you will find that you agree.

Anyhow, it was Rainier's mother who gave me the most important role of my life: the role as lifeblood between the Assouline family and my own. Let me explain. For two months, I brought them dinner. Often, I made it myself so the cook wouldn't be suspicious. Oui, you are surprised? I can cook. I can cook quite wonderfully. It was fall, so stews and soups. We were under rations at this point, but I did what I could. This is when I met your father, Jade.

Maurice. He was a dear boy, with those startling eyes. They were huge. Saucers. The right eye an icy blue like one of those Arctic lakes, the left murkier, blue pooled with brown. He didn't speak much, not to me, not in my presence. I felt him assessing me, and finding me wanting. Your grandparents were kind. Exceedingly kind. They kept thanking me, thanking me. What was I doing, other than what anyone would do? Helping people. My in-laws had a motive, perhaps, but for me there was none.

And then the baby. They called him Arnaud. He was not but one. He was the sweetest baby, the fattest. His thighs had their own postal code, that's what your grandmother said. His eyes were unlike his brother's—the palest green. They do say babies' eyes can change, fade to brown perhaps, like his father's, but his never did. He was always smiling, but he cried when he wanted the breast. Sometimes he grabbed at his mother's neck, and his mother told me once how he loved her necklace. How he used to love to play with it. But now her neck was empty, and we both looked away at that point. Me, for shame, of course, that we had taken something from her, when we should have just opened our doors out of the generosity of our hearts. Later I thought she looked away from shame, too—that she needed to buy her safety with jewels. That she and her family were entirely at our mercy. What a gruesome time it was.

I learned that Arnaud got fussy when he hadn't slept enough, and these were not comfortable quarters in which to sleep. It was freezing inside, so maybe he was also fussy because he was cold? That kept me up at night. The children in the cold. I brought them more blankets. When the blankets weren't enough, and rations were tight, I learned to knit and tried to make sweaters. It was an impossible time. A whole world to save, and mere knitting needles with which to do it.

One morning, I was having breakfast, when Rainier's mother announced the Jews had to go.

I choked on my tea. Had to go? What did she mean?

Oui. It's not safe. The Germans are searching. Anyone housing Jews will face immediate death. *She didn't look at me as she said it.* And you, Séraphine, will inform them.

I begged her, I pleaded. She couldn't send them away. If she made them go, she'd be signing their death warrants. She'd be sending them right into the hands of the waiting Germans.

She didn't care. Rainier didn't care. Nor did his father, whom I'd thought to be quiet but caring. He wasn't quiet but caring, as it turned out. He was just quiet. They are too big a risk to us. You are a naïve girl to urge us to keep them.

Finally, I summoned my strength. I went to Rainier's mother. I asked her to save the children.

Just how, *she asked me, irritated,* do you expect to do that?

I cleared my throat. Summoned the whole of my courage. I will take them. They will be mine. Mine and Rainier's.

You? *She peered at me over her eyeglasses with that condescending stare.* You are but a child. Nearly nineteen. And one year you have been married to my son and have yet to produce anything in your womb.

She pointed, cruelly. As if I was not aware.

So, they will be mine. You will have grandchildren.

Jewish grandchildren, *she said, her point entirely made.*

What if I am barren? *I shouted.* Then you will have none.

She looked at me with a cruel smile. Then I shall.

That afternoon, I hatched a tentative plan. I had a school friend from my girlhood whose family wasn't wealthy like mine. I arranged her work as a housekeeper in the chateau. We were close, despite the patent difference in our statuses, which was only exacerbated once I married Rainier. Still, she confided certain things to me, and me to her. She had told me once, inadvertently, that she knew a secret about Rainier's father. But she was too discreet to tell me what. But the morning after my conversation with Maman, I went to my friend. I told her what was taking place, beneath our own roof. I said, You have to tell me what you know. We must save the children.

I was meant to banish them that day, you see, Jade. I was meant to send them out to the wolves.

My friend, you know who she is? She died about ten years ago, but she was the grandmother to Raphael, my groundskeeper. You will understand now why I gave him a job, though he isn't particularly fit to be a groundskeeper. His grandmother saved your father. She saved me, too, that day.

She never told me what she knew, what leverage she had. But she went to Rainier's mother and soon returned.

You can have the baby, *she said.* The baby can be yours.

I nodded. I knew she could do it. She had seemed confident in the secret she kept. I hadn't even stopped to wonder what horrible thing my father-in-law had done to save the baby, in the end. My teeth were chattering, so hard I actually wondered if they could shatter. What about the boy?

No, *she said plainly. Her face was branded in pain, so I knew that no was an absolute.* Hurry, you must be quick about it. She wants them out by the night. You can take the older boy to an orphanage for Jewish children. I know of one near Marseilles.

It all happened so quickly. I had to tell your grandparents, Jade, what Rainier's mother had decreed. Perhaps they understood I wasn't to blame—I was an eighteen-year-old nobody. I couldn't make such a decision unilaterally. It had to be Rainier's parents. But then, your grandparents were on the precipice of decimation. Fighting for their lives, for the lives of their children. In such upheaval, did they make a distinction between who had ordered them out, and who delivered the news? And is it even fair, that I wanted them to?

In any event, they were stoic. In shock, absolument. Maurice was screaming, bloody murder, when his parents told him I was taking him away. His mother stared at him then, and he stopped. He had to stop screaming, or else they could have been ousted even sooner. I understood his anger, or I tried to, at least. What it would feel like to have your entire world swept out from under you. But then his mother crouched down and whispered to him for a few minutes in the corner. I don't know what was said. Only that eventually he came to me. I remember that his fingernails curled into his palms so hard that when he opened the car door and had to unfurl them, I could see he'd drawn blood. I took him to the orphanage. Back routes. It would have been dangerous if we were stopped and asked for papers, but we weren't. When we arrived, I saw that it was a stinking, horrid place, crowded with children. It felt unbearable to leave him there, but of course my pain is irrelevant in this tale. He wouldn't look at me, not on the way there, and not when I left him, with as much money as I could scrounge.

Before we went, I asked Rainier's mother for the diamond necklace, to give the child something of a start. But she refused.

When I returned to the chateau, it was I who had to force your grandparents out. Did I know I was sending them to their deaths? God, I hoped not. But did I suspect what awaited them? Yes, I did. The naïve girl I once was had gone the day they stepped into our chateau.

I couldn't even give them money. They'd insisted every last franc go to Maurice.

The baby was crying. Babies are so wise, aren't they?

I will never forget it, Jade, when your grandmother handed over her child to me.

Love him, she said. Love him fiercely. Love him twice, for you and for me.

I was crying. I couldn't stop crying. It was raining, and I felt like a fool, because I was going inside to dry, to warmth, with their child, and yet I was crying and they were not.

All these years, I have replayed the scene. They were in disbelief, no doubt. How can anyone process the events I catapulted them into? It doesn't matter that I didn't decree it, that I was powerless to stop it. I was the one who ultimately sent them away.

They hurried off into the night, and I clutched their wailing baby in my arms. I went inside. By the next morning, Rainier and I had new papers. We couldn't keep him as Arnaud, but I gave him the first letter, in homage. We named him Antoine.

Yes, Jade. Darcy's father, Antoine. Darcy is your first cousin. Isn't it unbelievable? And Antoine was your uncle. I am so sorry you never got to meet.

I did know that your father survived the war. I was overjoyed to hear it. You can't imagine. When I saw his name on a list of survivors, I cried very hard, for very long. So many times, I wanted the boys to meet. Brothers. Rainier wouldn't hear of it. Antoine would never forgive us. That was how he saw it. And perhaps he was right.

Add it to the list of my regrets. That list is long, indeed.

I did think that once Rainier was gone, I would revisit the subject. I hoped I would be a strong enough person to do what was right, for my son. Oh, how I loved Antoine. He was the best boy, the best man. I tried to raise him as his birth parents would have seen fit. With integrity. With love. He turned into a man to be proud of, a gentle, loving father, a kind person. I don't know if any drop of it was a credit to me. But I did try.

Antoine died just before Rainier. Both men in my life, in quick order.

And then you showed up in my house. It was altogether staggering. I remember it now—I was wearing the diamond necklace. Your eyes immediately fixed on my neck. Oh, I felt like the scum of the earth.

But please, allow me to explain. When Antoine was a baby, after his real parents were gone, he cried and cried. Relentlessly. A sweet baby became inconsolable. I was a stranger, and I didn't have breastmilk to soothe him. Sometimes he would paw at my neck, like he had done to his mother, but with increasing agitation. He scratched me there, so many times. Wanting something he would never have again.

I went to Rainier's mother. I demanded the necklace. And for some reason, she obliged. It was surely the most selfless thing she ever did in her entire wretched life.

So I wore the necklace, all day, every day, and my baby smiled again. It was like the necklace was his connection to the life he'd once had, and with it, he was my happy, bubbly Antoine.

I suppose I became accustomed to wearing the necklace. I associated it with him. Even after he died, maybe especially after that, I didn't want to take it off.

I understand how it must have looked to you. What you must have thought of me.

At Darcy's wedding, I saw you eyeing it. Darcy asked me for a duplicate key, and I had a hunch. I knew she'd figure out the code to the safe. Her father's birthday. When I returned, I wasn't surprised to see the necklace was gone.

My life has had many unspoken agreements, and this was one of them. The necklace was returned to its rightful owner. I am sorry I didn't give it to you sooner. I am sorry for so much.

I should have told you all this twenty years ago, when you first came to my chateau. But Rainier's mother drilled it into me, how much our good name mattered. It was only near the end of my life, *when I received my terminal diagnosis, really, that I thought about what it truly meant to have a good name. And I knew I couldn't die without you knowing what lies in my heart. I have wrapped the canvas up for you, with this note, in case something to happens to me. But as you will see, the painting must still be restored to the original. Speak to Victoria. Victoria will know what to do.*

You may still hate me after this. That is your right. Please send my regards to your father. Please show him this letter, and tell him how sorry I am. If I could go back and change things, I would. I would have stood up to my in-laws. I would have forced their hand somehow, made them see what was right. I wouldn't have let your grandparents walk into the night.

Oh, let's call it like it was. I wouldn't have banished *them into the night. To their deaths.*

Oh, how I would take it all back, if I could.

Yours,
Séraphine

———

It's all buzzing in my brain. What Grand-mère did. What Grand-père's parents did. What they did to *my* grandparents. I'm Jewish? Jade is my cousin? Her father my uncle? How can it be? How can it have been under our noses all this time?

I sink toward the ground, suddenly dizzy. As I sag atop the cement, my hand catches on the little basket in the bookshelf.

What in the . . . ? Oh yes, I remember seeing it when I entered. But the canvas wrapped in butcher paper beckoned first.

Now I dip a hand into the basket. I grasp a slip of paper on top. There's something else in the basket below. I hesitate, then look in. Immediately my heart seizes up. It's a plastic bag that contains surgical gloves. Also, a gray shirt I don't recognize, matted in something dark.

The basket plunges from my grip. I stand there frozen, staring at the wall, thinking but not putting anything together. Finally, I crouch down and pull out the slip of paper I saw on top.

It's from Grand-mère's notepad, and it's ripped partway down the page. This triggers alarm bells, but my nervous system is currently at its chased-by-a-tiger peak. So it's fuzzy, what the alarm bells are pointing to. My eyes refocus on the paper. I recognize it, of course. At the top is the crest, and Grand-mère's name. And below, in scratchy script that is unmistakably hers, there is one word.

Arabelle

"Arabelle?" I whisper, trying to make sense of it.

I am so confused, by everything, that I don't even register the footsteps.

"You called?"

And I look from the buttery suede boots in my eyeline upward, to see my friend—once my friend, at least—staring down at me, a little smile playing on her lips.

"Come out, come out, wherever you are," she says, almost playfully.

"What?" I hear myself stammer.

"Don't you remember? When we were kids, that's what I would say when we played hide-and-seek. When I'd ultimately find you."

My lips search for words, but none come.

"I always did find you. Didn't I?"

CHAPTER THIRTY-SIX

Jade

"**D**id I kill Séraphine?" I repeat, a bit stunned. "Do you really think I could have, Vixen?"

She is looking at the almond tree, and I suspect she's still transmitting it her waves of love. "I don't know," Vix finally says, slumping forward on the bench. "When I think about who could have done it, I keep drawing a blank. It couldn't have been Darcy. She loved her grandmother. She really did. I don't care that she inherited bazillions after her death. Arabelle wouldn't have done it—she has squillions of her own. And she never would bash Sylvie over the head." Vix rubs her arms. "Anyway, she's the only one of us with an alibi."

"Oliver," I supply.

"Ollie." Vix affects a French accent, with a hint of a smile.

I bite back my own smile. "If we can't laugh, we'll cry."

"The theme song of this week. Some reunion, huh?"

A laugh blasts out of me. "Some reunion, indeed."

Vix nods. "Sylvie is out as the killer. We can agree on that, right?"

"Agreed. There's no way."

"That leaves Raph. But he was in custody when Sylvie was attacked. . . ."

"So if he murdered Séraphine, that means someone else assaulted Sylvie, which—"

"Seems implausible."

"Highly implausible."

We sit in silence for a bit, digesting it all, the loop we keep cycling that has no discernible end. The almond tree blurs in my eyes, and I almost have to pinch myself to keep from drifting back into a time that wasn't even mine. But it feels like mine. It all feels so real, sometimes more real than the reality I am living.

"You haven't answered my question," Vix finally says.

"I didn't kill her!" I hear myself exclaim, in a defensive way that sounds like a confession of the exact opposite. "I swear," I say, calmer this time. "I swear I didn't do it. I mean . . . I'll be honest. I considered it."

Vix looks at me, wide-eyed. "You considered *killing* her?"

I nod, bite my lip. Then I tell her about what happened to Lux. How angry and scared I've been. But I shake my head. "I couldn't kill a person," I finally say. "I would never do that. It would mean I was just like her. And I'm not, Vix. You know I'm not. Besides, if I'd killed her, don't you think I would have asked her all the questions I've stored away my whole life? Whoever killed her took away my last chance for answers. What Séraphine did to my family, where she stored the painting, has all died right along with her."

Vix is quiet for a bit. Then she finally says, "I believe you, J."

"Good." I feel my chest heave with relief. And then the question bubbles up, an itch at my throat. "Did you . . . Did . . . ?"

"No," she says plainly, not defensive at all. "I loved Séraphine. I really did."

I know she did.

"I believe you," I say, even though I don't think she needs me to.

She nods, runs a hand over her breasts. She does that a lot. I'm not even sure she notices. "Who killed Séraphine, then? Some random intruder?" Vix sounds disbelieving, but a bit hopeful.

"No. I wish I could believe that. God, it would make things so much easier. But no. We know it was one of us."

"One of the two of us? Are we back there again?"

"No," I say honestly. "I don't think it was one of the two of us. I mean I know it wasn't me. And I don't think you did it."

"Well, if we didn't do it, then chances are the murderer is at the chateau now."

I shiver, but not from the rain now peppering us from the ghostly sky. "We should get back, then. What if something is going down?"

"Yes. We should get back," Vix says, but doesn't rise. "But can we sit here, just a little longer? I just . . ."

I reach over and squeeze her hand. I understand completely. There is something cleansing about the rain, and this moment, and this place. "Yes, let's sit here a little longer."

CHAPTER THIRTY-SEVEN

Arabelle

I pick up the scrap of paper with my name. Darcy's perfect green eyes are staring right at me, but glazed over, containing nothing distinct.

"*Arabelle?*" she says uncertainly, shifting back on the floor, away from me. "The note says *Arabelle?*"

"Yes, that's what it says," I say patiently.

"Arabelle," she repeats, like an incompetent child. Like someone very mentally slow.

"Yes." I motion with my right hand in a circle, like *get fucking on with it*. Do I need to spell everything out? Is everyone an imbecile in this house?"

"You mean . . . this is the top of the note the police found in her room? You killed Grand-mère? You *murdered* my grandmother? Oh my God."

Her face is fully readable now. You can see everything etched into it. The shock, the fear. She hides nothing, not from me. She has always been loved so completely, so unconditionally, for being her weak, spindly self. Well, maybe she hasn't been loved as such by Ollie. I've proven that. But by Séraphine, certainly. Darcy calls herself a warrior, but she is not. She has had infinite people, now infinite money, bolstering her up. That's not a warrior. That's a pampered princess.

"The note doesn't say I murdered Séraphine." I tap my head with my right index finger. "Think a little more critically here."

Her face has colored an almost blistered red, which, honestly,

275

doesn't suit her hair or pallor. She scoots back farther from me, across the stone. The wall is a few inches behind her. There is only so far to go.

"It says *murdered*." Her bottom lip quivers. "The note says *murdered*. Past tense."

"Yesss."

I can see by her face that she knows. She doesn't know everything, of course. She is too stupid to figure out everything, even when it's right in front of her nose. But she has found the note, and she can see it in my demeanor. In my words. I am done faking it with her. After forty years, I am so done faking it. But still, she's largely clueless. So I will have to help her along.

"You might want to look back in the basket," I suggest.

Her splotchy face rearranges itself into some variation of defiance. She is like a mother antelope, squaring off against a lion. The defiance is false. She knows it, and I know it. The lion always vanquishes the antelope.

"I'm not doing anything you say until you tell me if you killed my grandmother. And I saw what was in the basket. Bloody clothes. Gloves. A bag of evidence, no doubt pointing to you." She points at me in breathless accusation, like she has the upper hand.

I slowly take my left hand out from behind my back. Her eyes flinch.

Yes, I am holding a gun, and it is trained at Darcy. I am not playing around.

"Look in the basket," I say. "See what else is there. Underneath the bag you call evidence."

The color has drained from her face, now as gray as storm clouds, or headstones in a graveyard. Her coffin, slipping into earth. She digs frantically in the basket and slowly pulls out the note that was tucked at the bottom.

I see her eyes widen as she registers it.

A l'amour de ma vie, Sylvie

"You . . ." Her voice falters. I understand why it does.

"Yes," I say, because her lips are flapping now without ejecting words. "Yes, I am the one who hit my grandmother over the head. I hated to do it. But I had to, you see. To get the note before she read it. You'll soon understand."

"You . . . you . . . *bashed* your own grandmother on the head. You . . ."

"Yes, me, me, me. And I'll have you know, Séraphine is the one ultimately responsible for it. Before I killed her, the day before, I warned her to call it off, her horrible plan. But she refused. So anything I had to do to get the note back is on her. And really, Darce, *bashed* is such an aggressive word. I only put Mamie out for a few minutes, enough time to steal the note and get away. She is fine." Although as I say it, I do feel a flash of guilt. I never wanted to hurt Mamie. Of course not. But when Séraphine and I went to lunch a few weeks back, and she told me what she'd planned, she also warned me that she'd written a letter to Mamie. That if anything happened to Séraphine, that letter would still be sent. Little did she understand that instead of deterring me, she'd just given me a heads-up.

I'm impatient now. I wave the gun and move closer to my friend. *Friend.* That word is laden with meaning, but hardly sufficient to describe who Darcy and I truly are to each other. She needs to understand it all, once and for all. Darcy tries to move back away from me, from the gun, but that's the end of the room. Nowhere to hide. Not anymore.

"Read it," I say.

"What?" Tears are dripping down her cheeks.

"Read the note. No more secrets. Isn't that what you've wanted?"

Her fingers aren't moving. It's like her brain has gone slack. Can no longer communicate with her limbs.

Must I do everything?

I snatch the letter from her with my right hand, keeping the gun trained on her with my left. I haven't gone through all of this—oh, so much—to give her the slightest opening to fight back. No. I will snuff out the last of her warrior. Whatever flickers remain.

I shove the letter in between her fingers.

"Read," I command. God, it feels good to be purely myself. It's like taking off a Halloween costume that has been making me sweaty and itchy for years.

"You killed Grand-mère?" she asks for what feels like the ten millionth time, smudging the sleeve of her dress against her sniffling teary mess of a face.

"Yes. I killed your grandmother." I groan. "You're really slow, Darcy. Pick it up, why don't you? Gather up your brain off the floor and turn the switch on!"

I take a deep breath, try to calm down. It's natural after all this time, all these plans, that I would be a bit eager to commence the finale. Still, I spoke too loudly. This room is insulated, but less so after the renovation. Now thin wood covers the old doorway. They don't make 'em like they used to! It's why I asked Jade to switch rooms with me when we arrived. The small room by the stairs can pick up noises from this room. I knew Darcy would find it eventually. I always intended that she would.

And if she didn't, I intended to drag her here, at gunpoint. One way or another, it was always going to end here.

"Read," I say. "Fucking read."

"You . . . You . . ." Her teeth are chattering now. "You killed her with a *knife*."

"Yes. I wanted her to feel like an animal. I wanted her to feel pain." I think of it now, how much I pleasure I got, stabbing Séraphine, again and again. "She deserved it. Every last slash, she deserved. You, on the other hand, I'm happy to give a quick, painless death. If you earn it."

"You're going to kill me." She doesn't ask a question this time. Just states a fact.

"Let's see," I say, even though, yes, I'm going to fucking kill her. "If you're good, and do what I say, maybe I won't."

The gun is cool and smooth against my palm. With a silencer, of course. And untraceable. It was almost shockingly easy to procure, from a former guest at my inn. An unsavory guy from Marseilles, whose contact I kept just in case I'd need it one day.

"You're going to kill me," Darcy says, the fear in her eyes evident.

She's watched all those insipid detective shows. So who am I to tell her otherwise?

"I will," I finally say. "Yes, it was always coming to this. But for now, enjoy the air I am allowing you to breathe. And fucking read." I move closer, put the gun to her temple.

Oh God, that feels good.

"Read the note," I repeat. "Now."

And then I smile when she does.

CHAPTER THIRTY-EIGHT

Darcy

I feel my hands shaking, shaking, as I unfold the letter. The letter that Arabelle nearly killed her grandmother for. If she did that to Sylvie, she won't hesitate to kill me.

I need to fight back. But how? She's standing there, waiting for me to read the letter in my hands, with a gun trained on me. I've never seen a gun in person, only on TV. The gun is black, heavy. My mind drifts to this toy gun, silver with a black handle, that a friend from childhood had. I remember her brother, in a diaper and red cowboy hat, running and squealing around the apartment, amid *pop-pop-pop* sounds.

Will I hear the *pop-pop*, when the bullet is heading toward me?

No, don't go there. I can't go there. I summon the fight. The warrior. This psychopath isn't taking me down. I have Mila and Chase to live for. Suddenly it occurs to me—if I'm gone, and Arabelle somehow weasels her way out of culpability, she will have easy access to my children.

That makes me spring off my feet. I lunge toward her, toward the gun, and am surprised when it gives easily away. Oh my God oh my God oh my God.

"Back up," I say, the gun fumbling in my hands. She obeys. I am shaking wildly. She steps closer, her face impassive. I don't know how we were ever friends. How I ever thought I knew her. She is as impenetrable to me now as one of those wax figures at Madame Tussauds.

"Not any closer!"

She stops. "You won't." Her eyes are almost glittering, taunting me. I don't think I can do it. I can't kill her.

She steps closer again.

But if I don't pull the trigger, she will kill me. She's admitted as much. And I know it in my bones. She won't hesitate.

I summon my will, then I squeeze the trigger. My eyes close involuntarily. I've seen what happens in the movies. Splatters of blood, organs, flesh. But nothing happens. No bullet, no Arabelle flesh. Nothing. I try again, squeeze harder. Nothing.

Arabelle laughs and comes over, twists the gun out of my Gumby hands. "Safety was on," she says, and pushes me hard. I plunge to the floor.

I hear someone weeping, and I realize it is me. Mila and Chase. That's all I'm thinking about, their sweet, trusting faces, their pillowy skin. My cheeks are drenched in wet. My heart is squeezing so tight I expect it will explode.

"And besides," I hear Arabelle say, "I haven't loaded anything yet." I watch her pull what I can only guess is a round out of her jeans and stuff it inside the gun. It makes a sickening click.

"But you played to my hand exactly," she tells me, taking new aim.

"You wanted me to do that?" I ask, panting. I want to be cool, to show her I'm not afraid. But I'm terrified. I'm fucking terrified. And I still don't get it. There are still so many missing puzzle pieces.

"Of course," Arabelle says. "Now both our fingerprints are all over it."

"You're setting me up?" I say slowly.

"Yes. That way when I kill you, it will be in self-defense."

"But . . . But how?" I find myself babbling. "What possibly would be my motive?"

Arabelle retrieves the letter that has drifted to the floor. She places it in my hands. "Are you ready to read now? Because I'm losing patience, and you really don't want to die without the answers, do you?"

I am pinned down by fear. I try to respond, something clever, something warrior-like, but the link between my brain and my mouth has severed. Nothing emits.

She sighs. "Whenever I envisioned this moment, and it was many, many times, I'll have you know, I thought this would be more fun. That you'd be a more worthy opponent. All right, start reading. We don't have all day. Or at least, you don't. Soon it will all make sense."

I wipe my eyes, trying to create a window to see. *Help me, Grand-mère* is what I am thinking as I attempt to focus.

But in all likelihood, I am praying to the wrong person. Two letters from my grandmother I have now discovered, and neither was written to me.

———

Sylvie, ma chérie,

Oh, Sylvie. If you are reading this, then the worst has happened. Well, not the worst. But the thing I most feared.

I am writing this in English because I ask you to share it with the girls. I have gathered everyone here for two purposes. One is to make amends with Jade. You will soon find out the story. I have been too ashamed to tell you before. Please forgive me, ma chérie, *for keeping too many secrets.*

The other purpose we haven't spoken about. Before I die, in whatever manner that may be, I must make something else right. As right as it can now be.

Sylvie, my darling. I don't know how to start this. With my love for you? No, you know this. It is fact. You will never question it. Promise me you will never question it.

Everything I did was for you. Was to keep both our families intact. Hindsight is difficult, though. I am older, wiser. I know now different things. I would have made different choices. But you can't go back and scratch out the past and insert a better one, can you?

All I want to do now is protect you. And protect Darcy. And now you must do that for me. By this letter, you must expose what has been done.

If I've been murdered, then it is Arabelle who did it. Oh, I'm so sorry to say it. I know how you love that girl. But you don't know who she is. Or maybe you do. Because you know evil. And you know how evil spawns.

Do you remember the day Rainier died in the pool? Cracked his head on the statue? I saw it all from my window.

Later we spoke of it in private. The bastard was gone. He really was an evil bastard. You, in particular, were full of relief. I was, too, in different measure. I did love him once, in another lifetime, maybe. I loved him when I was young, and youth glossed over the tiny buds of his failings. But in the end, he had his mother's genes inside him, and oh how they bloomed in him. She was a horrible person, who sent Jade's family into the hands of monsters and didn't even give them back their heirlooms to barter for their subsequent safety.

Rainier was evil, in different ways. How he spoke to me, yes, in that demeaning manner. How he hit me, yes. I became très bien with my makeup application, to cover up my bruises. But you bore the brunt. I wish I had known, when it happened. If I had known he had raped you then, when you were newly married, I like to think I would have left him.

I don't know, Sylvie. I was weaker then, especially when he was still around to hurt and threaten me.

You might be thinking, why dredge all this up? Why bring up the painful facts of Rainier?

Well, because of how he died. I told you that he slipped. That was always what I said. Darcy was doing a handstand in the water. She'd gotten quite good, and Rainier doted on her. He was cheering her on. I always thought the best of him came out in Darcy. He did love our girl. The part of him that was able to muster love.

While Darcy was underwater, Arabelle came out from nowhere, sprinting from the house across the lawn. She didn't stop. I was paralyzed, watching, as she barreled toward Rainier. She shoved him, hard, and he cracked his head on the statue. It was deliberate, Sylvie. There was no other interpretation. And she didn't linger to marvel over what she'd done. She didn't stand there in horror. No, she sprinted away, as fast as she'd come, only stopping momentarily when her eyes caught mine through the window.

Yes, she knew immediately I had seen.

Well, it was a mess, as you know. I couldn't get down fast enough to prevent Darcy from finding her grandfather dead in the pool. And I didn't know what to do. Call the police immediately? Console Darcy? Protect her from Arabelle?

Darcy ran off so I couldn't find her, and after I'd called the police, Arabelle came to my room. I told her what I had seen, and she didn't deny it.

I asked her for an explanation, and eventually she gave me one.

She told me that she had overheard you and me speaking—you remember the conversation, don't you, ma chérie? You and I circled each other for very many years, before our mutual intentions were confirmed. In that conversation in the dining room, we bared our souls. You finally told me about the rape that created Arabelle's mother, and Arabelle in turn. We held hands under the table for the very first time.

Well, little did we know, but Arabelle was sitting behind the curtains, listening to everything. You remember how she used to find little corners in which to read? Always poring over those cookbooks? How she used to hide sometimes and read, behind the curtains?

She must have been jealous of Darcy from the start, but from then on, she couldn't stand her. You remember, of course, how Rainier doted on Darcy but ignored Arabelle. Even though he knew exactly who she was. I always thought that was despicable of him, but unsurprising. Many facts unspoken lie in the gulf of a marriage. This was one of ours. I pretended I knew nothing of what he did to you, and he pretended he had done nothing. And now, in the wake of his deeds, Arabelle knew Rainier was her grandfather, too.

After Arabelle killed him, she told me she was sorry. She was so very sorry. And I'll be honest, I didn't believe her. Was there a chance it was an accident? No. But I wanted to believe her. If I told the police it was her, it would have destroyed you. It would have ended her life, and yours, too. There would have been a trial. And it would have come out—what Rainier did to you. We all would have been mired in scandal.

I told her I would keep her secret, but that she was never to lay a hand on one hair of Darcy's head. That she would stay away from my granddaughter. And that I would be watching.

She promised.

But over the years, I've seen little things that have reinforced my belief that Rainier was not an exception to the rule of Arabelle's deepest inclinations, but rather the rule itself. I didn't like that Arabelle became ensconced in Darcy's group of girlfriends. I didn't like it at all. But that semester, I felt I had some control. When I saw the girls befriend Arabelle, I invited them, over and over, for weekends here. That way, I presided over things. When they visited me, I could keep my eyes on her. Later, they dispersed, and Darcy and Arabelle were separated by half the world, after all.

Still, I was discomfited, frightened at times. I tried to convince myself I was inflating things. Worrying over nothing. That what Arabelle did to Rainier was a gross childhood error.

But when I was informed recently that I don't have long to live, I decided to invite all the girls back to the chateau. That reunion is in a few weeks. I am both looking forward to it and dreading it more than I can express. Yesterday I called Arabelle and asked her to dine with me in town today, when you were out at the dentist. I told her I wanted to see her, before the other girls arrive.

Today at lunch I told Arabelle that I have a terminal illness. I wanted to see her reaction. I told myself going into it that if any instinct in me prickled wrongly, that I was going to go through with my plan.

I wasn't worried about her coming after our wealth. Some of it is rightfully hers, I suppose. If after my death I thought only that she would tell Darcy the truth about her parentage—that she and Darcy are actually cousins, equal heirs to Rainier's estate—I would have kept quiet still.

What I was really worried about was that, finally, without me to keep a check on her, to hold what she did as a child over her, she would target Darcy. And I wouldn't be around to stop it.

She was polite at the lunch, even sympathetic, when she learned that I was dying. But when we were walking out, I tripped a little, going down the stairs. She caught me. She was right beside me. But as she did, I saw something in her eyes. She hesitated. I saw her hate, how enormous it was. Clear as day. And I knew immediately that her hate burned just as bright for my granddaughter.

She walked me to my car, and I told her that I was going to reveal what had happened all those years before at Rainier's death. She was irate. She squeezed my wrist so hard she left marks. If my prior instinct hadn't convinced me, now I was certain of what I had to do.

I told her I couldn't leave Darcy alone without warning her before I was gone. I told Arabelle that if she was easy about things, I would urge any prosecutor for leniency. I would tell them she was young. That she'd been provoked.

She raged then, about her career, about how it would look, how it would injure her brand. She promised she wouldn't go after our money. I said it didn't matter. I'd made up my mind. And I told her I had written this letter to you, so she better not try anything funny.

On that note, I was lying. I am only writing it now, still shaken by our encounter.

I am scared, ma chérie. But I am a Demargelasse. That name has evil inside it, but never a backing down. I won't back down now, for Darcy's sake, and for yours. I know even you won't be safe with her after I'm gone. No one will.

People don't change. I saw how she shoved Rainier, callously and without remorse. No matter who he was, what he had done, I saw her evil in motion. And I am afraid for what else she has in store. Please forgive me, for everything. And do what must be done.

All my love,
Séraphine

CHAPTER THIRTY-NINE

Arabelle

I did wonder if all this would push Darcy so far over the edge that I wouldn't have to kill her. That she'd have a heart attack, or something else. She is fragile, like porcelain. And porcelain shatters easily. She's just never been pushed so far as to break.

Last night, as I lay in bed, I ticked through it all in my head. Jade and Vix were going to Van Gogh's sanitorium in the morning. Mamie said she was going to rest, still weak from the attack. There are certain moments in life you have to act. I knew it all those years ago with Rainier, standing there at the edge of the pool, all gleeful over Darcy's stupid handstands.

I knew it last night, too. That Darcy would want to confront me now that things had sunk in. And that I would confront her back. A final, lethal confrontation.

She is clutching her chest, heaving on the floor. Maybe she is indeed having a heart attack. How will that fit into my narrative, that I killed her in self-defense? I'll think of something.

"You . . . You . . ."

"I . . . I . . ." I taunt back.

I might sound heartless. I do, don't I?

It's just, you try living your whole life in the shadow of the *real* granddaughter. The beloved granddaughter. The one who gets the best of everything, both her grandparents' affection. And then you discover that contrary to what you've been told, you have a grandfather alive and kicking. Hell, he even knows all about you. And he couldn't care less. He doesn't even deign to look in your eyes. When you pass him in the hall, it's like you're not even there.

You are the illegitimate granddaughter. A stain on his good name. A reminder of the evil inside him.

And just this week, when I murdered Séraphine, after I searched to no avail for her letter to Mamie in her safe, I found a painting in her closet, with a letter addressed to Jade. I was intrigued, and I wanted to make certain there was nothing that would implicate me inside. I felt propelled to bring the package to this room, where I knew the police wouldn't search. Along with the upper half of the note Séraphine tried to hide in her bed, incriminating me. Of course, I saw it, when I arranged the murder scene. I tore the note apart, leaving only the bottom half. The bottom half was good. I saw how it could turn the investigation in a direction that would serve me.

Later, when I read the letter addressed to Jade, I received the ultimate blow.

Darcy wasn't the real granddaughter, after all. She wasn't even Rainier's, not by blood. And he knew it. He only had one grandchild by blood. Me. And he never acknowledged me.

"He deserved to die," I tell Darcy now. "I never regretted doing it. Just so you know."

She is coughing, heaving. I watch her. Let her have her moment. She knows, just as I do, that the clock is slowly ticking down.

"You killed Grand-père." She isn't looking at me, just pounding her fists on the floor, distraught.

"Ding dong, the witch finally figured it out," I say. "Is that the saying?"

"It's ding dong, the witch is dead," Darcy whispers.

"Oh." I laugh. "Well, that, too."

I am smiling at my cleverness, when suddenly, Darcy shoots up from the floor with strength I didn't expect and darts toward the door. On her way, she shoves me to the floor. I am taken aback. I fall.

Putain!

I scramble up. The gun is still in my hands, and I run out of the room into the foyer, where Darcy is screaming.

Putain, putain, putain!

I only pray Mamie has ear plugs in. She doesn't hear well, anyhow, but Darcy is screeching, her decibel high. Darcy makes it to the door. She is barefoot, and that gives her the edge over my booties. But I am the runner, and that gives me the ultimate advantage. I reach for her hair, but it streams through my fingers as she continues her flee. She escapes the front door, pounds down the steps, screaming nothing that makes sense, but sounds like a tortured prisoner of war.

I chase after, fast, down the steps, into the gravel walk bordered in pines. It's drizzling now, and the sky has gone white. I've always thought the entry of the chateau looks like something out of a Russian movie—but especially now. It is bleak, barren. You can practically imagine a birch forest in winter, blanketed in snow. As I run, quickening my pace, almost strangely enjoying this unexpected chase, I am reminded of a Russian cookbook I once read. I read different countries' cookbooks. It's fun. I like to sift through another culture's food, if only to confirm that French is the best. Sometimes I incorporate a wink to Italy, a nod to Finland. For Russia, I did a French take on the blintz. Naturally, my version was superior.

The point is, I learned in that cookbook a morbid fact. The author wove it in during a retrospective on Soviet food. She said that the worst punishment in Russia is being shot through the face and then buried in an unmarked grave. In my imagination, I see that grave in a birch forest. Or the front of the chateau.

It's the punishment I want more than anything to give Darcy.

Nom de Dieu, the girl is faster than I gave her credit for. I could shoot her now, but that would be messy. Someone could see. I want to do it in the room. That was my plan, and I'm not letting Darcy screw it all up.

Finally, I pump my arms, burst out with my legs, and reach her. I shove her to the ground. She writhes there for a few seconds and I can see her right cheek is scraped, bloody. I bend down and run a hand along her cut, slowly. She winces, cries out. When I draw my fingers back, they carry a fresh slick of blood. Then I grab her hard by her hair. I tip her chin up to me, so she's looking into my eyes, and I whisper an inch from her mouth, "If you make any more noise, I'll shoot you right here and now."

Then I drag her like a rag doll back to the house as she whimpers.

"Shut up," I hiss. "Don't make a sound. Not one little sound, or you'll risk Mamie's life, too. You don't want to do that now, do you?"

That shuts her up. The threat travels through my tubes, bumping not so nicely up against organs. I don't like threatening anything having to do with Mamie. I certainly didn't like hitting her over the head. I am not a monster. However I've been portrayed.

I am a wronged woman, and I am finally claiming what is mine.

We are almost back inside the room. One more second, and we would have slipped her by. But life has never been shy about serving me up curveballs. Dropping a little extra tragedy on my lap.

"Arabelle," Mamie says, and I swivel to see my grandmother, with a look on her face unlike any I've ever known.

She knows. Somehow she knows. And this little scene—the gun against precious Darcy's head—isn't doing me any favors.

Mamie's lips are firm in a line. She waves a note in the air. "Put down the gun, Arabelle. Put it down *now*. There was a second note. Underneath the plane tree. A box, we buried there, to . . . oh." The *oh* is a desolate sound, absent of hope. Like I am a lost cause, or something. "Arabelle, let Darcy go. *Now*. You . . ." Her voice dribbles into a cry.

"Right," I say, letting it all sink in. "Okay, then." I wave the gun at Mamie. "In with you, too. Come on, Mamie. You know I don't want to hurt you. But you also know what I'm capable of."

I am a little frightened, to hear those words emerge from me. As I watch Mamie's little frame tuck desolately inside the secret door, I feel a wave of genuine sadness. What a shame—how unfair!—that I will have to kill Mamie, too. I wanted to warn Séraphine that her note would only endanger Mamie. But that wouldn't have bought me the time I needed. When I hit my grandmother over the head, I was saving her at the same time. That note was her danger, not *me*. I love my grandmother. I do. Dearly. But love has nothing to do with anything now. I know what must be done. In order for me to have the life I deserve, there is no other way. And what is the alternative? Would Mamie live out the rest of her days in enjoyment with her flesh and blood, the one on which she has pinned the entirety of her hopes and dreams, in jail for murder? Put there at her hands? No. This is best. Mamie will go straight to heaven, reunite with her Séraphine. She will thank me for sparing her any further pain on this earth.

I'll be honest, I hoped it wouldn't come to this. But maybe I always wondered if it would.

CHAPTER FORTY

Darcy

Sylvie and I are sitting on the ground, our backs to the wall, while Arabelle and her gun loom over us. My body is still twitching, high on adrenaline and sheer terror. My gaze pings off the walls, then fixes on a sliver of light at the end of the hall toward the door. There wasn't light there before—at least I don't think. When Arabelle slammed the door, she must not have shut it properly. Or maybe I'm just seeing things. Imagining a way out of this hell, when hope feels down to vapors.

Sylvie is weeping. Waterworks. I understand, or at least, I can relate, on a theoretical level, although at the moment I am numb. All of the revelations, followed by my failed escape, have stun-gunned my tears. I'm not sure what I think, what I feel, anymore. None of that matters, though. Right now I need to keep Arabelle occupied so I can figure out how to thwart her before she kills us.

"I don't understand a few things," I say, willing calm into my tone. "How did you have an alibi during the time of the murder?"

"Oh, that." She smiles. "I really did plan it all perfectly. Having Ollie over. I knew it would expose us to you, too. When he had been reluctant to do so. It needed to come out."

I file that away. Oliver has been manipulated by her, just like the rest of us. But that doesn't mean he isn't culpable. He broke our family apart of his own volition.

"But the clock. It was shattered at the same time you said you and Oliver were . . ." I still can't force it out of my mouth.

"Having sex." She nods, like it's old news. "I smashed the clock intentionally, after I killed Séraphine. Then I moved the time forward an hour. I had some time then, to clean up my mess. I saw Séraphine scribbling something on her pad when I was looking in the safe for her note. I had a gun." She indicates the one in her hand. "To ensure she wouldn't scream. Plus." She smiles. "I told her if she screamed, I'd come for you next. But in the end, it was rather a brilliant thing for me that she wrote what she wrote."

"Arabelle murdered R," I say, because now it has all sunk in, far too late. "R as in Rainier. Not Raph. None of us paid much attention to the verb tense of *murdered*."

"Exactly. That's what I was banking on. I was going to take the entire note to conceal, but then I realized how it would be interpreted if I simply ripped off the top. I knew the police would search the chateau. My car probably, too. But how perfect to have the secret room to leave things inside. I told you that it had been covered up in the renovation. Mamie knew that wasn't true, but I knew it wouldn't occur to her to suggest to the gendarmes to look here. So I washed up in the sink downstairs, with my fingerprints already all over it. And then I deposited things in here. I'll toss the shirt once the police aren't swarming the house on a hunt for every possible clue. It was better to hide stuff here until they leave."

"Arabelle!" Sylvie's face contorts in pain. I reach over to grasp her hand. Her mouth opens, then shuts. I understand. Her granddaughter is a sociopath. What more can possibly be said?

"You brought Jade's painting here, too," I say. "But why, Belle? You wanted it?"

"No!" Arabelle's eyes narrow, like I've accused her of something despicable that her high character would so obviously preclude. "The painting belongs to Jade, of course. I wouldn't dream of keeping it from her. I just wanted to make sure the note didn't implicate me. I haven't done any of this for money. Though . . ." She smiles. "Everything in this place will in fact be mine. I am the only heir, after all."

"*Darcy* is the heir," Sylvie says.

"Yes, because you tried to keep secret my real identity. You kept all this from me!"

For the first time in my life, I hear Arabelle's naked spite toward her grandmother.

"Rainier raped me," Sylvie says softly. "That's the sort of man you wanted in your life?"

"Better than nothing!" Arabelle says. "Better someone to pay attention to me! Not that he wanted to." She turns to me. "He was only ever concerned for his precious Darcy. Not even the grandchild from his blood." She waves the gun manically, pointing the barrel at herself in punctuation.

I want to get her off this train. "So when you got back to your room, Oliver was sleeping. Naturally."

She laughs, almost conspiratorially. "Yes. You know Ollie. Dead to the world. I woke him up. We . . ."

"Yes, I know what you did."

She nods. Blessedly doesn't expand. "Afterward, I asked him the time. It was really rather perfect. I knew he'd remember. Back up my alibi. And there you have it."

"I don't have all of it, though. How in the world do you think you're going to murder me and claim it's self-defense? You think anyone will buy the accusation that I murdered my own grandmother?"

"Of course they will buy it," Arabelle says calmly. "You mean to say you weren't called into the police station to be interviewed as the prime suspect?"

"But what's my motive?" My heart sinks. I suspect what she will say.

"Money. You and Ollie are in dire straits. Don't act like this inheritance hasn't solved every one of your petty problems. And I saw the invitation on your bureau. Séraphine handwrote that she wanted to talk to you about her Will."

Shit. We never even got to have that conversation. Now I wonder if Grand-mère wasn't trying to give me a heads-up about Vix's inheritance. Or about my own? I'll never know.

"Okay, so money," I say briskly, trying to underplay it, even though

I feel shaky inside, at how neatly the bare facts fit for her ends. "But then, why did I hit Sylvie over the head? Why would I try to kill you? And if I had a gun, why would I kill my grandmother with a knife instead? Doesn't that aspect fall apart? You think the cops are going to buy that I killed my grandmother with such vengeance?"

Arabelle claps her hands, the barrel of the gun slapping her skin in a way that makes me fling my hands to my head, in protection. "Bravo, Darce. You're smarter than I gave you credit for. Why the knife? Well, you discovered something," Arabelle says with a terrifying glint in her eye. "Something that made you very angry."

"Oh, really? What's that?"

"That I am the true heir of Rainier. That's what your grandmother was going to reveal to us all. Séraphine was going to announce she intended to change her Will, to make clear that I would inherit half. And you needed to stop her, at all costs."

It rolls toward me, like an avalanche. The brilliance. The deception. That all of this makes a warped kind of sense.

"I'll take good care of your children," Arabelle says with a hint of a smile. "I promise."

I lunge at her.

"Arabelle!" Sylvie shouts, as I feel myself flung backward, landing in a twisted, horrible way on my left sits bone.

As I'm rubbing it, infuriated, petrified, I hear someone call, "Darcy? Darcy, where are you? I heard you shout. Darcy?"

Raph!

"Not a word," Arabelle hisses, waving the gun. "Either of you. This has a silencer on it. And I won't hesitate."

I know she isn't tossing out empty threats. My heartbeat is so loud that I pray he can hear it.

"Darcy? Sylvie? Arabelle?"

A shadow passes over the tiny opening at the door. Then the crack of light again. Hours seem to pass until finally, I hear footsteps recede. I feel my body slump forward. It's over. I'm never going to get out of here alive.

But Mila and Chase. I clap a hand over my mouth to keep my cry inside. I have to fight for them. But how?

I am furious at myself now, for my failed escape attempt, for how it has roped Sylvie into this, too. And how stupid that in my precious moments of freedom I didn't call the police. Call Raph! Who is on this property and has no clue what is going on. He's a security officer. He's the best person to save us. Contacting him is what I should have done, straightaway. If I can just message him without Arabelle noticing . . . Maybe Sylvie will distract her. But how? My phone is burning in my pocket against my hip. I stretch my fingers inside, grasping for it. Maybe I can just . . .

Suddenly Arabelle's gun comes level with my temple. "Yes, take out your phone."

"Take out my phone? What do you . . . ?"

"That's what I said. You asked me how I'm going to frame you. Well, there's one more thing I have in mind."

Slowly I draw out my phone. I have no clue what she means.

"Arabelle, this is . . . Arabelle, shame!" Sylvie cries, positively bereft. "Please don't do this. Please. See sense. You are a good person, at your core. You have to be! You have to be!" It is a hideous thing, to see a devoted grandmother in terror of her granddaughter.

Arabelle ignores her. "Pull up that Instagram account."

"The Fertility Warrior?" I ask, even though I know that's not what she means.

She waves the gun. "No. The Instagram account you thought you were so smart about. You didn't know it was me, did you?"

I swallow hard. "I thought it was Jade."

She smiles. "You found the scrunchie."

"You *wanted* me to find the scrunchie," I say slowly.

"Of course. And you wanted to get revenge."

I nod. What an inane plan. I can't even call it a plan. Just a burning desire to expose Jade in the most humiliating way. How wrong I was. How wrong I was about absolutely everything.

"Well, let's give you another motive to murder me, why don't we?

Because we haven't even talked about the best one. I stole your husband. Not only am I taking half of your inheritance, but I'm taking Ollie, too."

Oh my God. The perfection of what she is saying is enough to hoover up my breath. She's right. No one will believe I didn't do this. Not even Vix or Jade. And if Arabelle gets rid of me and Sylvie, she'll walk away scot-free. With both my husband and my children.

"Pull up the account," she says again. "Now, let's add one more post, why don't we? A final post, how about?"

My fingers are clunky, not moving properly across the screen.

"Come on, we don't have all day. Or at least, you don't. One post. Let's make it simple. Upload a square in red."

"In red?" I ask, not getting it. "Just the color?"

"Yes. Now."

I do what she says. What else can I do?

"No funny business," she warns me. "I'm watching. Not like you have any followers, though. Last I checked." She winks. "The caption will be one sentence. How about, *Blood is the color of revenge*."

Oh God. I stare at her, frozen.

"Go on!"

She turns away, pacing back to the wall, and I type quickly.

"Show it to me," she says.

I show her, praying with all my might.

"Okay." She nods. "Upload."

I watch the bright red square upload to the feed of the stupid revenge Instagram account I created back when I knew nothing about anything in my life.

"It's done," I say.

"Good. Give your phone to me."

Slowly, I hand it over.

"It's all fairly perfect, *n'est-ce pas?*" She smiles, and I wonder how I haven't always seen it, that perfect empty smile that hides a deeply disturbed person beneath. "The police will no doubt find this nice evidence. You hated me from the start of the trip. You've wanted revenge, even before you knew I was coming for your money. While you stood over me with a gun, you decided to upload one final post."

Just keep her talking. Keep her talking, and keep on praying. "What about the notes, then?"

"I'll destroy them, *bien sûr*. I'll say that you burned them but told me everything that was inside them, how I am Rainier's true grandchild." Arabelle turns to Sylvie. "Mamie, your note, please. How perfect that I get my hands on the unknown extra copy."

I watch Sylvie fumble as she retrieves the note from her pocket, her face disbelieving.

"What about the bag of bloodstained things?" I ask. "How are you going to explain that to the police? It will have your DNA all over it."

She cocks her head at me like I'm a moron. "I'll get rid of it. Put it in my car. It's going to be so clear-cut what happened in here that the police aren't going to do any further searching."

"Okay, but your fingerprints are on Jade's painting, too," I counter. "What do you think the police will make of that?"

"I was curious," she says calmly. "When I was waiting for the police, after I turned the tables on my attacker, naturally I felt curious to take a peek at the painting and the letter.

"Okay." She snaps her fingers, the hand without the gun. "You're not much use to me anymore, are you? And best be quick before Raph comes looking again, or Jade and Vix return. So let's commence the finale, why don't we? Or your finale, at least. It's time, at long last, Darce, for you to bid *adieu*."

Sylvie threads her hand into mine and I look at her, both of us teary. And I pray. I pray harder than I have in my life.

CHAPTER FORTY-ONE

Raph

I've been searching everywhere, ever since I heard Darcy scream. And something told me to keep refreshing Instagram. Just in case she sent me a DM.

She didn't, but she did post something creepy and cryptic to her feed.

Blood is the color of revenge.

And she tagged a random account she doesn't even follow. @underthestairs.

Under the stairs? I know the message is for me, but as I pace the foyer, I'm trying to no avail to parse what that means.

Where are you, Darcy? And *who* were you screaming at?

Suddenly, I hear muffled voices. I strain my ears. The voices are coming from the wall behind the stairs. Suddenly, I spot a small crack. A crack in a hundreds-year-old wall? I cup my ear up close and listen. I can't make out what they are saying, but I hear Darcy, and then Arabelle.

Darcy and Arabelle. My brain works, fitting disparate pieces together. There must be some hidden passage, a hidden room. I start to probe with my left hand, my gun firmly in my right.

I debated, after leaving the police station, about coming back here to the chateau. And then, when I decided I would, I debated further, about whether I should make a stop first, to retrieve my gun.

I know why I did both of those things. Even if I've been trying to pretend to myself there were other reasons. There weren't. It was for her. Ever since our first conversation by the cherry tree, I've felt an irrational need to protect her.

Finally I spot a crimson smudge on the gray wall—blood, unmistakably. I brush my fingers against it, still damp. At last I feel grooves. I push. I steel myself, then charge quietly in.

In war, in defense, surprise can decisively shift the balance of power. Best to strike the enemy in a way for which she is unprepared.

I may not know much, but I know now who the enemy is. And I've seen her handiwork. She won't falter.

Neither will I.

Her side is to me, her gun trained on Darcy, with Sylvie on the floor beside her. I am briefly startled by the presence of Sylvie, but I am trained to confront unanticipated elements. Darcy's face flickers with recognition. Relief.

Arabelle swivels toward me. Her face darkens. Then she pulls the trigger.

"*Non!*" screams Sylvie. In my peripheral vision, I can see her hands flinging up to cover her face, but my eyes are trained on Darcy, the target. "Arabelle, *non non non non!*"

I dive toward Darcy, at the same time as I shoot at Arabelle with one outstretched arm.

I crash to the floor. Darcy collapses in my arms. There is blood. So much blood.

Arabelle's blood, across the room. And more blood. Mine.

CHAPTER FORTY-TWO

Vix

Two Weeks Later

For the first time, I want to paint people. I've always done landscapes, but abstract stuff. Modern, but not the kind of modern that Van Gogh originated, where a person was a recognizable person, and a wheat field a recognizable wheat field. My stuff had slashes and shapes. Nothing wrong with slashes and shapes, but truthfully, I was never sure what I intended them to mean. Someone said an apple. Another person said a porcupine. I could see both. I felt the fury behind it. That was real. But I'm not sure I ever knew where I was going.

Now, as the light across the room from my new loft space illuminates Juliet's fluffy wheat hair, I know exactly where I am going.

I am painting a person. A corpse. Séraphine. Without the bloody murder. Instead I have seated her with a rigid back, at the helm of her dining room table, in the diamond necklace that is rightfully Jade's. Behind her, over her perfect curtains with their perfect ripples, it says in a brilliant ochre red, *It's Not Over 'Til You're Dead.*

Macabre, yes. Pushing boundaries, maybe sailing over them. But when I considered what I wanted to paint first after that horrific week, I knew it had to be Séraphine. She gave me so much. Not just money, but care. She loved me, in her own way. And she was brutally murdered. In all the secrets and lies that unraveled that week at the chateau, I left feeling distraught in so many ways, including how her death unwittingly took a back seat to everything else.

So I am painting her. Maybe it will be horrible. Maybe I'll go back to abstract. But I don't think so. I feel a rumble inside me that didn't exist before. Juliet's accusation when we parted that I lacked passion cut so deep because it was true. Somewhere along the line, early on, I got comfortable, and too afraid to really try. A lethal combination for any creative. In the end, France did, indeed, reinspire me, although not at all as I anticipated at the start of the trip.

Juliet smiles at me across the room, and I feel that still-fresh pitter-patter of cautious excitement that she is here. Real. After Jade and I returned to the chateau to all that blood, all those incomprehensible revelations, I called Juliet. I left her a voice mail. Later she told me it made its own strange sense, even though I was rambling like a lunatic. More or less I said that I'm not dead, so we can't be over. I know what dead is. I've seen dead—and it's final. It's really, really final, and please say that it isn't final with us. I said, please give me one more chance. Because no more secrets. No more lies. I promise on everything that is sacred and true.

And then I said that by the way, for a brief moment in time, I was set to inherit five million euros. But I'm giving it all away. So if you want to give us another chance, I'm essentially a pauper.

As it turns out, paupers are a big turn-on for Juliet.

And no, I wasn't lying, or exaggerating. I'm giving away my entire inheritance. I've been debating causes I want to contribute to. The story of Jade's family still lives at the forefront of my brain. So maybe something for Holocaust survivors. Besides, the money doesn't feel like mine, like I earned it, or deserved it. And I want to try to make something of myself on my own. I won't be able to live with myself if, at the end, I never know if left to my own devices, whether I would sink or swim.

Juliet tells me all the time now, in my moments of doubt, and there are many, that I'm a swim girl all the way. No sink in the vicinity. And you know what? I'm a fucking survivor, in more ways than one. It's swim, swim, swim, from here on out.

I stare at my canvas. A wave comes, of doubting myself. No. Swim, swim, swim.

Across the room, Juliet is threading a new earring for her jewelry line, her tongue stuck out between her lips. I stand, because maybe I'll go check out what she's doing, give her a little back massage. But she pins me down with her eyes. "It's not break time yet!"

I grumble but sit back down. Juliet's rule is that we work for three-hour chunks, and then take a little break. It's a switch. I used to do the opposite: work for a little and then take a three-hour break.

Arabelle would approve of Juliet's methods, is what pops into my head. She always said I just needed a little discipline, a little structure, and then I'd soar. I have so much fury toward my old friend, but I miss her, too, the person I thought she was. I haven't admitted that yet, not to Jade, and certainly not to Darcy. We've been talking a lot, the three of us, eager to reunite when Darcy returns. God, I can hardly wait to give the girls epic hugs, especially Darcy, and rehash everything again, because who else will ever understand but us three?

But I haven't broached Arabelle with them. It's too raw. Too delicate for texts. Still, I've been telling Juliet how I feel about everything else. No more secrets between us.

I pick up my paintbrush and stare out the open window of the loft, into the courtyard. I moved into a new space just a couple days ago, and Juliet moved in with me. We needed a fresh start, even though it was difficult to say goodbye to my tree that had grown so kindly toward the window of my old place. But there is a new tree, a sturdy oak, a ways away, just in my line of view. I watch it for a while, its leaves flittering in the breeze, my heart beaming it extra-powerful love vibes, replenished, as it has been of late, in the love department. And maybe it's silly, but somehow I think that in all those invisible ways that trees do their growing, its branches are already stretching toward our window.

CHAPTER FORTY-THREE

Jade

Papa is in his study, staring at the painting. I join him, put a hand on his forearm. For a while we are mesmerized. It doesn't matter how many times I look, there is so much more to see. The ecstatic feeling of the sketch pervades the painting, but on canvas it is amplified far beyond. It's hard to fathom unless you are in the presence of it, and finally, after so long, we are. I run my eyes over the smoke curling up from chimneys, the curved roofs, the imposing cypress thrust through the sky. Heaven meets earth, in the painting and now. Here.

"It's over," I tell Papa. "It's finally over."

I look over at him, but he's somewhere else entirely. I want so badly for him to cry. For the past to fade out of him. This painting—it was the apex of everything. I was trying to protect Darcy's family, while also protecting him. I should have exposed this long ago. I should have at least tried. We might have gotten our painting back sooner. Darcy and I—we might have known who we really were to each other. First cousins. She hasn't even met her uncle properly yet, just FaceTimed him from France. We've all lost so much time.

He turns to me, but his eyes aren't clear like I long for them to be, like the air after a good rain. "They're gone," he tells me, his lips quivering.

"Who is gone, Papa?"

"My parents. My brother. They're all still gone."

"Yes," I say at last. "They are all still gone."

We stare at the painting again, the thing that for so long has been my singular focus. A painting representative of so much loss and pain for a vortex of people. For the first time I regret bringing it back here. Maybe it was always supposed to stay in the past.

"Papa, do you remember how you bought me a piccolo?" I ask.

"Huh?" His face screws in memory. "Oh. Yes."

"I played it for three years."

"I took you to that teacher . . . *Merde*, he cost an arm and a leg."

"He lived out in bumfuck." I laugh.

"What is bumfuck?"

"Far."

"Oh."

"Papa." I screw up the courage to say what I've been thinking since coming back from France. I haven't even told Seb yet. "Papa, I've been thinking about doing something new."

"New?" he asks vaguely. "Like the piccolo?"

I smile. "Not the piccolo. My piccolo days are firmly behind me."

"Some other hobby?"

"Not a hobby, really." I pause. "I'm not sure. A new career, maybe."

"A new career?" Now he swivels at me. "What do you mean?"

I breathe in hard. "I might . . . I was thinking I'd like to . . . help people. People banished from their lands. People with no homes, no hope."

"Help people." I can see his head working, processing. "Like that Angelina?"

"Jolie?" How does he even know about Angelina Jolie? "Not like her. No. I'm not sure, exactly. Just, think what would have happened to you if Séraphine hadn't saved you."

"The orphanage saved me," Papa clarifies. "That lady of yours just took me there."

"She saved you, Papa. You read the letter."

His face suddenly droops, so despite his tan from all his walking outdoors, he looks old. He *is* old. But I'm not. All at once, I feel young and energetic and full of verve, and needing to make a different kind of difference. And not just for the privileged women who attend my spin classes.

"What does this mean?" Papa asks abruptly. "Are you going to leave Seb and your children and move to Africa?" He says it a bit derisively, but somehow, for the first time, his opinion feels strangely meaningless. Where before it could flatten me, or bolster me, now I realize, I am a forty-year-old grown woman. The only opinion that really matters is my own. That's how I want to live the rest of my life. That's my forty-ever-after.

"No," I say slowly. "I love my family. Of course I'm not deserting them. But the kids are older, and Seb works very hard. And the studio practically runs itself at this point. I want to do something more meaningful. I have a platform, already, on Instagram, and maybe I could leverage that. Think about what those kids did to Lux, Papa, and how worried you get when Mom goes to synagogue." Papa's eye twitches. I know that will land. Ever since the Pittsburgh synagogue massacre, he works himself into a tizzy every Saturday morning until my mother returns unscathed from her weekly synagogue stint.

"I don't want to feel paralyzed anymore. Helpless. Maybe there's something I can do, to spread awareness. To combat all the hate. I could fundraise, and try to help refugees, too. Maybe go to places where I am needed, places where people are being persecuted. And maybe . . ." I avert my gaze from Papa's, stare at the American Constitution proudly displayed above his desk. All of his hate toward his past and the country he felt betrayed him has been channeled into love for his adopted country, where he has been able to live in safety. Although safety, I know, is relative. I suspect that since the day Papa parted from his family, there hasn't been a safe hour—even minute— in his brain.

"Maybe I want to take French lessons, too, Papa," I finally say, and feel something loosen inside me with the admission. "Reclaim some of our heritage—*my* heritage."

As I finish my whole speech, I hear how grand and lofty it all sounds, how implausible. And I also feel it in the deepest part of me that this is right. That this is true. That somehow, I am going to move forward with different priorities and find a new way to make a difference.

"I'm going to take a walk," I say suddenly.

Papa's face shifts to something new. If I stop, if I give it twenty seconds, I can read his reaction. I can figure out how he feels about this plan I've proposed, whether he approves, or half approves, or thinks it's entirely absurd.

But I don't want to know what he thinks. For once, I don't really care.

I wander outside onto Gerald Avenue, the street where I grew up, that holds so many memories that sometimes it's like stepping into thick, punishing fog. I don't know where I'm going. I could go home, but Seb's at the office, the kids are still at camp. I could go to the studio, but I don't think I can cope seeing all those fit women, in their daily war with their excess two pounds.

I am that woman.

My mind lingers desolately on that thought. All those years, all that work, to nothing. Do I let it just drift through my fingers? Gone? For what?

My thoughts go when my eyes catch on the McDonald's down the street. The one I used to go to every week as a very young child, to get a McFlurry.

Suddenly I am walking there, faster, flying through the revolving door. There is a line, and as I wait, thousands of memories find me, cling to me. Me after a piccolo lesson, age eight, clutching my black case. Me after one of my father's episodes, when he threw a china dish of my mother's across the room. The shatter, the looks frozen on my parents' faces. My mother sent me down with a five-dollar bill, and that time I ordered extra OREO crumbles.

Once I reach the register, tears are rolling down my cheeks.

"OREO McFlurry, please," I ask the bored-looking girl who can't be older than sixteen.

There is no ceremony when, thirty seconds later, she plops the giant paper cup on the counter. I pay with my Apple pay, which is the only thing that feels different from over thirty years prior.

Out on the street, I sink onto a bench. I take my first bite and instantly moan. I can't believe how good it tastes. How long it's been. The next bite is more urgent. I am ravenous for the pleasure, and simultaneously devastated for the girl I was up until thirty seconds ago. The girl who gave up ice cream.

How could I have given up ice cream? How?

I watch a teardrop fall into the McFlurry. More teardrops, more. More ice cream, more. My eyes flutter shut. Something has gone from me. Something has come. I can't put an exact shape to either, but I can savor all the dreams that now swirl about my tongue—forgotten, buried. Risen.

CHAPTER FORTY-FOUR

Darcy

It is ironic that where I go to recover after the week of horrors at the chateau is Arabelle's stomping grounds. To the sea, to Nice. I did stop by her inn, say hello to Giancarlo. He was kind but quiet, which didn't surprise me. However shocked I was at everything that happened, I lived it. Living something gives it more access to permeate. He learned it all secondhand. Who can say which is better? Life isn't always a buffet. Sometimes you have to sit down for the meal that is placed before you.

I stretch out my legs, surprised at how tanned they've gotten just from playing with the children in the pool and walks by the sea. I tip my face up to the warm, medicinal Riviera sun. The first couple of days, I turned pink, and Mila did, too, having inherited my pale, freckled skin. I took that as a sign to return to our room, put the children down for naps, and take advantage of the bath. That's another thing old Darcy didn't do. She didn't linger in sudsy baths, pruning up, reading Jonathan Franzen. And she certainly didn't buy the chic, pricey emerald green jumpsuit in the hotel boutique on a whim, doubtful if it fit her style or body and where she was even going to wear it.

But New Darcy . . . well, I'm still figuring out who New Darcy is.

The children are eating pizza now, and Mila is hunched over her coloring book. My eyes hardly stray from them. They are here, yes, Mila inches away, Chase cushioned into me, so I can stroke his chubby little thighs, but still, part of me wishes I could slide them

309

back inside my womb. They were safe there, and I was safe, too. After the ordeal, I spent a couple of days with them in Saint-Rémy, exhausting their will for hugs and kisses. I was hungry for their skin. I still am. I don't know what it is, exactly. Something primal, I suppose. When you think about what could have happened . . . how close I came . . .

After that nightmare in the room under the stairs, when the gendarmes screeched in with their sirens, and there were questions and exclamations and me throwing up everything inside me, and then throwing up some more when I thought I'd finished, Officer Darmanin took me aside. Jade and Vix were hovering nearby. Perhaps they thought I might break. *I* thought I might break. I wanted to go to the hospital, to be with Raph, who'd been whisked away by an ambulance, and the police wouldn't let me leave. I was irate, and grieving, and a thousand other emotions. So I wasn't at my shiniest when I faced the officer again. At first, I thought she might apologize for having suspected me, or for not having caught Arabelle in time, but she didn't. She asked if she could give me some advice, and although I didn't particularly want it, it isn't in my nature to refuse that kind of thing. I said, *Okay.* She said I should walk out of the chateau and never look back. That she'd seen victims replay events ad nauseum for their entire lives. Eventually it becomes unclear in their minds who was the perpetrator and who was the victim. She said if I did that, I would start to blame myself. Think of a thousand little missteps, how things could have been different. *Leave it in the past. Walk forward to your future.*

My future. I had to sit with that concept often in the days that ensued. What exactly was my future?

After Grand-mère's funeral, Oliver and I sat at one of the local parks in Saint-Rémy, watching the children play, and he asked me if I could ever forgive him. I was surprised to hear myself tell him I already had. I could see his face shade with some relief. He reached for my hand, but it felt all wrong. Our skin didn't mingle right anymore. *No,* I told him, retracting my hand. *I forgive you, but I can't fight for us anymore.*

Now I gaze out at the iconic saltwater pool hewn into the rocks, the one I'd only ever seen in magazine photos of celebrities, or on Arabelle's Instagram. Beyond the pool, sails flutter out in calm sea.

"Have some *frites, ma chérie*?" Sylvie passes me the basket of fries a waiter has just deposited.

"Yes." I smile gratefully at her, my unfortunate partner in those horrific minutes in the secret room under the stairs. She is ensconced beneath a massive umbrella, wearing a white linen top and matching drawstring pants, with a huge straw hat. She has big, black sunglasses on, but she doesn't fool me. I see how she removes her sunglasses every so often to dab at her tears.

"Sylvie, look!" Mila shows us the page she's been coloring from the foot of Sylvie's chaise. On the page is an animal I can't place—a big, hairy animal with cartoon-wide eyes, waving, his tail flopping behind him. All animals look the same to me in these coloring books. Rascally, and kind. "Look how I did the tail, Sylvie!"

Sure enough, the yellow scribbles outside the tail are minimal.

"Good job, angel!" I say.

"*Magnifique!*" Sylvie says brightly, as she strokes Mila's hair. "*Que vais-je faire?*" she says aloud, to herself more than to us. *What will I do?*

"You have us." I reach over to squeeze her other hand. "What you will do, is be with us."

Sylvie shifts the cross of her legs, her hand limp in mine. "You will go back to America."

"Yes," I admit. "But here you have Giancarlo. He told you that what Arabelle did doesn't change how much he loves and respects you. You have him, and his family, and your friends. You'll get a place in Saint-Rémy. I'll help you. We'll make it a happy home. And you'll come visit us in New York, if you can. You have me, Jade, and Vix, always. They've been messaging me constantly, asking about you. And either way, we will all visit you, the girls and I, and the kids, too. You have always been a second grandmother to me, Sylvie. And now you are the only one my children have left."

"Yes." She smiles, though I can see it's an effort. "What about Oliver, *ma chérie*? Have you changed your mind? Arabelle . . ." She makes a strangled, grunting noise. "My Arabelle, she was manipulative. She was sick. Oliver . . ."

"Oliver was a grown man," I say. "He made his choices, and now we both must live with them. Anyway, it's not Arabelle who broke us, not really. Something about our relationship always felt like trying to paddle upstream."

If I think about it more, in all the ways it's not fun to think of things when you're wildly in love and laughing and trying to move forward to the milestones you want—Oliver and I were an almost. We should have stayed an almost. We had so many ingredients, but we were missing the glue. I could have fought forever, glued us together out of sheer will. But it would have taken every last ounce of my strength, and I would have had nothing left. Nothing for myself. It's hard for us women, especially in our thirties, when we stand before the potentiality of motherhood, the clock slowly ticking its demise. It's easier to grip onto an almost with all our might. But my fighting days are over. I am grateful for my children—for them my fight feels worthy, pure. But whatever lies ahead, it's going to have to be easy. And it won't feel like an almost. I don't know what an easy sure feels like, but I know about a hard almost. So hopefully I'll recognize its opposite.

"I am proud of you, Darcy." At last, Sylvie squeezes my hand in return. "Séraphine would be very proud of you, too. But tell me, *ma chérie*, what will you do with the chateau?"

A shudder wracks me, head to toe. I slide my hand out of Sylvie's and study my nails. I bit them down in the room under the stairs, crouched on the ground, with Arabelle towering over me. I am trying not to go there, to the panic, the fear. The gun. But I can't stop the flashes that invade. "Sell it. I'm sorry, Sylvie. I know it was your home. And if you want to keep it, I'll happily give it to you."

"I certainly do not want it." Sylvie laughs, a sad, guttural laugh. "What would I do with such a massive, burdensome place?"

"You have so many memories there."

"Memories live here." Sylvie taps her head, her eyes misting over. "Now tell me, you're not going to give away all your money, are you, like Victoria is planning to do?"

"No!" I laugh. "I know money won't buy me happiness, but it will help me be a single parent, send my kids to private schools. And it will enable me to expand The Fertility Warrior, to help so many women on their journeys to being mothers." Suddenly I feel a fire inside, something rekindled. It's exciting, I have to admit, to finally have the financial backing to give my business baby a real go. "I know I will still have worries. Money doesn't save you there. But at least I won't be worrying about money. And I'll be charitable, too, of course."

I place the basket of *frites* back on the table and recline once more in my plush chair. Then my phone blurts with a text.

It's from Raph. *How are you doing down there?*

I respond, *Fine, thanks. Hot and sandy and lots of ice cream and snuggles with the kids. How are you recovering?*

Immediately comes the ellipses of him typing.

It hits me again, like it does in the middle of the night. I didn't see the bullet, just Raph, crashing to the ground. I collapsed atop him. There was so much blood, an abyss of death all around. The doctor said if the bullet had lodged a millimeter away it would have hit an artery. And he wouldn't have made it. And Raph just did a combination smile/grimace from the hospital bed and said the bullet had hit him exactly where he'd intended. *Practically back to new. Even managed a sit-up.* Then a selfie comes through, of Raph in bed, propped up in pillows. His eyes are crinkled at the corners.

I zoom in a bit on his smile, crooked and warm. I write, *Back to push-ups in no time. If you need anything at all, I'll be back at the chateau in a couple days.*

"Raphael?" Sylvie asks, peering over my shoulder. "The groundskeeper?"

I tuck my phone back into my bag. "Yes. Just checking that I'm okay."

Sylvie nods. Then Mila looks up from her coloring book, all long, freckled legs, a bona fide real person. Overnight she has become such

313

a real little person. If Oliver were here, I would tell him that observation. A wave of sadness tidals at me. He is the only one who would get what I mean, how we are losing the tiny person she was, and gaining the one she is growing into.

"Mama, what do you think about ice cream?"

She's referring to the parlor a few blocks away, our new home away from home. Normally I wouldn't indulge the kids in sugar so much, but on this vacation, it's been ice cream every day. "I think that's a very good idea. Sylvie, what do you think? We'll go inside and shower off, then go get ice cream?"

"Ice cream!" Sylvie says, marshaling glee. "*Oui.*"

We start to gather everything up, all the towels and sunscreen and random items the kids collect, like Chase's new wooden frog. I'll hand one of the bags to Oliver, is what I think, and I look for him over my shoulder, before I remember. Suddenly, I halt. I take in this unexpected hand that's been dealt me—no husband, no grandmother, but the children, healthy and beautiful and mine, and wonderful Sylvie, and even this swanky hotel, that no way could I have afforded before. It's a new deck of cards, my life, and I feel frightened, and sad, and also another feeling that I can't put my finger exactly upon, something sprightly, though, like the first buds of spring. I shift one tote over my shoulder, slip another on my forearm, and then bundle Chase in my arms. As we round the pool, I peek back at my phone.

Raph wrote, *Don't need anything. But looking forward to seeing you.*

I stare at that for a beat, then reply, *Looking forward to seeing you, too.*

"Mama, will you get *citron gingembre* today?" Mila asks, hopping on one foot a few times, and then when she stumbles, shifting easily to the other foot. Flavor choices are very serious for us this trip. Sometimes we linger for half an hour, doing taste tests, debating.

I kiss her head, and with my nose in her hair, I breathe this new life of mine deeply in. "Maybe, angel, or I might get salted caramel. I think I'll try a couple and see."

CHAPTER FORTY-FIVE

Arabelle

Hate, I know, is like a volcano. It can lie dormant for a very long time, before it erupts.

He pulls back the metal chair, scraping it across the linoleum. As he sits, he rakes his hand through his thick, dark hair.

"You fucking sociopath," he says.

I don't respond, not even a tiny muscle twitch.

Did I know he would come to see me? Of course.

"I can't *fucking* believe you tried to murder her!" Anger flashes in those navy eyes—eyes I used to lose myself inside. No. Wrong turn of phrase. I never lost myself, not once. I've always known where I was aiming, even though it all went so completely off the rails.

"Yes," I say simply, agreeing with him.

"She's the mother of my children," Ollie says, his self-righteousness flaring so absurdly that I bite my lip to quell laughter. He lowers his voice. "You lied to me about so many things!"

"Oh?" I cock my head at him. "And you didn't lie to me? You didn't tell me it was me and you, until the end? Always?"

"I meant it, until I realized you're a fucking *sociopath*."

That word again. Now I feel twitches, jerks, my eyes, my knees. My hands, writhing in my lap. A guard passes by, hand on pistol. I force myself to still.

"Your lies changed everything," he hisses. "A couple weeks ago, before I learned who you are, I loved you. Or I thought I did. Maybe

315

that was a con, too. Your lies are staggering." He's fallen to such a whisper now, I can hardly grip onto his words.

"My lies?" I ask, incredulous but also almost amused at his hypocrisy. "Oh, you mean not telling you in Gordes about what I did to Mamie?"

His eyes narrow to slits. "How do I know you're not wearing a wire?"

"A wire?" I guffaw. "I don't need to wear a wire."

"How do I know?" he asks again.

In a flash, I lift my shirt. The guard is turned, speaking into his radio. We're in a blind spot to the camera. I anticipated this question.

"Nothing to see here," I say cheerfully as I drop my shirt and give him a tiny wink.

I can't parse his look, but it's nothing appreciative. Even though he once worshipped my tits.

He doesn't speak, doesn't even comment on the bandages covering my right ribs. Instead, he runs his hand under the table, then peeks beneath to be certain. He's smart, my Ollie. But not as smart as me.

"You were saying?" I say, slightly taunting. "My lies?"

"*Yes*, I mean how you lied about what you did to your grandmother. And obviously all that garbage about Séraphine."

"I never realized you were such a victim. I'm the one sitting in handcuffs here."

"You told me Séraphine abused you, Arabelle! You told me there was a pattern of abuse that stretched from your earliest memory. That she beat you, many times! That you were terrified when she'd come into your room at night! You told me she was evil. You said she was the one who killed Rainier—not you! You said she threatened to twist it, that the police would never believe you, when Séraphine handed over her manufactured evidence. You said her death would benefit both of us." He leans forward, his lips no longer emitting sounds, just shaping the words, as if I am a deaf person. "You suckered me into this! You made me help you. . . ."

I lean back in my chair, cross my arms over my chest. I can smell his cologne, Chanel Homme Sport Allure. My favorite male scent. I bought it for him once, as I did for Giancarlo, too. It's the one thread that unwittingly connects them—other than me.

"Help you? You're being awfully cryptic here, Ol. By help me, you mean, help me *murder* her? You mean, you planned the whole thing with me and held the gun while I looked in her safe for the letter that yes, I admit, I told you was meant to frame me? You mean, you watched me kill her, and didn't stop me? I believe the technical term is *accomplice*." Unlike him, I am not speaking without sound. My voice is quite normal, and as a result, it is almost comical how his head spins cartoonlike, trying to shut me up by wildly flickering eyes, while ensuring no one in earshot is paying us any attention.

"Shut up," he finally hisses. "Shut up, shut the fuck *up!*"

I just smile at him. "That's why you're really here, isn't it? Not to rail at me for trying to kill your precious Darcy. But to take my temperature. See if I'm going to spill."

"I did nothing." Now he smiles, flashing those cruel pearly whites. "You were the one who said it, weren't you? Leave not a trace. You said we couldn't even speak of it after, even when we were alone. We might slip up. Someone might hear. If we pretended we never did anything, no one would know. So don't try to threaten me now. You have zero leverage. You can't prove a thing."

"Oh?" I let my silence do the speaking.

"I'm right, aren't I?" But I can see him wobble.

I shrug. "If you say so. Well, I suppose you're golden, then."

I watch him trying to make me out, climb inside my motivations, but then he straightens. "It astounds me, how wrong I was about you. Everything you told me was a lie. We didn't even need that alibi, but you just blabbed it to the police. You were supposed to say you were sleeping during the murder, just like the other girls. The alibi was supposed to be in case something went wrong. And nothing went wrong! You had no motive to kill her, nothing ostensible. No one would have suspected you. It was going to be pinned on the groundskeeper, by virtue of that note—"

"Séraphine only had means to write that note because you tried to help me search in the safe, rather than stand watch with the gun, like you were supposed to."

His nostrils flare. "That note worked to our advantage!"

I shrug. "Still. A fuckup."

"Regardless," he says, exhaling deeply. "Regardless. I needed more time after the trip. I told you that. Darcy wasn't supposed to find out about us. I needed longer, for the—"

"For her inheritance to kick in. Yes, I know. It's why you really helped me kill Séraphine." I flutter my eyelashes in a way I know will bait him. Then I croon, "Money, money, money, *money*!"

He glares at me and looks furtively around. "Shut the fuck up."

"Money, money, money, *money*," I sing, a bit louder this time. "Stop acting like a fucking saint. You didn't help me kill Séraphine just because you were trying to protect me. No. I always knew the dollar signs were your main impetus. You're drowning in debt. Some stuff Darcy doesn't even know about. You figured she'd throw most of her inheritance into your joint account, settle all your mutual debts, and never even notice when you siphoned more away. Best laid plans, though . . ."

"Yes, about Darcy's inheritance." Ollie's lips curl with loathing. "You *knew* Séraphine was terminally ill, that the inheritance was coming to us soon in any event. Yet you kept that crucial fact from me, to rope me into your plan. You're such a fucking bitch."

It nearly flattens me, all of a sudden, to realize we have devolved into this. It was supposed to be me and him, forever. I loved him. A big part of me still does. I was all in, and I was certain so was he. He said he and Darcy were over. I thought—maybe I convinced myself—that he'd ultimately find Darcy's death at the end of things a neat, pleasant result. In a strange way, I even felt Ollie and I to be bonded by our crime. By his willingness to defend me. He watched me murder Séraphine. He knew my fury, and he accepted it. Later, after I'd showered, he even held me and vowed it would be okay. That we'd survive it—soon, be better for it.

Ollie puts his hands on the table, props himself up, like he is about to leave. Like he can just waltz out of here, unscathed, leaving me to rot here forevermore. "You're a sociopath."

"Sticks and stones." I sigh.

He shakes his head. "You repulse me. I hope they throw the book at you."

"Why did you come?" I ask him, even though we both know the reason. He wants to assure himself that his role will remain quiet. That there are no threads. Even though I, by virtue of my existence, am one big, superlong thread.

"To warn you to stay away from my family."

"I'm in prison," I remind him. "My lawyers say my chances are not good. The evidence is, unfortunately, overwhelming."

"Yes." His eyes flicker with uncertainty. He stands. "Okay, then—"

"Anyway." I smile at him. "If anyone is a threat to your family, it's not me. It's you."

Something gray passes over his face. He slowly lowers back to a seat. "What the *fuck* do you mean by that, Arabelle?"

"I mean, I have plenty of evidence against you," I say pleasantly. "Heaps."

I can see him waver. He thinks I am postulating, but he's unsure. He squares his shoulders, rock star mode. "You don't. We never texted anything. No emails. If you try to drag me into this, you'll just look stupid. My word against yours. No one will ever believe you, Arabelle. Don't even try."

"I recorded us when we planned it," I tell him simply. "In the Berkshires. My phone was behind my back."

His face goes as white as his wife's skin. "I don't believe you. . . ."

"Believe it. It's not on my phone now, of course. Nor in my emails. The police have scoured those. But I uploaded it to one of those websites. You know the ones, Ollie? That keep things private and secure for as long as you want them to. And I think the police will find it

319

quite interesting, if I tell them about the recording. Quite interesting, indeed."

"You're lying." But his lower lip is trembling.

"I'm not."

"What do you want?" he finally asks. "If you haven't turned me in yet, you must want something."

"Oh, you know me well. I do want something. A little something." I smile. "You know, there's a saying you Americans have. I think it goes, *If at first you don't succeed, try, try again*."

I can see the confusion swirl in his eyes. He doesn't get it. I feel my feet bounce against the floor. Oh, it will be fun when this sinks in!

"Should I put it another way? Sure." For this I finally lower my voice, even though the guards aren't paying us any attention. We're jilted ex-lovers in the wake of a crime, not exactly an uncommon scenario within these walls.

"If you want me to stay quiet about your part in Séraphine's murder, you'll have to do something for me. You'll have to finish what I started."

Ollie's eyes blink furiously. "What?"

"Darcy."

Immediately he spits fury. "You can't be serious. She's the mother of my children. You can't think I'll do *anything* to her!"

"You will," I say calmly. "At least I think you will, because you're a narcissist, and your instincts for self-preservation are strong. But don't think I won't hesitate to turn you in if you don't."

"You can't. . . ." His face pales. A ghost, a sheet. A sheet over the ghost, suffocating her. Or him. Either will do.

"You wouldn't," he breathes.

"Try me. I would. I will."

"How would I even . . . How do you . . . No . . ."

"That's up to you. I have faith in you, Ollie. You'll think of something creative. If I'm going to be locked up here for the rest of my life for something we both did, you'll have to make it worth it for me. And *this* will make it worth it."

"I won't," he stammers, but he doesn't convince me. "Mila and Chase," he finally whispers, his voice raw.

"Mila and Chase. Yes." I sigh. "It's really such a shame. Either way, your children are going to lose a parent. But it's up to you, Ollie. Which parent will they lose?"

Acknowledgments

To my agent, Rachel Ekstrom Courage, who was so supportive when I wanted to foray into suspense! I am enormously thankful for your enthusiasm for me and my books and for finding this one its most perfect home. Hoping this is finally our year to get to hug in person! And thank you to all the fantastic people at Folio who have helped catalyze my book dreams.

To my editor, Lara Jones, with whom it was truly love at first call! Thank you for all the passion and imagination you brought to this book. I haven't stopped smiling since we started working together. So grateful for you and the entire incredible team at Atria/Emily Bestler Books.

To Eden Adler, for making me the most gorgeous website and helping me conceive of this plot on the balcony on Zamenhoff—oh, how I miss you here. To Lexy Grant, for connecting me to amazing sources and being my #1 fan—let's always live around the corner from each other, 'kay? And to Eden and Lex, for the most epic book release party of all time—I will never, ever forget that magical night. To Jenna Golden and Rebecca Katz, for generously allowing me to pick your brains on all things Francophile. To Tracy Alexander, for ace brainstorming and tiger-button-type diagrams to help me through the weeds of yet another tricky plot. To Jaclyn Mishal, for writing comradeship and your fabulous Pink Pangea community and retreats. To Nicole Hackett: critique partner extraordinaire! To Lauren Klitofsky, for my favorite book club event and staying close even when we're far. To Jill Salama Handman, for how immensely you championed my first book—I cherish you and our creative brainstorm sessions. To

Acknowledgments

Rinat Spivak, Zo Flamenbaum, and Natalie Blenford, for sharing the writers' life and always uplifting me. To Linda Sivertsen, for your wisdom and endless inspiration, and to the ladies of our Carmel group, for your friendship—all I can say about that dreamy week in January 2016 is that the Universe knew what it was doing. And to my other friends and cousins, both in the US and abroad—each of you brings so much light to my life.

To Meagan Harris, for so beautifully promoting my first book. And to the wonderful readers and bookstagram community who greeted it with enthusiasm, with particular heartfelt thanks to Ashley Bellman and Lauren Lograsso.

To Jas, for gifting my first book to your customers and rooting me on every step of the way. Love our weekly chats—I can't imagine a more caring brother. To Nadav and Arica: Thankfully Suz and Jas have impeccable taste, because I would choose you two as my siblings any day. Ar, still can't get over those stunning PR packages, and Nadav, your advance reading and thoughtful praise are so touching. To Liad, Reagan, Griffin, and Noa—it doesn't get any cuter or sweeter than you four. I love being your Auntie Jac. And to my wonderful aunts and uncles, Nancy and Jeff Adler, David Newman, and Renee Potvin—thank you for being some of my loudest cheerleaders.

To my Bubsicles, for believing in me to the end. I adore you and your gorgeous punim and consider you a best friend as much as my grandmother. To your 120th, and then we can discuss. And thank you to my beloved Zadie, who feels so close to me, always.

To my parents, Cheryl and Alex Goldis, for our magnificent trip to Provence that inspired this book, a decade after the fact. And for the boundless love and support you have blessed me with all my life.

To Suz, my first reader and editor extraordinaire, whose invaluable insights make my books infinitely better. Thank you for carving out time in your very busy life to read, edit, and brainstorm—even if your epic watercolor covers have tapered off. It is my favorite ritual to finish a book, send it off to you, and trade voice notes as you provide the perfect measure of brutally on-point and deeply supportive feedback. Adore you, sisra—so excited to live in the same city at last!

And finally, thank you to my grandparents I never got to meet, Khana Vinarskaya and Shimon Goldis. Here is yet another story I have set in the long shadow of World War II and the Holocaust, with your loving hearts, courage, and perseverance at the forefront of my mind—living on in my characters, and in me.